MW01240887

# STREAM WALKER

by Greg Johnson

Dedicated to
my wife Molly and my son Michael
who read, edited, and critiqued every chapter
and inspired me to become a coach.

They are both hiding within this story.

Inspired by real events

Introduction

Although a few beginning chapters in this story take place in
Southern California and Arizona, they are only a little background
description, leading up to events that develop in the Pacific Northwest,
the part of America this story is really about. Many different and
seemingly unrelated things happen in the early chapters, but the end
reveals they are in some ways connected. Although I have tagged this
story as fiction lots of truth is mixed in. To put it another way, this tale
is not very tall. Most of what happened to the Blue Angels soccer team
is true.

This brings me to another introductory comment. Quite seriously,
some people of the Pacific Northwest have been entertaining another
name for their very special ecoregion. Around the early 1960s some
were saying the name Pacific Northwest just wouldn't do anymore. It
sounded too gray and boring: it lacked accent and majesty. The idea of
having a better name for the outland that encompasses the great Salish
Sea and its grand rivers that flow into the Pacific Ocean has been
discussed for more than a century... and now a name change is the
front runner: Cascadia.

People still debate the exact boundaries of a new Cascadia and
some wonder: why bother to change? What does the name mean?
When you say to a Texan you are Cascadian, what are you telling him?
The answers have not been totally refined, but a few things are coming
into focus. First, if you have a Cascadian soul you love and worship

salmon, the great wild fighting regalia of the Salish Sea. Just as a salmon will fight, a true Cascadian will fight to keep the genus robust. If anyone tries to ruin a salmon run, a Cascadian will get angry and call out those wronging the compelling fish. If someone interferes with the needs of salmon and proposes a hulking colossus of a dam he might want to be careful. Such project plans might get blown into confetti: not by ecoterrorism, but by the Cascadian spirit. If a developer builds a paved strip mall and ruins salmon habitat with impervious concrete, he too might want to be careful. It may bother the legal staff of a tribal elder who is also an American citizen. The elder holds a treaty and knows a treaty gives him the right to fish. And he knows a treaty is *the supreme law of the land.*

Something else looms large as the name Cascadia unfolds: sports. Cascadians are frenetic about sports. They play all of them it seems, but they are particularly fond of their scholastic and professional sports teams, too many to name. Here again the Cascadian spirit emanates as rowdy and uproarious as the great storms of the eastern Pacific. A typical Cascadian stands cheering behind his teams, heading for the stadiums, unwilling to miss a second, talking and jamming the air waves as if there were nothing else to mention.

Not too long ago Cascadia welcomed the world's best sport: soccer. Soccer… the sport of planet Earth… the sport of simple rules, minimal equipment, and superb conditioning. The sport small, quick people can play… the sport where there isn't much of an offseason. The sport that unites all mankind through the World Cup, where a final score of 0:1 leads to wild celebration. The sport women embrace as much as men. This story is about soccer.

Mossbacks they call them. There is another Cascadian subject worth mentioning. They love the rain and are not usually sedentary. They gleam with sweat mixed with rain and have rippled arms, V-backs, and go to a gym every day. They sometimes even fight in the ring. They hike, sail, swim, fish, and summit. To renew and unwind, they do the Pacific Crest Trail. They hit the streets in large numbers and stand up for what they think is right. A Cascadian groundswell is moving across the evergreens; the land is becoming more integrated. This story is about a people like that.

Sound like a lot of romantic emotionalism?

Cascadia is an emotional place.

# CHAPTER 1

April 7, 1998

Port Angeles, Cascadia

Two men stepped out of the local coffee shop full of hash browns and omelets, ready to work. They worked for an environmental consulting firm out of Olympia called Graham Hughes Environmental. Hughes assigned them to investigate a culvert salmon migration barrier that had been reported on a tributary to the Strait of Juan de Fuca. More important, the outcome would provide a report on the quality and quantity of the salmon habitat blocked by the barrier.

It was 7 am, and the two men loaded their overnight gear into the truck. They had already picked up lunch and were ready to begin a full days' work, having spent the night in Port Angeles. Both were a little excited about the coming work project. A worker never really knew what would happen on a full physical stream survey in the Cascadia woods. Not really. There was always some uncertainty. Something or someone could be up there. They could find a raging cougar, a rutting goat, an angry landowner, or a bush vet with a semi automatic.

Thomas Cameron and Trap Field planned for a long day. Both were concerned they could not finish a full survey of Little Elk Creek in one day. That meant a lot of trouble and a lot of hassle. So they left the Northwestern Motel an hour early and planned to work late, hoping that would do it. But their survey would begin after an hour's drive west.

Thomas slid behind the wheel of the white Chevy 4X4, and Trap, balancing a metal cup of fresh coffee, took shotgun. Thomas eased the truck into the US 101 morning traffic and started heading west. He continued through Port Angeles around the dogleg where 101 runs southerly and again west. Trap took a sip of coffee and took a long look over his shoulder at the great arc of Ediz Hook spit and the Strait beyond. This early in the morning, a thin layer of fog held over the Strait and there was little wind.

Trap thought to himself that they would be helped today by the weather. The Strait, from what he could see, was pretty flat and lay out to the north like a steaming sheet of bronze lit by the sun rising over the North Cascades. He could make out the high ground of Canada, 19 miles north, rising above the fog.

The two surveyors, for the most part, organized their own work priorities in their office in Olympia, and had decided this stream was worth taking a closer look. A double-barreled, concrete, round culvert under the Little Elk Creek crossing of State Route 113 had been identified as a complete barrier to salmon passage. It had been singled out by a preliminary fish passage inventory of culverts in Cascadia. So many culverts were found to block salmon that consulting firms were being used to handle part of the load.

Thomas and Trap had both worked for Hughes Associates a long while and both were good at what they did. The two men were not particularly good friends, though not disliking each other either. They did not have much tenure doing fieldwork together, just a few trips. Usually they each were leading a survey team with less training, but Little Elk was probably going to take an experienced team.

Thomas was pretty conservative and Trap, a political southpaw, felt it sometimes got in the way of things. The two did not see eye to eye on a lot of topics concerning the environment or politics, but they trusted one another in the field.

Thomas and Trap called themselves Stream Walkers: vernacular for a stream surveyor who had proven him or herself as a fast, reliable source of accurate information about Cascadia's streams. Thomas was the oldest (mid-forties), and Trap was a decade younger, but was more experienced at running a survey.

Thomas was a smooth talker, and could coax a pissed landowner into letting them pass on private property. Stream Walkers were notorious for trespassing and did it all the time. Asking permission took too much time when they needed to move fast. They would usually quietly slip through private property unnoticed.

Both men loved the primal Cascadia woods and looked forward to these field days. Today's survey appeared to go deep into the rainforest of the Olympic Peninsula. Walking the woods of Cascadia, a Stream Walker often finished a survey with a renewed sense of the moment. Trap often noticed the benefits he had learned about the Japanese modern day practice of "forest bathing" or "Shinrin-Yoku", which was simply a way to improve your health by walking in the woods and being completely engulfed in the moment. According to Japanese research, just being in the woods was thought to bring health by reducing stress, lowering blood pressure, and strengthening the immune system. The Stream Walkers also benefitted from inhalation of the aromas of essential oils in wood, thought to bring on bliss and promote calmness.

A Stream Walker experienced the forest like a wild animal. Every day was different, as was every survey. The landscape, the vegetation, the age of timber, and the animals all gave the survey singularity. The wind, the humidity, the heat or the cold, the approach of a new season, and especially the silence, would be somehow different. Every time it was new.

They both loved these streams. They were athletic, lean, and fit, and could move aerobically up through streams without yelling for help, complaining about the work, or falling. They didn't come to be known as Stream Walkers by making excuses to end a survey before it was complete.

Thomas and Trap learned long ago not to fight the stream by hacking the riparian zone with a machete. Instead they carried a small handheld pair of sheers for the rare vine really blocking their way. These two were faster and quieter than most and could survey several kilometers in one day, given good conditions.

A surveyor didn't get hired off a job bulletin for a Stream Walker in some personnel office. The term was more subtle and esoteric. One slowly became a Stream Walker in the minds of his or her peers, after many years of crossing, without injury or delay, some of Cascadia's most rugged country. They walk the stream itself—always going upstream, against the current—often to the source, or to a natural salmon barrier. They walked, climbed, and sometimes crawled in the stream without disturbance, and with strict procedure, ducking under large fallen cedar logs eighteen inches off the water, slipping through thickets of willow, blackberry, devil's club, sword fern, and vine maple. They were natural climbers, tackling steep rock cliffs or imposing ice covered rubble, and balancing over falls, log jams, or unstable beaver dams, and passing through silent inevitable swamps that lie upstream.

More important, the Stream Walker had to take organized, legible notes, and ultimately needed a good memory for what had been seen on the survey, how to access the stream, and what human-made features were in the headwaters. Eventually the Stream Walker would need to describe to a group of twenty technicians, biologists, and engineers what the stream was like and what it had to offer salmon should the barrier be fixed. Sometimes a solution could cost millions.

Tom turned right off US 111 to State Route 113 and again west. They had both taken this route many times. But there was no getting over it. SR 113 followed the shoreline of the western Strait for more than 40 miles, finally dead-ending at a historically rich Indian reservation. This was one of the most beautiful stretches of road in the state. Trap couldn't watch the road. Sipping his coffee he gazed over old growth cedar and spruce. Small clearings and many small gray wood home sites marked nearly every turn, some of them abandoned. It gave Trap the feeling that busy Port Angeles was far behind and he was going back in time.

Tom was being unusually quiet this first part of the road. Especially during the beginning of their survey trips, the freshness of the morning made people talkative. Trap decided to break the ice.

"Perfect day to do this," he said.

Tom glanced in the rear view mirror then at the side of the road.

"Yeah, I guess," he said, falling quiet again.

Trap thought for a moment there was something bothering Tom but he wasn't sure.

"This could be a long survey," Trap persisted. "From the map it looks like Little Elk goes up in this steep country about eight kilometers. It'll probably be about six meters wide at the mouth."

"Probably tidewater," Tom mumbled. Then again he fell silent.

Trap was now more certain something was bothering Tom. Usually he went on and on, with an opinion about everything and everyone.

The truck went around a hairpin turn and crossed over Eagle Creek culvert, a huge barrier culvert with a six-foot outfall drop scheduled for major work. Tom tightened his grip on the steering wheel as he accelerated out of the turn. He was trying to hurry, anticipating the long day. The road continued to twist and turn westerly. Then Trap asked Tom a question he'd never asked him before. Somehow he knew what was wrong. He knew today's partner, unlike himself, was a Vietnam veteran and was now lost somewhere back in the jungle.

"Ever think about Vietnam anymore, Tom?" Trap asked.

Tom flinched like coming out of a nightmare - coming to the present. He rubbed the stubble on the lower part of his face, and slowed the truck a little. He replied rather quietly.

"Christ, do I ever." He spoke calmly with no anger. "Do I ever," he said again, more like a whisper. Tom seemed to appreciate the question, as if Trap had struck the nail on the head.

"I was just thinking about it this morning, as usual. I mean, I think about what happened over there mostly in the morning." Tom glanced across the cab. "So what are you, some kind of psychic?"

"Well usually this time of day I can't shut you up!" Trap kidded. But he could sometimes read people pretty well, and that could get to be a bad habit. He had a rule about working with people. If you want to know how somebody feels, you have to ask them, or you're an assuming prick.

"Well Trap, I think about Vietnam every day of my life and that's a fact. You know, hardly an hour goes by without my blinking five times and hearing a helicopter go by, or maybe I hear an M16 rattle off a few rounds."

"You mind my asking?" Trap offered, not sure he was on welcome territory.

"No. It's okay. It helps me to talk about it, usually. The worst thing you can do is keep Vietnam all pent up inside you like some overstuffed drawer creaking at the seams—I've learned that much."

Tom looked at Trap and gave him a forced smile. "You know, especially in the morning, like now, it gets me. Or those nights when you wake up real early and can't get back to sleep. You just lay there and those bombs go off. It never goes away for me. I was a helicopter gatling gunner, and especially in the morning I think about the people I did over there as the sun was coming up."

He took a deep breath and rubbed his forehead.

"Sometimes I could just swear the next bullet that flies on this planet is for my head."

Tom began slowly shaking his head. "And after all these years, I still don't like Orientals."

Trap shot Tom a piercing look. His face tightened with anger, and he looked down at the floor, nodding. He started to speak but choked back the words.

Trap was half Native American and hated racist remarks. He didn't know if it was a weakness or strength. Sometimes it would cloud his thinking and he would have to clear his head for work matters, biting back his grating emotions. He knew what Tom had been through, and some of what his tour was like... or at least he thought he knew. Maybe he didn't know. Through his anger at Tom's racial slur he felt the digits in his fists but couldn't find it within himself to blame Tom for saying something like that. It was that damn war and these were the spoils. Tom was a high functioning casualty. He was marked for life like a branded steer, and there was nothing he could do about it... marked for life.

But on a deeper level Trap still felt some anger. What a bummer to feel so broadly about another race, he mused to himself. It was Trap's turn to be quiet as he thought about what Tom had said.

They were nearing the town of Sekiu: a remote village with the best salmon fishing in Cascadia. Both men knew the coho salmon fishing could get so hot in Sekiu they could limit a boat in an hour. If they were there the last week of August they could limit out before breakfast and spend the rest of the day walking the beaches next to the underwater forests of bull kelp just off shore. A salmon fisher could listen to the slow rising and falling of the sea, and feel the peace it brings... looking forward to fillets of fresh silver salmon.

The road dipped down and began running along the beach with Sekiu Harbor coming into view. Black silhouettes of boats tied up at the Sekiu pier could be seen to the northwest a few hundred yards off the beach. Both men were quiet for a time, wishing today was a day off, and wishing it was August instead of April. Listening to the gulls, Trap thought he could hear a cormorant calling out in the fog offshore. Their destination was only ten more miles.

Tom cleared his throat and muttered something about approaching Shipwreck Point.

"What?" Trap looked at Tom.

"I say I never go out past Shipwreck Point up ahead. You can sure tell when you're on a reservation in Cascadia."

Trap didn't like Tom's remark. He thought he was hearing another racial slur. He ran his hands through his hair. If there's one thing Trap knew about himself it was the fact that he hated bigots. Could have been his Native American side: the side the rest of the American squatters referred to as "the vanquished."

This time Tom had a remark about his way of thinking. Trap started to get pissed again, but it lasted only a brief moment. He rolled down the window of the truck and let the cool marine air blow back his black hair and lave the edges of his face, trying to simmer down. The fog was lifting and a gentle breeze came across the water from the west.

Perhaps a little humor was in order.

"You know what you need?" asked Trap as he nodded his head. "You need to get in a cage with someone who isn't white."

Both laughed a little. But an awkward feeling hung in the air for a few moments after.

"Didn't you know you were riding with a redneck?" Tom finally cut the silence.

"No, did you know were riding with a Native American?" asked Trap.

Tom was his partner: a trusted Stream Walker. He was someone he counted on. He was on his team and it was a good team. Keep your cool, thought Trap. Don't mess it up. Just simmer down. Trap took a deep breath.

"So you don't like Orientals or Indians. Is that it?"

Tom could tell he had crossed the line with Trap.

"Oh hell Trap, don't get your undies in a bundle. I say what I say and it just pops out. That's just the way I am. I'm right on the surface and I don't care who knows it."

Trap paused as the truck moved to higher ground above the Strait. He would say one last thing.

"Just don't repeat what you just said again when you're talking to me." Trap was hoping this was over. He clammed up, rubbing his hands together. Just skip it he thought. He didn't like this kind of talk, not at all.

"Oh chill out," Tom said, slapping Trap lightly on the shoulder. "What do I know?"

"Yeah I guess," Trap mumbled.

The truck dipped up and over a little crest and passed through an understory of sword fern with a canopy of douglas fir. Up ahead was a dip in the road and a double white hash mark on the pavement, marking the SR 113 milepost of Little Elk Creek.

Tom pulled off the road and got out, walking to the crossing.

"I was almost right. It's only about fifty meters across the beach to the salt chuck. No barriers downstream. That's for sure."

Two culverts passed the creek under the road. There were a couple of one-meter concrete rounds about four meters apart. They were set at a five per cent slope and the stream rifled through the pipes at about ten feet per second: a blockage to salmon. That velocity would double at high flow – the most important time for a fish on the move.

The two men dressed for the survey: hip boots with corkers, long rain jackets, polarized photo-brown glasses, and an assortment of tools necessary for taking measurements of the stream parameters, including a five meter stadia rod. The survey began with the tying off of a small thread from a hip chain, which could measure how far upstream they managed to get. Little Elk at the beginning of the survey was wide open and easy walking. The stream went wide, over gravel rubble, up around the corner. Mostly freshets were keeping the stream clear of large chunks of wood and thick vegetation. The two men worked easily upstream, taking what data they needed. The Strait sprawled out in back of them. The fog was lifting and they could see the coast of Vancouver Island in the distance when they turned to face the ocean. Small waves gently lapped the beach as a wind picked up out on the water, and the morning sun was beginning to warm the air. Trap was relaxing, leaving behind the unpleasant conversation earlier, and enjoying the hike. *Hike?* Trap thought; *this is a walk!*

The two men were having a remarkably easy time of it and within two hours of surveying were a thousand meters upstream. As they moved up through the gentle gradient they entered a more incised canyon section. The banks were vertical and composed of ancient compacted gravel, but the banks were far apart and walking the stream was still easy.

"Well this comes as a surprise," said Tom, barely breathing heavily. "This is the easiest survey I've ever done!"

The stream began to twist and turn a bit. Tom and Trap were at eighteen hundred meters when they rounded a sharp meander of the creek. A six-meter vertical falls loomed fifty meters upstream. It chattered loudly against a ten meter wide plunge pool about two meters deep, sending a plume of spray over the Stream Walkers as they advanced. A rainbow held over the falls. Tom and Trap looked at each other and smiled. End of survey! It was not quite noon.

"Well this is really something!" said Tom.

"A Stream Walker loves a survey that ends in a falls," said Trap as he arched his back, sending his gaze straight up. Then without hesitation, Trap took the stadia and climbed the falls along the moss-covered face of the adjacent cliff. Tom couldn't help but notice the style Trap climbed with. It was like he belonged there. He was clinging to the cliff like it was just another sidewalk. "Get us a photo," said Trap.

"This is the end of the line for any migrating fish," said Tom.

"Yep."

Tom snapped about six angles of the falls and scrambled to the top, sitting on a rock near the edge of the cliff. Covered with sweat from the survey, he snapped a few more photos and turned to Trap.

"Well Trap, does being a biologist feel like the way you thought it would feel when you battled your way through all of those brutal classes in college?"

"Not hardly buddy, being a biologist is like being a quarterback... the one to which all the blame lands... the guy who gets sacked!" Trap tightened his cheeks into a smile and nodded his head slowly. "It's like being a straw man for every frustrated blaming, logging, farming, fishing character out there."

They each broke out a sandwich and looked over the falls to the plunge pool. The huge flat Strait spread out in the distance. Trap wiped the sweat from his forehead. Though the survey was easy, it was enough of a workout to give him the glow a runner feels after finishing a distance race. He took a deep breath and savored the view. He could see about forty miles north and could make out the tribal land to the west. A big sloop, about forty feet, was making its way slowly up the middle of the Strait.

"Look—she's probably coming back from Maui, bound for Seattle," Trap said. "God, I love to sail."

Sitting on the crest of the falls Trap felt as high as he'd felt in years. Taking a note on his survey sheet he knew he would never forget this day.

He turned to Tom, finishing his sandwich.

"You're a coach, aren't you Tom?"

"Yeah, baseball. Little League."

"I've been asked to coach soccer." As good as Trap felt, there came a sudden pang in his stomach. The first meeting was tonight and he didn't have any excuses not to go. "I got a letter from Parks and Recreation. I did some summer work with them years ago. Trouble is, I don't know a damn thing about soccer. Not a thing!"

Tom smiled. "Watch out for the parents!"

He held the survey thread high overhead: the belt chain thread that revealed a Stream Walker had done this creek. He broke the thread that symbolically ended the survey.

"Done!" Tom exclaimed, and they headed down the mountain.

The drive back to Olympia was again quieter than usual. Trap felt good about the successful survey and the mind blowing views he'd seen this day. He decided then and there to accept the request to coach soccer. *Actually*, he thought, *no need to fuss, it's only an assistant coaching job*.

Tom loved to drive and kept the wheel. They were roaring down 111 again, southbound next to Hood Canal. Trap was finishing up his field notes on the survey. Some tension still hung in the air. Though he couldn't help feeling angry about a couple of racial slurs he'd heard, he was a Stream Walker, and that meant working with people and all races of people. Maybe today's talk had crept under Tom's thick skin. Trap started to calm down and enjoy the ride home—then he started to get a little madder again—then he would let it go. Then he would get mad again. And it was the same all the way back home.

CHAPTER 2

May 11, 1984

Sedona, Arizona

Reuben Sanchez twisted the throttle of his Harley Davidson with his right hand and accelerated his machine into the blazing Arizona heat. Southbound on Highway 17, he and his friend were just south of Flagstaff. Reuben was in an unusually good mood and was thrilled at the freedom he felt from leaving LA and getting a break from his job on the oil rigs. Loving the desert, he roared down the highway. On the open road with little traffic, he felt safe. He kept fully aware of front and rear, always kept his lights on, and made sure his baffles were good and loud so he could be heard if not seen. The evening skies of the southwest were deep cobalt chased by a polarized eastern horizon. No matter how many times Reuben rode this country, there was still a thrill that moved his spirit, and made him feel a bit religious. The sun was like a hot burning deity and the rock formations around him were like backlit black idols. Reuben felt tightness in his throat as he thought about the special place he was in. He had a sense of something new waking up within him.

"If there is a God he lives in the desert," Reuben said to himself.

The young man was covered from wrist to shoulder with tattoos, some of them obscene and graphic. He wore a sleeveless denim jacket though he bore no emblem of a motorcycle gang. There was only Reuben and his riding buddy Wade, from Newhall. Wade lived in the canyons east of LA. He followed close behind.

The hot wind splashed against Reuben's temples.

Reuben was half Mayan Indian, and half Apache. He was fluent in Spanish and English, but he knew a little Mam also from his days in Chiapas. Born in Mexico and for a time living on the Apache reservation, he moved off for good when he was in his late teens.

Reuben decided to join the ethnic diversity of America when he was a young man. Later he even joined the U.S. Army Reserve.

The two riders slowed a bit as they entered through a stand of Joshua trees. They communicated with hand signals to deal with the roar of the two Harleys. Wade signaled Reuben to take a quick break.

Both men were deeply tanned, especially their arms. Reuben's face was prematurely wrinkled from riding the burning southwest sun. They stopped their bikes and drank water. Wade pulled off his helmet and stroked his hair.

Reuben couldn't resist mentioning the section of road they just passed. "Did you feel anything strange on the last stretch of the road?"

"Yeah," said Wade, "Sort of like God was giving me a look see. The landscape spreads out ten miles in front of you. The horizon is an end-to-end sphere. Your body feels like it could float into space if you would just let go of the grips."

Wade realized he didn't know much about Reuben. "You got kin folk you think about while you're down here in the desert?"

"Did have, not any more. My ex is half crazy and lives with my baby son in Cascadia," grumbled Reuben, as the conversation took a less pious turn. "No offense against your lady but I'm full up with women. I don't want to see them or hear them."

"So she got away from you, hey Reuben? If it were me she would end up put in her place. Some women need to be shown how to act. To live with me they need to be under control."

Reuben couldn't believe his ears. "That's the coldest thing I ever heard you say, Wade."

"Watch me. I'll have her just where I want her," Wade retorted.

The two riders pulled back onto the highway and brought their bikes up to cruising speed. After a few miles Reuben noticed a car approaching from the rear, moving fast. It looked like an older car and sounded like it had no muffler. Or perhaps it had headers and cutouts. All Reuben knew is it was loud.

The driver sped up to the two bikers, following directly behind them. Reuben wouldn't speed up or slow down but identified the roaring vehicle as a two tone blue and white '57 Ford two door with no passengers. Reuben smelled trouble. He pressed his mouth into a thin line as he tightened his grip on the handlebars.

Without warning the Ford picked up speed and veered onto the left side of the highway. The man behind the wheel slowed as he came up alongside of Reuben and gave him a big grin, holding position for a long time. Glancing over, Reuben could see the grin turn to something else: a secret, ugly expression.

The driver gunned the engine, making Reuben and Wade well aware the motor had been worked over at the speed shop. It was perhaps a blueprinted late model Ford 427. The man revved the engine again like he wanted to race, but Reuben just waved at him to go ahead and pass. Instead of passing, the man in the Ford swerved a demolishing hard right into Reuben's cycle, the two machines colliding with a deafening crash. Smoke, sparks, dust and flying gravel spread about the site as the bike hit the road shoulder in shambles.

Somewhere in the cloud of dust there came a dull unconscious moan. Reuben's body had been knocked into the air and landed along the right side of the road. He let out another groan that sounded like he was unconscious. Wade was screaming, but his bike was unharmed. Reuben had his hands on the pavement with his forehead in his palms. He lay still. Wade Bode wasn't badly harmed, having stopped in time. The Ford roared as the driver floored it into the distance.

Wade's first reaction was to give chase. He lowered his head on the gas tank, and gritting his teeth started after the speeding Ford. Wade's rear tire barked between each gear. As he hit top gear he bellowed at the Ford, letting out a loud growl.

"Stop, you son of a bitch! God damn it, stop!" Wade roared. He was yelling at the top of his lungs.

Both machines were fast, and exploded with power and speed. But the modified Ford was pulling further away, and Wade Bode realized he was not going to get a license number or a mug ID on the driver. Thinking of his friend, he slammed on the brakes and turned around. After dropping the Harley into low, he gunned the throttle and started back to the scene where his friend was down. Then from behind, he

heard the tires on the Ford squeal as the car came to a halt facing Wade
and his cycle. Wade had the Harley flat out but he heard the back tires
on the Ford shriek as the front end came a foot off the pavement. Then
the Ford stopped. The maniac driver idled the engine. He was
apparently watching, staring, enjoying. Then slowly he pulled around
the corner.

Before long Wade was back at the wreckage dreading what he
would see. Dazed but not hurt, Wade jumped off his bike and ran over
to Reuben who was lying face down on the roadside. Wade nudged his
shoulder.

"Reuben can you hear me? Reuben! Say something—Reuben,
dammit say something!"

But there was no sound from Reuben. Wade reached around to his
neck to see if he could find a pulse. It was slight.

"Oh dammit," Wade moaned.

Though there was blood smeared across his face, Reuben startled
Wade by suddenly opening his eyes. Reuben's eyes were clouded with
blood and he glanced around as if trying to focus on something.

"Is it you, Wade? God... Wade, are my eyes open?" He croaked.
"My eyes... my eyes—are they open?" Wade was distressed by the
question. He felt in his stomach his friend was in the last moments of
his life.

"Yes, Reuben, your eyes are open," he stammered.

Reuben let out a feeble cry.

"Oh god... Oh god... I'm blind!"

Wade felt a choking tightness in his throat.

"I'm going to make the call!"

"I'm blind!" Reuben wheezed. He felt despair and agony take over
his body. He had been cruising down the road close to brethren with
God. Now he was covered with blood lying at the side of the road. His
chest heaved as he gasped for air. Reuben felt himself lose control of
his arms and legs. He felt himself slipping. He could feel a convulsion
coming, and he fought to keep control of his body.

That evening, Reuben lay motionless in the ER of Flagstaff
Memorial. Two doctors were working on him. A neurologist stepped

up to Reuben's face and looked in his eyes with a slit light. The pocket of fluid within Reuben's eyes was blood red. A doctor walked out to the waiting area to find Wade.

"Fella, he might have a slim chance. Might have a chance, I believe, but it doesn't look good. He is awfully banged up. You can see him fighting for his life. He keeps saying he is blind, but I've seen it before. His eyes are hemorrhaging and the clear fluid in his eyes is filled with blood, making him temporarily blind."

Wade felt a load of tension in his forearms and forehead. He spoke up, though his eyes were red and his voice was trembling.

"He got side swiped by a road rage maniac in a '57 Ford hot rod at 60 miles an hour." Wade was stuttering, and gasping for breath. He felt weak in the knees.

Wade wondered if Reuben was going to make it. *That maniac didn't get me*, he thought. But looking down at his hands it felt like both his wrists were sprained.

"I'll tell you one thing," he croaked to himself. "That doctor doesn't know how tough Reuben Sanchez is."

In the ER Reuben was not doing well. His head pounded and one of his ribs was like agony next to his lung. He was slipping away, deeper and deeper into a coma. Reuben was going away.

The doctor was trying to say something—something about his head draining—but his words were changing to colors.

*But where am I? Am I dead? I'm not sure I know. I don't know.*

Days and weeks passed. But Reuben felt nothing. For Reuben time did not pass. Time did not exist.

\*   \*   \*

Twenty-three days after the accident, Reuben opened his eyes as if jerking awake from a night terror. He could remember vivid images, colors and lights. He had made a conscious decision to fight back into life, though he felt for a time he had left it. He remained silent, staring at the ceiling. He had no words. His head was pounding. Could he speak at all? Something was very different. He continued to stare at the ceiling.

"My God, I can see!" He spoke in a hoarse voice.

Six months passed and it was near sunset on a Friday. Reuben was back at his modest one bedroom home on Placerita Canyon Rd, east of Los Angeles. His recovery after the coma was nothing short of amazing. He was walking around. His ribs were healed. He was missing a foot of his colon, but he could care less.

The only real problem was that his thinking had changed. He didn't want to go back to the roofing business where he had worked previously. There seemed to be flat spots in his thinking, and his memory was spotty at times. He would sit for hours on his small back porch and stare at the oak trees, not saying a word. He spent time considering what he would do next, and wondered why he kept thinking about working with kids. He had brief vague memories of playing soccer as a boy on the reservation, and he wondered why the thoughts came to him. Soccer didn't seem real; he didn't understand it anymore. It was in his subconscious but at the same time it was gone.

Something had changed while he was in a coma. He felt peace, and the peace came back with him. It was restoring him, healing him, giving him new thoughts and ideas.

There was a knock on the door. It was Wade.

"How's it going today buddy boy?" Wade asked cheerfully.

"I can't believe I'm still here. I just don't believe it. It's like I died and came back." Reuben said.

"You'll be okay," said Wade. "But you were nearly killed. Did I tell you they caught the maniac?"

Reuben looked blank. Wade shifted his stance, uncomfortable with the idea that Reuben couldn't recall. He looked out the window, very aware that Reuben had changed and would probably never be the same.

"Yeah, the Arizona Highway Patrol picked him up two days after we reported him. Some guy named Jimmie Creech," said Wade. "They nailed him on attempted murder, reckless endangerment, assault with a deadly weapon, and auto part theft, among other things. He had a bored out 427 with shaved heads, two four barrels, full race cam, and headers. Fast car. Now all he can do is make little motor sounds with his lips from a snug fitting little cell where he'll be for a very long time."

Reuben should have felt hatred, contempt, and a desire for revenge, but he turned his head and stared out the window at the oaks instead. Finally he turned to Wade and frowned.

"I'm through with this life, Wade. I'm through with working those oil rigs. I'm through with LA. My bike is for sale. As soon as I'm strong enough I'm going to move north. I think I told you I have an ex wife and baby son there. Maybe I'll see him sometime." Reuben's frown lightened slightly. "I've got to move on. I want to work with kids. I want to do something else with my life."

Wade reached out and sorrowfully shook Reuben's hand. It was obvious the two were going their separate ways, and there would be no more rides in the Arizona desert. Wade looked like a kid losing his best friend. Only eighteen, he would probably never finish high school.

"I'll come up to see you one of these days, see how you do with those kids," said Wade. "Maybe I'll go back to the tuna boats. Everything stinks of fish, but I feel free out on the ocean and it's good hard work. I'll be headed down to San Diego as soon as I can get my act together. I've got my gear stashed at my place."

"What about your girlfriend?" asked Reuben.

"Oh. She'll have the baby and move in with her parents again I suppose. Then she'll probably continue to gain weight until she waddles. She was always good at that. She's got a nice face if you blot out the zits. But man, what a porker."

"But Wade, that's your girl," said Reuben, "and you got her pregnant."

"I'm no father," said Wade, his eyes shifting to the window.

"Christ, Wade," said Reuben. "You told me her parents used to slap her around the house like a rag doll."

22

CHAPTER 3

November 28, 1984

Winsberg, California

The roads of Winsberg wound tightly and gracefully through the hills around the San Fernando Valley. Streets were lined with old eucalyptus showing their unraveling bark to motorists as they cruised up the canyons. Dead leaves rattled under the tires of overpowered convertibles, as an occasional blue jay or morning dove called out among jeering eucalyptus leaves. Arid trails meandered through the hills, gullies, and bluffs where homes had not yet been built. This was country for every kind of person, and the difference in the people would become apparent to anyone moving there. The smell of sage hung in the air, helping people to retrofit their smog-drenched souls. Sometimes the smell of smoke was carried through by blustery winds from the east. Then people would be on edge, fearful of the spread of fire.

Not everyone in the Valley was rich. Some were poor, some were angry, some were despondent, some were sick. It was a wasteland of secret affairs and domestic violence.

At age eighteen, Wade Bode did not need permission from anybody to marry. But Libby Sorenson was only sixteen when the pregnancy happened, so she needed parental consent. That would be her parents: Lon and Bette Sorenson, both hard drinkers. Lon was a violent man and not a suitable father.

If there ever was a cruel pounding that a young girl should not have to take, it was the evening Libby told her father she was pregnant. Libby fought back her tears as she explained to her parents she had not been careful and asked them for their help and forgiveness.

Lon and Bette, however, had a whole different take on the situation. Lon looked at her with contempt fueled by a few shots of bourbon. He exploded, his face creased with rage.

"Who's the father, you disgusting little tramp? You were probably on a one-night stand, right? Or let me guess, he picked you up next to a dumpster on the street downtown!"

Lon completely lost his temper. He gave her an opened hand across her face and came right back with a whistling backhand to the other cheek. Libby screamed as Lon got hold of her collar and shook. He shook until the wall pounded with her palms. Lon shoved a half conscious Libby against the front window and she heard it shatter behind her. She fell to the floor, and curled up into the fetal position hoping to protect the baby. Libby reached up, grabbed a kitchen chair, and pulled it over herself, hoping for some protection. Lon just kicked it across the room. He got down on one knee and put his face in Libby's. He rolled his lips at her.

"And what are you going to do now you fat little streetwalker? Lon's vicious beating continued. Lon's hand twisted into a fist. He came down again and Libby saw a black void.

She came to in two minutes, laying on the floor with her hands on her stomach. Her head was pounding and she could taste the blood in her mouth. She spoke quietly to her father with her teeth clenched.

"If you ever come near me again I'll kill you! Why don't you go beat on my boyfriend and see what happens!"

She couldn't stop him. She couldn't get out of his way. Libby promised herself she would never set foot in this house again. Bette just stood there with a mind numbing drink in her hand. Suffering from neuritis, she was too sore to take a swing… although she was plenty angry that day with her knocked up daughter.

This wasn't the first physical-emotional beating Libby had taken from Lon. In the past, he often got off work and got stupid drunk before coming home to Winsberg ready to sharpen his boxing skills on Libby. Now it was different than before. Now Libby was pregnant and vulnerable. Unthinkable things could happen.

Libby stumbled across the front room and found her way to her bedroom. She had time to gather her things and a suitcase. She didn't want to wait until he was at work. On her way to the door with her suitcase she managed to pick up her purse and her coat.

Without a car, Libby waived a taxi. Having nowhere else to go, she went to her boyfriend Wade, the father of the unborn child. Wade paid Lon a visit and threatened an assault charge. But he decided not to talk to the law; he had another plan. What he did get was quick parental permission for Libby to marry him. Without delay, the two were married, and she moved into his apartment in Kagel Canyon. But as so often happens to a brutalized woman, Libby married the same kind of man she left. Libby was a trembling wreck for weeks, and Wade didn't do much to help her recover from the trauma caused by her father.

Wade grew frustrated with Libby's erratic behavior. She was so overweight that he grew disgusted with her. Eventually he just carried on where Lon had left off. He continued to slap Libby around the house just as her father had done. At times it was worse. He was bigger and stronger than Lon. He preferred to attempt to control her, ordering her around the apartment. When she protested, he opted to wrestle her down until she couldn't move. There was no permanent physical damage, but there was a long-term train wreck in her soul. Libby tried to cope by eating and her weight problem grew worse. She was heading for severe obesity.

A few weeks later on a rainy day, Libby and Wade had a talk in the living room. He was slumped on the couch and she on the floor. Wade told Libby he was out of money. He had changed. His feelings for Libby had changed. To Wade this whole thing was a mistake. He didn't want to be a father, and he didn't want to be a husband. Libby looked terrible when she moved in, and he wanted a pretty woman. Her face was often black and blue from Wade's maniac slapping. She spent the better part of the next few months getting a huge belly and crying. He demanded she stop bawling all over the furniture.

Months later, a perfect eight-pound boy was born to Libby and Wade. They named him Morten.

Something happened to Libby the day Morten was born. It was like the house was burning—not with fire—but with a women's anger. Even so it was like a spirit had entered into the house. Over the next several months, people who looked at Morten said there was something special about him. One woman said she felt an old spirit wisdom coming from him, and that he had been here before. Other people also got a strong feeling that Morten lived in some distant past. Though she'd given birth to a perfect little boy, she remained deeply disturbed by the similarity between her husband and her father. How could she make such a mistake?

Libby would take Morten for walks in a stroller she bought from a local yard sale. Morten loved his daily rides, moving slowly along the serpentine roadside eucalyptus trees. Two doors down from Wade's lived an older, half-Native American woman who had taken a special interest in Morten. Her name was Privina, and she claimed to be a shaman. She told Libby of her many experiences in the spirit world and her communications with the animals that continually carried messages to her. Lonely, she would try to be on the front steps when Libby and Morten came by so they could spend some time talking. Libby loved to listen to her moving stories about life as a Native American shaman. The two became friends despite the age difference. Privina described her husband's death by aneurism three years ago; Libby talked about the domestic beatings from her parents and her husband, explaining the bruises on her face the day they first spoke. T hey would talk about Morten and the presence he carried with him.

Soon came the day when Libby really needed to talk to Privina. Wade informed her that he was running out of money and would be going back to the tuna boats.

Libby wheeled Morten back to the apartment where she found Wade on the front steps drinking a beer. Libby pointed at Wade in fear and anger.

"Oh for Christ's sake Wade, what am I supposed to do with an infant? How can I earn enough money for us to live on?" Wade clenched his fists while Libby started crying. She never felt so angry and defeated in her life.

"That's the way it goes," said Wade. "I told you to stop crying didn't I? Didn't I? You can keep the apartment and eat all the junk food you want. You pay the rent and the bills. I think I'll stay with friends when I'm in port, so you can have the place to yourself. Remember you're still my wife and you'll do as you're told. I just don't want this baby shit in my life. I can't sleep at night with all this crying going on. And lose some weight! You look like hell!"

"You would leave me alone with this little child? He is your son Wade, your son! What am I gonna do? I have no job, no income, and no way to pay bills!"

Wade scowled at her. He threw her on the couch and slapped her with his big right hand; she fell to the floor. What kind of monster did she marry? He was just like Lon: full of punishment. Libby blacked out on the floor, unconscious. In the blackness she heard herself screaming in despair. She heard loud noises that tapered to silence. She felt heavy hands falling on her face. Then there was emptiness, a vacuum so complete it didn't even take up space.

Finally, after several minutes, Libby came to. She lay on the couch and tried to breathe through teeth clenched with anger. *Goddamn monster*, she cursed. She made her way to the kitchen and grabbed a bread knife. She gripped the knife tightly, and a feeling came over her that she had never before experienced. She raised her upper lip like a wolf, ready to kill. Suddenly she stopped. She looked at the knife and threw it accross the room. She had reached a point where she had to change.

Instead of hacking Wade with a knife, she gathered up Morten and carried him over to Privina's, describing through her clenched teeth what had happened. Privina listened intently, silent tears dripping to her lap. Struggling to get a grip on herself, she tried to be there for Libby, who so obviously needed help.

"What am I gonna do? God, what will I do?"

It took a long time for Privina to respond due to the knots in her throat.

"Suppose Morten stays here, and you get a job. You drop him off in the a.m. and pick him up at quitting time," Privina said.

Libby's voice was shaky, "Yeah, but Privina, I'm only sixteen, I couldn't pay. What could I do for work?"

Privina got up from the couch and took a long gaze out the front window.

"We don't need that son of a bitch. That guy is a real son of a bitch. How could he leave you stranded with an infant? He is a rotten son of a bitch. We'll work this out, Libby," said Privina, as she made her right hand into a fist.

"Two of my sons are back on the East Coast now," said Privina. "but the middle one lives in Olympia, and nearly put himself through college as a painter, along with some student loans. He's still in the painting business with his own contracting company. Do you think you could work for a painting contractor? Are you strong and fast with your hands?"

"Well, I love art, and I love to paint," said Libby, looking down at the floor.

Privina picked up the phone and called her son Bibs the painter, and handed the phone to Libby. Bibs explained what commercial painting was like in Cascadia: relying on speed because summers are short, working high up on scaffolding, the all-essential clean up, spackling, puttying technique, followed by more speed. Speed is money, faster, faster. Finally Bibs said something to Libby that would change her life. Because she was a friend of his mother, he offered her a job, should she find a way up north.

Privina found an old set of weights in the want ads and set them up in her garage for Libby to improve her body strength. Libby would drop Morten off at Privina's and started hiking the Winsberg trails. Within days she began losing weight.

But painting season had not yet arrived up north, and a week later Libby had not found work. Privina took her to the Employment Development Center in Winsberg. They found some housekeeping jobs in the area where Libby could either walk or take the bus. There were a few nanny jobs also. Privina jotted down the phone numbers. As they were leaving, Libby started feeling pain in her stomach. She noticed her hands were beginning to tremble. Realizing the situation she was getting into, her breathing turned shallow. *What about Morten?* She thought. *My god, what will happen to Morten?*

Libby left Privina and Morten and went up into the trails. She hiked about three miles in and turned and faced the valley. Nauseated, she sat down in the center of the trail. She put her forehead on her knees and started breathing deeply. At first her breath came out in sobs. A few more weary breaths and Libby suddenly toughened up. She got to her feet and started quickly down the trail. Libby went straight to Privina's place because Morten was there. Privina met Libby at the door and threw her arms around her drooping shoulders.

"Libby, I have the most wonderful news. I found you a job! You'll be wanted to sign on with the Student Painters out of Northridge on Monday morning."

Libby raised her arms and pointed at the sky. Her eyes filled with tears as she hugged Privina. She was so relieved she had trouble speaking. Privina smiled a broad smile and looked happily at Libby.

"Come on my pretty, let's go teach you to drive." Privina gave Libby a broad smile.

CHAPTER 4

May 28, 1985

San Diego, California

Arcing behind the Sunset Cliffs and in the lee of Coronado Island is the beautiful tuna capitol of the west coast, Point Loma. The seas stretching to the eastern Pacific are the great sport and commercial tuna fishing grounds. Tuna fishing in Point Loma is as old as the city itself. The old fishers, set in their ways by lifetimes of hard work, don't want change.

Young Wade took on the past of the old timers without delay. He was offended, in fact outraged, by the strong interventions of the government to prevent the decimation of the great dolphin pods that marked the sign of tuna underneath. Walking the docks and beer joints of Point Loma, Wade would join other unemployed deckhands looking for a full ride on some local highliner. They hung out in the old sections of the port so they could steer clear of the sport fishing yuppies going out on the water in an expensive charter for a huge fee, only to up chuck the whole time. According to the local fisherman, you used to make fair money if you were willing to spend a few months on the ocean... harder now. On one occasion a group of Wade's fellow unemployed fishermen gathered at the local pub for several pitchers of beer. They spoke loudly, sounding like Brazilian Surdos.

"So anybody get on a highliner yet?" said a voice from the group. "It's getting harder every year... new fish finding technology means smaller crews. The stocks are tanking and all the government can do is count porpoises."

"Yeah, we've all got our own observer now with their fucking degree in marine biology and their scientific buzzwords: You should hear ours... 'given hypothetical theoretical unresolved frameworks?'"

That brought horse laughter to the group. One tuna boat deckhand stood in his heavy coat and raised his beer mug.

"Here's to tuna and dolphins," he croaked.

"Yeah!" said another slightly resentful Fin. "Don't forget to thank the scientific community for the mercury in our fish. Give a round for coal, cement, oil, mining, PVC, smelting, and sinter! Thanks for helping out!"

Wade had some difficulty getting a commercial ride. Big, strong, and aggressive, he had an overwhelming urge to run the show. As a team member most tuna crews thought of him as an asshole who would resent women, boatswains, and government authorities. He also tried to bully his way past someone trying to learn the ways of the experienced fisher, because he wanted to be top dog. He knew gear though and could show people how to get things done, even if it meant showing people how powerful he was. Aggressive was an understatement. If Wade offered a shipmate a drink and he politely said no thanks, he would pin him to the wall with his big arms and pour a bottle of whisky down his throat. Those who knew him were beginning to think sociopath. Few were really close to him.

More than anything, Wade was looking for another fishing trip. Too bad beaten and battered Libby tried to get in the way. He'd show her a thing or two. As his wife she would heel when he said heel. If not, she might end up getting worked over again.

Wade decided to sign on the Orion Sun out of San Diego. It was a purse seiner about 90 meters long, with a crew of 33. Fast and ready to punch ahead, the vessel had state of the art diesel electric propulsion. They would be fishing the eastern Pacific, which meant a government observer would be on board. In this case the observer was a 22 year old graduate student out of UCLA, named Bruce Hills. He would be estimating the dolphin incidental catch for the annual quota. As Wade stepped on board he saw the observer thumbing through his data sheets. He spat on the deck.

Observers and crewmen did not often see eye-to-eye. In some cases they clashed violently. State of the art purse seining techniques caused high dolphin mortality. Members of the crew knew it but did not want to change the rigging. They sure didn't want a snot-nosed kid with a fancy degree to tell them how to do their work. The crewmen loved their work, and they loathed anyone trying to interfere, especially a stuffy know-it-all college graduate. Wade never did have any use for observers and he daydreamed about a smooth drop-kick of Dr. Bruce over the stern, to be hopelessly tangled in the net. Wade's mind drifted into his hormones. He found himself sweating as he snapped out of his fantasy. Wade helped cast away the lines and the Orion Sun was under way. They headed south towards Central America and the open ocean.

Two days out the wind came up to about 20 knots and the seas rose to about 10 feet. If Orion had one flaw, it was to roll from side to side when the swell came up. On a day like today it was a challenge for Bruce to make his way from his cabin to the galley. If there was a place on the ship to get one's balance tested, it was the hallway that led to the galley.

At one point Bruce ran into Wade on the way to the galley for lunch. Bruce tried to introduce himself, but Wade just glared at him.

"Just stay out of my way, always! If you see me coming get out of the way," grumbled Wade, "damn college puke!"

Bruce stepped to the side of the hallway and started to step past Wade. Wade, the much bigger man, threw his shoulder against Bruce, knocking him hard against the wall. Bruce grunted from the impact.

"I said stay out of my way, didn't I?"

Bruce looked Wade in the eye. Though not as big as Wade, he was not about to submit to this abuse.

"You're looking for a whole lot of trouble, aren't you?" said Bruce. "You're gonna get yourself thrown off this vessel."

Bruce showed Wade he was not afraid of him. As Wade went for a third body check Bruce grabbed him by the coat and shoved him back. Bruce walked away looking over his shoulder at Wade.

A hundred miles offshore the Captain of the Orion made his first set. The net skiff made an arc around a pod of dolphin, as the captain suspected albacore below. They tried to dip the seine after having it pursed and a pod of dolphin passed over the net. Not all of them, however.

There must have been 60 dolphin mixed in with about 200 albacore. The captain noted from the wheelhouse that there was a wide variety of other species in the purse, as the crew used the boom to bring the catch over the turntable. A crewman released the bottom of the net and the rear deck was suddenly inundated with fish. Wade moved in on the catch as if he wanted to get the trash fish out. He grabbed a plastic tote and started throwing in all the undesirable species. It was a mess of slime, scales, and shredded fins. Bruce was close beside Wade.

"Perfect," thought Wade as he twisted his lips.

When Bruce seemed most involved in estimating the dolphin kill, Wade lifted the bin full of fish and dumped it on Bruce. He was literally covered in fish, down on his back, and struggling for his footing in the fish and slime. Bruce was coughing and gagging.

Wade leaned over to Bruce and said rather convincingly, "Oh shit, bud, sorry about that. That one got away from me."

Bruce looked up at Wade with a deadly expression. He took a step to the side and then to the other side. He seemed to be having trouble seeing. Wiping his eyes, finally he spoke.

"We need to talk this over in the rec room. I'll see you there," he said from deep in his throat.

Bruce waved his hand and told him to follow. "Rec room! We're going to have a talk!" Wade looked up at the wheelhouse and the captain seemed to be occupied. He picked up one of the clubs used to knock out the tuna and slipped it into his back pocket. Bruce was the older man at 22. Wade was only 18 but he outweighed Bruce by 50 pounds.

There was no discussion, and it was a short fight. Bruce raised his hand at Wade but did not have his footing. Wade reached into his back pocket for the fish club and planted it right on Bruce's forehead. Bruce, covered in fish slime, fell very hard. Wade struck two more times at Bruce's head, grazing the club off the side of his skull. Wade turned around as the captain peered into the porthole. Both men were in deep trouble for much different reasons. Hurrying back to the bridge, the captain called a rescue plane and requested a sheriff's deputy and a replacement observer on board.

The crew continued to work the catch while the captain took care of details regarding the fight. The second mate, as medical officer, didn't hesitate to provide aid to Bruce.

Wade stood on the deck for a moment and looked at the birds flocking next to the ship. He took a long last look at the ocean; the transparent blue seemed somehow perfect, and without end. Wade was just beginning to realize he had beaten a man half to death. The hardest part for Wade was that it was his fault. He was dead wrong. He was guilty as hell. The charge would likely be felony assault with a deadly weapon. He lowered his head.

Wade was brought up to the wheelhouse for questioning and was taken directly to his quarters.

*   *   *

Wade was taken to the county jail to await trial, where he was found guilty. The judge was harsh on him for his beating of a federal agent performing his duties and gave him a four-year sentence at the state prison.

Bruce recovered from the clubbing he received from Wade, but suffered a severe concussion. After being treated for disturbances in his vision, and after giving a statement to the police, he was released. He would never serve as an observer again and went north, working temporary jobs in Cascadia.

Libby could not grieve when Lon and Bette Sorenson died a few months later in a head on collision on that twisty road to Winsberg. Following the crash they were knocked off an embankment. The car rolled several times while a half full bottle of gin bounced around in the back seat, shattering in the package tray. From now on Libby would go it alone.

She did well to keep pace at her painting job, and was getting pretty good at it. She had become a slight distraction for her painting crew as she started losing weight. She could also get along with the others she worked with. The crew accepted working with her despite an inner anger that she sometimes displayed. They enjoyed watching her graceful movements, and appreciated her sarcastic sense of humor. Libby made a decision for herself during her time with the student painters. She would spend the next two years in Winsberg with the help of Privina. She would save her money, get Morten sleeping at night, and move to Olympia when she was 18 and Morten was two. There she would take Bibs up on his offer to work for him, and shed the miserable memories of the men in her life—or so she thought.

Over the next two years Libby lost 60 pounds and grew three inches taller. She had become a young woman with a curvy slim figure and a sensuous long neck. Libby joined a health club, hired a personal trainer, and started fitness training. Her workouts made her lean and shapely, her waist growing smaller as she lost body fat. At the same time, weights helped vent her anger. She would grit her teeth and strain against the leg curl universals. She did long sets of sit-ups while clutching weights with her hands. She barred the wolf-like snarl that marked her rage against Wade. Her arms and legs grew strong and tight. Her hair grew long, touching her waist. Libby was becoming a very good-looking young woman. Her unsubtle breasts were enough to get any man's attention. Her face was pretty, with high cheekbones and disarming dark brown eyes. Her eyebrows slanted naturally toward the bridge of her nose.

Though emotionally ravaged, Libby tried to avoid despair. Yet fear remained. Trying for a better life, she nervously divorced Wade while he was in prison. After turning 18, Libby changed her name, and Morten's. From that day on she would be known as René Coogman, and her son was now Riley. She wanted to live in the northwest where everything was wet and clean. Bibs let her know that people treated each other well in Cascadia.

René did her best, though at times she felt rather strange in a way that was hard for her to understand. She would try to talk Privina into going with her, but Privina would cry with simultaneous grief and relief. Refusing to go along, Privina reminded René she was a shaman and would continue to work metaphysically, helping her find her way in Cascadia.

Try as she might, she could not entirely escape her past. She was haunted by dreams of Lon and Wade. Sometimes she would lose her concentration in the middle of a conversation and drift off her train of thought. Sometimes she would act like she wasn't there at all. In spite of her new beauty she would not go out with a man, though they were falling over each other to get a date with her. Men were like Lon and Wade: they left you suffering. She was beginning to wonder if she could ever love a man again. After being beaten by a big, utterly controlling man, she was tortured by inner demons. She didn't know how to heal what was inside her. What could she do to avoid the night terrors, waking up screaming, completely convinced that Wade was in the room? She sure didn't need men. She loved Riley and that was enough.

## CHAPTER 5

April 2, 1998

Tumwater, Cascadia

Trap arrived early to be sure he had the right directions from the Thurston Soccer Club. He had a bulletin explaining that the first meeting of Soccer Team Four will take place at William A. Bush Park off of Yelm Highway at 5:30 pm on April 2.

William Bush was not really a soccer field, just a cattail pond with one-foot diameter fir trees lining a greater open area in the center. The park was also a popular hangout for wild geese, crows, and gulls, adding to the noise of excessive traffic from the adjacent highway.

Trap definitely had nerves in his stomach as he looked across the park. He was wondering how he managed to get himself in this situation without knowing the first thing about soccer.

There was an African-American man and a kid, probably his son, tossing a football back and forth at the east end of the park down by the cattails. As the man ran closer, Trap could tell he was stiff in the knees. But the man leaned back and gunned a perfect spiral like a professional athlete. Smiling, he then walked over to Trap and introduced himself.

"You with the soccer team?' he asked Trap in a raspy voice.

"Yeah, I'm supposed to back up the head coach, someone named Reuben Sanchez," mumbled Trap.

"I'm Jaylen, and my son over there is Deshaun. We signed him up for soccer. I'll lend you guys a hand coaching when I can, but I work a lot of swing shift. And I can't run all day like I used to— transplanted ligaments in my knees. Car accident."

Jaylen seemed bright and friendly, and Trap liked him right off. He had a very contagious smile. Trap thought perhaps Jaylen could sing, with a beautiful rasp to his voice, but he didn't feel right asking.

"Have you coached soccer teams in the past?" asked Trap, shifting his weight from left to right.

"Not a bit, not even a little bit" said Jaylen. "I just love sports and Deshaun asked if he could get on a soccer team. That kid is a natural athlete, and how hard could soccer be? You'll see, he'll be just fine."

*Boy do I love this guy*, thought Trap. *No clue about soccer either, but smiling and ready to go.*

Trap was beginning to relax when a man and his son pulled up in a Plymouth Voyager and opened the rear hatch. The man pulled out a netted bag full of soccer balls and cones. Next to him was a heavy-set boy with short black hair, helping his dad with the gear. Trap approached the man and cleared his throat.

"You're the soccer coach I would guess," said Trap, sticking out his hand. "Trap Field."

"That would be me. Call me Reuben." The first thing Trap noticed about Reuben was his arms. He was literally covered with R-rated tattoos. Reuben shook Trap's hand.

"I told the Soccer Club I would help you out, seeing as how your regular coach left the area. I've got to tell you, I'm not much of a soccer player." Trap felt a sudden pang of unworthiness. He had not even read up on the game. It became apparent to Trap he hadn't truly decided to do this until today.

"Well, I need help," said Reuben in a muffled voice. "I coach baseball, too. So I've got a full plate."

Reuben gave Trap a first impression: he looked like a Latino soccer guru. Trap could swear Reuben had soccer written all over his rugged features, like he had been involved in the game for decades. But Trap would later come to realize he was a badly needed assistant coach.

Coach Reuben unfolded a card table and chair, placed a stack of forms on the table, and dropped a stack of cones on the forms.

Parents were beginning to arrive with their kids, some obviously too young to be on this team.

Once a good crowd of kids and parents had gathered, Reuben spoke up, putting his fist on his hip.

"Could I have your attention over here please? My name is Reuben Sanchez and welcome to the Blue Angels U-14 soccer club. I want to say right off: I am a Christian and I plan to have a prayer circle before each game. I don't want to offend anyone, so if you choose, step back from the circle or join the circle, honoring the privacy of your own faith. Also, for you players, I am a safety guy. Chin guards, soccer shoes, and cups are required for you to play on this team."

One of the kids was looking around as if not quite understanding.

Reuben paused a moment and looked at the ground.

"Does everyone know what a cup is?"

One kid wrinkled his forehead looking totally baffled.

"What's that?" the kid asked.

Coach Reuben spoke right up. "Trap, could you take this youngster over yonder and explain to him what a cup is?"

Muffled laughter spread through the parents standing nearby. Trap tried, but he couldn't quite hide a grin.

"What's your name, buddy?"

"Kyle Heng," the boy said.

"Well Kyle, soccer can get pretty rough sometimes, and there's some places on your body you want to protect... like with a cup."

Kyle looked completely blank.

"You know, you have places on your body where it really hurts to get hit," Trap tried again.

"I don't get it!" Kyle shook his head.

Trap shrugged, realizing this kid was not the athletic type.

"You know, your balls, man," Trap was nodding his head and pursing his lips.

Kyle still looked baffled, but he finally looked up at Trap and asked:

"Why put a cup on a soccer ball?"

Trap was trying to hold back, but was quickly losing it. He buckled to his hands and knees and started belly laughing. Nearby parents were giggling as well.

"No… No… No! They're hanging between your legs… your balls! You're a boy so you've got balls. Ever heard of a low blow? That's when you get hit in the balls—that's what you need to protect!" The parents could not help but overhear all this and started to drown out Trap with laughter.

Even after all that, Trap wasn't sure that Kyle got the point, but he ended the conversation by pointing at his own zipper and announcing: "balls!" He walked away, the parents still laughing.

Reuben ran his hand over his mouth to conceal his laughter.

"Okay," he said in a loud voice. "Now that we think we know what a cup is, I'll need each player to fill out a form with me and have your parents sign it." He sat down at the card table and asked tryouts to form a line.

"I'll need your name, uniform size, and you'll need to verify that you're 14 years old or younger," said Reuben.

Trap became serious as he looked over the kids. He stood next to Reuben to get familiar with the sign up procedure. There was something very special about the line of children in front of him; something that stopped him in his tracks. The first kid to sign up was Latino: Gabriel Santa Cruz. Next was a Japanese boy, Kip Kamishi. The next three were brothers of Pakistani decent: Babar, Wahid, and Sajad Haq. Then there was an African-American kid, Willis Gray. Another Latino boy stood in line: Diego Torres. Next was a big white kid, JR Matigan. Then came Eyana Jones, a black girl. A kid of European decent, Riley Coogman, followed. Right behind Riley was an African-American, Deshaun Jacob, who looked like a running back. Next in line was Kyle Heng, of Chinese decent. After that came Nicolás Sanchez, son of the coach. Then another black kid by the name of Hines Chastain stood in line. And near the back of the line was a girl named Jerri Morgan. Two remained: a thin blond kid named Ralph Neil, and a big red-headed athletic kid named Kenny Finnegan.

Trap didn't know how to react. It was hard to believe in this predominately white town that his team looked like a world united team. This was the most diverse group of kids he'd ever seen in one place. He slowly turned his gaze to Reuben and then over to Jaylen. Jaylen just smiled back, knowing what he was thinking. Even the coaches turned out to be black, olive white, and brown. There was something uplifting about this team that all three coaches felt. The kids' diversity was off the charts, in this neighborhood. There was a kind of intangible feeling hanging in the air that this team was going to be something special. The kids, however, were completely unaware of the remarkable melting pot they joined.

Trap eyed the group of parents with a half grin and all he saw was nods and smiles. In the back of the group he saw a slim woman wearing a bulky blue jacket. Wearing big dark glasses, she looked rather awkward and plain, but somehow intriguing. She caught Trap's eye, and he quickly turned away so as not to be obvious. *It figures she'd dress in blue*, Trap thought to himself. He turned around and started introducing himself to the players.

"I'm Trap Field, but you can call me Trap."

But the kids weren't having any of that. From that point, whether on the field or off, the kids would call him Coach Trap.

Reuben spoke up again. "There isn't much time left, but let's get some dribbling going." He spread out some cones for the kids to weave around and announced next practice would be Thursday at 5:30 here at William Bush.

When practice was over, Trap made a beeline without delay to Yelm Soccer Shop. Inside, he bought a book of soccer rules and five videos on soccer basics. The salesman was showing Trap a catalogue of hundreds of soccer tapes he could order when the shop door swung open again. Trap looked up. To his surprise it was the woman in the long blue coat and her son Riley. This time Trap could not avoid looking at her without being rude. Getting a closer look, he was a bit taken by her pretty face. Her eyes seemed locked on Trap's dark eyes, though it may have been the other way around. He felt a wave of butterflies pass through his stomach.

"Hi," said Trap, choking back an urge to stammer. "Two Blue Angels?"

"Hi," she said. "One Blue Angel, one soccer mom. We thought we'd better pick up a cup." She broke into a smile. "And Riley knows what it's for." Both of them blushed as René dropped her purse. Trap and René both knelt to reach for it, but René was there first. In stooping down her bulky blue coat touched the floor and slightly revealed her dress and legs. Trap saw she was a shapely athletic woman, her legs lean and powerful in the dim light of the shop.

*Whoa*, thought Trap to himself.

"Yeah, a cup—you strap it to the ball before you kick off," said Riley, smiling and scratching his nose at the same time. Trap started laughing.

"Sort of an awkward moment for the first day," he admitted.

"And some soccer shoes, too. Don't forget the shoes, Riley. You did fine Trap," she smiled again.

Trap could not help but notice she looked a bit troubled, but he wasn't sure. He couldn't be. He might venture to ask her if they ever got acquainted.

"Well, we gotta check out the shoes, we'll see you Thursday. My name is René, by the way: Riley's mom." She shook Trap's hand and started towards the rear of the store.

Trap brushed his thick hair back and started out, but he thought he sensed her eyes on him.

CHAPTER 6

April 14, 1998

Bremerton, Cascadia

Trap received a job assignment from Hughes to take a construction representative and negotiate the removal of a perched culvert salmon barrier from a private landowner's property. First thing in the morning the two men headed for the Kitsap Peninsula. The meandering channels of Puget Sound were everywhere; its moody twisting and turning waterways seemingly went on forever. The waters rose and fell with the moon, loosely held in place by a bottom of till and edges of barnacle and rock lichen. The air smelled of incoming tide, brown algae, and salt. Trap was aware that some flow patterns in the Salish Sea are very complex. There are channels in the sound that always flow the same direction regardless of the tide's pull. Water from some channels clashes, spirals, and upwells into other channels, challenging a salmon's great current finding abilities. Experienced boaters took caution with this water. Most of the time the narrow channels form a great placid maze: the southern reach of the Salish Sea. Sailors can underestimate the sound when the wind blows. They occasionally find themselves trapped in a blur of howling wind, nasty chop, and white water.

The driver of the Hughes pickup was pushing north on Highway 3 along the edge of Sinclair Inlet just south of Bremerton. Trap and Charlie Bailey, one of the construction equipment foremen for Hughes Environmental, were headed for a small ranch near Poulsbo. There would be no stream walking today, but a task just as touchy. Still it was lucky for Charlie, who was 50 pounds overweight and in no shape to walk streams.

The two riders were quiet for a few moments, glancing over at the Naval Shipyard.

"You a native?" asked Chuck.

Trap didn't particularly like that question at all, although he'd heard it many times. He thought to himself maybe he was growing temperamental, having a Native American slice of the pie. You a native?... you a native?... you a native?

"I don't know, Chuck... what do you got to do to be a native?" Trap said as he wiggled his eyebrows up and down.

"You got to be born in Cascadia! You know, a real live native." Chuck raised his voice and gestured with his finger towards Trap.

"No hope at all, huh?" Trap smiled on one side of his mouth. "How about I get born again? It could be like some sort of religious thing. And there's my background: big points with the native crowd. Where do you think the term Native American comes from?"

"Well I'll tell ya," Trap went on with a little sarcasm, "My mother was a wheat farmer from Wenatchee." He straightened his cap and pulled it down over his eyes. "Dad was a salmon fisherman out of Westport. Just kidding buddy... I was born in Nelson B.C., and my mom was Native American. My dad was Irish."

"Have you ever been to one of these landowner meetings before, Chuck?" asked Trap, changing the subject.

Chuck thought for a minute, staring again at the Salish Sea Naval Shipyard. "Naw, but how hard could it be?"

"It's not hard, it's soft. You've got to be as nice as you know how to be. All kidding aside, you got to be like a headwaiter at the nicest fish house in Seattle. Walk on eggs or he'll run us off for sure. No matter what, don't tell them what to do, ask them what they want. Make no mistake, the whole outcome of this project depends on this meeting here today."

The truck roared past Bremerton and increased gradually in elevation. Trap thought to himself what a salmon graveyard this stretch of road was. The road fill was 50 feet higher than the dozens of small steep culverts, preventing salmon passage. This was not a particularly beautiful stretch of Cascadia, and Trap's mood usually sank when he crossed this section of highway.

44

The truck finally reached the Quick Stop called Four Corners and Trap turned a sharp right next to the convenience store and on up Big Valley Road to the Rich Eagan place. Mr. Eagan was standing in the front driveway. Trap was right on time as usual, and Rich seemed to appreciate it. As many meetings as Trap had with Rich, they always had the company of Danny. Danny was a nice kid, and he was developmentally disabled. He seemed to stagger more than walk. He always wore orange overalls and had trouble speaking due to an undershot jaw. But Rich Eagan always welcomed Danny to his onsite meetings and treated him with respect. That is why Danny kept coming.

The Eagan ranch was small and beautiful, the property split by Kingston Creek. It was thought to be a quality salmon stream by a Stream Walker who had previously surveyed the creek.

The four men shook hands and started toward the back of the house to the pasture. Charlie looked across the pasture and stopped, pointing across the clearing.

"Holy Christ!" he bellowed, "there's a camel over there. What's a camel doing in Cascadia's rain country? Look at him, he's got two humps too... Why do some camels have one hump and others have two?"

"Different species," said Trap, pointing his finger. "A one hump is a dromedary... a two hump is a bacterian."

"How did you know that?" asked Chuck.

"Mammalogy was a great class," said Trap.

"Stinking animals," said Chuck derisively.

Rich Eagan fell quiet, lowering his eyes to the ground. Trap shot a glance at Chuck hoping he would learn about working with landowners. He just didn't quite have the knack.

"Yeah," said Rich. "That's Habib the camel and he belongs to my neighbor, Abeni. She's the small African-American woman that lives on the other side of the county road. She's renting this pasture and she is just convinced she is going to make a bunch of money on that camel one of these days."

In the distance Abeni came down the stairs to her house, more out of curiosity than anything. Rich waved at her and she seemed to relax, sitting on the stairs that led to her front porch.

"Christ, now we got camels and pygmies!" blurted Charlie.

Trap spoke between clenched teeth, "What did I say back up the road?"

Chuck spat on the grass and pulled out a cigarette.

Trap was quiet, but inside he was getting angry.

The four men went through the side gate and to the barrier culverts. The meeting was short, but Trap explained the terms of replacement of the pipe. Rich, wanting to help, abandoned one pipe crossing altogether as part of the deal.

"What a fine man that guy is," Trap said to himself.

After the meeting the four men went back through the side gate. The camel came across the pasture. Abeni seemed to be getting nervous, still sitting on her front steps. She opened the gate on the far side of the pasture and started to jog towards the camel. Trap was walking in front of the rest wondering if he had fully covered the meeting. Abeni was waving her arms and yelling.

"Mean camel! Mean camel! Watch out!"

The camel charged. For some reason he ignored the three men walking closest to him, probably thanks to some familiarity with Rich and Danny. He was headed for the back of Trap's head and was getting close when Danny moved in on the camel.

Rich yelled for everyone to watch out, as Danny did the trick. He entangled himself in the camel's legs, nearly knocking the camel down. Now, Danny had one arm around the camel's neck but was mostly under the animal. The camel's two front legs buckled and he came down on in the middle of Danny's chest. Danny was wrestling the animal now, his hands gripping the heaving ribcage. In spite of Danny's struggling, the camel was heavy. Danny continued yelling and pushing the animal in the sides and shoulders. About then Abeni arrived. She went immediately to the right side of the animal and took hold of the camel's ear. She screamed.

"Habib, get up!" She tightened her grip on the camel's ear: " Habib, get up! Get off him!"

Finally Abeni, as small as she was, managed to twist the camel slightly to the right, allowing Danny to slide out from under the front legs of the camel. Enraged, Danny came out from under Habib with a look on his face like he would have fought that animal to the death. Both fists were clenched, and he was gasping for air. Trap and Rich went over to Danny to see if he was okay, while Chuck just shook his head and laughed.

"What is this, some kind of circus?"

Trap thanked Danny from blocking what might have been a severe head butt, or maybe a bite.

"He wouldn't hurt you real bad," said Danny dusting off his orange overalls, "they call him the kissing camel from Poulsbo."

Danny seemed fine—maybe even a little proud of himself. Trap moved over next to him.

"Thanks Danny," said Trap. "You really saved me over there and I owe you one."

"Probably would have gotten the old head butt to the back of the neck," said Danny.

Charlie continued to shake his head and let out a gloating, obscene laugh. Trap got Charlie off to the side by pulling his arm.

"Hey, take your hand off me!" said Charlie.

"Man, I told you to treat these people with respect. That means all of them!"

Then Rich Egan took a long look at Charlie.

"What's your name again?" He asked.

"Charlie Bailey," said Charlie.

"What is so funny?" Rich asked Charlie, his voice flat and even. "Are you laughing at the little black lady, or Danny?" Rich's eyes narrowed. "Or is it the camel and the project? Just what is making you so giddy?" Rich nodded at Charlie, as his tone became threatening. "You work on my property, you treat the owners like you are a guest, or you will not work here at all! I've got half a mind to throw you both out of here for good!"

Finally, Charlie shut up.

## CHAPTER 7

April 15, 1998

Lacey, Cascadia

It was the first full day of practice for the Blue Angels U-14 team. Trap was surprised again over the ethnic jumble of his team. He was amazed, in fact, just as he had been the first day of practice. How did this team come together by itself? Nobody planned for this, it just happened. He thought about it often.

The kids and coaches walked onto the Redfield Middle School soccer field. Reuben Sanchez, the head coach, had completed his move from Arizona a few years back and was now a permanent Olympia resident. Everything he said he would do after his road rage incident, he did. It was like he had morphed into someone else. He rented an apartment in Tumwater, started working with youth through the school, church, and county as a guidance counselor and motivational speaker. Reuben also coached soccer for a few years, with limited success.

Trap crossed his eyes, realizing how little he knew about the game. Personally, Trap had only a week's experience. In that week he bought or rented several videotapes on soccer and watched all of them. He was making some solid progress on understanding the game.

Trap was a fast learner and almost immediately started making some connections. One day he was walking on the Rails for Trails path and he got in a conversation with an older British gent walking a couple of greyhounds. It turned out he was a retired professional soccer coach. Trap convinced him to agree to answer questions from time to time, and got his address and phone number. Surprised by the information suddenly available to him, Trap thought this was really coming together.

A few days later, Trap met Nick Carson. Of all the people Trap could meet regarding soccer, it should be him. Though they hadn't met before, Nick Carson worked in the legal department out of Hughes. Nick was a a critical help to Trap. He was smart as a whip, loved sports, and had twenty years experience playing soccer. Plus, the guy loved to talk. As they talked, Nick grew to like Trap for his keen interest. When it came to soccer, Nick was a weapon in Trap's back pocket for sure. He could answer anything Trap came up with. In fact, he was happy to do it. Nick encouraged Trap to do a great deal of scouting of the teams the Blue Angels would eventually play.

As always, Reuben was determined to stretch everyone before playing soccer. Although he wasn't highly experienced, Trap showed them a few routine stretches. Some of the kids loved it, and some hated it, but it helped them to loosen up.

Reuben and Trap agreed on some dribbling drills, followed by passing drills. Trap showed the team how to kick soccer style.

"Kick it with your laces!" he repeated constantly. How to kick soccer style turned out to be one of the hardest things for the kids to learn. Later in the practice they had their first scrimmage. It was a bit of a mess. Kids were bunching around the ball. Kids were refusing to kick the ball in the penalty area. Kids were off sides.

Many of the soccer teams in the league had trouble with filling up teams with players. Even when they had a full roster, other teams had trouble getting players to come to practice. The Blue Angels had the opposite problem. They came out in diverse swarms for the Blue Angels. Young people were everywhere, tripping over themselves to get a shot at the team. Trap kept wondering why this was happening. Something was good. Kids could feel it when they walked onto the field.

"We need you fast and loose," Reuben was saying, "not tight and bulky. Try yoga a few times and see how you feel after, not before." Trap walked over and offered his hand. Reuben shook it and said:

"Well, here we go Coach."

At the end of their first set of drills, Reuben set up practice times and places and made the kids well aware he would keep them in line if necessary. Trap had a notebook full of stuff to work on.

"I've been thinking about you kids all week," said Trap. "I think about you a lot, and I think you can be a very special team. But you have to reach for it and you have to work for it. I've been watching a lot of soccer lately and everybody tends to praise the guy who kicks in the goal. Well, you just remember: that goal belongs to the whole team —not just the guy who taps it in." The kids looked at each other as if they hadn't thought of it that way.

Trap turned and headed towards the sidelines only to see René standing alongside his equipment. She was backlit by the sun dropping southwest. He could not help taking another look at her attractive face. Trap looked down and stroked back his hair. He looked again at René. She was wearing a heavy down jacket.

"Hi, René," he said.

"Hi Coach," she said, "how's it going?"

Trap found it hard to avoid looking at her.

"You know I never feel quite worthy when someone calls me coach. It hasn't been that long," said Trap.

"Oh don't be so hard on yourself, mister. You look like a coach to me. Maybe you don't have the Blue Angles game down yet, but when you talk to those boys and girls, it makes them feel good. You've got lots of talent where many have none. You know how to speak with them." She tilted her head to the side, shyly. Her expression was vague, unrevealing of what she might be thinking.

"And how do you know all this?" he asked.

"Whenever my son is involved, I catch on quick," she remarked, smiling on one side of her mouth.

"And besides, I think you'll find out my son Riley is very smart and he fills me in on everything going on out there."

"You have an informer?" asked Trap.

"Riley says there's something special out there on that field. He says there's something magic about the team," René said.

Trap again noticed there was a slight dimness to her smile. There seemed to be some pain in her face, but he couldn't be sure. Maybe it was anger...maybe rage?

"You know, he says the most amazing things to me sometimes. Years ago we were out rowing. Riley puts his finger on the water and says 'The silence of water is not a sound, it's a feeling. Don't listen to the silence with your ears.'"

"Sounds like a smart kid!" Trap shifted his arms to his hips.

René smiled gently and looked out across the soccer field. "Some people say he has been here before, that he was born a grown man."

Trap frowned and blinked several times. He said nothing.

Practice was breaking up, and kids were meeting their parents. René stepped a little closer to Trap and asked "Do you belong to a gym, Trap?" she leaned over and touched her toes. Then came up and arched her back gracefully, clasping her hands, and pointing her arms at the sky.

"Ah, no… too busy, I guess," he said looking down, shifting his feet from side to side.

"Would you like to go with me on a guest pass tomorrow?"

Somehow, Trap kept his balance. He swallowed. "Oh yeah, that'd be great. That's very nice of you."

"Pick you up at six," said René. "Be hungry!"

"I'll be… ah… hungry."

After René left with Riley, Trap walked along the sidelines picking up cones.

"Holy shit!" he mumbled.

Trap wondered about René's troubled expression. Then he remembered his old rule about working with people: if you want to know how somebody feels you've got to ask them, or you're an assuming prick.

He jumped in his minivan and headed down to the marina to check his sailboat, then on to his apartment. He was happy, exhausted, a little excited about the team, and of course, about René. "I guess she asked me for a date. She's so pretty she could have any guy she wants," Trap thought, rubbing his index finger along the bridge of his nose.

CHAPTER 8

April 16, 1998

Olympia, Cascadia

Trap, not knowing whether to dress for a workout or dinner, finally pulled on a pair of navy nylon soccer warm-ups, and a faded red sweatshirt with the sleeves cut off at the elbow.

There was a knock at the door, and it was René. For the time being the painful look on her face was gone. She beamed as if truly glad to see him. She was carrying a fairly large workout bag with her. Because she was already suited up, he wondered why the bag.

"Hi Trap, ready for a workout? This might seem a tad out of the ordinary, going for a workout and a dinner date, but not to worry. I've never done it before either."

She seemed like she was looking forward to the night. The vulnerable, bashful look on her face interested him. Right off, Trap got the feeling she liked him.

She had on black tights and a baggy blue sweatshirt that said "Trout Nut" across the chest. Trap couldn't help notice that she was a slim woman but she was wearing loose clothes to avoid showing off. For a moment, Trap just stared at her face. He swallowed, and felt a tingling sensation pass across his temples. He shook his head and tried to look away, but René's high cheekbones already had his attention. She tilted her head to the side and crossed her hands behind her back. For a moment her good looks had him speechless. She became slightly embarrassed as Trap looked at her. She looked down at the ground, causing her long light brown hair to fall across her shoulders. She looked at her feet and smiled.

"Trout nut?" said Trap. "I figured you for being a nut, but where does the trout fit in?"

"Well you're right, I am a nut. But I fish for trout. You're a fishy guy aren't you Trap?"

"Yes, it's what I do."

"Well I fish all over the east side mostly," said René. "I love the sage country. I use an old bamboo pole. You know hexagonal, and they break into three parts. That's me. An old fashioned trout fisher."

She started walking towards the car. "Well, anyway, want to head over to my club and get in a workout?" Trap liked the way she asked him to share a workout. His eyes were forced to drop to her back as she walked away. Her back tapered to her waist, no doubt the result of her work in the gym. Her hips swayed gracefully with lean muscular tone as she stepped into the car. She was facing in the opposite direction, but she could feel his eyes on her. She just smiled.

She thought Trap was a rugged good-looking man, but that's not what prompted her to ask him to go for a workout with her. It was that feeling she got around him. The same feeling she got at the soccer field. Other than just being a nice guy, there was something she wanted to tell him. But it was better to get to know him first. René remembered something Riley said about Trap and she felt herself relaxing.

Trap and René drove across town to the Olympia Fitness Center and had a workout. René stayed by Trap's side most of the time, like a personal trainer would—touching him gently on his back, arms, and legs to point at certain muscle groups. She didn't exercise much at first, keeping on her baggy sweatshirt as if concealing herself slightly. She showed him some of her favorite equipment and encouraged him to avoid overdoing it like so many do. She showed him mostly universal machines. When she did her own workouts René was usually alone. She usually worked her abs very hard. Occasionally she slipped over to the free weights for bench presses, curls, and other equipment, but tonight she concentrated on Trap.

René was distracted by one of the side rooms. Behind an acrylic wall was a boxing ring, with a speed bag and a heavy bag in the corner. Her face grew hard and her eyes narrowed as she eyed the ring. See nodded with a kind of certainty that came from deep inside her. Turning away, she showed Trap how to work his back, abs, and arms.

Just to show off for him, she did a set on the chin bar. She could do a dozen chin ups. *She means business,* thought Trap. *Angry... hiding something.* While hanging a foot off the ground she raised her legs to perpendicular, putting pressure on her abdominals. She looked rather like a gymnast as her backlit silhouette arched up and back. Her movements made Trap want to get in better shape. René cupped her back bringing her feet up with her toes nearly touching the back of her head. Sweat gleamed on her face as she brought her knees up to her chest, sometimes doing reps twisting to both sides. Trap watched her with sincere admiration as she dropped to the floor keeping her balance as a gymnast might. René was not a woman with huge muscles, but rather very lean with low body fat. Over the years she had changed that little pudgy girl. Happy with what she had done, she took a moment to give herself a rest. After a few minutes she did leg curls and groaned with determination as she completed five sets of twelve, causing her legs to hurt and making her calves and thighs tight. Pausing to get her strength back, she smiled at Trap, and went for two more sets.

"Done!" said René. "Wanna try it?"

"You look like a gymnast," said Trap, feeling somewhat humbled.

"Long time gone," said René. "Come on, try the chin ups."

René reached over and took him by the arm, pulling him toward the bar.

Reluctantly he followed her, and did pretty well considering. It felt good for Trap to take the risk and it made René smile. Trap was a fit man also. His arms and legs were powerful due to his many years of walking streams, but he didn't train with weights.

Suddenly René became a little distant and distracted. She took on a serious look and told Trap she had something to attend to. She grabbed her workout bag, walked deliberately to the personal training room with the boxing ring, flicked on one dim light, and vanished into a poorly lit corner of the room. Trap wondered what she was up to but walked over to the free weights, minding his own business. He fiddled with a couple of dumbbells for a time, but was all too curious. Before long he wandered back over to the room where René had vanished.

Not wanting her to notice him, he peered around the corner of the wall. René was at the back of the dimly lit room wearing boxing gloves. Moving in and out, she flailed away at a heavy bag in the corner. She gave a little grunt each time she struck the bag. She was mostly hooking the bag where her punches had power. There seemed to be temper in her voice. The blows continued for minutes as Trap watched her closely. His face grew serious, wondering what was going on inside her. She seemed to be venting anger and her punches were hard and experienced, as if she had worked out on a heavy bag many times before. Finally exhausted, she put her gloves on her knees, and Trap wandered off to the other end of the gym to do some leg curls. She seemed to be aggravated about something—acting out an emotion deep inside her—but he would not ask her about it tonight.

After leaving the room René stood facing Trap. Her face gleamed with sweat. She leaned on a vertical beam and stared at him. He had little body fat, dark hair, and wore a close cut beard. She could see he was part Native American. *He is not a pretty boy*, thought René. He looks like a handsome hard worker with black irresistible eyes. Still hiding in her sweatshirt she wondered how a man like that could be single. It looked to René like he would be the first one taken.

Trap and René jumped in her van and started down to the Olympia waterfront.

"Boy," said Trap. "Workouts like that could be good for my stream walking."

"Oh, we're not done! This is just a dinner break," she said.

"What?" asked Trap.

"Just kidding, mister… mister babbling brook stomper." René scratched her forehead, wondering if she had offended Trap by heckling him about his job. They had just met.

"You okay Trap? No offense."

"No offense... miss…"

"Miss Coogman," René said.

Trap appreciated being asked how he felt.

"Hope I didn't insult your work Trap, you seem pretty serious."

"Forget it René, I'm not the least bit offended. In fact I'm having a good time!"

René pulled into the Steamboat Bay Café, the least fancy of the waterfront joints. She hoped a relaxed atmosphere would help them get to know each other. Slightly embarrassed in their gym clothes, they slipped into a booth by the dock so they could look out at the boats. René cupped her hands on her chin and leaned her elbows on the window frame, looking out the window. Trap took a chance.

"Are you all alone, René?" he asked. She held her gaze across the blue air over the sound. A bit of pain crept down her cheek but she quickly tossed her head. She smiled very slightly and looked longingly at Trap with her dark brown eyes. Trap's heart beat a little faster.

"No, I've got Riley," she said. "He is just a pleasure to be with."

"But I mean how...?"

Trap fell silent.

"Some other time, Trap. I'm havin' a good time. It's been so long. Please let it go."

There was a long awkward silence. Then Trap spoke to her very gently.

"Hey, sorry René. That's none of my business for sure… forgive me."

René gazed at Trap. She really liked this guy. He was thinking about how she felt.

Trap made a big change in the subject.

"You know what's kind of nice? Did you ever notice you drop your G's? It's all walkin', fishin', goin'. It's really cute." Trap was glad to be on a more comfortable subject.

"Yup," said René, "must be my Irish roots." She seemed a little more cheerful.

"Okay miss trout nut, what do you want to eat?" asked Trap.

"How about some pan sized golden trout?" René smirked. Trap loved a sense of humor. He felt a hysterical giggle coming up from his stomach. René was sexy, and funny too. Trap couldn't help but give a chuckle as he dropped his head to the table. In the fading light she let out a long sigh. It sounded to Trap like she was beginning to relax.

"Hey, that reminds me. I've got a question for you... why do they call you Trap?" she narrowed her eyes with interest.

"Because that's my name," Trap looked up at the ceiling. *Oh no*, he thought.

"Really, Trap is your real name?"

"Okay, Okay... when I was a little boy I spent some time in a little waterfront shack on Flathead Lake in Montana. Talk about bear country, they're just thick. One was prowling our shack at night. You could hear him crunching the pine needles all around the shack. We left the garbage out, and by the next morning it was all over the yard. Tribal Wildlife came out with a culvert bear trap and set it up above the road. I was only about five years old mind you, and I saw this culvert thing about eight feet long, up slope from the shack. I grabbed my spear and went up to investigate. All I remember is looking into this gaping hole and smelling something. So I crawled into the pipe. Near the back I could see a slab of smoked bacon. I lifted my spear and heaved it at the bacon, and the trap sprung. And so I came to be known as Trap".

René put her hand over her mouth.

"That's a cute story," she said. "Really, that one is great—I won't forget it." There was a long pause as René studied Trap's masculine features. Finally she spoke. "So what's your real name?"

"Trap" he said, followed by more silence.

"Alright... my real name is Jess Field. But please call me Trap. I like my nickname."

The two each ordered a cup of clam chowder, prawns tempura, hot whole grain bread, and Caesar salad.

"Hey René," Trap said. "Want to take a walk on the dock when we're done with dinner? I want to show you something."

"Oh sure," she said looking down over the shadows of boats with their black reaching masts. "Any time, Trap," her voice seemed to be trailing off... wandering... lost.

"I'm glad you came with me tonight," she said, suddenly serious. "It's been so long," her eyes closed for a few seconds.

"What's been so long?" asked Trap.

"Oh never mind, please let it go. I shouldn't have said that. Sorry, Trap." She forced herself to hold up her end of the conversation. "So you want to walk down the dock?" René cocked her head slightly. Trap couldn't take his eyes off her. He wondered how she looked beneath her baggy sweatshirt.

The wharf was dark and a little cold. The two walked close together. René hooked her arm in Trap's. He got another rolling sensation in his stomach, but enjoyed her warm touch. It was dusk, and the water dead calm. The fir and madrone along the bay glowed an indigo color as the gulls and crows were settling down. The pilings on the dock were only lightly slapped by invisible waves. Barnacles anchored all over the black mussels holding to each piling. Fucus grew along the water's edge and put the smell of brown algae in the air. Two men in a small sloop were just pulling into her slip in the last few shades of daylight.

"What do you do for a living, René?" asked Trap. René put her arm around Trap's waist and drew her body close to him.

"I used to be in the painting business, but now I work at a sporting goods store. As soon as I can I want to get licensed as a physician's assistant."

"Sounds like you're doing pretty well," Trap nodded his head.

"Oh I could do better Trap, but I'm gettin' by."

"I was reading in the paper the sporting goods business is taking off," said Trap.

"I didn't know you could read, Trap," René giggled. It struck Trap funny, and he lowered his head laughing.

"Say, where are you takin' me? This is a long dark stretch of the dock. We could get mugged." She looked him in the eye and held his waist a little tighter.

"Well heck, I'm a political lefty. I try to see the other guy's point of view when I'm being mugged in an ally."

René burst out laughing, and covered her mouth in a self conscious way. So he wanted to clown around, eh?

"Hey Trap, mind if I borrow a quarter?" René pushed her hand deeply into Trap's front pocket. Trap started to step back but she was deep in his pocket her fingers groping around.

"Boy, are you a cut-up," remarked Trap.

"Yeah that's me", said René. "But then again, you're not exactly a straight man either." She smirked as a cool breeze slid over the dock.

"Hey Trap," she said. "I'm a bit cold."

Trap put his arm around her shoulders and pulled her closer. René locked both of her hands around Trap's waist. She had his heart going again.

"Trap, you're the nicest guy I've met in a long time," said René. He leaned over and kissed her gently on the side of her mouth. She drew in a slow breath.

A hundred feet down the Percival Landing wharf they were still holding each other very close. René started singing very quietly, but it was a song he didn't recognize. Suddenly a raccoon darted out of the brush and ran very close to René's feet. She let out a scream and staggered backwards, letting go of Trap and backing up a few more steps. René screamed again and started backing towards the van. Trap took a few running steps to catch her. She was definitely over reacting.

"René stop, please stop. It's just an old coon. It's nothing to worry about. Hold up, please, take it easy!"

Trap reached out for her and held her for a moment, kissing her on the forehead. He thought it was very odd the way she reacted so strongly.

"I don't know. That animal gave me an awful start. Oh… Oh my God, it scared me," said René as she gasped for breath; she was making a wheezing sound.

"Oh forget that old coon. Come with me, I have a surprise for you. This way," he whispered, and he brought her along the walkway to the floating infrastructure where the boats were moored. He unlocked the gate combination just as the evening lights were coming on all over the wharf. He brought her down the floating dock and walked over to a pretty little sloop sailboat.

"Here it is," said Trap. "*Mornin' Mist*, meet René Coogman. She drops her G's too."

"She is y… yours? She's beautiful, Trap."

"She's a Ranger 29. The hull has been painted a very light red, almost orange. The mast and spreaders are anodized metal flat black. I had the mast modified so the spreaders sweep back."

René slid her hand around Trap's arm.

"You're a lucky man, Trap."

Trap touched René on the side of her face. He felt another back flip in his stomach. She seemed to be calming after reacting so strongly to a raccoon. Trap unlocked the companion way and they went below.

René trusted Trap completely. Did she trust herself? Her attraction to Trap was growing.

*Mornin' Mist*'s cabin was big enough to move around in. Trap had a little floor heater going.

"Have a seat my friend," said Trap. "I've got a special treat for us. Come sit at the table." Trap reached under the table and brought up a bucket of ice containing a cold bottle of champagne, and two plastic glasses. Then he lit two candles.

"This is a great gift. Thank you, Trap, for bringing me here," said René.

Boy, thought René, what a date. This guy is too cute. She felt very special as she sat watching Trap open the champagne, and pouring her a glass. She looked up at him and blinked rapidly.

René looked at the floor of the boat and took a sip of champagne.

"Trap, I asked you to come out with me cause I had something to tell you. I get some of my information from Riley. If you haven't noticed, he is a very smart kid."

"That's because he has a smart mom," said Trap as he studied René's eyes.

"He says you have a gift for coaching that could lead to great things. I wanted to tell you because you're acting a little tentative out there. Well don't back down, and don't back off. Something's gonna happen. I can feel it. And Trap, Trap… Look at me. Don't let anyone tell you any different."

Trap shifted in his cushion.

"I don't know soccer," he mumbled.

He looked up as the candlelight flickered across René's raised cheekbones and trickled down the elongated muscles of her neck. The dancing light and dark shadows on her face seemed to amplify her beauty. He felt his stomach begin to dance once again.

"You sure are getting into this soccer stuff," said Trap.

"Because you coach my son," René spoke smoothly. "And another reason: I trust you to come through for us. I don't like many people, Trap. When you have a pretty face, men try to take advantage. But with you it seems different. I'm okay with you. Especially when I look at your eyes. I... I have a feeling about you as a coach."

"I trust you René," said Trap.

For a moment he thought he saw fear cross her face, but then she tilted her head to the side and smiled at the candle. Without saying a word, she looked at Trap's hands.

René finally spoke. "Trap, can we stay for a while? I love it down here, with the 'silent sound of the water,'" she softly quoted Riley. Trap was amazed that a six-year old boy had come up with that phrase. Sitting quietly, they could hear water splashing gently between the boat and the dock.

"Trap, you have no idea how special this is for me."

The heater was warming the cabin. René squirmed a bit in her trout nut sweatshirt.

"Getting too warm in here for you, René?" asked Trap. Secretly he was hoping she would remove that damn baggy sweatshirt so he could see her breasts.

"No, feels good."

Trap nodded, while feeling a bit disappointed. An impish silent voice inside him asked her to please remove her sweatshirt. He resisted an urge to smile.

René was feeling she could not resist him: gentleman, shiny black hair, a little playful.

René saw Trap looking at her. *Why am I so nervous?* she thought. *What was I thinking of?* Trap drew a deep breath. But the thought returned to him: *What does she look like under that baggy sweatshirt?* Trap cleared his throat. René could tell she had Trap admiring her. She smiled again, her eyes gleaming. It was her beautiful face that captivated him. He felt a few dozen butterflies making him a bit lightheaded, and cleared his throat again.

René leaned over her champagne glass. She giggled and enjoyed Trap looking at her. Smiling, René knew she had Trap's heart going. She knew because her own heartbeat was up.

"Why do you work so hard in the gym?" Trap asked.

"I just got really tired of being the little fat girl. Man, did I get tired. I work hard with diet and exercise so I'll never be that way again. And you know what? I like workouts. It's a good way to vent my anger." She put her hand over her mouth and let out a little cough. She regretted speaking of her anger. It was irritating trying to keep up a front.

"What are you so angry about?" asked Trap.

René's eyes pleaded with Trap to end this conversation. She seemed very sexy but mixed up, filling the cabin with confusion and leaving Trap's pulse pounding. He couldn't help but notice she again had that troubled look on her face. Trap wondered about this painful expression. He wondered why, on their first date, she seemed to be bothered by something. It was odd. Then she moved her shoulders back and forth.

"You wouldn't flirt?" asked Trap, smiling.

"Why not," said René. "I think I'll flirt with you some more Trap. You're just too cute for your own good." For a moment René was acting unsure of herself. Her eyes drifted a bit, looking out the window and over the water. In the last light of the day René leaned forward as a large bird sliced over the masts of the many boats moored in front of her. She saw a speck of white as the bird arced upward for higher altitude.

"Did you see that bird Trap, that was a bald eagle! Holy Jesus!" Trap looked quickly out the window, but the bird was out of his vision.

Trap started to get up, eager to go outside and have a look for himself. But he sat back down and turned his eyes back to René. His eyes grew larger and he cupped his hand over hers, as if something very important had just happened. For a moment he was silent, studying her eyes and glancing again at the window.

"René, I pay attention to the shaman. The shaman say that the animals all around us speak to us all the time. Shaman say they bring to us messages that help us find our way through our troubles and understand the meanings of our lives. Do you feel anything right now…do you feel the eagle said something to you…words that seem to come from inside you?"

René shifted her eyes quickly from side to side, but she heard nothing from within. She thought of making a joke, but the serious look on Trap's face made her think again.

"Well, my guess is you were just given a message. Next time an eagle comes that close to you, pay attention. Eagles bring many messages, but I think I heard him speaking and it was a voice for you. René, there is an opportunity for you that you are considering, and it would be to your advantage to act on it soon…there will be a new beginning in a positive direction, following a recent period of strife. There is an opening now for you to grow stronger because of recent anguish."

René looked at Trap's hand still covering hers. She was stunned by the truth in his words. She looked at Trap's face. He just smiled gently and patted her hand once.

"But what…but how did you know?"

"I didn't," said Trap.

"But you did? Are you a shaman?"

"No," said Trap, "I just sort of pay attention to the shaman. It's kind of like fortune telling…only when it comes to shaman, there is a big difference."

"What difference?"

"They tell the truth," Trap looked to the side then back at René.

Trap ran his fingers through his hair. René quietly glanced at him and took a sip of champagne. She got to her feet and made her way around the galley table to where Trap was, and sat very close to him. She stared at Trap for a brief time, touched by what he said. Responding to her affections, Trap ran his arm around René's side. He rubbed his hand up and down her waist a few strokes. Another deep breath came from within him. René let out a sigh also. She moved closer to Trap as she gazed into his dark eyes. Then she buried her face in his shoulder. She whispered to him. "I need a friend."

Trap felt like he was a train traveling at high speed, roaring through a tunnel, and he was trying to yell above the noise. He realized René had some problems. They were on a first date and she was not quite in the moment.

"Do you need to get home?" Trap spoke quietly.

"Not till we're done here," René spoke in more of a whisper.

Trap's heart pounded watching René's candlelit face. He had never been with such a beautiful woman.

"Do you want to go up front?" asked Trap.

René's voice could barely be heard.

"It's too soon," she mumbled.

CHAPTER 9

April 19, 1998

Lacey, Cascadia

On the first day of practice Reuben and Trap were both surprised again at the big turnout. More kids showed up for practice than were on the team. That was something pretty typical for the Blue Angels.

The coaches and parents standing around had a curiosity about this team. No one planned it, no one predicted it, and no one created it. It just happened. The kids didn't seem to notice the diversity of the players, as if that was the natural order of things – the way things should be. And, in the time the Blue Angels played soccer on the planet, there was never any ethnic trouble. It was as if prejudice had vanished, if only for a brief time…while some higher power stepped in, called off the nonsense, and added some clemency. Both Trap and Reuben had a sense of optimism as they walked onto the field.

Reuben was not fully recovered from his road rage attack in Arizona fourteen years ago, and he never would be. He had other health problems, including heart trouble. It wasn't long before Trap realized Reuben had large blank spots in his memory, both short-and long-term. He also struggled with his English at times, and even with his understanding of the game of soccer. Reuben had become a religious man since he relocated. Knowing he was in over his head with this soccer team, Reuben prayed for help and thanked God for giving him this assistant coach. With Trap on the team, Reuben had a load of stress off his back. Trap seemed to be a perfect fit, with all the qualities Reuben lacked, without taking away his strengths. One thing Reuben did have was discipline. He was sometimes harsh and uncompromising with his soccer team, making them run laps if they misbehaved.

In order to find the speed on the team, they measured out a fifty-yard dash. Reuben took one end of the little course they laid out and Trap took the other end with a clipboard and two stopwatches.

Reuben turned to the team and said, "All right ladies and gentlemen, we are going to find the speed on this team, so run like the wind!" Reuben selected two fast looking kids from the team: Gabriel Santa Cruz and Babar Haqim. Both ran in the low eights. Trap noticed something about Babar as he spun around to watch him finish. Babar, while not a big kid, had the most remarkable coordination for a boy. He was like a little man, with all the grace of a star athlete. Gabriel was more like a shot from a cannon, with the power of a jackhammer in every step. When he ran his face was twisted into a grimace, simply willing his legs to go faster. No one tried harder than Gabriel. There were only two faster kids on the team. The real speedster was Willis Gray. There was no anguish on his face when he ran, only a contented dreamy expression. Willis put his head down and ran with perfect poise. He ran silent, cat like, seemingly effortless, to a 7.9 second 50-yard dash. It didn't even look like he was trying. The other kid who was going to give his opponents a lot of grief was Deshaun Ward. Deshaun was tall and powerful. He was a strong running back for the middle school football team. Deshaun ran disorganized, like he was coming unglued. He was like a furious tiger in a cage with arms and legs flying in every direction. But he was nearly as fast as Willis with an 8.0 second dash. The others were spread between the low nines and high tens. The fifty-yard dash became a kind of cornerstone for the players. They would always try hard to better their time, as if speed was the bottom line in soccer.

"Okay strikers, we'll do this once a month and see who's getting quick as a mongoose. In the meantime follow me!" Trap walked to the center of the soccer field. Reuben went to work on the phone, talking to the league about practice field reservations, rule changes and new players. That became a template for these two very different men. Reuben, the head coach, was on the phone. Trap was on the field, spending his time building skills and working out strategy. Jaylen (Deshaun's father) would help when he could break free from his swing shift job. It could be said that Reuben was the manager of the team, taking on duties such as discipline and resolving arguments. Trap was the technical coach, bringing out skills and flaws in the kids' play. He also had a knack for teaching tricky plays. The combination of skills seemed like a good fit for the team.

"Blue Angels," said Trap, "I want everyone on this team to get up close and personal with every line on that soccer field. To play soccer you will need to know exactly what each line is for: kickoff circle, penalty arc, penalty area, goal kick box, corner kick."

Trap had the kids come to the sideline.

He had visited the Soccer Fair in Tacoma and picked up a magnetized miniature soccer field about the size of a legal pad. Each soccer player was represented by a magnetic button. Trap took advantage of the moment to explain the off side rule, letting the kids create various off side penalty scenarios. He also used the board to work out attack and defense schemes. Then, as would become the rule, they used practice jerseys, split up the team, and played soccer. Trap had a brief conversation with Reuben and ran out to organize two teams. He used a samba whistle, blowing three different notes to add some color to the scrimmage. Trap would ref, although there were many refinements to the game he needed to sort out with some of the experienced soccer people he had met over the last few weeks.

After practice, Trap was alone on the field using a bike pump to inflate all the soccer balls.

His stomach did a triple backflip as he saw René strolling up the sideline in a short cotton skirt. She was just beautiful. She had Trap distracted all the way across the field. Her long hair was waving in the breeze, and light from her high cheekbones danced across her face as she squinted at the sun. Trap exhaled and drew in a big breath. René looked down at the ground and smiled. Looking very fit while shifting her weight, she looked over the team and waved to Riley. But she covered her upper body with an oversized lime-colored baseball shirt gathered at her waist… still hiding her breasts.

As René walked, there was a mild disturbance in the crowd. Wives were elbowing husbands to stop staring. She kept smiling and gave Trap a slight nod. But René also seemed to be using her good looks to hide something else, thought Trap in his intuitive way. Behind the beautiful woman, something was wrong. Something was dark. Something was false. He saw it in the dimness of her smile. He saw it in her clenched fists.

Her short skirt was tighter than a shaman's drum, showing off her lean features. But that big baggy baseball shirt still hid her upper body. She had a beaded belt tangled loosely around her waist. When Trap came to the sideline she was embarrassed, fumbling with the buckle of the belt. She turned her back to Trap and smiled secretly.

"Can't seem to get my buckle."

Trap forced in a sudden breath and his heart began racing as she drew in her belt, revealing to him the extreme smallness of her waist and the hourglass that described her back and hips. Trap held his eyes on her waist, taking some quick breaths as she continued to tighten. He forced himself to look away as he shook his head a little. But he had to look at her again.

"Showing off a little?" asked Trap, smiling. "Why?"

René rolled her eyes. "Because I feel like it," she muttered. She started walking down the sidelines and cheering for the Blue Angels. Trap wondered to himself whether he could ever understand René.

It seemed to Trap that René would get in strange moods, and beat them back by getting men to stare at her. He couldn't help sneaking looks at her either. She looked back at him and gave him a broader smile before looking down, tilting her head in coyness. She liked him. After one date she wanted to bring Trap home to a warm fire. Trap ran his hands through his hair wondering what she looked like above the belt.

With his pulse pounding with thoughts of René, he brought his concentration back to soccer. The end of practice was approaching so she got into Trap's denim jacket.

Reuben and Trap had a debriefing at the end of practice. In Trap's opinion the team had a ways to go and not much time. Many of the kids were toe-poking the ball. Kids were also mobbing the ball like a fumble in a college football game. Some players didn't understand the penalty box. Others were chasing the ball all over the field with no regard to position.

Something more serious happened to the Blue Angels on the field on this day. One kid was calling his teammates "stupid jerks." Trap heard it and was getting ready to say something, but Reuben was on it.

"If you ever use that word in reference to a Blue Angel you'll run laps till you drop and then you'll be drop kicked from this team. That's not okay, and you burn that into your brain. See those kids out there? They are your teammates and you will treat them well or you're just not good enough to be a Blue Angel!"

Trap couldn't help but admire the way Reuben handled that. They shook hands, and said goodnight.

Hesitating, Trap walked slowly over to René and looked into her eyes. Then his eyes fell to her graceful long neck. Then lower to her long legs. Trap felt tension between the two of them.

"Hi." Trap said. "You look terrific in that skirt. What a perfect fit."

"Thanks buddy. See, I altered it myself cause the waist was way too big," said René. "I finally have something that fits me. It feels good."

Trap wanted to tell René she looked so good she was distracting the team and crowd, but he bit back his words. He had another insight, thinking René was vulnerable and very easily hurt. And besides, her presence on the sideline might help like a cheerleader. He said nothing and looked at her instead. Her expression brightened a bit, because she had Trap's undivided attention. He wanted very badly to just reach out and touch her. But René's eyes shifted nervously back and forth in front of the team.

"Need to borrow a quarter?" Trap asked.

"Yes please. I need to call my husband."

A look of surprise passed across Trap's face. His eyes narrowed.

"I had you going there didn't I, Trap?" René burst out laughing, and looked at the ground again. She shook her head.

"You like to play don't you," said Trap.

"Want to come over tonight for corned beef and cabbage?" asked René. "I'm really good at it. Irish, ya know. Riley is sleepin' over at a friend's. Why don't you come over?"

René squinted at Trap's eyes. Trying not to seem forward, she found his eyes so striking it made her a little nervous. She handed him a slip with her address and phone number and she went towards Riley. Trap watched her sway gently as she walked away.

Just behind René a cherry bomb went off sounding like a high-powered rifle. Then a voice came from a distance. "Cherry bombshell!" a kid mouthed off at René. René jumped like she had been whipped. She screamed and reached for Trap, clutching his arm. Her eyelids were fluttering as she whispered to herself.

"Oh God, not now!"

René clung to Trap's arm. As he regarded her seriously, she started trembling. He whispered in her ear, "It's okay René, just a cherry bomb."

René whispered, "I know, I know, just give me a minute. Loud noises bother me."

She kept her hold on Trap's arm. In a few minutes, she was a little better, though she looked flushed.

Trap arrived at René's just before dusk. He had on Levis and a navy blue flannel shirt with a gray tank top underneath. It was a warm April night and the green tree frogs were in full chorus, sounding like a thousand crickets.

René was renting a doublewide mobile home right on Henderson Inlet. It was a woodsy spot—high bank, but facing salt water. Many species of waterfowl called from the Sound, and Trap thought he heard a loon out in the darkness. Down below he could hear waves lapping the gravel beach. A quiet breeze came from the north and Trap inhaled the fragrance of the woods around René's trailer. The smell of wood smoke filled the air. The only sound was the lapping of small waves. For a moment, Trap felt a sense of peace from the salty marine breeze;

a Friday night, a crackling fire, and René Coogman waiting for him inside.

Trap tapped on the door and René poked her head out. "Hi Trap," she said giving him a welcoming smile. "Come in, come in!" Once they were inside she started flirting with Trap too soon. She knew it, but she couldn't seem to stop herself.

Wearing cowboy boots, she had changed her clothes to unwind from the week. She was intentionally trying to get Trap's undivided attention. To impress him, wore tight boot cut jeans. She had surprised him with her pretty face after their first date. At the first soccer meeting she wore a bulky coat with her hair up and big dark glasses. Tonight she wore a tight fitting tan rayon top with a low crew neck. On top of all her curves, she had upright breasts made lean by years of exercise. She had wide shoulders and appeared to have the features of a slim athlete, including an extreme V to her back. She took his breath away. She was too sexy to describe. On top of all of her other beautiful qualities her abdominals rippled under her thin rayon top. It was all he saw: rippled abs, sculpted thighs. Trap was still at a loss for words and could not stop staring. She giggled as Trap's pulse pounded. *All this is coming too soon*, she thought, but she couldn't resist teasing him at this point.

"Surprised, Trap? You look a little distracted. Can you talk? You aren't afraid of a girl are you?" she tilted her head.

"Wow," said Trap.

"I exercise a lot," René shrugged. She reached for his arm, but finally decided to ease up a bit.

"Want to go for a walk on the beach?" she asked. "It's such a warm night. Here, I'll get a flashlight and we'll take the chicken walk through the sword fern," she said.

René took Trap by the hand and started over the bank. She held his hand as tight as she could, like a schoolgirl with a crush. Once down on the beach, they walked for a short ways listening to the repeating harmonic waves. René slid her arm under Trap's right arm.

She turned around and looked out over the water, squeezing Trap's hand tighter.

"I love Cascadia. It's so dominated by water," said René. "And you, Trap: a perfect gentleman. How'd you get so nice?"

"I'm not always nice, René. Maybe tonight by the fire I'll tell you about it. But I have a simple rule I live by," said Trap. "It helps me from day to day: never think you know how somebody feels unless you ask them. Otherwise you're assuming that you're accurate in your thinking. People get it wrong every time. But the other part of the puzzle is you, René. It's the way you seem... it's as though your spirit is troubled. But I'm uncomfortable assuming anything... what's the matter, anyway?"

She wouldn't answer, but some deep anger surfaced in her face for a moment. She tightened her grip on Trap's hand again.

"There's a loon out there," she said in a distant voice.

Trap thought for a while, "You know René, the shamans say if a loon calls to you, it's asking you to pay attention to your dreams—especially those you remember during the day. Explore your subconscious and you will understand yourself better."

"I need that," she whispered as she nodded slowly.

René continued to whisper. "You know, I can see the northern lights from here. Over there, to the west, in the fall. Out over the water in the early fog, where your sailboat got its name."

"Same place," said Trap. "Would you like to sail her? I'll give you the helm."

René looked at the water out of the corner of her eye.

"I was wondering when you were going to ask me out. I've been trying for days to get your attention. But the answer is yes, I want to sail *Mornin' Mist* if you'll come along. I know how to sail, too."

"Really? How'd you learn to sail?"

"Riley and I took many lessons a couple years ago. I just can't keep off the water," she said.

She sat on the gravel beach, Trap beside her.

"How come a guy like you is 33 and not married? The ladies must be beating down the door!" said René. "Ever had a girl, Trap?" René put a hand on Trap's shoulder. She waited for an answer.

"Yeah, but there comes a point when you know you aren't going anywhere, and as painful as it is you go your separate ways."

"Guess you're right Trap, about knowing when the relationship isn't going anywhere."

Trap and René continued to walk up the beach just above a very narrow splash zone. Upslope, the frogs continued to chorus as the water surface began settling into dead calm. A harbor seal, barely visible, brought his head above the water and quietly watched them.

"You know what else the shamans say, René? If a seal watches you like that, it means you'll be folded in dreams tonight, clear and vivid, and all night long."

"You're a scientist and a shaman, Trap?"

"I'm not totally a shaman but some of my friends are. But I am part Indian, you know, and I listen to the shamans. Right now they're telling me I'm hungry."

"I've got the perfect answer," said René.

Inside the trailer it was toasty warm because René had built a fire in her woodstove. Her features were enhanced as she stood in front of the fire with flames dancing on the walls. She folded her hands behind her back and looked down at the carpet the way she often did. She crossed her ankles while standing in front of the fire.

"Let's be friends, Trap. I need a friend."

Trap backed away so he could see her looking at his eyes. Trap couldn't take his eyes off her, and she loved it. That was the second time she had said she needed a friend.

But he didn't understand her pleading behavior. He didn't know what to think. Aside from being such a looker, she seemed emotionally clumsy and inexperienced. He walked toward her and whispered in her ear.

"René, relax I am your friend. What's bugging you? You are very pretty but you don't seem happy. Should I say goodnight?"

René backed up for a minute. Her eyes were flashing and blinking rapidly. She started stuttering again and looked like she was frightened.

"Oh… T-Trap, I'm s-sorry. I was just feeling a little light headed. I haven't dated in so l-long I almost d-don't know how to act." Her eyes were still blinking rapidly. "I'm so sorry. Trap you aren't going to leave are you? I'm just a little mixed up and I wanted to see you again."

Trap put his hand on her shoulder.

"No René I'm not leaving. I'm nuts about you. I didn't mean to get you upset." René smiled and appeared to recover almost immediately; too soon, it seemed.

But Trap realized there was something wrong with René. A half hour later she was back to her cutting up.

"I'll give you something to look at." She grinned.

She rolled her shoulders back slightly and flexed her arms in a muscle pose. Her biceps were those of a very athletic woman. Trap complemented her for looking so fit. But Trap was curious. She looked frightened and forward at the same time. She was flaunting and teasing, way over the top, thought Trap, and at times he thought he again saw anger in her eyes.

She was having fun doing these sexy muscle poses in front of Trap, laughing through the whole thing. She turned to the side and took a deep breath. She flexed her lats and abs making her upper body look ripped. Her lips were pressed together and she looked meekly at Trap, who was so flustered he couldn't find any words. Looking at René, he felt more attracted to her than any woman he'd ever met. But he hardly knew her. All he knew was she could make a man's heart race.

René suddenly felt a strange sense of vertigo that made her fall to her knees, and she went down on all fours. Her eyes began blinking rapidly again as she shook her head. Trap watched her with concern. He put his arm around her shoulders and asked her if she was okay.

"Yeah, yeah, okay," said René, "I just felt a bit dizzy for a moment. Too much flexing I guess."

René shuffled over to the corner and sat on the floor close to the wall. She put her hands to her face and took a few shallow breaths. Trap moved towards her. But something told him to back off. Neither of them said a word.

Trap was concerned, but after a few moments he began to relax. He watched René. She looked much better. In fact she looked completely back to normal.

She had a dark complexion for an Irish woman. She wore no makeup and didn't pluck her eyebrows, making her face look natural. So what was wrong with René? Why the silent past? Why the mysterious moods? Why the overly sexy showing off and acting out? Why would she stretch into the tightest clothes possible, leaving every man around her with their eyes stuck to her? Sooner or later he would have to find out. He would have to ask her. A relationship was in motion, and he didn't want anyone hurt. He continued to gaze at René, his feeling for her growing stronger... yet he felt a hovering hesitation to engage too quickly with her.

Trap's face was also lit by the firelight. René looked down where he sat on the floor. His face brought to mind the roughness of a fighter. He looked up at her with black eyes lit up by the fire. His skin was dark from outdoor work and from his Native American roots. He moved with a kind of grace from his experience as a stream walker. He was slim and broad shouldered. René was interested in Trap's eyes. Her mouth began to tremble slightly. Finally she spoke:

"Well you're quite a guy aren't you, Trap? I think you are the best friend I've made in years. Come join me for corned beef and cabbage."

René was right. She made the most delicious corned beef and cabbage he'd ever tasted.

Trap wiped his mouth and leaned over to René, touching her on the chin, and kissing her on the cheek. She looked pleased while Trap finished her mouth-watering meal.

"I can't help admiring you René. You ever consider entering some sort of fitness contest with that figure of yours?" asked Trap.

Secretly she very much liked such complements because she'd worked so hard at diet and exercise, but she thought that remark a little forward of Trap.

"Some sort of contest?" asked René. "Well for starters, perhaps we should get some measurements," René mused scratching her chin.

"Sounds good to me," said Trap.

René walked around the corner and pulled a tape measure from her sewing basket. She walked up to Trap and asked him to please remove his shirt.

"What? We were going to do you," Trap started to chuckle.

"No, that's a waste of time," said René.

Trap continued to laugh as René helped him off with his shirt. She was stunned at how good Trap looked with his shirt off.

"Hold still, we need to be both accurate and precise," said René.

She cleared her throat. "Okay, chest 44", waist 32", hips 34", and then she broke off laughing. Both couldn't help but laugh. When Trap finally settled down he said to René, "Okay, so what are your measurements?"

"Well Trap, I've got you beat six ways to Sunday. I'm five foot seven, 125 pounds, and a size seven shoe. That's all I know. You know Trap, you're the one with the foxy body. Could you take the rest of your clothes off? I'd like to get some more measurements!"

Trap looked at her with his piercing eyes. "Well aren't you cute!" he said.

René raised her eyebrows. "No Trap, you really do have a foxy body. Can I have a feel?" She ran her hands over his bare chest.

"For real Trap, you make me feel funny."

He had noticed a time or two she was still visited by strange moods. Trap wondered about it. He didn't want to corner her.

"Hey Trap, want to have a brandy?" René smiled with her eyebrows going up again.

"Yeah, sounds perfect," said Trap.

René tip toed into the kitchen and grabbed two snifters. "Here's to my new friend with the foxy body," she said giggling.

"That's what I was going to say," Trap shrugged.

"Hey, I meant to ask you, want to join my gym?" René widened her eyes.

"Oh, I dunno," said Trap.

"You'll become even cuter. Maybe we could spot for each other and I could get in a few more feels. Maybe we could see more of each other," said René, becoming a little serious.

"Hey Trap?" She changed the subject. "How about I play you a song? Not that I'm trying to seduce you. More like undermine your world with erotica. It's just one I been working on," she said.

She went into the spare room and fetched her little Martin. "This song is perfect for us. It's about a half Indian/half Irish hermit that lived in the central Sierras in California during the 1940's." René fingerpicked an E minor 9 and a C major 7 and started singing. She had a soft alto voice, and was pretty well in tune.

*In the canyon cliffs away from you*
*I make my home*
*Where never a man will find me and I want it so*
*In my youngest days, I was raised by an Indian squaw*
*And a white man's son, I was born on the snow*
*Oh Wolf is my name I am the last of them*
*And the winter's rage let me in from the wind*
*Where the fire is warm*
*And if I stare at your woman, bear me*
*I am a lonely man*
*I will leave before the dawn.*

It's not finished," said René, setting down her instrument. Trap was surprised she could play guitar.

"You wrote that," he finally said, "and you can play the guitar and sing. Jesus, René what else can you do?"

"I used to play between school and workouts. I would play folk songs for hours, a lot of Irish and Scottish tunes. They sing about war, heartbreak, drinking, and human suffering, their love of the land," said René, smiling and looking down.

"Yeah Trap, I wrote that."

As the firelight danced warmly across her guitar, Trap started to look at her in a different way. There was more to René Coogman than met the eye.

"Who is Wolf?"

"His name was Monte Wolfe, the legendary hermit of the Mokelumne wilderness. I was just a little embarrassed playing for you," said René. "The way I feel about you, you're a big audience."

Trap smiled broadly. "Do I make you nervous?"

"Call it alert," said René. "Anyway, could you put your brandy down for a second?'

Trap lay flat on his back, the flames from the fire flashing in his eyes. René eased her head sideways on his chest, singing softly.

*Watch at the edge of the underwood*
*I will come to you*
*And Mokelumne moves in the heart of me*
*As I walk along*
*And the river below, I'll drink of her*
*And she'll keep me strong*
*There's a man who wonders*
*Which way I go*

René moved her head off Trap's chest and rested it on his shoulder so her mouth was very close to his ear, and she whispered:

*And there is nothing I am searching for, it's behind me now*
*And Coloma is done*
*and the grave of the man I killed is gone*
*And what keeps me here is the only thing that*
*I linger on*
*Let the truth be known or*
*I live on alone.*

René kissed him on the cheek.

"Who is Coloma?" asked Trap.

René kissed him again.

"The site where gold was first discovered in California," said René.

She cried a bit as she put her arms around Trap's neck. He felt the tears on his cheek and rose up to look at René.

"What's the matter?" asked Trap. "That was a great ballad, I loved it. On top of the beauty there's talent. You are just an amazing woman."

"Oh, nothing's the matter Trap, I just choke myself up sometimes," she said weakly.

She changed the subject again. "Trap, when we were down at the beach earlier you said you aren't always a nice guy. What did you mean by that?" René had a concerned look on her face. "You're always a perfect gentleman with me, and you treat me so fine."

Trap ran his hand over the back of his neck, taking a moment to think.

"I don't like bigots. So what else is new? Well I *really* don't like bigots. They make me fighting mad, and I find myself ready to take a swing. It's probably because I've got some Indian blood in me, but a switch goes off in my head and I get furious. It's getting harder to control. So far I've managed to keep it down to yelling, but it's getting harder. I've come close to blows. I think I'm going to hurt somebody."

René gazed into the fire, her face in the light. Trap was beginning to realize behind those fawn eyes there was wisdom. She put down her brandy and regarded Trap seriously.

"Trap, I think something is going to happen. Hear me out. This soccer team you're coaching—they are the most integrated team in the Puget Sound lowland. If you handle it right, Trap, maybe they can heal your anger. I mean, what kind of martyr trip is this you are on? Why do you stay awake at night hating bigots?"

"Sometimes I do!"

"Well you're overdone. I don't like bigots either, but things change slowly. Just let things happen and don't be so self important about it. Oh, but I can't just explain it away, can I Trap? Letting go of hatred has to happen to you. So you're defining bigotry for yourself in a different way. Where is all this bigotry going on anyway?"

"At my workplace."

"What about your soccer team?"

"That's the paradox," said Trap. "I go to practice and it's completely gone. I go to work and it bleeds over the yard like tule fog. At practice it doesn't even cross anybody's mind. Racial anger doesn't exist with the Blue Angels. It's like the older we get, the worse we get. It's the opposite of learning as we mature. Then I go to work and it's spic, nigger, slope, masada, dago, wop, wetback, coon!"

"Well, you think on it. You take it with so much rage you are apt to hurt someone, and that's not better than racist remarks. I can already tell, you go out on the field and there is a kind of magic; the team feels it. Where might that magic come from?" said René, before taking a moment to think carefully.

"Wow, you are surprising," said Trap.

"No, I'm nobody special, Trap. I'm just not stupid."

"No, you're somebody very special," said Trap.

"Trap, listen," said René. "How did you come to feel this way? What happened to you, that you won't just blow off a common racial slur?"

"I'll think on it, lady. But a couple of things come to mind. I grew up in a little town called Contra in Montana. We had a men's club in town where blacks were prohibited. And we had a fishing club down on the lake. If you had black skin you were not allowed to be a member of the fishing club. And I hear comments about Indians. If there's one thing I could put my finger on—excuse me—if there's one thing I could put my *fist* on, it's that."

René and Trap continued sipping their brandy in front of the fire. There was a serious nature to their recent conversation, and there was some tension in the room. And that was the last thing René wanted.

She wanted Trap. Trap made her feel so special that there was a humming going on inside her.

"We should talk on this race thing again, but maybe not now," said René. "I have a question," she continued. "Will you stay with me tonight?"

Trap inhaled a deep breath, and felt a great joy.

René sat on her knees facing Trap smiling.

His stomach did another swan dive.

Trap reached out and touched her. René welcomed his touch. She smiled and moved her body closer to his. He ran his fingers lightly down her sides, smaller and smaller, until he reached her waist. His head was swimming. Never had he held such a woman. Then Trap sat back and looked René straight in the eye as he grabbed his brandy. There were a dozen questions he had about this beauty, but he said nothing. He just stared at her. Their mutual attraction had grown deeper, and René saw in Trap's eyes he had burning questions. She went from smiling to a concerned expression. Trap didn't want to do that, so he just leaned forward and kissed her gently on the corner of her mouth. He decided to change the subject.

"Hey René, if I join your gym will I turn out looking as good as you?"

"Oh Trap, you already do."

Through the evening, the frogs continued to chorus, and a front continued to move in like a warm breath from the oceanic Salish sea. The air hissed gently, driving the smell of the forest into René's open bedroom window. The tide came in and mixed aromas with the rigorous white alder trees beginning to leaf. The woods breathed into the window. Lying in bed, Trap ran his hand over René's back, lightly touching her with his fingers. René smiled in her approaching passion and exhaled the woods. She nodded peacefully. Trap lay awake and felt the hushed beating of René's heart beneath his hand. He watched her without clothing on her back. He could feel the rippling of her back muscles. She exhaled the woods again, and with that Trap tried to move back to watch her. But René let out a low moan like the A-string of her guitar and pulled him closer.

CHAPTER 10

April 22, 1998

Pe Ell, Cascadia

Trap motored towards the Slade Creek Fishway off of State Route 13 near the town of Pe Ell. It was a short trip, just an hour from Olympia. He had a passenger on this day. A student from Evergreen State College named Raul had written him a letter asking if he could volunteer as an intern to get some work experience on his resumé. Trap liked these opportunities to show off his work and give a young student a chance to further his career. The smart students knew that a college degree looked good on a job application, but a college degree with a list of jobs looked much better... and the jobs were harder to get than the degree. The intern was Latino; he had come from Cuba to the US when he was five years old. Raul was full of questions as the truck rolled down the highway. Trap explained that Hughes was a consulting firm that got job referrals from state agencies, counties, and federal projects. They had their own heavy equipment, construction crew, engineers, and biologists. He explained the popular concept of the Stream Walker, vernacular for an extremely competent surveyor.

As they drove along Trap was a bit preoccupied by the thought of René. But this time it was different. Usually he was framing her terrific looks, but today he was thinking about more than that. He was thinking about what she said and what she didn't say. He had come to recognize her insight into things. René blew the heartthrob stereotype of empty-headed bimbo out the window. In spite of her lack of education, René Coogman was bright, creative, and sometimes she had penetrating insight into things.

"Blue Angels can help you... the Blue Angels can give back to you something you lost." Who was this woman anyway? During their time together he had learned little about her. How did she come to have a 14 year old son? It was all a mystery. She looked so vulnerable at times, and at other times she could be so completely attractive she could leave him tongue-tied. Her troubled smile was still an unanswered question. It concerned Trap the way she would cling to him almost fearfully in the middle of the night. One thing kept bugging him. He thought it wrong to be preoccupied with her bodybuilding. It is the mind, spirit, and personality a person is really attracted to. Despite his reasoning, he could not stop thinking about her fitness, even when he tried.

Feeling a little sidetracked, Trap brought his mind back to Raul. He explained more about the inner workings of Hughes. Perhaps he could get permission to have Raul survey with him in the near future. He told Raul he would be glad to drop him a line if a job opening should come up.

They rolled along Highway 13, a lonely drive west from I-5. It wandered past gray somber hills, mostly clear-cut or second growth timber. It was not a pretty stretch of road. The upper Blue River wandered next to the highway cutting a V-shaped channel through the riparian. Patchy clearings were being used for hayfields and cattle grazing. The Blue River was now an angry river and the high water marks were beyond belief. In some sections the river was breaking down its own banks due to erosion.

The weather was warming up. That was one thing Trap could feel good about. He was going to go swimming on this day.

Ranchers had ditched most of the creeks in the pasture areas along the highway. The ditching had removed the natural meander from the creeks. That meant a balance of pools, riffles, and a canopy of shade was gone. Several bridges and culverts were in poor condition and no one knew where the money to repair them would come from. Many logging roads were gated because unscrupulous people were driving house trailers deep into private forests, fully intending to set up methamphetamine labs. People wishing to avoid dumping fees were leaving old mattresses, couches, and hollowed out refrigerators full of bullet holes littering logging roads and yarding sites. Occasionally even the shell of an abandoned automobile could be seen rusting away in the otherwise pristine wetland seeps. If left alone, those little seeps could produce the sweetest water in the woods.

But the weather was something to feel better about. The sun stretched out underneath the rejuvenating spring sky causing steam to rise from the mass wasted woods.

On the right they passed a 100-foot bridge knocked off its foundation by a raging flood on the Blue. The Blue River was notorious for huge freshets due to the activities of man. The river, when swollen, was well-known for knocking everything out of the way within the high water marks.

But the weather was as blue as the Pacific. They were coming up on the Slade Creek Road turnoff as Trap shared his thoughts with Raul about upper Blue River fish habitat problems.

Trap explained to Raul what he was up to. Hughes was installing an attraction jet to provide additional flow to the recently completed Alaska Steep Pass fishway built to provide passage over a high falls on a tributary to the Blue. They needed a diver to bolt in place the lower sections of the metal jet assembly. The diver would be Trap. Then he got an idea.

"Raul, are you a good swimmer?" asked Trap.

"Yes sir, I am like a dolphin!" said Raul.

"You signed a waiver for this trip, didn't you?"

"Yes, I did," said Raul.

"Well I'll leave it up to you. If you want to do the underwater work, we have a dry suit on board."

There was excitement in Raul's voice and his eyes flashed. This would mean a lot to him. Trap had to admire Raul's eagerness to step up to the plate. The truck rolled along for another mile. After a bit Trap veered left into a driveway where a rustic cabin was perched above a cliff area.

If there was one beautiful place left near the Blue, it was Slade Creek Falls. It was a ten-foot high vertical drop incised into a cliff of smoke colored basalt. The cliffs around the falls were steeper than vertical, and small maidenhair fern and clumps of moss grew up side down on the rock. The spray zone from the falls held a rainbow. Trap was reaching the spiritual moment that he sometimes felt when he was around falling water. He went to his Indian side and rested a moment, listening to the chatter of the falls. He remembered why he was a Stream Walker.

A three-man construction crew was already on site when Trap and Raul arrived. While Trap and Raul walked the project through, Trap explained the fishway type and configuration, and why they needed extra water at the entrance passage. He explained the problem of salmon falling back over the falls after they had ascended the fish ladder. Trap pointed out that a study might be a good project for a Master's thesis.

Trap introduced Raul to Ed and two other men of the construction crew. They nodded half-heartedly. Raul took the dry suit up next to the cabin and began putting it on.

Ed, one of the crewmen, grumbled "Well, wet work ought to suit that little spic just fine."

Trap heard it, but he wanted to be sure Raul was taken care of. He got four bolts and showed Raul the lower end of the fishway. The lower section needed to be bolted to the side of the lining on the lower end of the existing assembly, which was completely under water.

Raul went to work, using the suction tube on his suit to achieve zero buoyancy. He took a bolt from Trap and disappeared beneath the surface, his legs kicking against the current. The three construction workers stood on top of a rock embankment above the lower fishway trying to get a glimpse of what was going on. After Raul had resurfaced, a shower of broken rock came over the cliff. Some of them were landing on Raul's head. He yelled, but Trap yelled louder.

"What in the hell are you doing up there, trying to start a landslide? Goddammit, get back!"

Raul disappeared beneath the surface, where he managed to install and tighten all four underwater bolts.

While Raul had his head underwater a voice came from the cliff above. "Why don't you tell him to swim up the fishway? The little wetback should be good at that."

Trap shook Raul's hand and the two men headed up the hill. He instructed Raul to get out of the dry suit, and walked over to Ed, looking him in the eye.

Trap spit on the ground. "You know, I get more sick of racial slurs everyday." He could hardly control his temper, and was breathing hard through his nostrils.

"Hell Trap, you know we don't hire Mexicans," said Ed.

Trap threw his hat on the ground and looked up at Raul to be sure he was still dressing.

"Listen, Ed. You take that line you just barfed out and you tell it to our personnel office. Be sure you include all the details, like his race, color, and creed. What do you think they'd say, Ed? You're the one who wouldn't get hired. If you did accidentally get hired in five minutes you'd be out the front gate. Boy I'm tempted to go to Personnel myself! Trap was still angry. He wanted to swing, but had sense enough to know he would be in big trouble if he did. He picked up his hat and walked off without another word. He helped Raul with the gear and the two men roared off in the truck.

The cell phone rang. Trap was glad he let himself vent a bit, and was amazingly composed given what just happened. It was René.

"Hey Trap, how's it goin'? Listen, I wonder if you could do me a big favor and pick up Riley today. He'll be at band practice until about 6:00. I'm working late until about 9:00."

"Really," replied Trap.

"Trap, I've got a chance to make some money. The editor of Runabout Monthly spotted me in the store and asked me to audition for the cover page. Trap, it's good money. I told you I want to go back to college. All I have to do is put on a bikini!"

"Okay angel, I'll do it, but only because you're so polite. You're gonna make that bikini look really good. But I have one return favor. Do you think you could teach the Blue Angels yoga?"

"Oh—oh. I don't know, shit, Trap, they'll cat call me."

"Aw, nicest bunch of kids on the planet, but you are required to wear a bikini for these lessons too!" Trap put his hand over his mouth.

"Well aren't you just the cutest little cut-up," René whispered and she hung up.

With the time remaining Trap and Raul swept over the upper Blue. He was glad René had called and cheered him up a bit. Raul could sense something was bothering Trap, but said nothing. The two men rode back to headquarters in silence.

When they were unloading gear, Raul seemed discouraged. Trap stuck to his rule and asked him how he felt. Raul put his hands behind his head and spoke.

"Trap, thanks for taking me on an outing. I know what happened at the fishway." He turned and walked away.

Trap wanted to go somewhere and get drunk, but instead headed out to pick up Riley.

CHAPTER 11

April 27, 1998

Olympia, Cascadia

Trap was beginning to settle down by the time he reached Redfield Middle School where Riley was having a late band practice. He felt like he had vented a bit, and a feeling of calm followed. He did feel concerned about Raul, but recalled René's comment that it was not his business.

"Own what's yours," she would say, "and to hell with the rest!" Though he still demonstrated his contempt for bigotry, René helped him. Sometimes a friend can tell you just the right thing, he realized. Just a few words and it can change your way of thinking—help point you in a new direction—just a few words.

*Boy, that René Coogman, she could be spot-on*, Trap thought. It was as if she could see into the future at times. She had that kind of foresight.

Trap strolled inside the gym where practice was breaking up and walked over to Riley, who was putting away his trumpet.

"Hi, Mr. Coogman," said Trap. "Your Mom asked me to give you a lift home so she could do some night work."

"Yeah, she called me earlier," said Riley, draining the spit valve on his instrument. "She got a modeling job up around Fife. I think it's pretty neat: my mother, a model."

"It should bring in some extra money, if all goes well," said Trap. "You hungry Riley? We could get a burger before I drop you off."

"Yeah Trap, that would be great! Can we go to the Bovine Burger Barn?" Riley smacked his lips.

The two headed over to the burger joint. Riley turned to Trap as they pulled into the parking lot.

"You really like my Mom, don't you Trap?" asked Riley.

"Yeah Riley, I'm fond of her. She's so smart…"

"Smart, huh? You sure it's not because of her body?" asked Riley. His hand went over his mouth hiding a grin.

"Well, hey I'm a guy," said Trap. He had to laugh. Trap reminded himself he was dealing with a very bright young man.

"It's okay Trap. Sometimes the son makes things difficult when a new man appears on the scene, but in your case I like it that you and mom are together. There's something very interesting going on. You and mom are alike, with an ability to get into people's minds to make them clear and strong, like they've never seen what's right in front of them before."

"You sound older than your years," said Trap.

"I get that a lot. People say I've been here before. They say I'm reincarnated, like the Dalai Llama. Do you believe that?"

"Yes I do. I believe some of us come back after we've gone," said Trap. He narrowed his eyes and gazed out the window.

"Hey Trap, I'll let you in on a little secret just between the two of us," said Riley.

"Yeah, what's that?"

"René is nuts about you, too."

They pulled into the Bovine Barn and went inside to order a couple of bacon cheeseburgers.

"It's nice to hear she's got feelings for me, Riley, but she won't tell me a thing about her past. Why the big mystery?" asked Trap.

Riley took a bite of his burger and showed some anxiety on his face.

"You've got to ask her about that, Trap, and don't be in a hurry. She doesn't like to talk about her past."

"And you, Riley are you as big a mystery as she is?" asked Trap.

Riley set his gaze out the window and choked back his emotions.

"Whoa, Riley," said Trap, "I'm sorry. I guess it is none of my business. I apologize."

"It's okay, coach. And about mom I don't know, Trap, no doubt she'll tell you when she's ready. Just be patient and gentle because she's been through hard times," said Riley. "So what about you? What sort of mysterious past have you been through?"

"Your mom knows most of it Riley, but I'll tell you some secrets if you like. Boy, you sure seem wise for a 14 year old."

"Anyway I'm 6'2," 195 lbs. I'm 1/2 Native American with mostly French and Irish in there. I went to UC Berkley and got a degree in biology. I used to be a fighter for the UC boxing team. When I was 21 I signed on a Swedish freighter and worked my way to Japan and back. Japan is where I got familiar with the Japanese practice of Shinrin Yoku. I have a Master's degree from Humboldt State in marine biology. I spent some of my youth in the Sierra Nevada range after moving there from Montana. It was my mother who taught me to fish and my father taught me to work with tools. But I owe my career to my mother. They are both gone now. I played football and track in high school—I was a pole-vaulter. Also, I used to be a commercial abalone diver for a short while, and I was an observer on a salmon troller on the high seas."

"Do you have any family, Coach?" Riley seemed to hesitate on the question.

"I had one brother who was quite a bit older than me, but he has gone on with my parents." Trap said shaking his head. "But I have some friends and cousins scattered around."

Riley felt a little pain at Trap's being so alone, but he brushed it aside. He was fascinated with Trap's stories.

Riley was quiet at first, then he spoke slowly.

"I'd like to have a life like that. I've also got this clarity of mind when I listen to your stories. You talk to me and I get pictures in my head."

Riley crossed his arms, "That's why this soccer team we're on is such a burning mystery. There's a feeling about the Blue Angels that's deep in my mind. I can't understand the way I feel about it."

"So you're happy being a Blue Angel? How about your position?" asked Trap.

"Blue Angels are like no other team I've ever been on," said Riley. "I wanted to be a striker, but I realize now I'm a better fit for midfielder. The fifty yard dash we did I was only a 9.2. But believe me, I've got a kick like thunder."

"Do you think about the racial diversity?"

"Well to tell you the truth it never occurred to me, or any of the rest of the team, at least as far as I can tell."

Trap was stunned like he'd run aground. A group of teens are indifferent to race, and a consulting firm preoccupied by it. Now what the hell was that about? Trap would think on it.

"Well Riley, I better get you home. It's after 7:00," said Trap. He drove Riley home, thinking he'd just talked to the smartest 14 year-old he'd ever met.

Trap went home exhausted from the full day. After parking and opening his apartment, Trap got a beer from the fridge, plopped back into his chair, and watched an old movie.

# CHAPTER 12

April 29, 1998

Olympia, Cascadia

René called Trap at home just after work and let him know that she would teach the team yoga. She had decided she was being foolish to be afraid she would get heckled. Even if someone did say something, Reuben would make them run laps until they dropped. She pulled on an old pair of sweat pants, a shirt, and a pair of Riley's leftover soccer shoes that were a close enough fit.

Trap called Reuben to discuss yoga for soccer warm-ups and agreed it was a good idea.

Everyone showed up at practice on time including Deshaun's father Jaylen. Reuben started off by letting the Blue Angels know there would be three practices a week for the month of May, and competition would begin in four weeks. Trap introduced René Coogman as a yoga instructor, who was going to loosen the team up at the beginning of practice. Trap warned the team to give their respect to René with no mouthing off and to pay attention to how they feel after they practice yoga. René felt warm inside listening to Trap and his baritone voice protecting her. She could also tell by the sound of Trap's voice that he thought a lot of her. She felt a calmness when she was around Trap.    Even with ragged faded sweats on, René looked fit, with her long hair reaching her waist. But her expression still held a stubborn, troubled dimness.

René lined them up in two rows and started through a difficult yoga strength workout. She wanted to get the message across to the kids that yoga is a tough physical workout, not an eastern dance. She wore a serious expression and the Blue Angels were about to get a workout they didn't expect. The kids were about to find out how strong René was too. She rose to mountain pose, plank pose, downward dog, upward dog, cobra, lunge, side stretch, shoulder stand, child's pose, arm balance, proud warrior, tree pose, half moon pose, and finally namaste hands. Then they would do it all over again. After finishing and holding namasté, she stood perpendicular to the team so they could see the pose. Silhouetted by the sun she bent her right leg to perpendicular. Her left leg was stretched straight and far behind her. Then she clasped her hands and reached as far up as she could as if trying to touch the planets. Her eyes slowly followed her hands and she bent her back into an arch also. René was like poetry. Then she eased her left leg further back, bringing her hands down for the moment. René reached the pose for all she could, arching her back towards her back foot. She always liked to add a little color so she held her arms in a circle like a figure skater. Many on the team could not help but admire her, and they looked at each other after watching her graceful movements.

"And this is the final pose, the final winning pose: exalted warrior!" she raised her voice. As the Blue Angels held exalted warrior, René walked up and down the two lines adjusting some of the kids' positions. Then René added her own pose. She asked the team to imagine a bright light was coming from their hands while their arms were held skyward. Then she asked them to slowly open their hands letting them fall to the ground and imagine a beautiful arc of light would come down touching their forehead, cascading over their bodies. They held their faces to the sky.

Then she said, "I feel somethin' special about this team. Have a great practice."

"What a looker," whispered one of the defenders to Riley.

"She's old enough to be your mother," said Riley.

After she was finished René ran over to Trap and asked him if he would drop off Riley. She had another request to appear in a magazine layout, for more money.

Trap said Riley was good company and he would be glad to. René had one more comment before she took off.

"Jesus Trap, there's a presence out there. They're so racially mixed it makes you feel the team is real uncommon. I'd propose a nickname: Blue Jets. Can a team have a nickname?"

"Sure they can." Trap said to himself, "UW dawgs, Seattle hawks."

Reuben called over to Jaylen and Trap and told them he had a new player named Kyle coming to practice.

"According to what I heard, he's a big strong kid, and a bit of a bully. Could you do me a favor and speak to him?"

Jaylen and Trap walked Kyle around the adjacent baseball backstop. Jaylen wore a frown that could melt Mount Rainier. Trap took a bit lighter approach.

"So your name is Kyle and you want to be a Blue Angel, huh?" said Trap. With two big men standing over him, Kyle had apprehension in his eyes.

"Well we take our soccer real serious, and the first part of that is respect."

Jaylen, who was very close to Kyle's face, intervened. He'd heard the word bully and he was not having any of that.

"Do you know what respect is Kyle?" Jaylen yelled in a hoarse voice. "Do you know what a bully is? Someone who jerks people around and picks on people smaller than him? Does this sound familiar Kyle?"

"Okay Kyle," said Trap. "Just show us you can be a respectful player and we'll be proud of you. Go out there and show us what you can do."

Trap slapped him on the back. But the searing words of Jaylen changed Kyle's attitude about the Blue Angels.

After going over mistakes from the last practice, Trap said "I'm gonna take this up a notch and show you some things on the field."

He gave Diego the ball and asked him to dribble downfield a few steps. Trap showed his team the difference between the near and far post, and explained why the far post was so vulnerable. Trap formed the kids into two lines, one at the near post feeding the ball to one at the far post.

"Okay Blue Angels, you've got a deadly weapon, we'll call this the far post play. Now pound the far post." The kids enjoyed this drill, and found it to be one of the more popular weapons throughout the season.

"Okay Blue Angels, well done, deadly weapons!" and he clapped for them.

"Over here," he hollered.

The kids ran after Trap and gathered around him, eager to see the next soccer move he had up his sleeve.

"Okay, before we scrimmage I want to show you another secret weapon. It's called a false nine. The two center strikers push forward getting right in the face of the two defenders, maybe even look them in the eye. Now with or without the ball, fade back towards the penalty arc. Watch carefully. If the defender follows you as you fade back it's working. As they try to cover you, the middle strikers, they will leave open the goal. The shot comes from an outside striker, or a mid-fielder. This can be used with a far post shot if needed. This drill is all about watching the other team. Watch the defenders and watch the goalie."

Trap pulled out his samba whistle and started blowing the three different notes: this was the signal scrimmage was about to begin. To Trap's disappointment, the nets had been removed from the post frames.

He put Gabriel and Babar together as the two most dangerous strikers, so they could learn to work together.

The Blue Angels exploded with the same energy that coaches felt as they watched. They were kind of random, using the notorious toe-poke and kickball technique, both dubious in soccer, but they were running hard. Trap refereed the game, but would stop play to make a point. As he expected, Trap was watching Riley think his way around the field. What he lacked in speed he made up with a powerful and accurate foot. Diego was not as aggressive as needed yet, but he had classic form. Gabriel was the most aggressive player, sprinting, and getting all he could out of his body. Babar was so well coordinated that everything seemed to come easy for him: speed, deception, and accuracy. Trap thought of Babar as a fourteen year-old professional. The defenders were big. One defender, JR, was fast and big, with the ability to punch the ball 50 yards. Although he was a toe-poker, he was learning and had the aptitude to change. The other three defenders were as tough as they come: Andre, Will, and Nicolás.

At the end of scrimmage Reuben said he was working on a preseason game with the Velociraptors, and that match would probably come in about a week. Then he introduced Kyle as a new team member, and the group clapped for him. It made Kyle smile. Reuben was going to get soccer nets from a friend, and he asked Trap to pick up some velcro tape.

Trap told the players, "René loved helping us with yoga and she thought you were an amazing team. She nicknamed you the Blue Jets." The kids seemed to like it.

"I'm going to work more on the field strategies next time like jockeying, overlapping, and direct forward play."

With that Trap gathered up Riley and they headed out for a burger. While munching down a salmon burger, Riley probed for a bit more information.

"So do you still have a crush on my mom?" asked Riley.

"Sure do, yep," said Trap.

"Well she still likes you to. At least I'm 99% sure she does. Women are kind of hard to figure sometimes. But she is acting dizzy and dreamy all the time, and singing and dancing around the house. I think it's because of you. I've gotten together a list of stuff that might help. Here, I'll read it to you."

Trap leaned over as if about to hear a well kept secret.

"Okay, first: let your hair grow longer, she loves long hair on a man, especially your shiny black hair. It's got her in a kind of trance," said Riley.

"Should I put a rush on that one?" asked Trap running his hand through his hair.

"Funny," said Riley.

"Second: get her a necklace, but don't buy the finished thing. Get the pieces and help her string it together. She'll go nuts!" said Riley.

"Will do," said Trap.

"Third: take her to work when you go into the woods. She's fascinated with this business called stream walking. You know how fit she is? She could handle it, I'm sure."

Riley lowered his voice. "Fourth: she loves it when you go to the gym with her. Boy did she love that—she wouldn't stop talking about it."

After dropping off Riley, Trap headed home. He felt a gentle glow about the team and the inertia that seemed to be following it.

About a half hour passed and there was an unexpected knock on the door. Though he was stripped to the waist, he ambled over to open it. To his surprise it was René, only a much different René. She was wearing a trench coat. Her face was decked out in mascara and lipstick. Her hair was shampooed and streamed down her back. She wore hooped earrings. She also had some sort of darker color to her skin. "Hi Trap," she said, handing Trap a rolled up paper with a ribbon on it. Looking at Trap with no shirt, René hummed quietly to herself.

"Hi René. Boy do you look different," he said in that silky baritone voice.

"Yeah, that's what they do before they put you in a magazine," said René. She looked at the tight muscles in Trap's abdomen, and she felt a surge of passion for him.

"You know what Trap? I come in here all made up and dressed up, and you are standing here with nothing on but a pair of jeans, and you're the one who is the looker."

"Not even close. I could never look as good as you. But thanks for the compliment," Trap scratched the back of his head.

"What's this?" He said looking down at the paper.

"Open it," she said, bouncing on her toes.

Trap did. To his amazement it was a diploma, certifying him as a full-blown soccer coach with all rights and privileges bestowed upon him. Trap giggled.

"Where did you get this?" asked Trap.

"I made it just for you. I'm qualified to give out awards you know, and thought you deserved one," said René.

"Let me be the first one to complement you on your great coaching!" she said.

Trap regarded her seriously for a moment and looked down at her coat. "Well thanks, René. Thanks for the confidence."

"Hey Trap, do I look like a magazine model?" René unbuttoned her trench coat and opened it fully: she wore a teal colored nylon/spandex bikini. She also wore a shiny gold chain tight around her waist. Her bikini was small, hugging her figure... making her waist look tiny and her breasts look huge. Trap couldn't help admire her as she padded across the floor to the kitchen for a glass of water for each of them. She became serious for a moment.

"Trap, I gotta go. I've got to spend more time with Riley. I just wanted to show you my swimsuit and give you your diploma, and say thanks. It's like there's a humming inside my body. When can I see you?"

"Let's go sailing Saturday on *Mornin' Mist*," said Trap, "and ask Riley."

René was about to leave, but Trap held her waist.

"Wait, a second, I haven't got a kiss yet," he said. Trap tilted his face towards her, placing his hand gently on her breast. She put her lips on his, but kept her mouth open as if wanting to say something.

"Oops," giggled René. "Your hand isn't quite big enough."

She closed the front door and left.

CHAPTER 13

May 2, 1998

Olympia, Cascadia

Percival Landing is the southernmost reach of Puget Sound. Trap sat in
the cockpit of *Mornin' Mist* sipping a jug of ice water. He couldn't
wait for René to show up. He could not stop thinking about her. She
seemed to reflect a stronger more independent woman. Everything she
said seemed more intelligent, every note she sang with her guitar made
him feel a chill. Every witty remark seemed funnier. There were
probably many other things she was good at. It seemed he would
discover a new talent every other day. And that was only what he
managed to pry out of her. She remained a mystery, and Riley kept her
secrets.

But as Trap watched her approach the boat he thought she looked a
little off today. She seemed to be bothered about something. Or was
she? Trap knew the way René sometimes expressed a mood was to
show off a little and dress to turn every head that walked by. But deep
down there she could be in a dark place.

It was early May, and the warm spring sun sliced across the clear
water of Salish Sea.

A great blue heron stood motionless at the water's edge looking like
a branch of madrone. Red-breasted mergansers and horned grebes
were carving wakes in the water down next to the pier.

Trap felt good sitting in the sun, and could see René taking long
strides down the ramp. Other people working on their boats stopped to
watch her walking towards Trap. Later, when his fellow sailors
commented on Trap's being lucky to have such a beautiful girlfriend,
Trap would simply reply, "I feel lucky!"

Trap sometimes wished his stomach would stop the stampede and
his heart would stop pounding when he saw this woman. René walked

up to him and gave him a hug. She seemed to get Trap more interested in her with each coming day.

René felt like she was falling in love with Trap. As they stood facing each other she caressed his arms and pulled his wrists against her stomach. Her grip on his arms was very tight.

"René, you have a death grip on my wrists. Is something wrong?"

"Oh shucks," she looked down at his right pocket. "Empty!"

"Well, not exactly," said Trap. "You have to reach further to your left."

"Oh well aren't we just a cut up," René smiled on one side of her face.

"Where's Riley?" asked Trap.

"He said he had soccer practice today." René put her hand over her mouth.

"Are you kidding me? Oh I get it, more Coogman humor."

Rene giggled, and her eyes were glancing about the marina.

"Riley said he'd take a rain check so we could be alone together," she told him.

"What do you suppose he wanted us to do, just the two of us?" René giggled again as she lay in the cockpit and pointed her leg straight up toward the sun. She looked at Trap. "Well angel, did you bring champagne with you this time?' asked René while she put sunblock on her arms and legs.

"Boats and liquor don't mix young lady," said Trap as he squinted at the light slanting over the water. Trap wore faded jeans with deck shoes and a navy crew neck sweater.

"However…" he cleared his throat. "However, on account of your looking so lady like, I'm going to make an exception. Of course I make this exception every time *Mornin' Mist* and I get together, but she knows me, she understands me."

"Yeah I suppose she's in love with you, too. It'll never work out. She's gonna leave you any day now," she said as she ran her hand over the starboard winch.

"Well you got to admit," said Trap. "I mean *Mornin' Mist* has really nice lines."

Trap guided Mist out of her slip. It quickly became obvious René knew how to sail. She took the tiller between her legs and unsnapped the main halyard while Trap took off the main cover. René cranked up the main by herself. Trap watched with admiration while she did most of the work, her chiseled muscles glistened in the sun due to the sunblock she had on. She grinned and flexed her bicep at Trap.

"Done," said René. Trap rigged up the jib. The lines were leading aft, so René handled the halyards and winches while Trap put the jib into the head foil and hooked it in place on the deck. Mist leaned to starboard as a moderate fifteen-knot wind came from the northwest making for a good beat up the inlet. René let out a holler as the increasing wind began roaring across the sails whistling in the stays. The jib was luffing as Mist came closer to the wind. René took a strong grip on the winch handle and cranked the headsail tight: half a foot off the spreader. Mist picked up speed, started healing to the toe rail, and began slamming the waves into spray, tossing them high in the air. René was getting wet but she was having a terrific time. Trap was impressed with her and complimented her on handling the lines alone. Mist continued to collide with fetched up waves as water sprayed across the bow pulpit. Trap knew there is nothing like the sound of a sailboat wake as a boat hisses and knifes through the water. René felt a moment of joy as Mist moved strongly into the wind. She yelled again. Droplets of spray passed across her face.

René thought to herself how much her life had changed since she met this adventurous man. *But more than that*, she thought, *is the way he treats me*. She could not recall ever being treated so kindly, and after a past like hers it meant the world to her. *It's as if I'm precious to him,* she thought as she watched the jellyfish mass along the boat's wake. She hadn't said the words, but she was getting ready. Just a little while longer and she would tell Trap something about these new feelings she had.

All lines secure, Trap worked his way back to the cockpit where René had the tiller. As she kept her eyes out front, Trap held René very gently and lovingly with his arms around her.

"René, you're a sailor too?" he asked. René started to kiss Trap on the neck.

"Careful," said Trap, "those houses up on the bluff all have nosey people with telescopes for spying on people who are making out."

René gave Trap a cute smile. "Yes, sir. But do we really care?"

Trap and René eased Mist up close to shore in Gull Harbor where they could not be seen from the eastern bluffs. Trap went up to the bow and dropped anchor. He went below and brought up a couple of sandwiches and the bucket of champagne.

Trap started in on a pastrami sandwich. René complained about the heat and took off her short sleeve top, revealing a blue bikini top. Trap's stomach did a cartwheel.

"Did you have a goal in mind this morning when you put on that bikini?"

"I did it for you. I thought you could use a little cleavage. Trap, you're the nicest man I've ever met." René said meekly as she smiled and looked down at the deck.

Trap slid over next to René and watched her.

"Was that hard for you to say, Angel?" as he put his hands gently around her waist.

"Want to go below, skipper?"

René could make Trap want her loving anytime she wanted. Just sucking in her stomach could leave Trap with his heart acting like a bass drum. But today it was different. There was something bothering him, and René didn't have a clue.

"No," he said. "René, I think you're a great lady, but I would like to know something about you. Who are you? Why are you shutting me out of your past? All I know is you're from Southern California and went on a diet that revealed a cute girl inside." René stiffened. She was not expecting this.

"Oh Christ Trap. What are you going to do, strangle it out of me? Can't we just love each other without dragging me over the coals about this? I don't like… I don't think… I can't." René suddenly went blank.

She stared over the water and wouldn't say a word. Trap had never seen her look so troubled. She started crying, but Trap heard a different cry, more like screams in short bursts. He was alarmed when her screams got higher in pitch. Trap's expression twisted in disbelief as her crying became even more frantic, and the sound bounced off the glacial till of the eastside cliffs. Gradually the screams turned to terror and she fell on the floor of the cockpit. René covered her head as if trying to protect herself. She intertwined her fingers in the jib sheets and held to them as tightly as she could. She stopped screaming only to gasp a few breaths and then started up again. Trap sat down next to her and held her gently, his hand on her back.

He was shocked.

"Come on, René, talk to me. What happened, what did I say? Come on, let's go below so you can lie down."

Trap lifted her and carefully carried her down the companionway. René put her arms around Trap's neck, which Trap interpreted as a good sign. He laid her down in the forward bunk.

Suddenly René said a few muffled words.

"Well aren't you going to kick the shit out of me?"

"René, what is happening? You're my angel and I… I—I love you!" said Trap. In that moment, with René helpless in the forward bunk, he realized she might hyperventilate.

Trap checked her pulse and it was racing. Her breathing was also fast, with a chilling groan between each breath. René started to sweat and tremble. She was staring at the inner hull but her eyes couldn't focus, they just jerked back and forth, rapidly opening and closing. Then she yelled loudly again, and with all the pain that had suddenly come to the surface. Trap looked at her.

"René, look at me! René look at my face."

René could not. She was trying to breathe through her teeth, her eyes were rolling and her face was wrinkling and twitching.

"It's me, Libby and Wade; time to bloody my face and beat my eyes till they won't open. Blind me, go on!" said René.

From the sound of her screams, Trap couldn't be sure her airway was clear. René was making a strange gasping sound; her hands were opening and closing at a rapid rate. For a moment it occurred to Trap that René could be in life threatening trouble. Fighting panic, he checked her vitals again. No change. Trap cursed himself for not getting a radio for Mist. She started gasping, and expecting her to vomit Trap took a bowl from the galley and held her forehead. Then she moved her hands above her head and waved them up and down like she was trying to block punches. Finally René drew her knees up to her shoulders and curled up in a ball, just as tight as she could get. She was silent for a moment, then hissed a few sounds.

"Don't harm the baby!" René whispered. "For God's sake!"

Trap fetched a towel from the head. But René grabbed it and started flailing it back and forth like some sort of flag.

Trap started for the cockpit when René called out. Trap made his way up to the fo'c'sle above her. He got her to lie on her back and he reached under her with a smooth massage. He bent over to her ear and told her he was sorry, that he'd had no idea.

"Trap! Don't leave me! Just hang on to me for a couple of minutes!"

Trap went below and held her as tenderly as he knew how, rubbing her back and massaging her neck and face. René was coming out of it.

He asked her in a clear loud voice. "René, what are you doing right now?"

Trap's hand felt so good, but she was exhausted and she started drifting off to unconsciousness. Just before she blacked out she looked up at Trap and said, "Don't hit the baby."

Trap tried to calm himself. René was unconscious but her signs were okay. He headed Mist back to Percival and an hour later pulled into her slip. At least the tide was in, and he had an easier time carrying her to his car. He debated taking her to the emergency room, but decided to head to René's trailer and monitor her there. Riley was home when Trap arrived. He carried her into the bedroom and put her to bed, where she slept on, out cold. Trap went to the front room and sat down with Riley. The boy shot a piercing gaze at Trap.

"What happened, coach?" asked Riley.

"I'm not sure, she had some sort of convulsion, or panic attack, or something," Trap mumbled.

"Did you start asking her about years ago, and why she wouldn't talk about it?" asked Riley.

"Yes, I did. I love her, but I feel I don't know her."

"Coach, I told you not to do that, remember? When we were at the Burger Barn I told you she'll tell you when she's ready, that she has had a terrible past. Remember? I told you she'll tell you when she's ready. Now is the time to believe it," said Riley.

Trap felt a surge of anger at Riley.

"All right Riley, no more fun and games. Your mother is badly traumatized and we have got to know what to do next. Now tell me what happened! Does she have epilepsy?"

"I wasn't even born yet," said Riley. But I remember Privina, my nanny, telling me my mother was brutally beaten when she was young. René, my beautiful mother, beaten black and blue—and I guess it was many times."

"Has she ever checked herself into a clinic or hospital?" asked Trap.

"She hasn't got any health plan, coach. She always tried to tough it out. She tried her best to be a good mother. See, I got no one else," Riley's eyes welled up.

"Well you've got me, Riley," Trap said. "Let's be tough. Has this ever happened before?"

"Yes. I think she's like a battle-weary soldier," said Riley.

"So she has these attacks and then comes out of it and is okay for a long time?" asked Trap.

"Yeah," said Riley, "but only recently. She didn't have these attacks until ten years after I was born."

"So she has these spells and then comes out of it, and after she is perfectly okay, is that the picture? No aftershocks. Has she ever gotten professional help? You know, a psychiatrist, counselor, crisis intervention?"

"No."

"Well, let's make a pact. You and I are going to get your mom over this." He shook Riley's hand.

"I'll take Monday off, and find her a doctor." Trap stood up before continuing. "So René was badly beaten on a number of occasions when she was pregnant, and the stress surfaced ten years later?" asked Trap.

"I think so, yes," said Riley.

"Riley, do you have any trauma or PTSD of your own? Anything at all?"

"No."

Trap went into the bedroom and sat on the bed next to René. She slept.

"I'm sorry angel, I didn't know."

Her heart was steady. Her breathing was a bit slow and raspy. Her hands were cold, so Trap pulled the covers up.

Trap left Riley at the trailer and headed back to button up Mist. He picked up some Chinese orders to go and stopped off for his sleeping bag and shaving kit. When Trap returned to René's trailer she was still asleep. Riley was quietly watching TV.

"At least tomorrow is Sunday. Do you feel up to going to school Monday?" asked Trap.

Riley nodded.

"What's your mother's work number?" Riley said she only had a home phone, and could not be reached when she was at work.

Trap turned around to see René standing behind him. She had a weary expression on her face, like she wasn't fully conscious.

"So now you know," she mumbled. "I wanted to impress you with all those sexy clothes and look what happened instead. I'm so sorry Trap. I really messed it up didn't I?"

Trap moved quickly to René. He gathered her in his arms and felt a lump in his throat. His eyes were moist.

"Thank God you're all right, precious angel. I love you. I found that out today. Only now I find myself not knowing what is happening. I don't know what to do. I figure we rest Sunday and better see a doctor Monday and get a referral. How does that sound?"

"I'm not sure; I have no health plan." René pulled a baggy trout nut sweatshirt over her head, covering her bikini top. "Smells good."

"I got you some Chinese, wanna try it?"

René took a single bite and put her fork down.

CHAPTER 14

May 4, 1998

Olympia, Cascadia

René was badly shaken, just like the last time she had a whole lot of trouble in her life. But this time there was plenty worth fighting for: a very bright son and a very big-hearted man who said he loved her.

Trap suspected that René had a bad case of PTSD and would have to deal with it. She skipped work and soccer practice. One thing was different now. Trap had told René he loved her and it meant a great deal to her. Despite her beauty she had not dated much since leaving LA, and the reason was now becoming clear. Trap had broken that barrier and perhaps, just perhaps, more good things would follow.

René wanted to be around Trap as much as she could. She was frightened over what had happened on the boat. His voice seemed to melt right through her soul and comfort her the way it always did. Trap took the day off to support her. He made some phone calls and got a referral for a specialist in trauma. He was very fortunate to get an appointment allowing René to get in within a few days. He told her he would pay for the therapy as long as she needed him to. In the next few minutes René fixed them some coffee, yogurt, and granola. She got a grip on Trap's arm and walked him to the sofa. Trap sat down and René sat in his lap. She put her cheek against his and started to cry. She cried hard until she had to gasp for breath, and then she sobbed until she had no more tears.

Trap was quiet through her weeping. Then finally he spoke.

"C'mon angel, let it out. You sure feel bad, don't you? You know I made a pact with Riley that he and I are going to do whatever it takes to get you through this. I'll always be here to help so long as you want me to."

Trap spent the next several days confused and distracted. Trying to put the pieces together, he thought about the odd behavior: dressing to attract attention but never really connecting, obsessive exercise, avoiding talking about her past life with him, and that smile—that terribly dim smile, her irrational fears of noises or animals. What did it all mean? Did he fall in love with the wrong girl? Was René insane? He thought not. Was she troubled, emotionally exhausted, shattered in some way, suffering from panic attacks? That seemed much more likely. But sticking to his rule about people, he would have to ask her; he would have to get it out in the open. As deep as he could reach within himself, he knew he still loved her. She was so beautiful—how could she be so troubled?

Trap helped René up to the car a few days later. After arriving at the clinic he held her hand up to the doctor's office. She was trembling, so Trap filled out the paperwork for the receptionist. Then René was called inside, and she would have to do this alone.

One hour passed. After René rejoined Trap, they drove back to her trailer as she quietly stared out the window. She was usually so comic that it was difficult to see her depressed, and Trap felt tight in the back of his neck as they headed back.

"Well, René, what happened in there?" Trap frowned and looked hard at her.

"Could you swing by the drug store? I have to take some medication for a while," she said in an even tone, then stared out the window.

"Oh, I get it… the silent treatment again," said Trap.
René exhaled hard through her nose, and Trap got the point.

"You don't smoke, do you?" she murmured. "I could use a smoke right now. Oh, don't worry about it. I hardly ever smoke… just when it hurts bad."

"Okay, okay," said Trap. "You're a big girl. Do what you need to do. Do you want me to pick you up some rum, too?"

"Yes," she said without hesitation.

"Let's make you a necklace," said Trap. "Maybe a choker would look good because you have such a pretty neck."

"Not now," said René. "I need to be alone. I'm going to the gym." Trap watched her fists tighten.

Once home, René grabbed her workout bag and went quickly to the gym. She went straight to the heavy bag in the back room. She raged against the pain she felt. She leaned into every punch and barred her teeth. Her back bent forward and she yelled with each swing of her fists. Her eyes narrowed and appeared black. She swung her fists on and on until her body spattered sweat on the floor. She looked down at her breasts and long hair and cursed them for being in the way as she hooked the bag over and over. She wanted her body hard. Finally, after twenty minutes, she stepped back. Gasping, she bent her back to rest her gloves on her knees. *Rum and cigarettes sounds good*, she thought... *rum and cigarettes*.

\* \* \*

Again more kids showed up for practice than were on the team. Reuben announced that they would start the season with a preseason battle on Thursday, May 7 against the Velociraptors. He asked Trap to set up the Blue Angels' favorite drill, the 50-yard dash. Every last kid wanted to be fast. The drill seemed to bring out the unique personality in each player and gave the coaches new ideas for individual coaching, which was beginning to get Trap's interest.

JR lined up at the start against Will. One would have thought JR with his overweight power would have no chance against Will, a wide receiver for Klamath Middle School. Trap blew his samba whistle and hit his stopwatch. JR exploded off the start, kicking up bundles of grass. He strained for speed, lowering his forehead as veins stood out on his neck. Air rushed past his cheeks and pushed his lungs. Small groups of people were gathered at the starting line. Some were yelling for the players. Will was a much different runner. He smiled when he ran, with a peaceful look in his eye. Will's stride was perfect and everything about him seem poised. He seemed to be having the time of his life when he ran. To everyone's amazement, JR crossed the finish stride for stride with Will. It was a shock and a joy to Trap and Reuben that JR made such an effort. Trap bumped fists with both boys. He looked at JR.

"Do you realize what you just did?"

Next up was Riley against Ben. Riley was determined to break nine seconds, but he had looseness in his lower body that was hard for Trap to figure. Riley looked double-jointed when he ran. Ben had some speed but ran with his toes out slowing him down. While still over nine seconds, Riley continued to develop a thunderous kick, as if a running disadvantage became a kicking advantage, possibly coming from his extra high wind up. Riley got Ben this time, 9.3 to 9.1. But Ben's problem was easy to correct. Both boys improved their sprint time.

The rest of the boys and girls finished their sprint. Trap took the sprint times over to René's place and studied the results. Trap tried hard. Knowing his inexperience, he studied the game until his temples ached… looking for the secrets of soccer, the world's most celebrated game. Over and over he looked at the times and got new ideas for the players. Something about the way the players ran taught him. He could see into them. He could see them clearly. To Trap, each young man or woman is an individual, to be treated as such regardless of their differences in race, color. The cowards of bigotry just couldn't get it. Trap learned he could understand a lot about these young athletes by studying the way they ran. Time and time again, as he stared at the sprint times, he would get a mental image of a kid running and begin to see strengths and flaws in their style of playing soccer. One kid had fast sprint times, but as Trap watched him play, he reasoned that the kid was perceiving the ball as closer than it really was, causing him to consistently top kick the ball as his foot came up… a huge power leak that was ruining his game. Trap would talk to him next practice. He soon came to realize that speed is one of the keys to soccer. Kids run from the heart, and you can't always predict their time and speed. They run like racehorses. Sometimes they're like a charging locomotive. Other times they just can't get moving.

After the sprints, Trap sat the team down in a circle. He found himself strangely nervous, probably because he was so worried about René. He forced himself to the moment.

"Okay, champion sprinter for the day is Gabriel Santa Cruz with an 8.0. The slowest time would be coach Trap. He hasn't made the finish line yet." The kids laughed.

Trap nodded, but he had something else on his mind.

"We spend a lot of time working out attack strategies, and not enough on defending," he said. "While it's true defending is more an instinctive part of the game, I want you to use this strategy. So the other team has the ball and is attacking. Defensive captain, use the word 'mark' to pick the player you will stop. Use the word 'cover' to get within three feet of the attacker, and use the word 'defend' to take the ball away with all your power."

Trap worked on several other keys to defending.

"To intercept," he said, "attack the ball from an angle. To front block, confront the blocker straight away with your inside foot. Don't be afraid of contact. Get in there and mix it up. Slide tackling in this league is prohibited. Chest nudge will not cause penalty, go for it. Work on jockeying, or getting in the attacker's way when he has the ball. Now, I've heard the officials in this league do not take solid control of the game. In other words they do not call many penalties. Use a shoulder check, a hand to the chest, a side cut with a push as legal play, viewed by the officials as incidental contact. Okay attackers, I want you to learn my favorite play: the wall pass."

Trap showed them the give-and-go of soccer. He went over several other deadly weapons such as roll and step, overlapping, fast combination play, close down space. There was something about Trap's friendly determination the kids really liked. He didn't yell at them. They almost expected to be yelled at, but Trap was too busy talking at them, calling the Blue Jets a deadly weapon. He heard other coaches on other teams use the most self-defeating language. One coach he overheard kept saying: "I've got better things to do!" every other sentence. Trap just shook his head at such negative coaching.

Trap blew the samba whistle three times and the scrimmage was on. The team was looking good for the most part. There were three main things that jumped right out at him: Deshaun was toe-poking, Will was playing kickball, and many kids were picking up their heads before contact with the ball, causing a power leak. Trap got busy pulling players aside to correct these problems. After a good scrimmage the sun began to sink towards Capitol Peak. Reuben, who was arranging a trip to the Tacoma soccer fair, called it a day. Trap was eager to see René, and called to Riley.

"Hey Riley! Want a ride?"

The two were headed for René's place when Trap turned to Riley.

"I want to stay with you guys for a few days, just to make sure your mom is alright. Is that okay with you?"

"Yeah. She really likes you, and that's as good a judge of character as I need."

René was finishing up a shepherd's pie. She hugged her boys when they came in the front door. Riley headed for his room and clicked on the TV set. Then he changed his mind and clicked on his PC instead.

René gave Trap a weak smile but took a firm grip on his hand. She got in his lap again and spoke slowly. She was still trembling.

"Trap, I've got to get out of this. What if I lost my job? What if I go crazy?"

"René, I won't let anything happen to you, I told you. I talked it over with that very smart son you have. He said this has happened before, and you always get better in a day or two," said Trap.

That seemed to calm René down.

"The doctor said to bring to the present one small part of my past, about once a week. But just one. Bring it to the here-and-now, tell it to someone you love. Write it down in a journal and show them what you wrote." She cried for a few moments then got hold of herself.

"That's you, Trap." She cried a few more moments. "Okay?" she asked.

"Okay." Trap gave her a little smile.

"Okay, well here goes. I never finished high school!"

René hesitated, as if waiting for a tornado to strike, but nothing happened. She took a sigh of relief, suddenly feeling like she would sleep well tonight. That short sentence was a huge accomplishment for René. Trap held her very tight in his lap. He tried to convince this woman that she would be able to pull through. Looking over her shoulder, though, Trap had a very troubled expression.

"I can already see another way I could help you. From now on cross-examining you about the past I will not do, unless you ask me to. I brought this attack on with some pretty personal questions. That's because things are certainly personal between you and me."

"Well, let's get some pie," said René. "I'll get Riley."

During dinner Riley asked his mom whether she was going to be okay. It was the most serious Trap had ever seen Riley.

"Coach and I will protect you, and I mean it. I figure in a couple of days you'll be back to work where you used to attract so many customers, and back to modeling where you attracted even more customers. After that it's the GED. What do you think?"

For the first time since her panic attack, René gave Riley a smile as he went back to his room.

After dinner René pulled out the bag Trap gave her and scattered a few dozen pieces for her necklace. Trap got an assortment of ebony pieces, puka shells, lapiz, long pieces of bone, and black beads, with a thin elastic line and a clasp to fasten around her neck.

Riley tip toed out of his room and came over to check on the necklace. He looked over at Trap and winked. Trap gave him a nod.

"Cool," said Riley, "can I have one too?"

"Soon as I swing by the jewelry store," said Trap.

"How about a tattoo, can I get a tattoo?"

"How about later, much later," said René.

"So you want to make a choker?" asked Trap.

Trap reached for the sewing kit and pulled out the tape measure. René's neck was 12.5 inches, so he set up the very small line to thirteen inches. René enjoyed sorting through the various pieces. Trap waited until she had them arranged in a way that pleased her, then tied the various necessary knots. When he held it up, René grinned and led Trap to the bathroom.

"Okay, put it on," said René.

Trap gently moved her hair to one side and clasped the necklace.

"God it's pretty. I don't want to take it off!"

"Please don't, it's just for you. Do you think it's possible for someone to look too good? If that's the case, you're in trouble lady," said Trap.

"I love all your compliments, Trap. You can bring me back and make me feel special. I've never been treated so fine as you treat me. You can bring me back from the void, just like you do to those kids, and I love you for it."

"I love you too, pretty girl," said Trap. "Why don't you lay down on the floor and I'll give you a back rub."

"Wait a minute, let me build a fire." She went outside to get some paper and kindling, followed by half a dozen logs. Riley made off to his room to finish up some homework, and to give Trap some privacy.

The wind came from the north, blowing fair weather with it. Out in the endless blackness coyotes were yapping. Tiny needles of douglas fir rattled against the side of the house like rain. Teal and canvasback were settling in on the sound, chuckling quietly. The waves from the water below them sounded harmonic and calming. Trap took his elbow and put it in the center of René's back.

"This would work better with your shirt off," said Trap.

"Yeah but Riley," said René. "I know." She went into her bedroom, pulled all her clothes off except her panties and a T-shirt, and dashed out by the fire to lay down on her stomach. At times she looked tough as black leather, and other times she shined with soft femininity, as gentle as could be.

Trap put his elbow on her spine again, running it from the depressions in her vertebrae. Then he moved to her shoulders and used a little force along her clavicle and scapula, finding several knots of tension there. René moaned, and Trap wasn't sure she was signaling pain or pleasure, so he used his low voice in her ear.

"You okay René?"

She giggled a bit then sank into Trap's massage. Her sinuses were congested the way a good massage does. Under Trap's touch René wafted into the anonymous past and future, and she let her wild imagination mingle with Trap's touch. With firm pressure to her neck she sailed a west wind up the Columbia River gorge looking at the columnar basalt cliffs. René felt she was in a dream. She could swear she heard the Great Basin flood and a deafening roar of water. She went over Multnomah Falls, tumbling head over heels in the silver column of froth, landing on her feet in the rocks within the chatter of the plunge.

Trap took René's right arm, folded it around the small of her back, and began rubbing her hands, including snapping his fingers over each of hers. René saw herself graduating from the UW physician's assistant program dressed in a purple gown. He placed his strong hands under her arms and followed her broad back down to her small waist. René was playing her guitar and singing at the local hotspot. The crowd was quiet, listening.

Trap worked his way around her pelvis and ran some strong strokes down her legs, especially the backs of her knees.

She was working at a medical center in Brazil, treating the sick with precious antibiotics; working hard and enjoying it. Trap moved to her feet and started crossing her pads with his fingernails. René cried at this, but only because it felt so good and because she had Trap sticking up for her. He let her lay still and walked across the room without saying a word. He started going over his clipboard of 50-yard sprints, the running times serving as a kind of primer, stimulating new ideas.

René was noodled out, groaning with pleasure, sounding like a DADGAD guitar chord still face down on the rug.

"Trap, you've got magic in your fingers. You can do that to me any time, any place. It puts me in a world of fantasy. Can I tell you something else? Just one line and then I'll shut up for a week. You know I love you, don't you Trap? Well I used to be married. Now I'm divorced. And he used to be in prison."

Trap looked up at René but didn't visibly react.

*Wade*, she thought, and her fine relaxed massage was gone, shoved aside by black anger.

"I'll see you later, Trap. I want to go down to the water." René grabbed the smokes and the bottle of rum and headed down the chicken walk.

## CHAPTER 15

May 7, 1998

Lacey, Cascadia

The two teams arrived at 5 pm Thursday at Deschutes Soccer Complex for the first and only preseason game. The kids were in uniform and couldn't wait to get started. René forced herself to get up and deal with her problems. She wanted to see the beginning of the soccer season, so she made her way to the game. After telling the kids to relax and play loose, she flexed her way through a dozen yoga poses to warm them up. After what she had been through, Trap couldn't help but admire her for hanging in there.

Reuben and Trap discussed the starting line up, who would sub in, and at what position. After warming up Reuben gathered his team into a circle. He said a prayer for the safety of the kids on both teams. Trap knelt and gave a few last words before play. He urged the kids to play spread out, to get in position to receive, and whenever possible to use the deadly wall pass.

Then he mentioned the main ingredient: "Attack—always attack, and be relentless. Don't let up on them. Don't let them come up for air. Goalie, you know what to do if your team gets winded. Watch out for our team getting exhausted. That is the one danger in this kind of play. Watch the Velociraptors. See if they're getting gassed and pour it on if they do. If you have them on the defensive they should tire more quickly than you. Use direct forward play."

Trap asked them to form a tight circle and had them bump fists and spread out to their positions.

This being a preseason game, Trap was forced to be the referee. That was not his first choice, but he gave it a shot. He gave René a quick frown and ran out on the field. Trap blew a few short blasts on his samba whistle. The Blue Angels would kick.

Both teams being ready, Trap gave a loud whistle and the game was on. Babar ran hard at the ball and kicked at it, but intentionally only nudged it a foot forward. He then took off running. All strikers charged the Raptors goal. JR was hiding behind Babar, first delaying, and then sprinting to the ball. He kicked it high and Babar was under it when it came down about 20 yards to the goal. Babar was getting in traffic, so he flipped the ball to Gabriel who one-touched it to Diego. Diego did not have a clear shot, so Babar got in the face of the goalie with defenders at either side.

It was a good false nine situation. Gabriel and Babar stutter stepped backwards. Two defenders followed, leaving the goal exposed. Diego looked back at Riley and sprinted as fast as he could to the far post, leaving the ball behind. Riley let loose the first shot on goal. It flew high and hard, typical of Riley's power. Diego was at the far post. The ball slammed into the crossbar and was caught by the goalie. Diego shook his head as he realized he had run off sides.

The coach of the Raptors scratched his head as he eyed over the whole Blue Angels team. He thought they looked like an international hit squad melting its way downfield. The coach wondered where in the world the Blue Angels found their ethnic diversity.

*Christ, they're intimidating,* thought the Raptors coach. *They're so quick and diverse they seem hard to understand. They're all scattered about and at the same time together.*

The Raptors, however, were no pushovers. By half time they had the Blue Angels two to zip.

Trap brought Gatorade with ice for the kids. The kids rehydrated and caught their wind. Reuben called the kids into a circle and he described what he knew of the Velociraptors.

"They are usually strong in the first half and score most of their goals during that time. Then the most curious thing happens: they tend to go flat, run out of gas, and give up. So now is the time to take a deep breath and really pour on the attack soccer."

Trap walked over to René. She smiled weakly and looked out across the grass.

"We're going into a stronger direct forward play," said Trap. "Watch how hard the Blue Angels can press."

The Blue Angels took the field for the second half. Deshaun (goalie) watched the Velociraptors take the field also. The Raptors were looking gassed. Deshaun gave the hand signal to go hard. The Raptors kicked directly to Will, who started downfield. The team went into hyper drive. It seemed to suit them; weeks of scrimmages were paying off. Babar headed a corner kick from the right side and it went in the net, making it 1 - 2. After the second kick Gabriel got cleated in the shin for a penalty kick. Much of the team got in the penalty area for a block. But Riley, understanding there was no off sides rule in a penalty kick, was parked at the far post. Gabriel, watching the defenders, lobbed the ball high overhead. It came down on Riley and he gave it a little tap into the goal.

After that the Raptors seemed to grow even more tired. The Blue Angels took over with their speed and stamina. They were all over the field, seemingly unstoppable. The final score was 7 – 2.

The Blue Angels slapped hands with the Velociraptors. The team was really high, smiling and grinning at each other. Reuben had to settle the kids down so he could debrief.

"This is the kind of play I want to see all season. How many of you got seriously gassed out there today?" asked Reuben. No one raised a hand.

"Okay then, I mean we can play a half this way, no problem. Trap any comments?"

"Great start Blue Jets," Trap said. "Think about those first two goals they got on us and we'll talk about it next time. Remember each and every goal today belongs to the whole team. Next week we start league play, so let's be ready."

The sun was creeping along the row of poplar trees that lined the soccer field. There was a mackerel sky that was quickly scorched into an orange sunset that splashed all the way back to the grand mountain of Cascadia. Trap looked into René's eyes, put his arm around her waist, and pulled her close against him. In spite of her muscle tone she felt to Trap like a helpless kitten in his arms. Trap felt a rush of confused emotions for her…as she arched her waist and flexed her tight core muscles in his arms he was overcome with passion for her. But at the same time he felt deeply sorry for her, knowing she was bleeding somewhere deep inside. He pulled her head against his neck and kissed her forehead. He put his lips against her ear and said: "I won't quit on you René." She put her hand on his chest.

"Thank you, Trap."

"Hey, we looked good today didn't we?" he changed the subject.

René watched Riley running up to them being pursued by Eyana the African American girl. Eyana shoved the ball at Riley and said,

"Come on. I'm calling you out, dude!"

Eyana lunged at the ball but Riley blocked and she tripped over his foot. Eyana burst into laughter as she hit the ground. The sunset over their heads was beginning to close the day. Riley flipped the ball to Eyana and she started laughing louder when he took it away. Her laugh was contagious and made Trap laugh also. Riley and Eyana both had a foot on the ball, but Riley shoved it forward and then raked it back. Eyana fell down again and howled with laughter. Her mother came walking up, and could not stop laughing either. The sky was turning deeper red and the field was growing quiet. All Trap could hear was Eyana's laughter bouncing off the school building.

Trap held René and didn't say a word. The sky darkened. Although still feeling a bit down, she walked next to Trap as if there was nothing in the world she would rather do. René started humming a soft tune. She was sure she could beat the trauma she felt from the horrific events that came when she was pregnant 14 years ago. Of all the bad days she had lived, she thanked God for this day and this dark haired spirit who had found her.

Trap, René, Riley, Eyana, and her mother walked off the field together, smiling. René smiled but the dimness was still there. She walked awkwardly. It was late so they all went for a burger. Eyana and her mother came along. Eyana was having a good time taunting Riley for a rematch.

In the table across from Trap the rest of the group recognized a young girl named Corin. Corin walked up to Trap's table and said hello to Eyana. Corin sort of nodded in Riley's direction. Eyana got the point and introduced Corin to Riley. Corin smiled at Riley, her eyes half open. She mumbled out a hello, but she made it obvious she was a bit taken with this good looking 14 year old.

The three of them, Trap, René, and Riley, headed home. René raised one eyebrow and turned back to Riley who was in the back seat.

"I think someone back there kind of likes you," she said. "Someone named Corin. Boy is she cute. Tell me true son, do you know the birds and bees? If not I could take you for a walk on the beach and explain it to you."

Riley turned beet red and Trap burst out laughing.

"All right grown-ups: here's the bottom line. I know every little detail there is to know, all right?"

"Good for you Riley," said Trap. "I'm still trying to get it figured out myself. Women are really complicated."

"Well, don't worry about me," said Riley. "Besides you don't get this info from your parents, you get it on the streets!"

The car pulled up at René's trailer. Riley ran inside while Trap and René sat on a bench overlooking the sound. The aromas of night had already settled in, and a cool mist rose up the high bank and mixed with the willow whips planted five years ago after a near disastrous slide. The whips rustled to the mist and made Trap feel good.

Trap turned to René. "Can you swim, angel?"

"Well, I'm not exactly shaped like a boat so I cause some turbulence while moving through the water, but I get by. I swim once a week at the fitness center. I'll bet I could give you a run for your money," said René.

Trap felt a giggle coming up from his stomach. He continued to love René's humor.

"Yeah, but can you snorkel?" Trap asked.

"LA swimming pool snorkeler," she said. René started to wonder what he was driving at. She smiled and shook her head a little. "My mother was a trout," she said giggling, "and I can out swim any land animal you can name. But what gives with all this swimming?"

"I would love it if you would help me do a summer steelhead snorkel survey Monday," said Trap. "You have to sign an insurance waiver and be issued a guest pass from Hughes. I've got all the gear you'll need: fins, snorkel, goggles, and a wetsuit custom designed to fit a turbulent lady," Trap chuckled slightly.

René nodded. "Yeah, if I can get off work I'll go with you. I love these adventures. You're a lucky man Trap to have the life you live."

"Can I have another massage tonight? My cerebral cortex needs a rubdown."

"Coming right up, I got a special massage for you. And you're right, I am lucky."

CHAPTER 16

May 11, 1998

Olympia, Cascadia

It was Monday morning. Trap picked up lunch and all necessary equipment and loaded them into his pick-up. René had to fill out a form as a volunteer, and they were off. A veil of high fog hung over southwest Cascadia about 800 feet up. It had the appearance of cotton candy and kept Trap confident that the skies would clear by noon. The two were unusually quiet the first part of the trip. René was preoccupied with V-formations of Canada geese flying north over the black freeway and under the clouds. She could hear the wild cackling in spite of the road noise, and she was craning her neck to watch them. René listened to the cackling but she looked at Trap, studying his handsome features. Something about the geese overhead overwhelmed her with a very passionate feeling.

"Trap, those geese are wild," she said with an adventurous look in her eyes. "Why don't we follow them? I know we're behind them, but maybe we could catch up." She moved over very close to Trap, putting her arm playfully around his neck.

"René, it's hard to drive like this," said Trap smiling.

"Having a tough time?" she whispered, kissing him on the side of his mouth.

"René, we're in the company truck!"

"Be wild, Trap. We won't hurt the truck. Just drive. I'll ask the questions."

"René, this is unprofess—" She cut his word off, cupping her hand completely over his eyes.

"René, I can't see!"

"Use your left eye," she giggled. "Now we're on a wild goose chase!" She squeezed his arm tighter and moved her hand around his back.

She moved closer to him, her whole body pressing firmly against him. "It might help if you catch those geese. Wild goose chase! Don't break the speed limit, Trap!"

She was acting much different from yesterday, putting her hand on his leg. He gushed out a big sigh and laughed. He tried to keep his eyes focused on the road. Before things got really out of hand, René backed off. She rested her head on Trap's lap with her eyes closed. She stayed there a long time.

She whispered quietly, "Wild geese, I'll always love the sound of wild geese."

Acting a bit stuffy he spoke to her, "René, I'm a biologist, a scientist if you will. But make no mistake. Along with my ancestors I pay attention to the spirit world too. I'm not a shaman, but I pretend to be. If a Canada goose is behaving strangely around you, it's an omen. Something is coming, and you can hear what it is by listening to the voices you hear around you. A Canada goose also tells you to let go your inhibitions and sing at top of your lungs."

René was thinking about how lucky she was to have Trap bringing adventure and romance into her life. She never felt about a man the way she felt about Trap. It was his duality. He was strong and athletic, and Riley told her Trap was a fighter in college. But he was always so gentle with her at times it brought her near tears. When he held her it seemed to René as if he cherished her. She had never in her life felt so special. René blessed her fortune to have found such a man. But she was not over the hump where PTSD was concerned.

"Hey Trap, after we get done with the survey, could we eat our lunch someplace really pretty with a view? I have something I want to talk to you about," said René.

"Sure, I know just the place," said Trap. "What gives?"

"When we get there," said René.

Trap pulled off the freeway and headed due east on Highway 23. The wide flood plain closed into a canyon as they came along side the

Moccasin River. The river was cool and quiet and steaming slightly beneath a heavy over story of willow, alder, hemlock, and cedar. The sun was breaking through the low clouds, its flashing rays burning against the bark of the trees, filling the air with the aroma of wet cedar. René was a pleasure to be riding with because she was so fascinated with the natural world. They came around the corner and Mt. Rainier showed herself for the first time today. It towered up in front of them, still heavy with snow and scalded by the bright sun.

"Trap, let's climb it someday, right to the summit, just you and me."

"Okay angel, you and me," said Trap. "And a guide."

He turned right on a logging road and started heading south over the Moccasin River bridge.

"Maybe up at your viewpoint we'll talk a little about me, but for now how about we talk about you," suggested René. "How do you feel about this soccer team now that you're about six weeks into it?"

"Best thing I ever did," said Trap. "I didn't expect to get so involved. Two months ago I knew nothing about soccer and nothing about coaching, and nothing about you. But now a lot has happened."

The road dropped down into a dense cedar grove. Due to saturated soil in the ground, the trees were buttressing. They grew so close together they blocked out the sky. They held out sound and wind so all that could be heard was the crackling of tires on the rocky road. A presence swept over the site and made Trap and René both feel odd.

"Do you feel that?" asked René.

"Yeah, we're being watched. Probably a cougar."

A raspy growl came from the shadows. It initially sounded like a dog. Then the barking sounded like a wild animal.

"What in hell was that?" blurted René, unnerved by the unusual sound.

"Coyote. They sound weird when they make that raspy growl, don't they?"

Trap stopped the truck and asked René to follow him. He pulled the truck off the road and stepped out, following a little clear stream. They stepped on moss and clover. With the truck stationary, René could hear the slightest moan of wind high over their heads. The cedar trees were mature. They were huge, with a 16-foot circumference base, sending their tangled branches upwards.

Trap put his hand on René's shoulder and spoke in his low quiet voice.

"René, have you ever heard of forest bathing? Better known as Shinrin Yoku? It's a Japanese modern day wellness practice. If you walk in the woods and inhale the various organic chemicals in the air, you'll feel much better. If you're sick, they say you can be healed.

René lowered her head.

"I could use some help, I guess."

Trap regarded her seriously.

"Sorry you're having a tough time, René. Things are bound to improve as you work through the pieces of this. I understand your feelings have been buried for some time, and I know it takes courage to pick up each part to evaluate what it means to you now."

The two continued up the little channel. Trap was extremely interested in the color of the water.

"There's groundwater here," said Trap. "lots of it. There's nothing better you can do for salmon than create habitat out of groundwater." As they followed the swale, the understory got very close: a mat of willow, blackberry, and vine maple.

"Ready to do some stream walking?" said Trap.

"You bet," said René.

They started upstream through a boggy area. Trap went down on his chest and crawled like an amphibian under a thicket of salmonberry. They were coming to flowing water, forcing them both against the right bank. There just wasn't enough room to stay dry, so Trap and René were forced to drag their bodies over the water. Lacking the experience to avoid them, René was taking stinging nettles in her face and arms. Nettle stings immediately, but later that night it is bound to get much worse. Finally the thicket broke up, and the understory mat returned to clover and moss. They came to a little half-acre pond at the upper end of the swale. It was heavily brushed on the right bank again, but a boulder cliff lined the left edge of the pond.

René marveled at the clear sweetness of the spring water. It was so clear and still she could not tell where the surface met with the air. She wanted to touch it, so she took a few handfuls and splashed her face, easing the nettle burns. The spring pond bottom was lined with pebble and rubble. Stones were different shapes and colors; some white, some black, some brown, some violet. René put her face close to the water and studied the rocks on the bottom. Each had a mosaic design of its own. Each was unique, special, with it's own identity.

René thought of Riley, who had told her that you don't listen to water with your ears. She felt a kind of peace that was unfamiliar. As she followed Trap along the edge of the cliff, she felt something welling up inside. She had found love after all these years, and it was just a few steps away in these shadowy woods.

"I'd like to find the source of this spring if I can. Follow me," said Trap.

They made their way along the edge of the cliff until they reached the end of the channel. The spring seemed to be perking water from the main river and at the same time, a substantial flow was coming from the rocks along the hillside, tumbling down the hillside making a small white cascade.

René was pleased with the beauty of the spring and the ancient forest all around. It was dark and silent and filled her with a deep satisfaction. Trap was taking notes and photos, but René pressed her body against his back and whispered her thanks for bringing her here.

Something was moving at the head end of the pond. To René's amazement it was the coyote, only it was a light-colored coyote whose fur coat looked flecked with paint. The coyote was a female, her tail hung straight, and she had slanting eyes. René poked Trap in the ribs and pointed across the pond.

"Holy Jesus! Look at that!" said Trap.

The coyote was looking at René. Trap pulled her very close to him and stood up as tall as he could, making his hands look like claws.

"Maybe it's rabid!" said René.

"No, see the look in her eyes? When an animal is rabid they have a look of madness in their eyes. Look at her, she seems peaceful."

The coyote craned her neck a little to get a better look at René. A kingfisher chattered in the distance. The coyote started calmly walking along the edge of the pond. She would not take her eyes off René. Losing her fear of this animal, René asked Trap to stay a few steps away from her. She and the coyote were locked on each other's gaze. The coyote continued inching her way towards René. René ran her hands over the animal's head. Soon she pulled back her hands and put them to her own face.

"Jesus Christ," said René, "she smells like eucalyptus!"

"There's no eucalyptus in Moccasin River headwaters." Trap settled down on one knee, pausing to consider the situation.

"My God," he said. "The old Native American shamans say an animal can be a messenger for a human spirit. An animal spirit can bring a healing message from the other side. Consider what she might be saying to you." He looked up to gauge her reaction. "You know René, they say when you experience a visit from a spirit coyote, she is asking you to forgive your past mistakes—the things you're not proud of—and to look at them as positive learning, which will help you in the future."

"Smell, smell my hands!"

Trap did so, and there could be no question the animal smelled like eucalyptus. "Most eucalyptus grows in central and southern California. What would that smell be doing in Moccasin River headwaters?"

The woods grew quiet. Even the birds stopped calling. The temperature dropped, and the air remained still. The coyote looked straight into René's eyes. René knelt and put the coyote's muzzle over her shoulder. The coyote let out a low whine coming from deep in her chest, then started panting as she rested her muzzle on René's shoulder. The animal started heaving her chest while resting on René.

"Are you crying, sweetheart?" asked René. "Or are you happy? I can't tell."

Trap wanted to keep his distance but he spoke up.

"Looks like she is both. Don't expect her to act normal. I'm pretty sure she is an animal spirit, sent to you from the other side, René. Think what it could mean."

"Smartest animal in the forest," said Trap. "Can you make anything of that? She clearly wanted to touch you."

"Holy Christ, let me think on it," whispered René. "Maybe she was just a tame coyote."

"I have never seen a coyote act like that in my life," said Trap.

Trap took both René's hands and deeply breathed in the scent on her palms.

"So now you know what I do," mumbled Trap as he jotted down some notes. "Let's get at the big job here and talk about this encounter on the way home."

The road got narrower and rougher as they headed south into Swift River country. The road became mid-slope as it headed down Bull Run Creek, finally spilling out onto the main line. Trap drove two miles from a spur road and left a mountain bike hidden in the sword fern. Then he headed back, pulling the truck off on a dead end spur road.

"Well this is where we go in and go downstream two miles. I think you got how to identify a steelhead: elongate body, patterned spots on the tail, white mouth." Just go real peaceful and easy or you'll spook them. You count on the right bank and I'll take the left."

He handed her a basket full of diving gear. René stripped down to her shorts and T-shirt while Trap was on the other side of the truck, getting geared up. As much as Trap wanted to admire René in tight shorts and snug T-shirt, he stayed put, trying to convey a sense of dedication to the job. René squirmed into her neoprene suit and asked Trap to zip up the back while she braided her hair. They both headed down a steep rocky embankment to the river. Trap stood on the bank.

"Well angel, looks like we got low water, and that'll make it easier. See the stake for mile six? We go to mile four, which will be a big stringer bridge with a big four on it. In case we get separated. Got your fish counter?"

"Got it!"

"Okay, slow and easy."

They both disappeared into the river. As the cold water rushed down her back, René struggled to get her bearings and to get the right distance from shore. She tried to imagine a three-foot fish holding in the water just below her. The river was dropping rapidly, the surface rough and hissing slightly. The water was beautiful, taking on a deep yellowish green color. The sun's rays slanted through the surface, partly obscured by old growth forest. To René's surprise, the bottom of this section of the river was almost pure bedrock. She could feel the shallow bedrock warming the water ever so slightly. Within a hundred feet the bedrock came to an end, tailing out into a large deep pool. They went over a short patch of white water and burst into the deep pool. René surfaced, blowing her snorkel clear while she quietly moved. She disappeared under the surface. The water streamed past her face, its rejuvenating freshness caressing her cheekbones. She sounded deep, clearing her ears twice to get to the bottom. Beneath her, two dark shadows crowded towards the edge of the bedrock drop off. They were heavily spotted on the tail, with white mouths. She clicked the counter twice and kicked for the surface. René looked over at Trap holding up two fingers, and yelled to him.

"Two steelhead on the bottom."

René noticed the cliff behind Trap. It was black but covered in maidenhair fern growing upside down. Spanish moss hung from the old growth tree branches and lay along the cliff. She saw that they were heading into a slot canyon. She surged forward with another stroke and dipped her head beneath the clear water. She surfaced again and exhaled a cleansing breath. The water seemed to glow with the medicine René needed to recover from her trauma. The canyon closed tighter and darker into a slot, the river ten feet deep. The cliffs became soft, composed of ancient compacted gravel. Hundreds of insects hovered just above the water surface, but didn't seem to bother René.

Trap slipped through the water and watched René glide over to his right. Though she seemed to be having the time of her life, he worried about her ongoing battle with PTSD.

It was a little intimidating to both swimmers. The river flowed slow and silent except for the soft echoes of their splashing as they stroked downstream. The banks were vertical, perhaps 20 feet high, and the river was only about 15 feet across. The swimmers could hear mourning doves up in the sunny warmth, and an occasional crow or blue jay up above the moss covered cliffs. Soon the slot canyon started opening up. René sounded down into the darkness of the shaded river. She closed her eyes and felt the tiny increments of current. René asked the river moving past her to help her recover. In that moment she believed it would, and a tear ran down her cheek underneath her face mask. Not wanting an emotional display, she cleared her mask and went back to her survey. She had seen five summer-run steelhead, but the run was just beginning. She completed the last of the survey in a kind of euphoria. René looked up at the sky and let the river close around her face. Trap was swimming next to her. He thought to himself that an animal messenger had visited René today. It was usually a good sign from the other side. But it was not always good: sometimes it was a warning.

René paddled down the river into a stand of old growth. Douglas fir spread two hundred feet into the air with their bases roughened by old bark. The river grew wider and swifter. René spread her arms and legs out to give her stability. The broken water rattled against her mask as she raised her head above the surface. Below there was a deep dark green pool, and below that was the stringer bridge. René took a deep breath and dove for the bottom, sliding quietly deeper and deeper. At the bottom of the pool she counted more lively summer steelhead, and as she broke the surface she signaled to Trap: four more. That was a total of nine, a good day's work. Both Trap and René got out of the water at the bridge. It was amazing to René how warm she'd managed to stay in neoprene, as warm water spilled from her suit at the ankles.

"Let me help," Trap said as he unzipped the back of her suit. She removed it. René had on only a wet T-shirt and soaked shorts. Trap watched her stand up straight with her T-shirt clinging to her fresh skin. She looked like the winner of a wet T-shirt contest. But Trap said nothing. René smiled at him, reading his thoughts.

It was 2:00 pm, and both Trap and René were starving. Trap headed the truck up to Antelope Creek Falls. It was remote, beautiful, and about 40 feet high. Both of them were still soaking, so Trap pulled the truck into a sunny spot where they could dry off. René looked at Trap in a very serious way. The falls roared in the background, sounding like a distant cheering crowd.

"Well Trap, I guess it's my turn to talk, only I'll go slow. I don't want to have another attack."

She diminished her voice into a squeak at the end of her sentence. "First off I love you, more than anyone I've ever known, and I don't want anything to happen to you." René's throat tightened up and she was fighting back tears.

"Y—You know I used to be married, Trap, when I was only sixteen. His name was Wade Bode. He used to hang around with bikers. Trap, my name used to be Libby, but I had it legally changed to René. W—Wade beat a fisheries observer half to death and got sentenced to four years in a state prison. Then he assaulted a prison guard, and got himself another 10 years. I divorced him while he was in prison. T—Trap, he's just been released. I'm afraid he'll come after me, or you, or Riley. He is one mean SOB, Trap, bigger than you and two years older than me. He'll find me. I look a whole lot different now than when I was 16, but he'll find me if he wants to."

René began to choke a bit and her hands started clasping at a rapid rate. Her face began to grimace. Trap saw what was happening, and he slid over next to her, using René's favorite massage on her neck and back. He turned her toward the passenger side window. She sounded like she was choking, as if she had the wind knocked out of her. Trap dug his fingers into her back and shoulders. He tried to talk to her.

"C'mon René, hang on, try to get your breath. René I love you too, and I won't let anything happen to you." Trap pulled René across the seat of the truck and started to work on her legs. As he touched her legs he found them strangely tense. René started yelling in frustration while Trap bundled her in both of their coats. René kept yelling, but

Trap noticed it was a different kind of yell, laced with anger instead of despair. She started kicking the inside of the driver's door, screaming back at her anxiety. René coughed from deep within her lungs. But she seemed to be clearing. Seeing she was better, Trap lifted her to a sitting position.

"Trap, you're a darling, but could you let me be alone for a few minutes?"

René sat up, staring into the sun. Her breathing was irregular but growing steadier. She gritted her teeth. But it was her eyes that were different. Maybe it was just the way Trap was looking at her, but they seemed bigger and slanted towards the bridge of her nose. Her upper lip trembled in anger. Trap could see after watching her that she was getting better. René turned her head slowly towards him.

Trap studied her face, and despite tangled hair and tears smearing her face, she never looked better, because just for a moment the dimness in her face was gone.

* * *

After dropping off the diving equipment, they got in Trap's Chevy van. René seemed to be doing well. She would not smile, but was looking deeply at Trap, as deeply as she could, down to his DNA. She would not take her eyes off him. It was a look of thanks.

"You know Trap, even though I nearly had an anxiety attack today, this was one fine day in my life."

Trap drove home, leaving supplies and equipment at Hughes before continuing on to René's trailer. René was quiet, musing, wondering what had happened today. What did it mean? What was the coyote that acted so strangely? Why did she feel so good even though she panicked today?

Trap and René stepped inside. René went to the back bathroom and took a hot shower. She dressed in her tight jeans and a gray sweatshirt cut very wide at the neck. Trap was facing the salt water of the sound while working up some data sheets on today's snorkel survey.

Riley came in and looked at Trap, smiling.

"You took her stream walking today, didn't you? Did you listen to the water with your senses? Excellent move. She's yours now. You got her thinking now, coach!" said Riley.

"Have you got anymore hints for me to help sweep her off her feet?"

"Yeah, take her to the Hoh Rainforest, take her salmon fishing, and protect the bluff in back of the house, because mom worries about a slide."

Just then René walked in gracefully and said hello to Riley. She was wearing the choker she and Trap made. Trap put his hand gently on her chin and held it briefly.

"Look, Riley, have you ever seen a more beautiful woman." Her eyes were wide and warm, and her rising cheeks softly reached her reflection in the window.

"Any nettle burns, angel?" Trap tenderly held her chin, turning her face to one side then the other.

Suddenly, René's eyes grew wide open.

"My God, my God, Privina! A female coyote, a painted coat, the smell of eucalyptus... get me a phone!"

René dialed Privina's cell phone. It rang a long while. Finally a man's voice answered.

"Hello, is this Privina Moody's number? Is she there?" René's hand was shaking.

"And this is?" said the man's voice.

"Well, this is Libby. Privina helped me through a bad time a long time ago. She's like my mother. Is she there?"

"Oh, Libby. I gave you advice about commercial painting years ago; you're the one who worked as a painter," said the voice. "You worked for me in Olympia for a time, but you changed your name after you moved. What was it Racheal or something?"

"René."

"Right. René, I'm afraid I have bad news. Privina passed away yesterday afternoon. Her aorta burst and she went real fast."

"Oh God, I knew it, I just knew it. I had a sign today," said René.

"Libby, the room right now is crammed with people, all of her friends. Please don't come down. She wanted no ceremony. I can tell you she wrote you a letter, but she never got around to finding your address. If you give me your mailing address I'll send you the letter. Libby, are you there?"

"Ah… you're Bibs, the middle brother who was a college painter. You coached me on how to be a painter. You gave me a job in Olympia when I first came up here."

"Yep, that's me. Listen, Libby… Privina left you $20,000 in her will."

"Well I'll be damned." René gave Bibs her address and they hung up. Bibs went into the kitchen and made himself a drink. A big man standing in the corner walked to the phone where Bibs had just taken a message. A hand clawed up the message, and Wade Bode walked out into the night.

## CHAPTER 17

May 14, 1998

Lacey, Cascadia

It was first game time, and the sky slammed shut with a thick layer of clouds. *This is not bad for soccer*, thought Trap: diffuse light over the field without sharp shadows. Heat is a killer in soccer and an overcast sky helps reduce it. It looked like they were going to get a breeze. The air rattled through alder and mixed fir leaning to the north. The Puget Sound lowland nearly always has puffy winds rolling in from the ocean and the southern Olympics. Trap strolled out over the field and took in a deep breath, thinking *this is the beginning*, and telling himself that the Blue Angels will not be dominated.

Gulls and crows perched over the eastern half of the field, fighting each other for a place to ride out the coming freshet. Robins were scattered about, foraging on the playing field, and an occasional mourning dove called out from the surrounding alder trees. Trap could swear the birds were making a racket as if to preview the contest to come. A clap of thunder moved slowly across the sky over the soccer field, sounding like a landslide of granite from the Cascade highlands.

Babar, Gabriel, Nicolás, and Riley were the first players on the field. The four of them were the captains of the team. Alongside one another the four of them did a slow jog around the field, talking to each other and keeping in stride. It was moving to watch them turning the corners of the field. People started filling up the grassy area, including parents coming over to watch the Blue Angels. This was opening day, and Reuben seemed badly stressed about something. Trap agreed to start the team and take care of the substitutions.

Reuben was feeling extremely dizzy, and he moved his feet around to keep his balance. Trap watched him. Nevertheless, Reuben called over René to tell her Wade had called him and had her address. René let out a wheezing gasp and her eyes went immediately to the horizon.

Then her attitude changed. She took on a hard expression, like she was ready for a fight. Then she changed her expression again and fear swept across her face.

René had just returned from an intense two-hour workout when she headed to the soccer field. She looked good to Trap... her muscles lean and tight from intense lifting. Rain fell on her limbs and her body gleamed in the moisture. She had worked harder in the gym this day, but she felt the same nagging anger that she always felt. After her workout she had gone to the main desk to join the boxing club, and paid extra for individual training. René always knew what was making her angry. Now she was going to do something about it. She spat on the ground. No one would ever beat her again.

It was a warm rain and René strolled up the sidelines wearing jeans with a blue tank top representing the team's colors. René had "Blue Angels" sewn on her shirt at the local T-shirt shop. She turned her face up to the droplets on her forehead. She let the rain soak her clothes and hair. Trap watched her and could swear there was a light focused on her body, singling her out. She wore an amulet on her upper right arm so no harm would come to her. Despite the frown, she looked different. She looked rough. Her hair was like a wet tangle of weeds. One little girl walked up to René and asked if she could take her picture. René let go of her anxiety for the moment.

"Sure sweetheart, but why me?"

"Because you're a pretty lady, and I want to look just like you when I grow up," said the little girl.

René swallowed and blushed, feeling really flattered. It was a familiar feeling for her. She thought of the coyote, the one that passed through the membrane of her body.

"You'll do fine, and you'll be a beauty. I promise," said René.

Trap stepped next to Babar and gave him a few words of encouragement. Babar was a striker of Pakistani decent, the second oldest of five children. He moved like a graceful dancer but with speed and power. Of all the soccer players Babar was not only a formidable weapon; he was a perfect gentleman. Trap thought of Babar as someone who would someday turn pro.

Gabriel lived in a small apartment with a small bilingual Latino family. He was a driven boy, his face twisted and contorted as he pounded his way up and down the field. He was determined to succeed and often spoke of going to college to study architecture. With handsome and athletic looks, Gabriel was also a bit of a ladies man. He was going with one named Rebecca. She was mature for her age, and dressed to attract attention. Reuben was Gabriel's godfather and tried to keep him out of trouble with his attractive, teasing girlfriend. She was a constant distraction and she often had Gabriel running through the streets and movie theaters of Lacey holding hands when he should have been at soccer practice. Reuben pushed Gabriel to stick to his dedication to soccer. Rebecca tried to lure him away with false eyelashes, makeup, tight clothes, and constant phone calls. She was hard to resist.

Nicolás was a big defender. He was actually too big, and needed to lose weight. Like JR, his weight became an asset in close quarters on the field, but he lacked speed. A casual observer of soccer sometimes doesn't realize what a hard contact sport soccer really is. Nicolás was a shrewd player and always seemed to make the right decision. He was not quick but he fit in with the unique Blue Angels defense. His strategy was to be smart and strong. The defenders never came to midfield, but stayed back about ten yards, set up for power without speed.

Of all the people out on the field Nicolás liked Trap. Something about those two worked well.

Deshaun, the goalie, was the tallest and most sensitive black kid on the team. He was the perfect goalie, but he carried with him a curious vulnerability. As tough an athlete as he was, Deshaun was easily upset. He usually cried out of self-blame. His father Jaylen had to be careful when Deshaun got into trouble or he would get extremely emotional.

A light rain continued falling and a wind swept along the field. More people showed up. A number of families arrived, making the crowd as diverse as the team. Trap and Reuben were surprised at the turnout and both scratched their heads. The referee arrived: a teenage kid from the soccer select league. The Black Badgers took the field as a mild cheer rumbled across the crowd as if to mark the beginning of the 1998 soccer season.

Riley ran into Corin, the pretty French girl from the Burger Barn. She hooked his arm and leaned over to kiss Riley on the cheek, but Riley wasn't quite ready for that. Then she let her hand drop into his and squeezed.

"Good luck," she said looking into his eyes without a bit of shyness. "I'm gonna watch you the whole time."

Corin was so willowy and cute Riley couldn't help liking her a little: just a little.

It started raining a little harder, and a seeping warm wind came in from the south. It moaned through the fence surrounding the soccer field.

It looked to Trap like Reuben wasn't feeling well, and he ran over to make sure he was all right. Reuben still complained of dizziness. Trap checked his pulse, both on his neck and wrist, then shouted for René. She came running out of the crowd.

"Trap, what's the matter?" René asked, looking concerned.

"Reuben's not feeling too well. Could you take him to St. Jude emergency if he gets any worse?" asked Trap.

"Yeah, sure will Trap." René took Reuben by the hand and walked him down the sidelines.

"Any chest pain, difficulty breathing, or sweating? Can you tell me what day it is?" asked René.

"Reuben, what day is it? Reuben?"

"Thursday," mumbled Reuben.

"Do you want to go to the hospital, Reuben?" René had urgency in her voice.

"*Tu eres una buena mujer,*" said Reuben.

René held her finger on his pulse.

A few umbrellas popped up from the crowd, but no one was about to leave.

The Blue Angels took a prayer circle and won the toss. Babar signaled all strikers and midfielders to charge the goal. The kick came very high and suddenly there were seven ready to strike. The Black Badgers were somewhat surprised by so much aggression and were struggling to catch up. Riley received the ball in the right corner kick area. He kicked the ball so hard he grunted as the ball flew across the goal to the far post. Babar headed the ball, twisting his body as he yelled. A gentle lob fell into the goal. In the first 30 seconds of the season the Blue Angels had already scored. The crowd cheered. René jumped up and down, the rain soaking her shirt.

There was an outburst from the crowd along the Blue Angels side. This really frightened the Black Badgers and the very next kickoff they started getting nasty. One of them planted a foot right in Kyle's groin. For the time being Kyle was out, writhing in pain. The ref caught the foul and red carded the offending Badger. Gabriel had a quick on field meeting with the front four. He proposed to serve as a sweeper and striker at the same time, going deep in his defense to break the ball loose. Gabriel was fast and would terrorize the other team's defense because he was almost impossible to mark. It seemed Gabriel simply never got tired. He just kept coming.

Reuben was not out of trouble. René grabbed a folding chair and got him to sit down. She stood behind him, put her hand on his left shoulder and ran her hand down his left arm.

"Any pain around here, Reuben?" René touched Reuben around the wrist. She was getting more and more convinced that he was having a heart attack.

"Yes, a—a little." Reuben grabbed his own shoulder. He changed his sitting position, his face screwed up.

"Trap! He's showing signs! I'm taking him to Emergency!" She got her hand around his back and she took his arm around her shoulder. Babar's father Ashar saw what was happening and rushed over to René, helping them to the car. Reuben was sweating and feeling some chest pain. Nevertheless he kept encouraging René not to cause a fuss with his situation. He asked her to make sure the Blue Angels continued with the game. Because Saint Jude was only two blocks away, she decided to quickly drive him to the emergency room. Once they arrived, the cardiac unit didn't waste any time. They were monitoring his vitals almost immediately. In a matter of minutes he was given a stent in his right coronary artery. From the ER Reuben was made a priority for a bed. René decided to stay with Reuben rather than return to the game. She stayed by his bed, telling Reuben he would be all right. A nurse dropped off a print of his heart where the new stent was located. Everything looked good.

Meanwhile the Black Badgers were no match for the Blue Angels. The Badgers seemed to be having trouble getting focused. As for the Blue Angels, clumps of grass flew and sweat spattered over twisting bodies. They pounded the Badger goal posts with near misses, giving the appearance the post was going to come down. Jaylen was present on this day. As Deshaun's father he had managed to make the game by taking time off at work. Jaylen regretted his career ending accident but kept a smile on his face loving a good sports event. He told the kids his story but held back the ending, because he wasn't done with his fight. He had an incomplete story, never telling the team how long he was in a wheel chair. Those donor ligaments enabled him to walk again. Running on a football field was a different story, one that would never happen. Jaylen was fun to be around, frequently cutting through the air with his African American raspy voice and quick wit.

Trap noticed that the crowd had grown larger. People were walking over from adjacent fields to watch this team that played with such fury and with so many tricks. They complimented Trap on building such an energetic team.

Final score: Blue Angels 7, Black Badgers 0. Not everyone was happy. Trap found that a full-size field was big for 14 year old kids. The main opportunity to substitute is an out of bounds, but the ball did not often go out of bounds. If the coach was not ready he would miss his chances to substitute some other kids in the game. As a result many kids did not get enough playing time. Those who don't get a chance to play had some really angry parents on the sidelines ready to keel haul the coach. Several parents complained loud and clear. Trap learned to be prepared for substitutions, and over time the parents understood that the team played to win. Kids who were playing sluggishly or foolishly, or ignoring their training, were unlikely to play as much in games, instead getting harder training at practice.

The Blue Angels did a little cheer for the Badgers and slapped hands with them. It had rained hard enough to get both teams muddy from the knees down. The coach of the Black Badgers came jogging across the field and shook hands with Trap. She introduced herself as Kay Robin.

"Great team, Coach, they really fight out there, and they seem to have a plan. I must say, I've never seen so many different races in the pot. How did you manage to put together this team?"

"Well, we didn't do anything. It just turned out that way by itself. Just so, the way you see it. It's so improbable in a predominately white community, I know," explained Trap. "Our national origins are from all over the world. You couldn't get a more diverse team than this one, and it's all just serendipity. I've never seen a group of kids play off each others skills like these youngsters do."

"That's the way the ball bounced, huh?" Trap was beginning to wonder if Kay believed him. "Well, my real job is a reporter for the South Sound Herald. Would you like to do an interview next game? What is it, the 19th?"

"The head coach is in the hospital," said Trap. "Why don't you let me talk it over with him?"

Reuben was resting comfortably in intensive care. René stood over him, fidgeting and studying his face. She called Trap who said that he, Riley, and Nicolás were on their way over. Reuben reached over and took René's hand.

"René, *mujer dolce*, I talked to Wade Bode a few days back. He's got your address young lady. He got it at a little wake they were having for your adopted nanny."

René looked down at the floor. Though she had not seen Privina for many years, she choked up. She thought of Privina and simply knew that the coyote had been a spirit messenger sent to cure her of PTSD. She could feel the spirit message glowing inside, helping and protecting her. Shamans were known for their ability to reach the other side. What really mattered was their ability to bring great truth and miraculous healing from beyond.

"We'll have to talk, Trap," said René, "you too Riley."

"Nicolás, your dad will be treated here about six days if all goes well," said René.

"Do you want to go home, stay without your dad? Can you get to school, to practice?" asked Trap.

"Yeah, I'll ride the school bus and get to practice with Gabriel. The grocery store is a block away. I need some cash, though."

"I'll give you a ride home now, and I'll stop by tomorrow. Hope your dad gets better," said Trap.

Riley, René, and Trap started home, picking up crab sandwiches and fruit juice on the way back. After arriving, Riley went after his homework while Trap and René sprawled on the floor.

"Want to be alone tonight, René?" asked Trap.

As beautiful as she was, René was also very affectionate. She wrapped her arms at Trap's waist and squeezed as hard as she could. Trap could feel her strength as he put his hands on her shoulders. Her tank top was still wet from the earlier rain.

"No, I want you, come join me. I love you, Trap. And it's hard to know but I felt like I was getting better, until this crap has to come up," said René.

"What crap?" asked Trap.

"Okay, here goes Trap: Wade Bode found my address. Remember a few days ago when I called Privina, because she is a shaman? Well, she's probably the one who sent the coyote. I talked to her middle son, who taught me to be a painter. They were having some sort of wake for Privina and I gave them my address so they could send some inheritance. Then the paper with my address disappeared."

Now that she was on the subject, René would not stop talking.

"Listen Trap, he'll track me down just as sure as hell. He's big, powerful, and cruel. Along with my father, Wade is the cause of my PTSD. He beat the shit out of me many times and he'll do it again if he has the chance." René let out a weak sound. Trap reached out to hold her and bent down to her ear. She was beginning to feel lightheaded and told Trap and Riley she had to stop talking. She looked at both of them, and more words tugged at her lungs, demanding to be spoken or they would choke her to death. Then she barked them out like an enraged dog.

"They beat me when I was pregnant!" her voice shook the room.

Trap backed up a few steps, and clenched his fists. He moved over to the couch and began to pound the back. René saw for the first time how fast Trap was. His fists were like two claw hammers pounding the back of the couch. The pounding of his fists did not frighten René. It made her believe Wade was in for trouble. She had never seen such hand speed.

"Remember, angel. I told you and you got the word. I won't let anything happen to you. Do you and Riley want to move into my apartment?" asked Trap. At those words, René felt a warm glow all over her body, her love for Trap growing.

"No trap, I want you in my house. I want you next to me, and I want you with me."

Trap leaned over to René. "I'm really sorry this happened in the past and it's happening again. This Wade guy is a savage...he was taking domestic violence to an underworld level. He is a reptile from a crack in the ground! So you think he is coming back? If he comes back here and tries to even come close to you I'm not going to have a heart to heart talk with him. There aren't many times in my life I really wanted to fight a man. That was a lot of talking you just did about your past. You feeling all right? Can I rub your back?" asked Trap. "How about you take it easy now. Forget about this guy for a little while."

"OK Trap...I'll try to get him off my mind...and my back. please, Trap, my back feels like granite. You think Reuben will be okay?" asked René.

"I think so, but of course I don't know so. By the way, the newspaper wants to talk to us next Thursday. They'll want to take our picture. Would you pose with us? I mean you'll sell out the paper! I'm pretty sure Jaylen will go back on swing. Could you serve as temporary assistant coach until Reuben makes it back? You just have to answer the phone, maybe give some rides to practice and warm them up with yoga, maybe set out nets and cones, all that sort of stuff."

"Yeah, sure Trap, but I'm not sure you heard me loud and clear when I mentioned Wade. He is one bad bambino and I can feel the anxiety creeping up on me. You used to fight, and believe me I'm strong for a woman with a decade of weight training. Trap, I want you to be with me right by my side." René leaned over Trap's shoulder.

"I'll get that bastard," said René under her breath.

Ever since the coyote had visited her she was growing stronger. Her tears dried shortly and she and Trap finished the sandwiches.

"Trap, you give the most wonderful back massages. I actually think it's helping me to get well. I owe you big time."

"No, you don't owe me, René. I said I will take care of you and I will," said Trap.

"Can you do my front side this time?" asked René, looking up at Trap.

"Lets see what we can do." Trap grabbed her feet and crossed her lower legs. He gave a light twist to her and flipped her over on her stomach. Then just to lighten things up, he crossed her legs again and flipped her over on her back. René let out a cute giggle. Trap reached his hand between the floor and René's back. When he had reached under her back to her spine, he began alternating his finger pressure against her back and the floor. The result was a kind of keyboard rhythm up and down her spine. Trap seemed to know just where to touch her to send her into euphoria.

René closed her eyes and began to drift away above the rain forests of the north coast. It was green, so remarkably green that tree trunks and highways were green. She cried from the pleasure of Trap's strong hands, raising her head to let the sun bless her with green. Then with eyes blinking the whole sky and all the clouds turned an opaque green that came down and spilled over her. She felt baptized by nature, and she continued to grow stronger.

In her fantasy René strapped on a pair of boxing gloves and started in on a heavy bag. Each powerful blow sounded like a nail gun while the room flashed red. She fantasized her work in the gym giving her blinding quickness: able to duck and dodge any cruel man she might encounter. Trap ran his fingers gently over her lats and across her serrates anterior.

"Touch me, Trap," she said smiling with her eyes closed.

"Nope. You have to be careful how you handle a bombshell," he said.

Trap looked down at René and put her head in his lap. He had her front side up. He reached over her face and bent down. He massaged her hips and waist. This hold was special. Trap would not touch her breasts: claiming it would interfere with his massage. He moved up to her neck and face. Although she had never done it, she found herself windsurfing over the surface of a large clear lake. There was no limit to her speed, the board galloping across the water like a murder of black crows. Then she fell, and collided with the chopping water. She dove beneath the surface and down into the yellow gold of Montana's water. She turned her face to the sun from under the water. A school of kokanee fingerlings all swam in front of her. They shimmered in the light, and there were thousands of them.

"Oh Trap. That was wonderful. My nose is all stuffed up and I feel miles away. My God, there's magic in your hands. Where did you learn that?"

"Oh here and there. I'll get you for phase two next. After 25 or so massages you'll be trapped in a spell from which you can never escape."

"Oh yeah, what kind of spell?"

"You'll see."

"Sounds like a bunch of B.S. to me. Hey Trap, want to hear a song?"

"Yeah, sounds great. Where's Riley?"

René walked by Riley's room where he was working at his computer. She grabbed some dry clothes for herself.

"So you think Reuben will pull through okay, Trap?" asked René. "Maybe we should talk more about Wade and what we should do. Do you think we should get pepper spray, or a couple of clubs?" René gave a concerned look to Trap.

"Let's think about self defense, and I'll get some of this stuff from town. René, please remember you're my girl and I won't let anything happen to you."

"Trap, let's relax and take it easy." she raised her hand to her forehead. "Here's to your first victory as coach of the Blue Angels. Excellent job. I feel like something is gonna happen with this team." René grabbed her Martin guitar and smiled at Trap so warmly he fell deeper in love.

René strummed out a few major 7th chords.

*Did you ever feel that you were*
*One of the hands on one of the feet?*
*Of a centipede*
*Come join the stampede*
*Come join the stampede*
*Yeah join the stampede*
*Be one of the feet*
*Of a centipede, of a centipede*
*We got a hundred legs to run the race*
*And you just got two*
*You're bound to lose*
*And you'll get trampled to boot*

"This here song is about invertebrates and soccer," René giggled. "Needs another verse. I'm working on it," she said as she set the Martin on some pillows in the corner.

"You wrote that?" asked Trap.

"Yeah, guess so Trap."

CHAPTER 18

May 19, 1998

White Salmon, Cascadia

The weather was cool in the Columbia Gorge, typical for late spring in the northwest. The creeks were falling vertically over the cliffs, turning to vapor and spray as they slid into small lagoons adjacent to the mighty Columbia, the fourth largest river in the continental U.S. The walls of the Gorge were straight up, carved by glacial hands during the great 15,000 year-old floods, sending clouds of brown silt and endless chunks of ice rampaging through the enormous gap in the Cascade Range.

Today the wind howled from the west. It blew so hard clouds of relentless dust flew into the air. The wind roared like a huge bear down this massive canyon. It blew hard, but not hard enough to stop the wind surfers as they joyfully fought the wild gusts and white-capped water. Trap had tried windsurfing in the past, and gave it up due to the traveling expense. But he remembered the peace it brought him, out there on the chopping waves. Out on the water there were no thoughts and no unhappy memories, just a peaceful all-consuming focus on the present moment.

The whole canyon seemed to moan when the wind blew in the Gorge. Repeating wind waves blew hard from the west. The green basalt cliffs stood more than a thousand feet high.

Traveling east on the Columbia the weather grew slightly warmer, venting up the face of the Gorge matted with oak and sage.

Trap rolled his window down and breathed in the fragrance of sage.

Missing René, Trap headed his pick-up north to highway 115. The clouds were breaking up, the somber gray fading away. But what was behind was not blue sky. For just a half hour the sky was a radiant yellow, seeming to add color to the wind. Trap swept past the upper end of the Gorge, where the wind, spray and the river fell silent. Trap turned left and headed away from the Columbia and up Silver Creek. He took a brief break and swung by the Silver Creek Falls. He rested his chin on his hand and watched the Native Americans dip netting for spring Chinook as they jumped at the white falling water. *They're a bit early*, thought Trap, as he rested his arms on the door of his truck. Some of the Native Americans turned around and waved at Trap, or so he thought. On closer inspection he realized he was being flipped off. He was a little offended given his Native American birthright. He headed about fifteen miles up the highway to the Wolf Tooth Saw Mill.

Wolf Tooth Mill was a very strange place: a sawmill that burned down three years ago. Charred concrete and iron remains still stood on a huge concrete slab about one half-mile square. Back then the whole mill went up in flames and no one ever determined the cause. It remained a mystery to this day. Every year, black remnants of wood and steel changed to a further decaying level of charcoal. Blackened cement ruins that appeared haunted were scattered about. Some buildings were still standing and were streaked with spray paint graffiti. Other buildings wound through dark passages and empty corridors. Some passageways were pitch black scorched by the fire, where animals scurried about in the bowels of the remains.

Wolf Creek was channeled as a 2,500 foot long flume through the middle of the concrete slab where the mill used to be. The flume was an outrageous fish passage barrier, where the designers of the mill had completely ignored the fact that Wolf creek was a salmon stream. The flume usually put the creek into a sheeting flow situation where fish simply do not have the depth of water they need to power up and swim. It always put off Trap when he looked at this sight. He shook his head, disgusted because the burned sawmill was the worst example of fish passage ignorance and abuse. Hughes was awarded the contract to rehab the entire lower creek for fish passage and completed the project two years after the fire. Some buildings had to be demolished to allow access to the flume with concrete forming and pouring equipment. All in all there were 26 concrete weirs, one dam deconstruction, and two culvert replacement jobs all spread out in tandem over the lower creek.

The Hughes work was completed a year ago, but when a Stream Walker inspected the site to check construction and look for fish presence, he or she felt very strange, like something alive was present. There were two steep high elevation hillsides on either side of the mill site. Both hills were simply huge. Many animals frequented them: cougar, bear, bighorn sheep, and plenty of rattlesnakes. Walking up the creek Trap felt watched: held by wild eyes. Something was watching from the hills. Something was unafraid, ravening.

Trap waited below by the flume for the construction foreman Charlie Bailey and a heavy equipment operator. Finally they arrived and started upstream making comments on the configuration of the weirs and anything that might interfere with the flume. The equipment operator said it looked to him like the banks to the flume should have been sloped back which would require demo of most of the slab.

"Not a bad idea, but it would kill a good nigger to remove the whole slab," said Charlie.

Instead of coming unglued, Trap thought of René and what she said about race—that the Blue Angels would stop him from ownership of every racially charged situation. Still, he was seething and it showed. Charlie looked down at Trap from the top of the flume.

"What's a matter half breed? You look mean. Did I say something offensive?" asked Charlie.

"Just back off before there's real trouble," said Trap.

Trap was standing in the shallow water at the bottom of the flume. The foreman jumped down the six-foot ledge and slowly rose to face Trap.

"You got a problem with my pale face you college half breed? You know I'm puking sick of you so-called biologists! Are you going up that creek? You know the grounds keeper told me there are sink holes up there in the canyon, three feet wide and fifteen feet deep! When you go under and your waders fill you'll be the one who's in real trouble!"

"I get in trouble all the time, Charlie, and I'm not going anywhere," said Trap.

"Come on, Trap, we all have a little racist in our blood from time to time." Charlie glared at Trap. Holding his gaze, he took a step closer.

Trap circled out towards the center of the flume. He watched Charlie carefully, expecting him to charge at any minute. Trap spoke evenly.

"So you want to fight, Charlie. Is that the picture? I'll tell you Charlie, I don't fight at work. You want to fight me, well do it somewhere else. To help me get riled up bring along some of your racist remarks. I'm going to inspect the upper flume."

"You chicken shit," mumbled Charlie. That remark nearly turned Trap around. A wave of rage passed through him, but he turned and continued walking upstream.

Charlie left in his truck with the equipment operator. Trap was alone. Charlie really didn't want to fight. He knew if he charged Trap he would get worked over pretty well. Trap was a young man, quick and strong. Charlie really just wanted to mouth off.

Trap shook his head. Sometimes being a biologist was not what he thought it would be like. Sometimes it was a real hot spot. It seemed like frigging everybody was on his case. At times every government worker was pissed at you. Every farmer, forester, every irrigation district, every frustrated fisherman couldn't wait to single you out.

Normally Stream Walkers work in pairs, but Trap was disgusted and just plowed up stream alone.

"Anywhere but work, fats," he mumbled.

Trap thought of René again as he moved upstream. He couldn't stop thinking of her beautiful face, her long slender neck, and her voluptuous figure that stood out so well. Though she was not there her image hung in his mind. She gently pressed against his arm and whispered:

"The Blue Angels are going to save you."

Trap walked upstream past a breached dam and a designed channel meander further up the creek.

He felt emotionally down standing in this charred place. The Blue Angels showed him what it's like to go through life without race hanging over his head. Hughes construction people had shown him the opposite. The Blue Angels were 14 years old and were outperforming Hughes six ways to Sunday when it came to racial attitudes. He

walked passed the first bridge and inspected the footings for cracks.
Even in the cool air he was hot and thought he would walk down to the
creek. He splashed his face and hair with water, trying to shake away
the mood he was in. It didn't help. Trap put his hand in the water and
listened for the silence, but the creek rattled along like rough static on
the radio. He climbed the bank. He ripped off his long sleeve shirt and
rubbed willow bark on his body to mingle with his sweat, protecting
his skin from insects. The willow bark would act as a stimulant for
Trap, and relieved a headache he was working on. It would also hide
his scent and might give him a better chance of spotting some wildlife.
With a little lift from the willow bark, he hastened up Wolf Creek
towards the second bridge. He passed the half buried culvert that was
taken out when the bridge was placed. It sat in a flat area 50 feet from
the flowing creek. Trap glimpsed into the culvert.

"Hey what the hell?" came a voice from inside. "Who's out there?"

"Just me," Trap mumbled.

A man dressed in overalls stumbled out of the pipe. He was actually
sleeping in the culvert, and gave Trap quite a start.

"What do you think you're doing way up in here?" said the ragged
looking man as he crawled out of the pipe. Trap noticed he had on a
revolver.

"You know it's my legal right to kill you for standing on my
property. I could kill you where you stand!"

Trap just shook his head. What a day he was having. "Where's the
owner? Did he sell to you? I have an agreement with him to inspect the
bridge and footings and to survey the creek for salmon and evidence of
slope failures upstream. Is that okay with you? Do you know the
owner?" The man loosened his revolver in his holster.

"I'm using this pipe for shelter and this is old Wolf Tooth land. I
used to work there until commies like you burned it to the ground.
We're going Communist! Can't you see it? Look at this mill site. I said
look at it!" the man bellowed.

Trap was feeling so foul he was tempted to take the gun away. He
sized up the situation to make his move, but his better judgment took
over and he just glared at the man.

"I'm going up the creek. It's my job and I'm going to do it. We'll take this up later."

Trap turned and left, ambling across the bridge checking crossbeams and concrete footings. Everything looked good, except the streambed shifted lower about one foot under the bridge on Wolf Creek. This meant a bed load shift had occurred. That would have to be monitored in the future.

Trap felt lousy.

Wolf Creek was a good size stream, and judging by the maps he had studied it wound through the canyons for about ten miles. The original survey noted a high falls at about mile two. He thought he would head for that falls, verify, and look for fish. As he worked his way up stream, he looked for bank failures, erosion, or any other sign of instability. Because there were no herbicides in this stream section, butterflies were more than plentiful. There were thousands. Trap spotted an otter playing on a rock near the center of the creek and thought of an otter's spirit message, "confront your demons with courage." Trap thought that fitting.

He made his way through a clump of fireweed, with skunk cabbage, and a bit of common devil's club mixed in. Wolf Creek was in the transition zone between the rain country and the desert: lots of sun and lots of rain and the riparian choked with vegetation. As Trap followed the creek, bluffs narrowed the stream width, making it deep and swift. A vast mat of blackberry closed over the creek, completely smothering the channel. Thorny vines dragged the surface of the creek. The blackberry was so thick that the underside of the bramble had died due to lack of sunlight. What remained were whips of stiff, dead vines an inch thick.

Trap groaned, knowing he was going to take a beating from this survey. He was lucky he had long sleeves and cotton gloves. Getting out his pruning clippers, Trap started up the center of the creek. Dead blackberry was just about the worst thing a Stream Walker could find in a creek. The vines were so brittle and thick they were almost impossible to cut. Trap fought the brush with his arms and clippers.

Thorns grabbed and tore his shirt, some of them clawing into his skin. Here and there Trap bled from the scratches on his arms. One blackberry vine snapped back after he cut it. The thorns hit him in the forehead, knocking off his hat. It floated quickly downstream and Trap let it go. He was more concerned about a deep scrape in his forehead, blood trickling down the bridge of his nose. He pulled out his bandana and wrapped it over his head, covering the deep scrape near his hairline. Reluctant to back off and knowing someone had surveyed this creek before him (probably in the winter) he pressed on through a 100 meter stretch of blackberry, the ugly invader from Armenia. Finally he reached the upper end of the thicket. He stopped to catch his breath, tend his wounds, and get the thorns out of his clothing. He could feel the nasty sting of nettles on his face.

*Jesus Christ, what a survey*, he thought. Trap was bleeding but still pushed on upstream. Continuing to walk, Trap saw something in the creek. He was pleased to find two old decayed salmon carcasses together on a sandbar. The smell was bad, but Trap was glad that fish had made it this far upstream. The creek grew steep and flowed over its cobble-sized bed material. Trap kept going. He noted that the bedrock was oozing clear water just like the little spring seepage he had seen with René the week before. That meant the stream would flow well in summer. Looking closely, colors of the creek bottom seemed to blend together. Looking closer yet, the stream gravel revealed again the most complex matrix of color and shapes. Trap reached out, overturned three rocks, and made note of many caddis flies and stoneflies clinging to the bottom of the cobbles. That meant lots of fish food. More stream banks were soggy from spring water seepage. Spring water does not stop flowing in the summer, and maintains nearly the same temperature year round.

"Son of a bitch squatter thinks he can kill me because of where I stand!"

Trap pounded his fist into the soft mud on the stream bank. He looked wearily at the sky and wiped the sweat from his forehead. His ears seemed to be ringing. Or was it the sky that was ringing? What did that mean? He couldn't tell.

He continued upstream and picked up the smell of urine. Something was around the corner. He continued slowly, not to frighten whatever it was. The urine smelled warm, as if only moments ago something had passed in front of him. The wind was blowing lightly down the canyon and he moved beneath the understory of tall black cottonwood rattling in the breeze like a field of dry corn. Because of the light wind Trap could not be heard or his scent detected. Up higher in the watershed the landscape was turning into bluff country with its cliffs of gravel and flat-topped terraces. This was the kind of landscape where waterfalls commonly form: the kind of landscape with shade and flat benches made of ancient gravel. As Trap rounded the corner he could hear panting. Up on the bluff was a full grown cougar. It was lying on its side in the shade. The animal turned its head in Trap's direction, seemingly watching him, but it seemed reluctant to move. Trap took a few more steps upstream and stepped into the stream itself. The cougar's eyes were empty, as the animal seemed to stare into space. The eyes were black and dilated. Finally the animal got slowly to its feet. Trap could see that it was in exceedingly poor condition. The cougar was hideous, its face scarred with apparent burn marks. Possibly the cat was caught in the mill fire. Staggering as he stood up, his ribs were showing. The cougar tried to move away, but rammed his head on the back of the overhang. The animal appeared to have lost most of its eyesight. Trap could tell the cat could not see him well. Was it just old? Trap stepped out of the stream and took a few strides towards the cougar. The cat sniffed the air. Trap stepped closer and could make out burns over the cat's face. He made a note of the location, and when returning to Olympia he would notify a wildlife crisis organization. The cougar was behaving strangely and Trap's Native American side recognized the message he was receiving. Friends, acquaintances, and the rest of the world needed support from him.

Trap continued walking the stream while rubbing more willow bark on his clothing. The canyon got closer as he worked his way up. Some large trees had fallen parallel to the stream. Trap jumped onto the tip of

a downed ponderosa pine and started upstream towards the root-wad
end. He looked down into the clear water, thwarting the light reflecting
on the surface. Then he angled his head and neck back and forth to get
the light right. This water was remarkably clear. Watching, he saw
several juvenile fish darting near the bottom. Trap studied the fish, but
there was another simple rule he went by: never attempt to identify a
juvenile fish species unless it is in your hand. Trap listened for the
silence and put his hand on the surface. His low spirits lifted very
slightly and he held the same position, remembering Riley's comment
about water. He recalled what Riley thought: the silence of water is a
feeling.

The creek was growing shallow. The streambed was fresh and loose
only at this location, indicating some spawning.  But upstream of the
disturbed gravel the creek flattened in gradient. The canyon was still
narrow, giving the water some velocity. He came to a large beaver
dam. Above the dam spread out before him was a large canary grass
swamp. Trap wheezed and wished he had another Stream Walker with
him. Canary grass swamps were difficult to walk, with three-foot high
shoots, tangled root masses, and unpredictable depth conditions. Trap
stepped into the swamp, unable to see the water surface due to the
extremely dense mat of vegetation. He was tired from the blackberry
and the channel was completely gone, though he could feel tiny
increments of current pushing past his boots. He could even hear some
current drifting close to him. The bottom was mud and in his next few
steps the water grew deep, the muddy bottom clinging to his ankles.
Then the bottom gave way, and a sinkhole opened up. Trap tried to yell
but no sound came as his head disappeared below the surface. He went
quickly to the bottom because of the surveying gear he was carrying.
Trap's waders filled instantly. Clouds of mud fell with him into the
hole, obscuring his vision. The slow moving current was enough to
push the grass he had fallen through over the top of the sinkhole, as if
to seal him in darkness. Trap knew if he tried to get out of his waders
he would drown. In near total blackness he rolled his eyes around the
hole he was in, searching for a way to orient his vision in the grass and
muddy water, hoping he was looking at the surface he tried to swim up

only to bury his head in the mud that lined the hole. He couldn't see…
not even his bursts of air bubbles which might point him towards to
the surface. He put his hand over his mouth and exhaled a bit of air. He
felt the bubbles slide across his hand and face and heard the
increments of rising bubbles showing him where the surface was.

Sinkholes were rare, but they did exist. They occurred most often in
urban areas where flows were very high and the riparian zone mass
wasted. Sometimes they could be found in the proximity of lava tubes.
Feeling for the sides of the hole, Trap spat out a round gasp of air and
carefully watched the silver gush move to the surface and scatter in the
grass. The hole was too narrow to swim, so Trap planted his foot and
opposite hand into the mud lining the hole and pushed upward. With
his boots full of water he could still get leverage against the hole.
Slowly, unable to breathe for thirty seconds, he pulled hard to the
surface like he would climb a corrugated pipe. Enraged, his head split
the surface. Trap coughed out a series of cuss words that were so loud
they bounced up the sides of the greater canyon. Still cussing, he
ploughed across the swamp and climbed the smaller bluff near the
creek. Trap was pissed and embarrassed, and he knew he could not sit
still.  It was too cold. Without hesitation he turned upstream and
walked the bluff.

"Damn rat trap creek," he grumbled. "Damn lousy Stream Walker!"

For another kilometer Trap fought the logs, brush, and devil's club,
finally coming to a huge falls and plunge pool perhaps eighteen meters
wide and three meters deep. The falls was about five meters high. This
was the end of the line for salmon or steelhead. Trap built a fire with
the waterproof matches in his first aid kit. He pulled off every stitch of
clothing. Though he was wet, he pulled a French roll with salami and
cheese from a zip lock bag, and perched himself on a large flat rock
near the creek. Trap was getting warm and the surface of the rock next
to the fire was an inviting place to finish his lunch. A Stream Walker
knows he can get warm by sprawling on rocks. They held heat even on
a cool day. Trap looked into the chattering falls. Certainly he deserved
a lunch break and a quick dip. He dove in the plunge pool. Trap

cleared his ears and sounded to the bottom. The bed sparkled with mica. The cold water soothed his body as he came up under the falls. There was some momentum to the falls that was scouring a small cave behind the pool. Trap crawled behind the falls and listened to the roar of water. The area was covered with wet moss and angel hair fern. He stood directly under the falls letting the water cascade over him, and tilted his head back as the water massaged his face. Then Trap dove through the falls and swam to the bottom of the pool again. He dried on the hot rocks, dressed, and started back down the trail. Trap's foul mood was gone. What he had been through on this survey was not unusual.

CHAPTER 19

May 21, 1998

Olympia, Cascadia

René finished a session with her therapist and walked out the door. All the counseling she got only made her more angry. She could swear her rage was growing stronger. Taking her gym equipment, she headed for the ring. She stormed into the boxing room and began on the heavy bag. She pounded it with round sweeping punches until she was ringing wet with sweat. A young smallish latino man stepped into the room and watched her.

"Hi René," he spoke in perfect English. "Come straight at it with combinations."

"Gee thanks, pal," she grumbled. "Want to go a few?"

From that day on she was in the ring every day, sometimes sparring with a man.

Thank God there was Trap. René never felt about a man the way she felt about Trap. Even her love for Riley was different, maternal. She was in love and in lust with Trap… the way he was always beside himself looking at her body… the way he was so gentle and protective with her.

And her counselor was revealing. René was working with an older woman who had insight into the kind of trauma that causes years of human suffering. She was empathetic in her style and had extensive experience with PTSD and battered wives. She also used cognitive therapy to show René that people will love you for your weaknesses as well as your strengths. She explained to René that everybody takes a beating now and then, and that René had been extremely vulnerable to an attacker at the time of the beatings because she was pregnant. She got René thinking about meditation and what it can be like to go deep without thinking.

"There is great peace in meditation," she told her. "It can rise from your feet and creep up through your body feeling like new life. But you might have a need to find someone within your meditation to act as your mentor."

René walked outside the gym and sat in the sun on one of the benches. She closed her eyes. She again thought she was beginning to recover. René was finding it easier to talk about past events. Getting up in the morning she had amazing clarity of thought lately. She could calmly remember details of her past that she hadn't thought about in years. Through her therapy René realized she was overwhelmed with burning anger. She was surprised to hear her therapist agreed that she should learn to fight. Even strapping on gloves and beating the hell out of a heavy bag would help her externalize her anger. And Trap, a trained college fighter, could help her learn to swing her fists. Knowing she loved Trap and knowing he would help, she would have a talk with him about her anger. René was running up a huge bill with these therapy appointments. They were helpful, but she would not use up Trap's savings, and with no insurance she could not pay herself. This would have to stop.

René walked down to the hospital and up to the fourth floor where Reuben was sprawled on a hospital bed watching TV in Spanish.

"How ya doin' coach?" asked René, feeling a little concerned.

"I'm feeling okay pretty lady," said Reuben. "They put a little culvert in my heart and you know the pain went away almost immediately. I should be out of here in a few days. Do you think you could score me a pair of pajamas? I hate my gown. Split up the back with my butt showing." René giggled that cute laugh of hers.

"My pleasure, hombre."

In a half hour René returned with a pair of blue pajamas. "Your color is blue, I presume."

"Pretty lady, could you spot me five minutes while I change?"

The two took a casual stroll around the fourth floor. René held his arm to help steady him.

"I'm gonna help Trap coach the team while you rest up," she said, "so you better get well. I don't know much about soccer."

Reuben had an overwhelming urge to talk to René about Wade, but at the moment he had a wave of dizziness. He tried hard to shake it off. It wasn't often such a young woman tenderly held his arm.

Reuben took a long look at René, almost studying her face. She had the highest cheekbones and prettiest brown eyes he'd seen in a long time.

"You sure are a looker, Libby... I mean, René."

René turned her head sharply, looking at Reuben.

"You called me another name, what was that?" René's eyes narrowed.

"I'm sorry pretty lady, I get names wrong. I can't remember anybody's name. The doctors said it was on account of my motorcycle accident 14 years ago. Put me into a coma."

Reuben felt a surge of pain at telling this to René, because he knew why he called her that name. Reuben's mind went blank. He felt his knees giving way, folding under him. René saw he was going down and got a firm grip around his waist. She took a wide stance and flexed the powerful muscles in her back to stop him from hitting the floor. Reuben was half conscious and took a weary look at René.

"God bless you, Libby," he mumbled.

Then René bellowed down the hallway.

"Nurse!"

Very quickly Reuben got the attention of nurses in the vicinity. They determined that he had accidentally taken a double dose of his blood pressure medication. He was given a stimulant and was showing improvement when René made for the soccer game.

"Come back and see me, Libby!" slurred Reuben.

René stopped in the doorway and looked back at Reuben.

"Please don't call me that name, Reuben. My name is René... René."

René took a big breath as she left Reuben's room and decided to try to let it go. This was no time for an emotional conversation. *Let it go, let it go*, she thought. Still, she heard him correctly and his words hung in the air.

Unable to let it go, she headed over to the soccer field in her Astro van. She couldn't quite shake Reuben's words now that she was alone. Why would Reuben call her Libby? She hadn't known him before she changed her identity.

Trap was alone on the field looking at an attack strategy they had been practicing for the last week. He called it attack soccer.

"Hey Trap," said René. She had that old scowl on her face.

"Hey Angel, what's up?"

"Reuben blacked out over at the hospital while we were going for a walk. Trap, could we jog around the field a couple of times? I need to clear my head."

"I thought you never ran," Trap lowered his eyebrows.

"Just two laps; it's important Trap." She looked serious.

The two started a couple of easy laps.

"Trap, there's something I have to tell you," said René.

"Angel, I got a head full of soccer, can't it wait?"

"No, Trap. Dammit it can't wait! I'll keep it nice and short. I'm almost sure Reuben was Wade's riding buddy down south! Up there at the hospital he called me Libby about ten times!" She took a couple breaths before continuing. "I never met Reuben down south. He never came around. I didn't even know his name. Wade always referred to him as 'his riding buddy'. Maybe 'cause of the baby reminding him of his kid. Reuben must have seen me over at Privina's house after my big weight loss. Wade and Privina were acquainted but not particularly friendly. Reuben must have heard Wade mention my name."

Trap fell silent while they slowly jogged around the track. Just as they were finishing, Trap put his arm around René's waist and spoke in a whisper: "Stick close to me. I won't let anything happen to you. Let's talk tonight."

Kids and parents started arriving. The size of the crowd amazed Trap. It seemed like the word was out on the team from Olympia called Blue Angels.

In 15 minutes the team arrived and Trap got them in a circle. Trap asked René to raise the red flag when the ball goes out of bounds.

"Okay Blue Jets, today we're playing the Bankers. They are a highly defensive team. Let's use our direct forward play attack soccer to start and show them they can't stop us. Remember, don't pass back. Keep the momentum forward, always forward. Press them hard and don't let up. Shoot high. Expect to shoot over Bankers. Try to shoot by the sixth pass. Pound the far post. You're a fast team so use your speed. If you guys are getting gassed, kick the ball out of bounds. Goalie, hold the ball as long as the ref will let you to let the team rest. Remember your team is in attack mode. I want one sweeper on the defensive side. And remember, too: the goal belongs to the team, not the guy who kicks it in.

Trap wasn't much for praying but he had them bow their heads.

"Dear lord, please protect these young athletes from harm in the time of their intense competition. Give them strength and the endurance to win. Bless the Bankers as well and prevent them from injury. Ready, break," and the kids clapped their hands.

Riley called out "Blue Angeles A," which meant a wall pass kick off. Babar tapped the ball to Gabriel who wall-passed it back. Babar stopped the ball and left it under his foot, as the whole team charged the goal yelling "Go! Go! Go!" Babar held the ball as long as he could and let loose with a high kick in front of the goal. There were three shots on goal. Two slammed into the crosspiece, jarring the support beams. Gabriel could bend the ball and wrapped a shot around the goalie. He kicked with his laces, but caught the inside of his foot. His kicking leg crossed in front of his other shoe and he landed on his kicking foot, adding to the spin. The ball curved like a fish hook and rattled into the net. The Blue Angels mobbed each other as they ran back to the defensive half of the field. Trap was clapping and René pumped her fist at her team.

The Bankers were a loud, trash talking team, making remarks like:

"You guys are like a bad check."

"You guys are overdrawn!"

"You don't look like Blue Angels to me, you look like Neapolitan ice cream!"

Gabriel was the hothead of the group and he clenched his fist hard. He was as good with a right hook as he was bending a soccer ball. He singled out the kid on the Bankers team making all the noise: a short pug nosed red headed kid.

The Bankers started down the field with possession. Gabriel went into his sweeper mode and was the usual pest to the other team. He stopped near the red headed kid and glared at him.

"Don't talk that way about the Blue Angels unless you want a whole lot of trouble," said Gabriel. He had a look in his eye that was unfamiliar to Trap. He looked savage. Trap could see trouble, and René walked over and whispered in his ear.

"Trap, if this keeps up they're gonna fight! I've seen it before."

The next out of bounds, Trap pulled Gabriel out of the game. Gabriel was pissed.

"Coach, did you hear that garbage?"

"Listen, you have to cool down. Do you see that camera over there? That's the South Sound Herald. They asked me last game if they could do a story on the Blue Angels. Don't spoil our chance to make the paper. Now there's a way to handle this without getting red carded and missing the next game as well as this one. Tell the referee that the Bankers are shouting and harassing to create an advantage."

"Good move, coach," said René.

Gabriel looked at the horizon and nodded. Trap put Gabriel and Eyana in the game, and Gabriel went right to the referee who then visited the opposing coach. The coach argued but seemed to come around after a few moments.

Play went on and both teams cooled down. The Bankers continued their strong defense but it was no strategy to cope with the Blue Angels and their attack soccer. The Blue Angels just swarmed the Bankers goal and caused them fatigue by the middle of the second half. Gabriel continued his dual role as defensive sweeper and offensive striker, and he seemed to have the endurance to do it. That was legal play but was very difficult to defend. Gabriel had the Bankers tied in knots trying to cover him. As the Bankers grew tired, the Blue Jets seemed to get stronger thanks to the technique of stalling at every chance to let the team recover. Both teams were pounding the turf so hard they were kicking up dust. There was a lot of contact in this game, but the Bankers coach convinced his team to stop mouthing off or they would be facing ejection. The end of the game whistle sounded. The final score was Bankers 1, Blue Angels 5.

Trap told the Blue Angels to come back for pictures after slapping hands with the Bankers. Gabriel slapped hands, but when he came to the red headed kid that rabid look returned to his eye. René saw Gabriel's eyes turn savage and could only describe it as terrifying.

Trap organized the team into two rows in front of the goal. Spruce trees moaned behind the goal posts. Several doves also moaned from the trees. Trap knew the messages he was receiving. They were saying that this is a time for great vision, and that he would be able to see the future clearly.

René squeezed Trap's hand and said to him, "Listen to those doves coach. I've never heard such joyful mourning. I think they're proud of you. I know I am. Attack soccer, huh? Have you been cramming soccer behind my back?"

Kay Robin, the newspaper reporter, came running over with a cameraman alongside her. She shook Trap's hand and looked over at René.

"Could I have a few photos of you and the team, and maybe a short interview?"

"Sure, can we get the kids first? Some of the parents are waiting. But Riley can stay late if need be."

The cameraman took twelve photos of the team from different angles. "Could I get your names and ages please?"

"I'm Trap Field age 33, and this is René Coogman, age 29. Our head coach is Reuben Sanchez, but he is in the hospital with a little heart trouble."

"This is such a powerhouse team, they seem like they can't be beaten. What makes them so electric?"

René feeling some pride, stepped over next to Kay.

"Trap probably wouldn't say this but he works real hard to understand the game, and he works hard to make the kids feel special, like a real team where everybody gets the credit. He likes to say: when the ball slams into the net, the goal belongs to the whole team, not just the guy who taps it in."

René was so photogenic the cameraman took about two dozen photos of her. René loved the attention and wished she had dressed nicer. She did give the camera her smile. It looked dim as usual.

"And Trap, this is the most ethnically diverse team in the state. How did you get so many racial backgrounds on your team?" asked Kay.

"We didn't do anything. It just turned out like this by itself. The soccer association assigns most of the players to the team. It just happened like magic. Some teams have trouble getting kids to practice. On this team the field is swarmed with kids and the same ethnic diversity grows with every new kid that wants to play. We almost called ourselves Blue Magic. I can tell you our diversity gives us strength. Because I'm a big football fan over most of my life I use schemes and trick plays like you might see in a football game. We use codes, huddles, assignments, and triggers."

"But they seem so charged with energy they make me want to test their circuits. How do you get them on fire the way they play?" asked Kay.

"We never yell at the kids unless one is really behaving badly. Lots of coaches try to motivate kids thinking they can yell like a D.I. in boot camp and make them try harder. Kids don't respond to that kind of talk."

"And you—is it Riley? What do you think of your soccer team?" asked Kay.

"There's a kind of a presence on this team, like a mysterious power. School comes easy for me. But I never tried harder at anything than I try on the Blue Angels. René is my mother but she looks like my sister and she treats me like her best friend. She helps me at everything I do. Trap and René are sort of going together, and what they feel for each other motivates the whole team."

Riley's head went down to stare at the ground and he kicked the sod with his spikes.

Riley and René rode home in the Astro. Trap followed in his old Chevy van. The three of them caravanned back to René's place, where a pot of beef stew was simmering.

After dinner Trap and René went out to a spot over the bank and sat in two picnic chairs. It was low tide and before dusk. Rene looked out over the primal ooze and smelled the dewatered mudflats. A large flock of redknot shore birds flew across the inlet flashing their colors of mottled brown and red. They flew with amazing speed and sudden changes of flight pattern that made the whole flock flash to white as they all changed direction. It was as if they had group soul with a natural communication and could roll sideways together at any moment.

"Isn't it wonderful the way they're so completely free. They have no troubles, no anger, no PTSD. You don't see any long faces. When something happens they just glide away and disappear," said René.

"There's that sad pretty face again," said Trap. "Bird flash is called murmation," he said.

"Oh, sorry for the sad face, Trap, we should be celebrating a victory. Hey Trap, the team looked you really good you think? They're a kind of sandpiper. Can you hear them speaking to you? Listen carefully. The spirit message is to dance...your moving towards an experience when you feel a period of masculine energy. Exercise very hard. Hold your ground in an emotional time. Don't give up and pay close attention to someone young. Now who might that be?"

"You know, sometimes I wish I were just plain, like one of those anonymous birds out there, fading into a flash of white."
René looked at Trap and smiled a weak smile. Then her head sunk down.

"Okay René, I know what this is about. It's about Wade. I'll talk to Reuben and speak with a lawyer about a restraining order. I'll buy some pepper spray and a couple of baseball bats to keep close to you.

One in the house and one in the car. Do you want to take a self-defense class downtown?"

Rene didn't say a word. She was already learning to fight and had kept it to herself. It was like her secret. It came from a selfish toughness, waiting and waiting.

"Trap, when Privina died, I talked to her son Bibs. He said Privina wrote me a long letter and willed me $20,000. I haven't received the letter or any sign of her will."

"Is it a probate situation?" asked Trap.

"I haven't the slightest idea," said René hanging her head.

"Let me call Bibs," said Trap. "René, how do you feel about guns?" Trap shifted awkwardly in his picnic chair.

"I hate guns, I don't ever want to be around them. Just to look at one makes me sick," said René. She put the palms of her hands over her eye sockets.

"Well that's the way you feel, and you'll probably continue to feel that way over the rest of your life. That feeling is telling you something, and you should never go near a gun, no matter what. But René, listen to me. You're strong. Look at those legs, that rippling back. I'll find you a women's self defense class. Give me Bibs' phone number."

CHAPTER 20

May 25, 1998

Olympia, Cascadia

Trap was sitting in his office reading his mail. It was 10 am and he thought, *time for a break*. It was a good time to get his personal business done. He dialed Bibs' phone number on his cell phone.

"Hello."

"Hello may I speak to Bibs Moody," Trap asked.

"Yeah, this is he."

"Hi Bibs, You don't know me but my name is Jess Field. I'm a very close friend of René Coogman. She used to be called Libby Sorenson."

"Oh yes, Libby who became René. She worked for me in Olympia. I'm glad you called, she called down the day after Privina passed. You know it's the damnedest thing. René is in Privina's will. I jotted René's address down and left it on Privina's end table. It disappeared. I searched high and low and it's like it got up and walked away."

"Okay got something to write with? It's René Coogman, 1627 Swayne Ave NE, Olympia, Cascadia 98516. Phone (360) 555-0112."

"Excuse me Jess, why is she not making this call?"

"Well I care for her very much and I'm trying to give her some support. She has trouble talking about her time in Winsberg. She may start crying when we get on the subject."

"Well in spite of that, I'll have her confirm this call."

"One more thing Bibs—do you know a Wade Bode?" asked Trap.

"A little. I think he's fishing now. Tuna I think. Why?"

"Oh, I think he's acquainted with our soccer coach, but I don't know. Thanks Bibs, maybe I'll talk to you later," said Trap as he hung up.

Trap quickly dialed Reuben's number at the hospital. Reuben picked up.

"Hello."

"Hi Coach, it's me Trap. How are you doing?"

"Oh Hi Trap. I'm doing really well. I'll be outta here in a couple of days."

"Listen Coach, do you know of a guy named Wade Bode?" asked Trap.

There was a long pause.

"Well yeah, he was my riding partner in Winsberg. He did some time for two assault charges. I know he got out recently. He calls me from time to time. I think he's out tuna fishing these days. Oh, I know why you are asking me questions. It's René isn't it? René used to be married to Wade, but I never met her. I was always off somewhere with him. Swear to God I never saw her face. Back then her name was Libby," said Reuben. "He talked about his wife and kid and complained about marriage."

"Coach, this is important. Is Wade trying to find René?"

Coach gave a long sigh. "I know he has her address. He apparently took it from Privina's living room the day after she died, or that's what he told me last time he phoned. They were having a wake for Privina. He said the note had René Coogman and Libby Sorenson written on it. That was more than a week ago," said Reuben. "He talks about coming up for a visit."

"I'm hoping we can avoid trouble, Coach. Will you let me know if he's coming?"

"Yeah, I'll let you know. See you, Trap." Reuben hung up.

No sooner did the phone hit the receiver than Trap picked up again. He had the number of the Olympia Self Defense Studio. Not knowing René was already doing some training in the ring, he arranged to get René in one of the women's classes. She was very strong from her many workouts, but he thought she was no fighter. The kind of training she did was for leanness and body sculpting. For Trap, one thing was of grave concern. What if fighting brought back her episodes of trauma? What if she went back there? What if the whole thing backfires? That was no way to think. Trap rolled his fingers on his desk, staring out the window. There was her steady improvement. You could see it in her brightening smile, and it was such a joy for Trap to watch. There was the healing animal messenger from Privina. There was the cognitive work with her therapist, and she had a lover to raise her spirits. And there was no doubt René loved him. He could feel it in his bones. *She'll learn. If she ends up facedown she'll just get up and keep fighting.*

Then he was struck with an idea. Maybe he should get her a dog. But he would have to talk to René and see how she felt about it.

Trap then called Thurston County Superior Court and started the process for a Restraining Order against Wade Bode.

*     *     *

Trap was a bit proud of all he accomplished as he tapped on René's door. Riley answered.

"Oh hey, Trap. Mom got another photo job. She'll be back in a couple of hours. You want to help me dig some steamers while you wait?" He grabbed some of René's clamming gear for Trap and they started over the sword fern to the chicken walk. They walked through a forest of ash, cedar and maple trees with an understory of sword fern, blackberry, and buttercup. As the hillside steepened they were getting into dogwood and they moved through columns of willow. As Trap walked he took some deep breaths filling his lungs with the woods. They stepped out on the gravelly beach and the smell of marine air was soothing to both of them. Riley squinted up at Trap and got a serious look on his face.

"Hey Trap, are you in love with my mother?" asked Riley. "I mean the kind of love where you get married?"

"Maybe. She's talented, smart, and funny, and man is she good looking," said Trap.

"Well don't worry, I've got more helpful hints for you," said Riley. "And if you marry my mom, you'll be my father. I'd like to have a father. Sometimes I need guidance." Riley started groping in the gravel looking for steamers.

Trap got a lump in his throat.

"You're a great kid Riley, and I would be happy to be your father. But let's wait and see what happens when your mother gets to know me a little better." Trap changed the subject. "Hey Riley, I have a question. Do you like dogs?"

"Yeah, I guess so. I've never had a dog."

"Let me talk to your mom."

René drove up 45 minutes later. She saw the boys, hurried to get out of the dress she was wearing, and pulled on her levies and a couple of tank tops. Eager to see her boys, she dropped over the edge of the bluff and joined them.

"Steamers for dinner, huh?" she asked, puffing a bit from the steep climb to the beach.

"Get out the garlic, butter, and French bread," said Riley, "these are special."

"René, want to take a walk down the beach for a while?" asked Trap.

The heat and marine air made the beach pebbles steam a bit. Several alder and madrone trees last winter slid off the steep bluff and were out on the beach. Trap and René climbed over a tangle of branches and roots. Trap held René by the shoulders and spoke to her.

"You're going to be fine, René"

She didn't respond right away. She was looking at the red knot birds again flashing to white.

"You treat me so fine, Trap. You just don't know what it means to me," she finally said.

"How have you been feeling lately? I mean regarding the PTSD," asked Trap as he kicked a few pebbles out in front of him.

"Pretty fair. Yeah, I'm feeling better," she said as she wrapped her arms around his waist. "And I've got you to protect me from Wade."

"Good, cause I have some stuff to tell you. I got on the phone at work. You're enrolled in class for women's self defense. But I worried it might bring back visions of the past."

"I'll be okay Trap, actually learning to brawl might be helpful in a way that's hard to describe. I'm so angry sometimes I can't sleep. But

I will never take it out on you!" she nodded her head slowly and looked down at the rock pebbles at her feet. They walked together to a large log lying parallel to the shoreline. Both of them sat in the sand and leaned against the log, taking a moment's rest. René leaned against Trap. She looked over at him and waved her hand over his eyes.

She frowned and asked Trap why he had such a long face.

"Okay, René. Brace yourself," said Trap. "Wade has your address and both your old name and new name. And it turns out that Reuben is an old friend of Wade's. Wade calls Reuben every so often and he's thinking about coming up for a visit. Remember when you talked to Bibs at Privina's and you gave him your address and phone? Well that's where he got it."

René started blinking rapidly and there was a stutter in her voice.

"Oh Christ… just what I needed to hear. I swear that man is going to ruin the rest of my life too," she said in a low voice. She threw a pebble into the water.

"Here's the good news. I filed a restraining order with Thurston County Court. You better know Wade doesn't want to go back to jail, or that's what I'm lead to believe. We'll get a temporary order followed by a permanent. But René, you'll likely have to appear in court. Do you think you can do that?"

"Will you go with me? I swear to God Trap, lots of people have tried to help me, but you're the one. You're the one who can really help. You know, I didn't date a man for fourteen years after I left LA. I hated men, until you showed up with those dark eyes and wishful talk."

"Now here's a big question." He rubbed her neck where she loved to be massaged. "Would you like to get a guard dog? Some of them are real strong and if you bond with them they will sure as hell defend you." Trap paused to take a breath.

"Let's do it," René said with some confidence returning to her voice. "A dog would be nice to have around here."

"Angel, I hit you with a lot just now. I figure you deserve a long massage tonight in front of the fire. And then we'll have steamers."

"You did all that for me today?" she grinned. "I'll be darned. Look me in the eye, Trap. Do you have a crush on me?"

"Slight understatement," he said as he looked back to check on Riley.

René tightened her arms around Trap's waist, her eyes following another huge flock of red knot.

"Look at their flight, they're like a single organic entity. The whole flock would streak across the water like they were one, playing with the inshore beaches. They seem without a care in the world, and suddenly they're all flashing to white. Each one has a perfect relationship with the other and the flock seems to know itself like I know the back of your hand," said René as she lifted Trap's hand and stroked his palm.

"Trap, there is so much trouble in my life, I sometimes wonder if my head will ever be right." René's eyes took on that troubled look.

Trap felt a surge of pain at René's remark, because he knew she might be right. But he was not about to admit it.

"Well, pretty lady, you seem to me like you're almost there. Have no fear. Let's get this done. I located a German Shepherd breeder in Little Rock. It's called Bernie's Kennels. Let's get you a full-grown female about two years old."

Riley had a half-bucket full of steamers.

On Tuesday, René headed to the Hughes Associates yard to pick up Trap. Together they headed to Little Rock. Bernie's mostly had pups for sale, but a few mature dogs also. Bernie took them for a walk past eight kennels containing older dogs after René explained she wanted protection. Bernie stopped at one cage containing a fit looking female.

"This is Caro. She has some training as a K9 but she was released from the program due to mild hip dysplasia. She would feel pain and would miss some of her commands. It seems she began limping after a days work and couldn't keep up with the other dogs. Don't get me wrong. Many dogs have hip troubles and make perfectly good pets. Caro is gentle and loving if you bond with her. She's very fast until the pain sets in, and even then she'll keep pushing herself. Caro responds to commands in German, and she knows the attack command. But you must be very careful to give her wise commands. Keep her on a leash. If you're faced with an attacker, yell 'Fass' and take her off the leash. She is trained to go for wrists and ankles. She won't kill a human, but she'll give an attacker a hassle like you won't believe. Because of her hips she is selling for $250, which is real bargain. K9 units fully trained can sell for $18,000. And if you're wondering why I'm going on this way, it's because I used to be a trainer. "

"What do you think, Trap?" asked René.

"Well Bernie, if you're a trainer could you spend some time with us to show us how to handle her?" asked Trap.

Bernie suddenly became very serious.

"Folks, there are lots of complications in my selling you a dog that has training." He leaned over to René and lowered his voice. "To tell you the truth, I don't think it's legal. But Caro is a special case, not being fully trained. The authorities would probably put her down if they knew. But they don't know and I'll be damned if I'm gonna see Caro put down because she knows how to defend her master. I'll give you four two hour sessions for free. Saturday only. I'll teach you all the appropriate commands and how to use them. I'd look forward to it. Training a dog is pure joy, and I've never done anything more satisfying. These dogs are unbelievably smart and their sense of smell will amaze you. Take a tablespoon of sugar and drop it in a swimming pool and this dog could smell the sugar. But remember folks, keep this between us. Don't tell anyone and you'll be saving her life."

René looked at Trap. Her eyes were glowing with excitement.

"Let's do it, Trap, but can you float me a loan?"

"I never could resist you, but is the backyard fence in good shape?"

"We got it! The fence is seven feet all the way around."

"Okay, we'll do it!" said René.

René leaned over to Caro's kennel.

"Didn't make it through high school, huh darling? Neither did I. Well that makes us a perfect match. Maybe someday we can take the GED together."

"One more thing: her name is Caro. No pet names. No sweetie, no darling', no knuckle head. Always Caro or she might get confused. You must bond with Caro. You eat when she eats, she sleeps where you sleep, give her plenty of good food and even more love. Bonding is the secret. If you do she will love you to death," said Bernie as he opened Caro's kennel and snapped a leash on her collar.

"Oh by the way, she is spayed. See you this coming Saturday."

René was tentative at first, but Caro was a perfect lady. Caro let the leash go slack and heeled by René's side, her shoulder gently brushing her thigh. Caro brushed her wet nose across René's palm, catching her scent. She gave an affectionate little whine as if she knew she had a new master. Already René was feeling some affection for Caro as she put her hand on the dog's head. René thought of the coyote spirit messenger sent to her by Privina and how it got her on the road to healing. Then she looked down at Caro and she felt her emotions move once again. She thought this was a great move. Her heart started beating fast, and she knew Trap had come through for her again.

Caro jumped in the Astro and they headed back to Hughes where Trap had left his van. Trap picked up dinner for René, Riley, and Caro, and headed for the trailer. As soon as she got home René took Caro in the trailer and introduced her to Riley.

"Pretty cool, Mom. A real German Shepherd."

"Yeah. Just between us she has a little K9 training. I want you to be protected from the likes of Wade. Remember, Riley, Wade could go after you too. We've all got to take a little mini course on how to handle Caro." Riley knelt down and looked Caro in the eye.

"She has a foxy face and a friendly expression." Caro calmly looked at Riley, her tail still, her face curious.

"I want you to bond with Caro, also. You'll need to give up a few Saturday mornings for a while. Bernie's Kennels is going to give us some more training," said René.

She took Caro out to the chair overlooking the sound. Caro followed, walking with a slack leash still brushing her shoulder against René. She was looking so intently at René it seemed she was about to speak to her. René was watching the huge flock of red knot gliding over the sound. She felt good.

CHAPTER 21

May 28, 1998

Olympia, Cascadia

Reuben was back. He called Trap on the 26th and said he would be at the game scheduled for Thursday the 28th. Just in time.

Trap was writing up his monthly assignments. Trap's boss Paul Herwich invited him into his office. Trap took a chair adjacent to his desk. Paul rolled his fingers on his desk and started clicking his pen.

"This one is going to be a bit of a challenge, Trap. The Government has put in a special request to us. A situation has developed where I'm going to need your help. As you know, coastal salmon sampling is in full swing."

"Yes, I did work for them when I was in my early twenties," said Trap.

"Well, they've suddenly lost two samplers. One quit due to all the harassment she was taking from the charter fleet. The other they fired for falsifying data. You know the sampling program is at the core of the catch quota, catch per effort, and tag recovery programs. We got a call from the Columbia River Marine Fisheries Cooperative to provide two salmon samplers while they get a couple more hired and trained. All the trouble is at the mouth of the Columbia at Port Clark."

"Paul, I'll do it, but I'd like to make a special request too. I have a girlfriend I'm crazy about whom I suspect has a stalker. Seriously Paul, this guy was once married to her, and he's already been in prison for two felonies. Both of them assaults. Can I spend my nights in Olympia?"

"Sounds serious," said Paul. "How about we put you on four ten hour days and fly you down and back in the twin engine Beach Craft. Leave at seven, be back by five. I'll get another experienced sampler and fly you both down. We'll get reimbursed for everything."

Trap's stomach rolled a little, but not like the pleasant butterflies he got when he was with René. He even had a moment where he regretted agreeing to this. Trap knew sampling, and he knew how rough it could be on the docks: fights, drunks, nasty people cussing in your face, lying, and other very difficult people. Worst of all, people die out there on the Columbia River bar all the time— *all the time*. But Trap made up his mind he would go down there and do the best job he could.

Trap drove to René's after work and found her with Caro in the front yard. Knowing Trap was coming, she tried to look her best. René was a little intimidated by a dog with so much training. But she hung in there practicing *foose* (heel), *site* (sit), *blieb* (stay) *platz* (down).

Trap walked to the lawn and started petting Caro. "I'm starting to get fond of you," said Trap as he looked down.

"Yeah, well thanks Trap," said René.

"I was talking to the dog, darlin'." Trap let out a hysterical giggle. "But now that you mention it, you do look kinda cute," said Trap. She had on boot cuts and a tan nylon top tucked at her waist. She saw Trap staring at her so she tilted her head and pressed her shoulders back. Her waist looked smaller than her thigh. Trap wheezed.

René grinned, "Still afraid of girls, buster?"
Trap took a few steps forward. He placed his hands under her arms, feeling her strong wide lats, and followed the tapering V down her sides to her waist. He squeezed her waist until his fingers nearly touched. René giggled as his hands continued around her hips, fully outlining her figure.

"Let's do it… right now!" She said impatiently.

*　*　*

Later that night, Trap gave her the news about this new job assignment and told her what it was like to work on the docks.

She shrugged and said it sounded exciting.

Trap blinked his eyes a few times and looked at René while shuffling his feet.

182

"Hey René, don't you work at the sporting goods store across town?"

"Yeah… part time. I'm getting more modeling jobs, too."

"Well what hours do you work?"

"Oh, well whenever they need me," said René, looking out over the water.

"Oh… Okay, just curious," said Trap. "Going to the game?"

Trap and René launched into a discussion about the Blue Angels. They agreed there was something special happening with the team. The Blue Angels had momentum on their side. They seemed unbeatable and always ready to compete.

The game attracted a bigger crowd yet. It seemed the word was spreading on this energetic team. The Blue Angels had become local celebrities. It was a pleasure to watch them work so efficiently together. They were like a well-oiled machine, which made them fun to watch. Because they practiced so much they were hard to wear down, and could bring forward new plays Trap taught to them. Trap thought soccer was an ailing sport because of passing back: giving away precious seconds to the defense while the offense took even more time to get tidy and organized, with everybody in a picture perfect position. Trap was not buying all that, and taught a different kind of soccer: a high entropy, relentless assault, with synergy so intense the Blue Angels would be ringing wet from sweat at the end of the game. Trap always brought an ice chest full of sports drinks and could not believe some of the opposing teams would play dehydrated. At half time the Blue Angels would literally swarm the ice chest. There could be no doubt it was helping them.

Today they would go up against Los Gauchos, known to be a pretty good team. The ref blew the whistle and Los Gauchos started working downfield. Nicolás put his shoulder into the abdomen of one of the attackers, knocking him to the ground. Nicolás got a big loud yellow card and Los Gauchos took a free kick close to the Blue Angels goal. The attacker bent the ball and it flew like a great black and white arc into the net. Deshaun the goalie got burned. As big and fast as Deshaun was, he was also extremely sensitive. His eyes welled up, his face tightened with frustration. Reuben saw it happening to Deshaun and he pulled him out of the game. Reuben was a bit hard on Deshaun on many occasions, much to the dismay of the other players, but this time he spoke evenly.

"Deshaun, for God's sake, don't get so upset out there. You're one of the biggest, fastest kids on the team, but the winning team is the toughest. It's not about the guy who gets knocked down, but the guy who gets knocked down and gets back up ready to fight back. You have to be able to lose as well as win to be a good goalie. Now when something bad happens, when you make a mistake, you shake it off, and I mean right now. You don't have a second to spare. You recover right now!"

At half time things were looking pretty bleak: 3-0 Gauchos. The crew gathered in a small circle. Trap spoke up.

"Okay guys, listen up. I watched this team a month ago. I can tell you they're another first half team. They don't seem to have stamina and they grow flat in the second half. I think it comes from poor, disorganized practice without much competition."

"Well not us!" shouted Babar.

"That's my point," Trap responded. "The score makes it look bad, but you can take them. Push up that attack soccer and watch how they go flat."

As the Blue Angels proceeded to clobber the Gauchos in the second half, Trap kept looking at the horizon. For the first time, Trap thought he was truly a soccer coach. He realized that to coach doesn't mean knowing every rule in every rulebook. It was how he talked to his players.

He looked at René with her new friend. Caro was heeling on a slack leash. René was practicing by softly giving Caro the command '*foose*' just to practice, but Caro knew what she wanted. Caro put her shoulder against René as if to thank her for giving her a home.

The final score was 7-3 Blue Angels. This was a common score in U-14 soccer. In professional soccer the goalies are big and fast, with good hands. Pro soccer skews towards the defense and scoring is minimal. But youth soccer is different. In the younger teams Trap had seen scores as high as 23-0.

René and Caro came running over to Trap.

"You know what, Coach?" said René. "You are a coach. You know what else? Caro has a slight crush on you. Of course I explained to her you're already taken."

René hooked her arm around his and walked beside him as if there is nothing in the world she would rather do.

"How's the self defense class going?" asked Trap.

"Well, being as strong as I am, I have a big advantage over the other girls."

"Strong in the armpits?" Trap nodded and looked at René.

"Oh you're real cute, Trap, especially your feeble attempts at humor!" René looked up at the sky and smiled on one side of her mouth. Although reluctant to admit it she liked Trap's quirky jokes. She let out a little giggle.

"No really, the first thing they taught me was the eye thumb gouge. When you do that your attacker has to react with both hands or suffer eye damage. That's when you come up hard with the knee to the jewels!"

"Seriously René, are you having any trouble with your trauma?" Trap ran his hand over the back of her head.

"You know, just a few minutes ago when Reuben spoke to Deshaun. Get knocked down get up fast and keep fighting. That's how it feels. It feels good, like fighting back," said René as she took a few cheerful jabs into the air. "Hey, here comes Riley, and he's with a girl. Look Trap, it's Corin and they're holding hands." Trap and René looked at each other and smirked.

Riley smirked back at them.

"How long do we have to look at those obnoxious grins?" asked Riley.

"Hi Corin," said René.

Riley looked at his mother, "I asked her to come over tonight and walk our beach and maybe have a fire."

"Would you like to have some enchiladas with us first, Corin?"
Corin nodded.

Trap headed for his van and René offered a ride to Corin and Riley.
All of a sudden René's jaw dropped.

"Trap, could you come here please?" She spoke in a low voice.

Trap walked over to René. She gestured with her head at the van.
Someone had taken a sharp metal object like a knife or key, and made
a gouge all the way around the surface of the side panels and doors of
her van. Trap shook his head in disgust. He thought it must have been
sore losers. Or was it?

Reuben started loading his little Dodge with soccer equipment.
Trap walked over to Reuben and spoke in a near whisper.

"Reuben, someone just keyed René's car. Do you know—" Trap
hesitated. "Do you know where Wade is?"

"No, I haven't talked to him in weeks." Reuben said as he got in his
car, slammed the door, and drove off.

Trap and René headed home with the two kids. They had a
delicious Coogman dinner of enchiladas, salad, and lime juice. René
fed Caro some chopped beef at the same time the kids dug in. It was
supposed to help Caro to bond.

Riley and Corin headed for the beach. There was still plenty of
light. Riley showed Corin a nasty slide that had taken place to the
north of the trailer. The slide had overturned trees, root wads, boulders
and a tangle of confused sword fern. The slide was oozing with spring
water. Corin could hear water seeping onto the beach like pennies
hitting a table.

Corin turned and faced the huge expanse of dewatered salt flat and
turned to Riley.

"Look, the tide's out. We could walk the flats and watch the moon
come up."

"Don't walk out there," said Riley. "Please, never walk out there.
You can walk the deep mud and suddenly it gets really deep, and
you're trapped in a wallow up to your chest. You can scream bloody

murder and if anybody hears you there isn't usually time to get you out. Then you know what happens? The tide comes in!"

"Scary Riley, right out of a creepy movie. You're a good storyteller. Let's go up and build a fire. You could tell me more scary stories."

They started back up to the trail to the house. A dove moaned in the trees up ahead. Then something big moved in the trees to the left. The brush thrashed and cracked as a big animal moved towards higher ground.

"It sounds like two legs walking through the woods," said Corin.

Riley froze, Corin grabbing for his hand.

"It sounds human, doesn't it?" asked Riley.

"Yes!" whispered Corin.

Riley cupped his hand at Corin's ear.

"I think it's our neighbor two doors down. His name is Lester something or other. He comes down in these woods and gets drunk and acts real strange. I don't like the way he looks at my mom."

Caro heard something too. She was sniffing around in the back yard when she heard movement just to the north of the house. She let off a series of loud barks, sounding primitive and vicious. Trap and René would have to get used to it. She sounded ready for action. Something was walking on the dead leaves making a crunching sound: *crunch… crunch…crunch*. René kept the leash tight. Deep down in Caro's throat there came a menacing growl as she stared out into the growing darkness. Back in the woods something was limping and wheezing. But the sound grew faint, and all at once there was nothing.

Trap spoke above the growling. "René, clip onto Caro, bring her out front."

Caro stood on the front porch and started that low growl. This time Caro leaned against her leash, and René felt how powerful the dog was. Caro crouched; the muscles in her haunches were ready to spring. René felt it was a moment to speak German to Caro.

"Platz" She said, and Caro rested on her stomach.

"Trap!" said René. "This is one bad ass puppy!"

"Well you can handle her," said Trap.

René cut him off. "Quiet… what's out there?"

"Time for Corin to go home. C'mon sweetheart. Let's all go," said René.

Trap drove. They were all quiet in the van. Then Trap broke the ice.

"Whatever it was out there, it was no Stream Walker. I figure a big man, clumsy in the woods."

Trap was thinking to himself. Whoever it was in the woods, he was not used to brambles and blackberries. He seemed to be hiding, feeling guilty.

Riley commented that the person got up suddenly, like he had been waiting and was suddenly surprised. They drove past the house two doors down: René's neighbor, Lester was standing in the kitchen window. He looked up as the van passed by.

After dropping off Corin, Trap noticed René was showing some anxiety.

"It's a deep friendly massage for you tonight. I've done it so much I know where your tension is."

"Yeah, but first I want to thank our special lady for her work tonight. No prowler would come close. Caro, Brava, Caro!" cried René.

"Don't call her 'special lady,' don't call her anything but Caro. Sometimes I get the feeling she knows everything we say," said Trap.

Caro sprawled out on the living room rug. René sprawled on the sofa. She was understandably anxious about the prowler outside. Trap got down on his knees and started giving René a rubdown. She was pleased by Trap's touch.

CHAPTER 22

June 1, 1998

Olympia, Cascadia

René got up with Trap, fixing him poached eggs and toast with coffee. She looked at Trap and made him promise he would not be late.

"There's something out there in the woods," she said. "Sometimes I think I hear something, and it turns out to be the wind or a round rock rolling down the cliff. But something tells me our visitor will be back. But hey, Trap—I've got some good news too. I've got a chance to get into online advertising. I'll learn more after I do some modeling auditions today. This is a good opportunity for me. Online ads are going through the roof!"

"One look at you and they'll zap you up in a heartbeat!" Trap raised his eyebrows and gave René a little smile. René blinked and smiled back.

"Hey, where's Caro?" asked Trap.

"Caro is shacking up with Riley, and they're both sound asleep in his room," René let out a giggle.

"You sure this is a watchdog, now?" Trap ran his fingers along his jaw.

"Well she likes to stay up late and sleep in in the morning," said René as she rested her chin on her hand. "Boy, it's early. I'm going back to bed. Good luck Trap. I heard those charter fishermen are sometimes hard on people doing research."

Down at the airport Trap yawned and climbed in the plane, taking a back seat. He stared into an eyedropper and squeezed, trying to brighten his bloodshot eyes for a day where anything could happen. Except for the pilot he was alone in the plane, so he assumed Hughes had not located another experienced sampler. He stepped into the cabin worrying about René and the sound of heavy footprints in the woods just north of her trailer. He would go into those woods as soon as he got back.

He liked the plane though, and was surprised how quickly they got to the port at 180 knots. The airstrip was just across the state route from the harbor. Trap met the remaining three samplers before boats started to arrive; they were equipped with data sheets, hemostats, serrated knives, and salmon nose tags. Two of the samplers were young women.

The idea was to count the boats going out, create an expansion number for the fish caught based on the number of boats sampled, recover scales to determine age of the fish caught, and recover fish tags. This would yield data on catch per effort, total harvest, and place of origin. Trap was lucky he had done this in the past, or he would have been lost. One of the samplers asked Trap to spend four hours covering the east end of the harbor, including a commercial buying station, then switch to the big commercial canneries in the afternoon.

Trap sat on a bench waiting for the first charters to come in with their catch. He looked over the harbor and the river stretching before him to the south. The water sparkled as a light west wind roughened the surface. The water looked peaceful, and it was difficult to picture the angry waters of the Columbia River bar. Flecks of light bounced off the small waves. Gulls were gathering in great numbers and were quite noisy, as if calling the charter boats home. To a gull, an approaching boat meant fish and plenty of food. Trap bent his leg, put one heel on the bench, and rested his elbow on his knee. He was trying to recall what it was like ten years ago when he spent months at the port as a sampler. He remembered how bad he felt some days if he miscounted a boat. He remembered drunks in his face refusing to let him search for marked fish. He remembered being filled with resolve, unwilling to record false data. He remembered one classy charter boat skipper who was friends with John Steinbeck many years ago. He respected biologists and treated them like welcome guests aboard his boat, telling his charter about the benefits to the fishery the biologists provide.

But that wasn't exactly the routine for a charter boat skipper in this reach of the river. There would likely be no outward racial slurs at this port, but there would be plenty of anglers who hated fisheries managers and research teams. There would be plenty of angry people, plenty of hostile faces.

Trap recalled that the harbor was similar to any coastal harbor, only the boats tended to be more beat up because they had to cross the Columbia River bar to fish.

The Columbia bar was one of the most dangerous boat crossings in the world. It stretched out before the fleet and there was always fear in the air as the boats prepared to make the crossing. Vessels going out would raft up just inside the bar, and the skippers would search the waterline for evidence of those notorious rogue waves. The bar would look flat when suddenly a gigantic wave would rise like a big gray beast, slamming the jetties so hard that five-ton rocks would shift out of position.

But the most dangerous time on the bar was the return trip. It was a frightening time when the stern of the boat faced the Pacific and a big following sea. On the way back to port a wave could come from nowhere, suddenly cresting at 15 feet high off the stern. Boats were sometimes knocked sideways by a breaking wave and would often roll, drowning half the crew and buckling the hull. Then there were other rare waves fearfully talked about by fishermen. Waves that came up out of the ocean moving across the water at high speed, only inches high, but gradually slowing and growing bigger as they crept into the shallower bar. Trap heard sea stories like the event of the Seagull II charter.

*It was the summer of 1989. A small charter boat with a woman skipper was limited with salmon and coming in to the harbor. So the story goes: it was a foggy day—visibility limited—so the skipper stayed close to the south jetty. The jetty varied in height due to the huge, irregularly shaped pieces of riprap. It came in the fog: a huge breaking wall of water 25 feet high. It picked up that little charter and threw it completely over the jetty. The boat was crushed on the riprap on the south side of the jetty with the screeching and splintering of the little boat's hull. Most of the crew managed to struggle to safety; only the skipper died in that incident. She was catapulted off the flying bridge, crashing headfirst into the riprap and tumbling into the ocean south of the jetty. She was dead before anyone got to her. Dozens of pieces of the Seagull II remained floating in the water, eventually washing up in small pieces on the beaches to the south.*

The smell of dead fish drifted east where Trap was going over his data sheets. The smell was mixed with bleached wet wood as fishers cleaned their kicker boats and hosed them down. Over the months in which he sampled, he learned he learned it was possible to like a bad smell. The harbor smelled of man's relationship with the sea.

Trap also recalled those tainted Saturdays. The effort tended to surge with inexperienced weekend anglers. He recalled hearing the sirens of ambulances racing out the road to Fort Shaffer. He was only left to speculate what had happened. Someone might have slipped with a bait knife. Maybe some deckhand took a gaff in the face and went overboard, screaming. There was always some fear crossing the bar. Maybe somebody had a heart attack or stroke and collapsed over the side. Distorted rumors would end up back at the port on what event warranted an ambulance being dispatched to the Shaffer camp boat launch.

Trap waited.

At 9:00 am the first charter boat appeared to be heading in: an old wooden charter named *Mad Man*. Trap remembered it from ten years ago when he was a young sampler. It was a hard boat to sample because it seemed the charter was always noisy and rowdy. Certain kinds of people seemed to be associated with certain boats and certain skippers, depending on how the charter did business. *Mad Man* backed into her slip while Trap handed the deckhand the stern line. Trap walked up to the side of the boat and introduced himself. No one heard him so he brought his voice up to triple volume.

"Hi folks! I'm helping out on a research project and would like to look at your catch to see if I can find any marked fish," he said.

"Who the hell are you? We haven't seen you before!" said the deck hand.

"Well two of the port samplers left, and I'm sort of a temporary substitute."

"Well shit. You're not near as cute as that little blond that was here yesterday," said the skipper.

A thought ran trough Trap's mind, going something like, *yeah, neither are you sucker!* But Trap bit back the words and gave the skipper a hoarse laugh. One young woman up near the bow of the boat looked at Trap and took exception.

"But you're not too bad, either!" she said.

Trap smiled and said to the crew, "Wow, a compliment. Give me a minute to celebrate!"

The crew laughed and began to unload the catches, carrying their fish in large plastic bags. Though it was only 9:00 am, one old man was absolutely sloshed. He stepped off the boat and started to pull back his plastic bag when Trap touched his fish, looking for adipose fin-off salmon. He obviously didn't listen. That was something Trap learned a long time ago. He had a problem with drunks. It might even be called a bias, something Trap tried to avoid. Drunks don't listen. When Trap had to deal with someone who had too much to drink, he felt uncomfortable because it reminded him of bad experiences at the port. The old man staggered to the boat ramp and almost fell in the river at one point.

Trap held up a map and asked the deckhand to point out where on the map he caught these fish.

"Pacific Ocean," yelled the deckhand, rolling his lips in anger.

"Did you catch any shakers today?" asked Trap.

"Negative, negative, amigo!" said the deckhand. Trap felt a cold spot in his neck, knowing he had been lied to. He turned and walked away.

Trap went down the pier to where *Morning Star* was backing into her slip.

"You're new," said the deckhand, and he stuck out his hand and stiffly shook Trap's.

"What happened to Rachel, the pretty blond?" said the skipper. "I was gonna ask her to marry me."

"She's a goner, my friend. She was getting a lot of heat from someone and went back to Alaska to work on a gill netter."

"Well you're welcome to come aboard to look at our fish," said the skipper. "Do you want to come out with us sometime?"

"On my day off maybe, but I have to go back to Olympia every night. My girlfriend is having some problems."

"Well get it over with and give her a rock!"

Trap laughed. "They call me Trap."

"Hi Trap, call me Rusty: the fishing pole. Get it?"

"Got it."

*Well, that was a breath of fresh air,* Trap thought as he walked away. He made his way to Walt's Fish Company buying station. Kicker boats converted to little commercial trollers usually sold their catch at Walt's because he was located close to the smaller slips. As he walked inside a kid in his late teens was cleaning a catch of about twenty fish. He was the fastest person at cleaning a salmon Trap had ever seen. The kid had lightning hands and a razor sharp knife. Trap watched him briefly and timed his speed as he cleaned the fish: 20 coho salmon in 100 seconds.

Shaking his head, he made his way back to the weigh station to do some commercial catch sampling. Inside was a friendly looking man who called himself Walt. He turned out to be a schoolteacher who was getting extra income as fish buyer. Walt too was known for his speed at weighing salmon and making out fish tickets. He was hard to sample because he was so fast. Trap was keeping up with him at first, but catches were coming in quickly. Then it came. Trap had his hands on the last two fish of his sample when a scale full of fish came tumbling down on his hands, arms, and face. Trap was suddenly enraged. His dark eyes knifed at Walt's face. He was covered with fish slime. Trap stood motionless, glaring at the schoolteacher. He

194

convinced himself to back off, though it appeared to have been done on purpose. Without saying a word, Trap walked out and cleaned up at the public restroom.

The day wore on and Trap was beginning to recall some of the tricks of sampling. Charter boats were the hardest to sample. The greatest hazard was counting the fish. People gathered around the sampler asking what he was doing. Meanwhile the sampler was trying to keep two counts in his head. One count was for coho salmon, and the other for chinook, not to mention the occasional humpy or sockeye that would show up in the catch. It was extremely difficult for the sampler to keep his numbers straight. Trap opted for a little debriefing meeting with the skipper to be sure the catch sized up the same. A skipper would get bent if he was miscounted, and usually appreciated a debriefing in case he had questions about fishing regulations.

The day was winding down. Exhausted, Trap made his way back to the plane and home.

René suspected Trap was going to be bone weary when he got home, so she made him a high protein meal of barbecued sirloin steak, garlic bread, and vegetables.

"I got some work today," said René.

"Yeah, so did I," said Trap, rubbing his face and hair. "Boy it's crazy down there! What kind of work did you find?"

"Oh, a couple of modeling jobs."

"Want to walk a bit, Trap? I'll get Caro. Riley, you want to go for a walk with us?"

"No, thanks, got to write a paper."

Trap, René, and Caro went north into the woods. They were underneath fully leafed out sprawling maples, their trunks covered with moss with an understory of horsetail and sword fern. Trap slipped through the shrubs with very little noise. René took Caro off her leash. Caro moved slowly through the woods her ears forward. Trap sensed something else. He sensed a kind of presence in the air. Maybe it was newly broken branches freshly hacked vines still oozing fluids. There were darkened maple leaves laying on the ground but overturned, with their black side showing. Something had been there not long ago. Then

René heard Caro barking from a good distance away. They both ran to the sound of barking. Far back in the woods at the end of an old driveway was a little shed. It was in exceedingly poor condition. The windows looked as if they were blown out from the inside. Cautiously, René wedged the door open and gave Caro a command.

"*Sook!*"

Caro slipped inside the shed with Trap and René close behind. There was no one there. There were a few unopened cans of pork and beans. In the corner on a small table was a neatly folded newspaper. Trap flipped open the front page, which read San Diego Hunting and Fishing News.

"This place is creepy," said René. "I've got a feeling something has its eyes on me right now."

They made their way back to the road.

Trap and René took an easy stroll up past Lester's house. Lester noticed them from his kitchen window and came out to meet them by his driveway.

He stunk of bourbon and his pupils were so small Trap could barely make them out. His eyes were weird, with a strange taper to them. The outside of his eye twisted up and the inside twisted down. The bourbon had reddened and yellowed his eyes. It was hard for René to look him in the face. There was something there beyond bourbon, something illegal.

Lester liked René, and his eyes seemed to undress her. He liked René too much.

"Hi folks, how's it going?" he slurred.

Caro was looking at Lester, the hairs on her back starting to hackle. She let out a soft growl. Trap could barely hear her growling.

"*Ruhig,*" said René. Caro stopped growling.

"I know that word. It means quiet. What's your fucking mutt growling at me for? I'm not an illegal alien!"

Trap grew tense. There was that ugly bigot again, two doors down. Trap recognized that sore spot on his shoulder again. He didn't say a word, but his temples ached.

Then Lester's eyes fell on René again. She tried to fold her hands over herself but Caro was pulling against her leash. She gave the leash to Trap, shifted her weight to her other leg, and taking a half step back folded her arms to cover her figure.

Trap kept his eyes on Lester, watching his face. There was an awkward silence. Finally Trap spoke up.

"Have you been stomping around in the woods north of us lately?"

"No sir, not me." said Lester. He began coughing.

"Have you heard any loud noises out in those woods?"

"What you say?" said Lester. Trap thought of the drunk he had to deal with on the charter boat today. *Drunks don't listen*, he thought. Lester was still staring at René. Trap had enough.

"Lester, would you please stop leering at my girlfriend?" Trap cocked his right fist, ready to deliver a right cross.

Lester rolled his eyes and looked at the ground.

"Sorry Trap, I been getting weird lately."

Trap tightened his right hand. Then he thought better of it. He really didn't do anything except look at René, and she was usually attracting attention. But there again was that racist slur growling in his stomach. Trap knew despite helpful conversations with René he still had that same chip on his shoulder. *It's just the feeling I get around Lester*, thought Trap. He decided he was overreacting and let it go.

"See you, Lester. We're going to walk," said Trap as he started up the hill.

Trap, René, and Caro continued to stroll up to the crest of the hill in silence. The air was still and cold and the tree frogs were chorusing again. Trap gently put his arm around René's waist.

"You okay René? Listen to those frogs; there must be a thousand of them. You know, according to the shaman frogs are spirit animals, and if they surround you with their music it's a signal that your old life is passing and a new life is beginning. Your next life will be filled with abundance."

René smiled. She loved Trap's shamanism.

"Did Lester scare you?" asked Trap.

"Yeah a little. But you know, since I've been going to the self defense class I really can handle myself better. I've learned all the soft targets that a man has. When I cross paths with a jerk and he starts acting funny I get a little plan together what I'm gonna do. And then I'm not so scared. I've learned eye and throat gouges, ear pops, mouth, nose, and throat claws, moves to the groin and to the fingers."

Trap put his hand on her bicep and was impressed as she grabbed his hand and showed him a grip that would enable her to break his finger if she wanted to.

"Of course, this is all hypothetical. I would never beat you up Trap, you're much too cute. By the way, will you stay over? I can't wait to show you my scissor lock!"

"Okay Angel. But man am I tired. Can we have a brandy, candle, and massage?"

"Yeah, and maybe a little soft guitar."

198

CHAPTER 23

June 3, 1998

Lacey, Cascadia

The Blue Angels were on a roll. They remained undefeated after three more games. The crowds were continuing to grow as the relentless pursuit of aggressive, out of control soccer continued. Their reputation grew within the league, with many talking about the way they played. Trap got his ideas about confusing agressive soccer from the huge collection of videos he gathered. Attack soccer was not a new concept; Trap had borrowed the idea from a major league soccer analysis called 'direct forward play.' The strategy broke apart the defense, leaving teams confused and unprepared. As Trap worked with his team, he was becoming more confident as a coach. Not only could he coach soccer; his strategy seemed unstoppable to opposing teams. Though Trap still lacked a boatload of experience, he was beginning to feel steady with his soccer team.

Trap had a trick play called the 'tie your shoe' play for corner kick situations. A kid would stand in the corner kick area ready to shoot with another player slightly upfield. The kicker would suddenly delay play and make an announcement:

"Just a minute, I've got to tie my shoe!"

As he bent down, ever so slightly he would nudge the ball onto the field of play about six inches and fiddle with his shoe. Soccer players have to deal with exhaustion and will take every possible opportunity to rest. Waiting for the corner kick, the other team would take a moment to pull up their socks, straighten their shirt, wave at their girlfriend, talk to each other. But all this time the ball was in play. The kid upfield would rush the ball and kick it into a bunch of players not paying attention. Even though the off sides rule applies to this situation, it is still a surprise play. Staying on side, the Blue Angels would crowd the goal and get ready for a header, or a full volley.

Sometimes it would catch the other team off guard, and sometimes it would result in a goal.

They had another trick play called 'the argument.' Babar was very good at kicking the ball high. In close situations where a foul had occurred near the goal, the Blue Angels would start arguing among themselves over who was going to kick the penalty shot. The deception was intended to put the other team off guard, laughing and shaking their heads at the Blue Angels for apparent foolishness. Babar would swoop under the ball with his toe and kick the ball very high, lobbing it to the far post and over defenders' heads. Riley would position himself at the far post and volley the ball into the goal. This worked extremely well, and the Blue Angels scored several times this way.

If the Blue Angels had one weakness, it was a lack of size. Some of the kids were 13. Of the three brothers of Pakistan decent—Babar, Wahid, and Sajad—only Babar was 14. The other two were twins aged 13.

Thanks to nearly constant scrimmaging, the team was in shape—with a couple of exceptions. JR was too heavy but had a thunderous kick. Nicolás needed to lose weight, but his instinct for soccer was good and his wit above average. He usually did the right thing given the situation.

There was another problem with the Blue Angels. Reuben seemed to be ailing. He had trouble with endurance, and would sometimes complain of a strange vertigo he felt. A couple of times he called on Trap to take charge of practice. When Reuben didn't make practice, Trap would miss him because Reuben took care of all the discipline. Trap hated to make the kids run laps for bad behavior. Even worse, he couldn't stand yelling at a kid. Still, Reuben did not seem well.

But the team held on to the magic they had. If anything, they were more diverse now than at the start of the season. A couple more Asian-American kids joined mid season and were strong and coordinated, bringing more punch to the team. Standing in the center of the field, Trap would get strange feelings he could not explain. It was their diversity that seemed to give them an edge, and from Trap they learned subtle ways to communicate. Just a nod or whisper here and there was all that was needed. Trap learned something from these youngsters he hadn't thought of often. The more the kids were different from each other the better they could cover the field. Trap would sit on René's couch looking at videos, studying sprint times. He would think about each player and make notes on what his or her needs and flaws were. He would note a key midfielder was perceiving the ball as closer than it really was, causing him to top the ball every time. This would result in a chronic power leak. Other kids were still toe-poking the ball. What seemed like an easy fix was actually one of the hardest bad habits to break.

"Kick it with your laces!" was soccer basics, but some kids stubbornly continued to toe-poke the ball every which way.

\* \* \*

June 5, 1998

Trap got off the Commander and ambled towards the port. Government officials informed Hughes that they had hired and began training two new samplers who would be ready next week. This would be Trap's last day of sampling. He was not disappointed. He had his fill of port sampling years ago, and he found himself worrying about René. There remained the possibility that René was being stalked by that tuna fisherman, Wade. It was heavy on his mind. Every day he was in a hurry to get back to the trailer.

Trap walked out on the paved strip that bordered the docks. He sat on a bench in the morning sun. The tide was low and the wind blew from the east for the moment, bringing with it the smell of oyster shells and fucus. The gulls and crows were more vocal. One gull was close to Trap. Standing on one leg, the gull kept staring at him. Something occurred to Trap. The gull seemed to be acting strangely, putting thoughts in Trap's head:

*You don't know it all, Trap.*

The gull lowered his other foot and flew over the cannery. Trap was restless this morning, even a little on edge. He walked completely around the port trying to shake off an apprehensive feeling that was bugging him.

The first boat Trap sampled was not funny. The charter *Posey* was being backed into her slip when Trap grabbed the stern line. The deckhand took the line and spoke to Trap in a low voice.

"Maybe you'd best move on to another boat. I'm afraid there might be trouble."

Trap didn't back off. He gave his little talk to the charter and waited. The first half of the anglers passed Trap quietly. Then a young man stepped off the boat and glared at Trap. Trap noticed right off he was carrying a bait knife on his belt. Trap finished counting about half of the take, including a pair of marked chinook salmon. The kid walked towards Trap and said nothing.

Trap spoke in his usual friendly manner.

"Hi, mind if I check your fish?"

The kid finally spoke. "No thanks, and get out of my way."

"What's the matter, friend?"

"I told you to get the hell out of my way! Do it, you son of a bitch!"

Trap counted his fish, but had not checked them for marks, ruining the sample. Trap looked at a couple more bags of fish. He glanced over his shoulder.

"I'll call you a son of a bitch any time, anywhere! Sink any more boats lately?" The kid had his bait knife out, holding it tightly in his right hand. Trap had not finished his sample yet but he let the other fishermen pass without looking at their fish.

The kid was so young, but his eyes were cloudy from too much drink. He stared at Trap.

Trap looked the kid straight in the eye. When he was angry, there was something in the way Trap stared people down. Something primal in his expression. His eyes were black. When he was angry, the look on his face was like a black cave. Trap stood his ground, and stared, waiting for the kid to move. He saw fear in the kid's eyes and began to think it was over.

"Fuck you, son of a bitch," and he walked away still holding his knife.

Trap relaxed and wrote a big "VOID" on his data sheet, because he had not checked the kid's fish for marks. Trap would not falsify data. But he walked away from *Posey* feeling pretty low. The skipper ran up to Trap and grabbed him by the arm. Trap jumped at being touched until he realized it was the skipper.

"Sorry that happened, buddy. His boat sank on the bar last year and he blames every official in site."

"Well thanks, skipper," said Trap. "It helps to know the why."

Trap took a break to try to settle down. He went into the local coffee shop and took a booth, ordering a bagel and coffee. He stared around the room, his eyes shifting from fisherman to fisherman. He felt like a man whose profession was ridiculed and hated. He couldn't help but think dismal  thoughts. Trap's hands-on experience forced him to accept that research projects in a fishing town were not always held in the highest respect. In fact, there was often outright contempt for those trying to limit the catch to a sustainable harvest. It seemed to Trap like many fisherman held a resentment for those aspects of an education they didn't understand, resulting in a mocking contempt … contempt for those trying to save their way of life.

The wind turned west as the next charter boat came in: the *Jester*. Trap was surprised to see it was a BFO, short for 'bottom fish only' trip. This was the kind of trip where salmon or other pelagic fishes were not targeted. Rather, they were going for lingcod, halibut, china and black rockfish, cabezon, cod, tomcod, and other benthic dwellers. As Trap walked up to the boat, a member of the charter posed a question.

"We have a bet going," the angler said. "Which fish on board is the ugliest? We want you to decide!" The charter was like a party, with voices rising up somewhat loud and partly intoxicated. Trap took his time looking over each bottom fish while the charter grew quiet. Trap nodded thoughtfully.

"Man, we got an ugly catch today don't we?" said Trap. "Well it may be my upbringing, but I always thought a cabezon looks like a mud fence with fins. Good eating though!"

Trap laughed. As he pointed to the cabezon the charter roared, as if a huge amount of money had just changed hands.

One of the fisherman reached over to shake Trap's hand and said with a grin, "You just won me a pile of money, man. Here, have a twenty."

Trap smiled and told him no thanks. He walked away giggling.

Trap continued to sample a few more charter boats without any particular event. Then in came the charter *Tyee*. The deckhand was stripped to the waist. As Trap walked down the dock towards *Tyee* he passed a pretty girl with black hair. She wore tight clothing and was walking slowly towards the boat. She seemed unsure of herself, and looked out of place with her high heels and heavy make up. Suddenly the deckhand jumped off the stern and hurried past Trap towards the girl. Though Trap could not make out what he was saying, he was clearly yelling something at her. The deckhand put both hands on her waist and lifted her whole body high in the air. After a moment he then threw her off the dock into the Columbia River. People on the charter, including some women and children, stared in silence. Trap hesitated to get involved, but finally walked back and looked down at the girl. She had her elbows up on the dock but didn't have the leverage to lift herself out of the water. Her face was a mess of streaked and running make up. She lifted her hand towards Trap and he could see the despair in her eyes. He lifted her to her feet. She gave Trap a simpering thank you and ran off down the dock. Trap turned and the shirtless deckhand was standing behind him.

"Don't get involved," said the deckhand.

Without saying a word Trap gave him a long stare... a long, savage stare. The deckhand backed up a few steps then moved off towards his boat. Trap walked the other way.

During the last few hours of the day Trap sampled the commercial catch at the cannery. One of the female samplers was already on the

buying float. She was in tears, her face wrapped in frustration. The
young sampler had her sample nearly done when the buyer threw a
monkey wrench in her work by sending half the catch up the conveyor
before she could count them all. She was just as devoted to protecting
the fish runs as anybody on the dock. But when the buyer wouldn't
show support she tended to come unglued. At that point she nearly
quit, but decided to stick out the season to make her resumé look
sharper. But on that day she decided that she would never take a
sampling job again.

As Trap walked to the cannery, a man about his age noticed that
Trap was carrying his sampling gear and walked over to offer a hand.

"Hi. You look like one of the samplers. Pleased to meet you, I'm
Bruce Hills. I'm gonna get me a charter and head out for albacore. I'm
slowly getting used to the northwest; I lived in southern California for
a few years. I was an observer on tuna boats. Boy, what a fire drill that
is. Almost got my head split open once, working that damn *Gabriel R*
tuna boat."

Trap regarded him seriously. "What happened?"

"I got into it really bad with one of the fishermen and he clubbed
me in the head. I heard he went to prison for felony assault."

"By any chance was his name Wade?" asked Trap.

"Yes! For God's sake, how did you know?"

"Well I'll be damned!" Trap's eyes rolled with surprise. "Where are
you living now?"

"I live with my girl friend in West Olympia, but eventually we plan
to go to Alaska to buy a purse seiner," said Bruce.

"Would you recognize this Wade guy if you saw him?"

Bruce said it was years ago since he'd seen him, but he might
remember.

"Well I got a plane to catch." said Trap. "Call me—it's important!
Here's my card. Oh wait, I'm with a friend these days," he wrote
René's number on the back of his card.

"What's this about?"

"Just call me, please!"

"Hey, I heard from one of the other samplers that you're a soccer coach. I played soccer a lot when I was younger. Great game. I was a high school player way back when," said Bruce.

Trap hurried over to the twin engine Commander.

The plane engine roared. Trap was quiet, staring out the window. He didn't talk the rest of the way home. Trap rubbed his eyes in their sockets and reflected on the week. He recalled that he had not seen a racial minority in the week he'd been at Port Clark. Why, he couldn't say, but he also thought he had just been through one of his toughest assignments. Trap thought about the young kid with a knife in his hand. All he could think about was the contempt so many people on the docks showed him. And there was a clue about Wade.

Trap arrived at René's exhausted. She had dropped off Riley and Corin at the movies and hurried home to meet Trap.

"Well how'd it go, baby cakes?" she said.

"Whew, that is one crazy place. Over the next few months I'll tell you about it, one story at a time," said Trap.

"Well I've got some news. I got a call from Thurston County Superior Court today. A process server found Wade in port in San Diego. He was served with a restraining order a week ago."

Trap looked down at the rug and folded his hands on the back of his neck. "Well I'm not sure it will help, but it sure can't hurt. You can bet that felon doesn't want to go back to jail. Do we have any wine?"

"Let's eat first. I made you breaded veal cutlets with mashed potatoes and country gravy. I got strawberries too."

"Have you thought about Riley? What are you going to tell him about Wade? Or does he already know?"

"He knows most of it," said René. "He knows his real dad went to prison on felony assault. He knows his name was changed from Morten to Riley. He knows his dad was a tuna fisherman, and he knows we are from southern California. You know Trap, I could never tell Riley his father beat me real bad. But he knows I have PTSD. I—I can hardly hide that."

Trap hardened his fist. He never hated a man more and they hadn't even met. René looked at Trap. She was trembling a bit. She looked beautiful with her dark eyes, and despite her well-defined limbs she looked vulnerable at the same time. She hadn't seen him angry very often. Trap's face turned fierce and his black eyes burned.

"I've got to pick up Riley. Calm down my friend, you've had a really hard week."

She hurried out to the van with Caro. Trap poured himself a glass of merlot and settled down in a rocker in front of the fire.

Though it was early June the nights were still cold and Trap knew René had built a fire just for him. She knew he would be completely worn out from a week as a port sampler.

Trap was tired, but his exhaustion was mixed with a deep satisfaction that he pulled off the assignment. Nothing is better than being completely spent from a job well done. Trap kicked off his boots and stared into the soft glow of the simmering coals. He recalled a voice that seemed to come from within him.

*You don't know it all.*

Friday night. Trap took a sip of wine and let his head fall to the back of his chair. A restraining order was served. Trap doubted it would even slow that fist-flying maniac down. But at least he could call the police in certain situations. At least he could keep himself out of trouble. He was angry enough to beat hell out of Wade. Trap took another sip of wine. *Relax, it's Friday night*, he thought. He threw another log on the fire and listened to the coyotes yowling out in the dusky northern woods. He listened to the rising and falling waves in the inlet below him. He could hear Caspian Tern calling 50 feet over the water for the last pass of the day.

René, Riley, and Caro pulled up in the Astro. As they stepped out of the van, there was a rustling in the woods. Caro, unleashed, jumped into the heavy foliage. Someone was running in the darkness next to the house. René gritted her teeth in anger. She'd had enough.

She bellowed into the dense brush. "*Fass!*" she shouted. "Caro! *Fass!*" Caro started a hellish barking. Though she couldn't see, Caro went straight for the sound of someone running. Then a big Harley

Davidson started up the spur road that led to the old cabin. The black trees towered overhead as the bike dug in for enough traction to make it up the hill. Caro bore down on the motorcycle, increasing her speed. The German Shepherd lowered her body for more power. She barred her teeth as the motorcycle shifted into second gear and the baffles sounded like hail hitting a tin roof. For the moment Caro was gaining. She had amazing speed, unafraid of the noise ahead of her. She smelled the stench of exhaust. Rotten leaves and chunks of mud and gravel hit her in the face. The rear wheel of the bike was side slipping as the woods opened up into a wider, flatter section of the old spur road. Caro was still gaining as the cycle began to wind up in second gear. She put on a last burst of speed, and left the ground.

Caro only succeeded in snapping at the cycle's rear shock absorber. She flipped head over heels as the bike pulled away, but she jumped to her feet instantly, snarling. Above the sound of the bike pulling away she could hear René yelling "*Heir!*" and Caro ambled back to the sound of René's voice. "Bravy! Caro, bravy!" said René. Trap heard the commotion outside and was struggling with his boots when René and Caro came in through the front door.

"Trap, someone was back in the woods, again, someone with a motorcycle. It could be him," said René, her voice trembling. "Caro tried to run him down but couldn't catch him." René looked out into the woods fearfully. "I'll just bet you it was him."

She reached down and put her arms around Caro's chest. Caro was still breathing hard, but she put her cold nose on René's palm. Trap walked outside and took a long look at the pitch-dark woods. His eyes narrowed.

CHAPTER 24

June 6th, 1998

Olympia, Cascadia

It was Saturday morning and René sat on the edge of the bluff
overlooking the water. She was fingering her guitar, but not paying
much attention to what she was doing. She bowed her head on the
soundboard of the little instrument and started crying. She was
showing improvement over the last couple of months. But she felt low
today because she could swear the next person she ran into in Cascadia
was going to be Wade. Her doctor said it was good for her to cry. She
cried about Wade and her father beating the hell out of her. Down
through the years René went, back into the past to experience what it
felt like to be pregnant, her father rearranging her face with his fists.
She just kept going back. Even against her will, the work of a shaman,
and a counselor, these thoughts still remained an angry voice in her .
head.

Trap was inside, sleeping in from an exhausting week. René didn't
expect him up for hours. Caro nosed open the front door and trotted
towards René. René saw that she was dragging her back legs a little
from last night's chase. Bernie from the kennel had said that Caro
would have hip soreness lasting a few hours after putting on her
amazing speed. He had warned her to be careful with Caro when she
was sore, as dogs don't do well with pain.

René was finished having her little cry when Riley poked his head
out the front door.

"Hey mom, want some bacon and eggs with hash browns? I'm
cooking today. You get a break."

"Shhh, Trap is fast asleep!"

Riley saw that his mother's face was streaked with tears. He came
out to the bluff and sat down beside her.

"Crying about my nasty old man? That was probably him last night wasn't it, even though he's been served?"

"Probably," she mumbled.

"You know you're sure an okay mom. I'm thinking you're 29 and I'm 14, so we're both still young." Riley tried to change the subject. "Mom, do you ever notice how time speeds up as you get older? Is that what Einstein meant when he said it's all relative?"

"You know I didn't finish high school Riley. There's a lot I don't understand."

"Did you know the Earth moves around the sun at 67,000 miles per hour?" asked Riley.

"No, I didn't know." René stared over the water. "I don't know a thing."

Riley looked hard into his mother's face.

"Come on mom, we're going to make it. Don't be gloomy."

"I'll try Riley. Life is really precious. I found out when I broke my ankle when I was about 21. I was roller-skating with some friends and I took a bad fall. Shattered my ankle. I was taken to the hospital and as usual I was broke. But the doctor said he would fix my ankle and worry about the money later. He told me he would write a letter explaining that I had no health insurance, so I could go to the welfare office and ask for help. That isn't something a surgeon would generally do… he knew I was overwhelmed by the costs and he was extra kind."

René continued, lost in the memory. "During the surgery I was under a strong anesthetic, knocked into oblivion for six hours while they tried to put my ankle together with screws. I was so far gone I couldn't feel time passing. I couldn't see, dream, think, or hear. When they woke me up it was like one second had passed from when they knocked me out. You know what, Riley? I miss those six hours because I never got to live them."

Trap woke up to the smell of bacon frying. He rolled over on his side, feeling rested. He pulled on his pants and walked into the kitchen where Riley was cooking breakfast. Riley turned to Trap and told him that René was on a bit of a bummer this morning. He handed Trap a plate of food and asked Trap to give it to his mom.

Trap went out and sat next to René, handing her the bacon and eggs. She took one bite and set down the plate.

She looked at Trap and shook her head.

"You know Trap, it just plays over and over in my mind. My father beat the shit out of me, a real anger management case. So what do I do? I leave him and move in with a guy who's even more violent. How does my mind work? What was I thinking? How could I have done that?"

"Well René, didn't your counselor say a woman will often do that? I mean leave a violent man only to move in with the same kind of jerk she left."

"Yeah, that's what I did all right. But thank God Riley came along. He raised me up as well as I raised him. He is such a remarkable kid. He made me strong enough to change my life. And I did. At least I can say that. You know I really got us out of a bad place. But now it's come back to visit again."

Trap looked at her and nodded slowly. "Yes you did René. But now if that son of a bitch comes around, we are ready. You are fit and strong and have a little training. I won't let him harm you and you've done a great job with that dog."

René closed her eyes for a long time. When she looked up there was still some dimness in her face, but her eyes held a steady determined gaze across the water. Feeling a bit better, she shrugged.

"Why don't we get Riley and head over on the east side today. Let's swim and maybe fish until twilight," suggested Trap. René was still feeling down but was open to the idea of a fishing trip. *Yeah*, she thought. *To hell with this moping around.*

"I'll get the poles. Eh, excuse me. I'll get the rods and we can do some fly-casting. As a bonus we can smell the sage," said Trap.

René was slow to get up, still closing her eyes for long periods, but she agreed. Riley asked to be dropped off at Nicolás's (mostly so René and Trap could be alone).

Over on upper Hat River, René cast a stone fly imitation out over the flat dark ends of the pools. René liked to fish the lower ends of pools where it was cool and dark and the surface unbroken. She held the rod high, making the fly carve a V-shape on the surface of the glide. She continued to use her three-piece bamboo rod though it must have been a half-century old. She was a strong caster and had her rod balanced with a shooting head fly line. She wore a Danish stripping basket to help with her distance on such a large river. She crept among the aspen, putting her hands on the cold white bark and listening to the softly quaking leaves in the hot light wind. There were some steeper sections of Hat River where the water rattled over huge boulders. These boulders formed pocket pools. René cast her dry fly accurately into these fishy looking backwashes that were so much fun to target with her line. She looked over the clear green water and realized she liked Trap partly for his profession of taking care of streams and rivers. She thought of Riley's description of a river, claiming water is a feeling, and it made her grin as her eyes scanned the horizon. Trap caught her smiling. A trout split the surface and bit down hard on René's stonefly. She jerked back as the line tightened and felt the weight of a big trout pull back.

René let the sound of the riffles sooth her, and the warm sun heal her, and by the end of the day with a creel full of rainbow trout she felt fine. They fished until dark, as trout fishing is an evening show, the opposite of salmon fishing. René's back cast was nearly perfect. She brought it back low, then brought it high over her head. At the very subtle tug of her back cast, she eased her line forward and let the scope in her stripping basket take her fly sixty feet over the river to fall gently on the surface. Trap watched her in the sharp angle of the sun and he took a mental snapshot he would never forget. She was such a beautiful woman, with such a perfect cast on such an open stream. The crickets were sounding off as they got in the van and headed home.

René slept in the back most of the way home. She was exhausted and filled with the pleasure of catching some pan-size trout.

Trap was humming softly and thinking he might take up a musical instrument. Maybe he'd try the recorder, so he could gig with René. Then that voice in his head came back.

*You don't know it all.*

On Sunday morning Trap and René were sleeping peacefully when the phone rang. It jolted Trap awake. It was too early for a friendly phone call. Trap rolled over with a feeling of urgency and shook his head clear as he padded into the kitchen and picked up.

Someone on the other end was gushing with tears: choking to find words to speak.

"Trap!" the voice finally got out a word.

It was a young man's voice.

"Trap!"

Was it a Blue Angel?

"Trap, this is Nicolás," his voice tapered off. "Coach, brace yourself...my father is dead! He'd been complaining of dizziness but wouldn't see a doctor. The spells were getting worse. This morning I got up and he didn't get up for church. I went into his room and he was really stiff, like he'd been dead for hours!"

"Oh my God! Nicolás, did you call anyone? Hang up and dial 911, they might be able to revive him. Let me get dressed and I'll be right over!"

"No, he's dead dammit, my dad is dead! Yes, I called 911, they're here now and they won't let me go into his room. Looks like they're loading him onto a stretcher. Trap, they won't let me in there," Nicolás sobbed.

"Nicolás, hang in there, buddy. I am on my way now! Let me get dressed and I'll be right over," said Trap.

René called from the bed.

"Hey Trap, what's the matter?"

Trap drew a long weary breath.

"Reuben died last night."

"W—what? Oh Christ! Wh... what happened?" asked René.

"He slipped away in his sleep." I guess some EMTs are there now. There's a big emergency truck in the driveway. I'm going over there to find out more!" said Trap.

"Oh... Oh, god! Do you want me to go with you?" asked René.

"No, just stay here and tell Riley. Lock the door and stay with Caro. I'll knock five times!"

Trap took off. René explained the events to Riley and asked him to get his baseball bat. Riley leaned it next to the door.

Trap returned after about two hours. He knocked five times and confirmed the bad news. Coach Reuben Sanchez was dead. "Nicolás told me his blood pressure was sky high and his heart failed while he was sleeping."

Word spread quickly throughout the team and the parents. Reuben and his wife had divorced years ago, but she still lived in the area. Nicolás was not very happy moving back in with his mom. She was a wild one. But for now it was the only option. Trap borrowed Reuben's cell phone and took down the name and number of everyone on the team. Then he started calling. He got through the list fairly quickly. Within a half hour he had word to everybody on notice coach Reuben was dead as of June 7, 1998.

Trap agreed to cancel practice and get together Wednesday the 10th, the day before the next game with the Cow Stampede. He made a point of telling the parents and team members that the next game would be in Reuben's honor.

The wind shifted from west to east. Reuben Sanchez was buried on Tuesday, June 9. René and Riley were there along with the Blue Angels. In a simple gravesite ceremony the pastor of Reuben's church did a reading. Nicolás and Trap said a few words about how Reuben would want the Blue Angels to keep fighting. All of them: weeping, shaking their heads, turning their backs so no one could see their screwed up faces. Crying was tough when you are a fourteen-year old athlete. But these kids didn't hide their feelings. Gabriel leaned over to Trap and said this was the end of the Blue Angels. The end.

As the group walked back to their cars with their parents, a man in a hooded sweatshirt and a denim jacket walked through the middle of the group. His hood partly obscured his face. He was carrying a handful of flowers past them. The flowers looked like they were gathered from the brush around the parking lot. As they walked onto the parking lot René turned and looked over her shoulder at the man walking towards Reuben's grave. She turned and hurried towards her car. A Harley was parked on the other side of the lot.

Only five kids showed up for practice on Wednesday. Heads were hanging. Nobody wanted to play. Trap urged the kids who did show up to get up and keep trying. It was something Reuben was always hammering on. He would say when you get flattened you get back up. That's the mark of an athlete. An athlete just keeps coming. But there could be little doubt a great shadow had fallen over the Blue Angels. Trap was unsure if he could manage the whole team with all of the phone calls and arrangements that had to be made. Now the words that kept ringing in his head made sense to him: *you don't know it all*. He finally understood the meaning. Reuben was the discipline on the team. He was the order. He didn't take nothin' from nobody. It was true, he didn't know much about soccer. But that wasn't all. He ran his team like a business. He took all the hard stuff while Trap had all the fun.

On Thursday the Blue Angels forfeited. Only four Blue Angels came to the game. The minimum number to compete was ten. Gabriel and Babar were both missing.

A sudden heat wave settled over the Puget Sound lowland. The rivers warmed up and many cold water salmon species suffocated. Many mossbacks love these flashes of blazing heat. But just as many do not. Some fall into heat exhaustion as soon as the air warms, and won't come out of the shade. Day after day the air grew heavy and humid, and the outside temperature climbed past 100 degrees. René had no air conditioning so all three of them sweltered in the heat.

The phone would not quit ringing: mostly modeling agencies wanting René in a bikini. Some of the offers she got were racy. Although she didn't tell Trap, some were topless.

The heat just would not stop. It burned the sidewalks. Bonneville dam was power peaking due to thousands of air conditioners running simultaneously. As René gained popularity she started taking jobs that meant more time away from Trap and Riley. She could model anything with her looks, helping to sell whatever happened to be the product of the day. She was photographed in an occasional fashionable dress, on the hood of a fast car, and using high-end sports equipment, along with occasional workout clips. Though it was hot she continued her daily two-hour workouts. The heat made her face, neck and waist grow slimmer. Wet with sweat, her body would glisten in the sun as she slimmed her thighs and hips and gave her legs more definition.

The Blue Angels were on course for a total breakup. Practices plummeted to zero. Trap seemed powerless to stop it. The heat sweltered and the air grew toxic and still. Trap's spirits were low; it was all he could do to show up for work. René was troubled about Trap's depression as she continued her trips to Tacoma and Seattle. She was very concerned about Trap. René started spending more time in Seattle, asking Trap to drop Riley off for the last days of school before summer. It angered Trap that she was away so much, ignoring the needs of her son. Perhaps he felt a bit left behind also. One day after dropping off Riley, he stopped off at a local bar for a couple of doubles of tequila.

As Trap sipped his drink, he had a foreboding sense that things were really turning bad for him. He was falling behind at work from leaving early to pick up Riley from school. He was also worried about Nicolás, and resolved to check in on him. A few days later, Nicolás answered a call from Trap sounding almost despondent.

"My mother is a real freaked out mess. She smokes constantly. She's always slamming things around the house and jabbing her finger at me. Everything is always my fault. It started to get bad as soon as I moved in and it's not getting any better. I'm not sure I can take this much longer," said Nicolás.

"Well you hang in there, buddy," said Trap. "Let's get together for dinner and talk this over. How about tomorrow night?"

Nicolás agreed.

René came home late again. She apologized to Trap, but this time he glared at her.

"Oh, I see, working late at the sporting goods store again? Tell me the truth, René. You never did work at a sporting goods store did you?"

"It's not a sporting goods store, it's a boat dealership," she could see Trap's face changing to real anger.

"And what do you do there?"

"Same thing I always do. I get into a bikini and show off my cleavage with a nice boat in the background!" René shrugged. "It's all I'm good for, so go ahead and look. In spite of my looks I'm a mental case!"

"Goddammit, René, you lied to me every time you walked out that door. Have you been doing muscle magazines too? Topless? All this time I've been here with you and you just looked out over the water when I asked you about work. Your waist is getting smaller. What are you doing wearing a corset? What is next? What would get you more of that kind of work? Don't tell me, let me guess."

"Not on your life, Trap, get over it! I just wanted some money! And I need money! I haven't got any money!"

"What about the inheritance money from Privina?"

"Oh, it's in p—probate, haven't you heard?" she said. René swallowed hard.

"Do you mean to tell me you have been flaunting that body of yours all over south sound, and that's all? René, why didn't you just tell me the truth? Have you been lying about anything else we should know about?"

"I used to work at an espresso booth. Guess what I wore there?" René gave Trap a sneer, "a little bikini! Oh man, Trap you should have seen them line up for a cappuccino... until I got fired!"

"For what?" asked Trap.

"Excessive absenteeism. I was always out looking for a job. But when you don't have a high school diploma it is really tough. So you're leaving me, is that what I'm hearing? Is that what's gonna happen? Is that what you're after? Well you picked a fine time! Did you see the strange man at Reuben's burial? That was almost for sure Wade Bode! And you're going to leave. Thanks for the encouragement, Trap. Right when I need it most!"

Trap was enraged. "I don't like liars or bigots! Come to think of it I don't think I like you teasing me with your bombshell figure! I've got to think this over. I'm going back to my apartment!"

He started towards the door, but paused. "What did your therapist have to say about your phony little sporting goods store?"

"I quit seeing her!"

"You what? You never told me this."

"Yeah, she billed me! It's too much money! I can't afford it!"

"René, I told you I would pay for it!"

"Well, you can't afford it either!"

"So, another filthy little lie. Why didn't you tell me you stopped seeing her?"

"Oh hell, get out then!" she turned away from him.

Trap stormed out into the night shadows. It was still too hot to move. He hurried up to his van and headed back to the apartment. Once inside he slumped in his chair. The apartment smelled old and dusty from neglect. He'd spent most of his time recently with René. He put his head in his hands. He clasped the back of his head. The heat was stifling and he struggled with his breathing. He felt sick. There was a distant feeling in his mind. It felt like he was going to pass out. Ringing wet from head to toe, he walked to the refrigerator and took out a beer. René, his beautiful lover, was a damn quitter and a liar. She had pulled the wool over his eyes with her killer looks for weeks and weeks. How could she do this to him? He was no longer convinced that she was in love with him. Now what? She probably got a good laugh out of taking him for a ride while she teased him sexually.

Back at René's trailer she was kneeling on the sofa, when there came a knock on the door. Three knocks. That meant it wasn't Trap. René froze, while Caro let out a low growl. René walked to the door.

"Yeah, who is it?"

"Hello in there. It's me, your neighbor."

218

"Lester? I don't feel like any company." René put Caro on the leash. "Not tonight, Lester. I want to be left alone."

"Oh come on, I got a great bottle of chardonnay. I'll share it with you. Looks like your redskin friend is gone for now... you must be glad to be rid of him. Where did he go, to a reservation?" Lester said, smiling.

He gripped the handle of the door and rattled it back and forth. "You sure are a foxy lady. I just want to be friends. Come outta there!"

"Lester, get out of here!" yelled René. Caro scratched the inside of the door.

René leaned down and spoke to Caro in an angry voice.

"Caro, *voran*!"

Caro let out several angry barks, reminding Lester that René was not exactly alone.

"Caro, *ruhig*!" Caro went silent.

"Lester, you're slurring. You're going to be sorry if I open this door. I know just the word to tell Caro!"

Caro was studying René's face, looking up at her, waiting for the next command.

"Okay, okay, back off lady. Christ, I was just being friendly, man! I got some mushrooms too! See you later. I'm outta here!"

Lester walked up the steep sidewalk to the garage. He thought he heard a sound from the dark: far back in the garage.

"Who is it?" said Lester. "Who's there?" He heard a cat yowl and kept walking.

Then a soft whisper came from within the darkness of the garage. There was something else in the there, and quickly a man in a hooded sweatshirt moved towards Lester. One fist flew. It came hissing through the air directly into the face of Lester. The blow sounded powerful, almost professional. Lester's face twisted and distorted. His vision turned crimson... then black. The last thing he heard was a dog barking, hoarse and relentless. Along with the barking there was a low mumbling.

"You come near her again I'll kill you!" said the voice.

Lester collapsed in the roadside ditch. Then there came a whisper.

"I'll kill that dog with my bare hands…"

The next morning Riley got up and went to school only vaguely aware that something had happened late last night.

After Riley left, the phone rang. Hoping it was Trap, René hurried over to the phone and picked up. It wasn't Trap, but it was a call for him. A guy named Bruce Hills wanted to know if Trap was there. René referred him to Trap's apartment and hung up. She walked into the living room with her morning coffee and sat down facing the beautiful view of Puget Sound. She watched as dozens of hooded mergansers poked about near the shore.

"Those birds don't have to worry," she said, looking over the bluff.

Trap was miserable. He didn't sleep a wink but got up and dragged himself to work. Bruce called that afternoon and left his number.

"Think, René," she said to herself in a soft voice. "What are you going to do? How did things get so mixed up? A few days ago I was on cloud nine with the man I love. Now Reuben is dead, the Blue Angels are history, and Trap left me. My God, Trap is gone."

She was silent and continued watching the mergansers. Her stomach began growling and she realized she had been sitting there alone for two hours. But she was so upset she couldn't eat. Instead she went to the gym. She added extra sets to her leg curls. She locked her teeth and did as many deep knee bends as she could do. Then it was sit-ups. She repeated the sit-ups until she was exhausted; her stomach muscles stood out like a washboard. Her whole body glistened with sweat as she stepped up to the rowing machine. She had only rowed for ten minutes when she decided to quit. As she walked out of the gym she could feel men watching her walk away. She smiled a wry smile to herself. Then just as quickly her smile fell, and she frowned at the carpet. She thought to herself that she could have any man she wanted. But she didn't want any man. She wanted Trap.

René sat in her van and leaned her head on the steering wheel, her eyes wet with tears. A few more came down her cheeks, and she started to feel better. A good workout always helped her when she was feeling low.

Exhausted as she was, René was getting ready to go to her self-defense class when Riley got home from school. Riley saw that she was leaving. He grabbed her arm and spoke softly.

"Mom, I need to talk to you. Can you skip your class tonight?"

"No, I've got some soft targets to learn. Could come in handy real soon. But thanks for asking. It's only an hour and a half, and I'll pick up some fish and chips on the way home. Then we can have a long talk. Remember Caro eats with us. I'll be back."

At class, René learned how to break fingers in a desperate situation. She also learned a few moves to the groin. She spent the rest of the period sparing. René got in the ring with a small Japanese woman who was disciplined in kickboxing. René was getting worked over by this small woman, but learned a lot from her. Although René was the larger woman, her sparing partner was taking care of herself and was not even a little afraid of the size difference. She taught René that size was not necessarily an advantage. Larger people lack quickness, and sparring goes to the one with hand speed. René began stopping her smaller opponent and asking her to show her how each move was done. The Japanese woman was very polite, very gracious and showed René a half dozen ways to fight a bigger opponent. The woman told her to practice her new moves until she had them down.

René was not done. She walked over to the heavy bag and stood in front of it giving it a few weak slaps. Then she exploded with a flurry of vicious hooks while cursing with frustration. She arched into the bag with a dozen quick uppercuts. The sweat poured off her body as she started hitting the bag with all her might. She grunted hard and threw some hammering crosses. The bag started swinging back at her so she gripped it and brought her right knee against it. She started screaming with every punch and crazing with anger. She backed up and rifled jab after jab at the bag. Soaking wet and gasping, she finally backed off and left the room.

René left the self-defense studio feeling better. She began to think Trap was just pissed at her and he would be back. Sometimes Trap was high and mighty about his self-taught principles. Once he realized she wanted him very badly and she was just trying to impress him, he would come around. She had come at him very hard with her sexy acting out. Now he was just finding out she was human and made her share of mistakes. Most of all he would remember that she loved him and wanted him back. She almost went directly to Trap's apartment and tried to talk to him. But she had promised to have a talk with Riley. She picked up dinner and turned for home.

Riley and Caro were waiting for her. René and Riley sat at the kitchen table and ate in silence. Finally Riley spoke up.

"Mom, we've got to reunite the Blue Angels. Everybody feels terrible and we can't let our soccer team fall apart. Reuben wouldn't have been happy at all over this breakup. We've got to think of a way. They're too good of a team and they stand for something greater than themselves. They meant something the whole world is trying to accomplish: learning how people who are very different can work together. We've got to stop this!"

René thought for a minute. She wanted to cry for her love of her extremely bright son.

But René was tired of crying. She didn't care what the doctor said. She was sick of it. It seemed like it was all she did anymore. She got up and paced across the living room. She looked out the windows at the Cascadia landscape and nodded her head to Riley.

"Why don't we take Caro for her walk. Anybody trying to stop us will get cross examined by Caro."

The three of them headed up the hill. Lester crept out between the shrubs and folded his arms while watching René. He started to speak when René cut him off.

"You want some more German, Lester?" she said. Then she noticed he was bleeding. She also noticed Lester's eyes were strange. They were blue and oversized. His pupils were so contracted it looked like there was no pupil at all: just an empty splash of blue. René jumped back and the sudden movement put Caro on guard. She let out a single loud bark and pointed her snout at Lester. Caro could smell what René could see. Lester was drugged.

Caro crouched. She could also smell the human sweat that just knocked on the trailer door. She could smell the stench of whiskey, and the aroma of blood. She looked up at René seemingly to ask if she should rip this guy apart. Caro held her eyes on Lester. He didn't say a word as René walked away.

René turned to Riley. This was about the tenth day of stifling heat. René was remarkably calm with this protective dog at her side. So long as Caro was around, no one could touch her. She headed back to the trailer and sat down with Riley.

"Okay Riley, let's write a letter. I'll get the name and address of everybody on the team. I want you to draft it and I'll look it over. Write a letter to lobby the whole team to reunite. Propose a meeting. Players only."

CHAPTER 25

June 11th, 1998

Olympia, Cascadia

Trap hardly slept the next night. He only dozed a little in that area which is neither sleep nor wake. The morning was already heating up. Trap spent the night lying on his bed on top of his sheets. He made up some coffee and English muffins and sat on his couch in his underwear. He crossed his legs and closed his eyes, taking even breaths. He wondered how all this could have happened. René's deceit burned in his stomach. What else did she lie to him about? Did she really love him or did she just sweep him off his feet like she had done to a dozen other guys she was not telling him about? How could such a beauty not go out on a date for so many years? She may have been telling him just what he wanted to hear for these few months. That way she could get him into bed only to finish it by ripping his heart out. Maybe she just plain hated men because of her case of PTSD.

Trap was going to be late for work and he hurried to his van. In the 20 minutes it took to drive to work he realized something. He was not being true to his rule.

*If you want to know how somebody feels, you have to ask them or you will get it wrong every time.*

*Your damn sure I will,* he chided himself. He realized he had to talk to her to get the answers right. But maybe he would wait a while. Maybe she would just tell him some more goddamn lies. Maybe he would just give it a few days. Maybe he would wait a few weeks. But what about this anger management monster, her ex-husband? What if he got to her despite the restraining order? What if that ice man managed to get to her even though she had Caro, who despite her shallow hip joints was one tough K9?

Trap made it to work in time and was asked to assist the Bloods Creek fish hatchery in driving the fish tank truck. The truck and driver would be needed to transport young salmon to the Willow Creek Rearing Pond run by the 'Fins For All' volunteer group. Trap was a bit reluctant at first because he was tired and feeling unlucky. He hadn't slept much in two days and those trucks full of 400 gallons of water could be hard to handle. Trap didn't like those fish hauling tankers at all. The rigs were very flawed in their design. There was no insulation on the top and sides so the water in the tanks would warm easily on a hot day. Also the lids did not latch down making the hatchway rattle in the wind and flop open on a large bump or rut in the road. And the flatbed trucks being used were not designed for such weight. Large payloads tended to be top heavy, making the trucks unstable and at risk for rolling. Occasionally wheel bearings and studs on the drums would break and an entire wheel would come off, rolling down the highway completely out of control.

The old veteran Tom Cameron was working with Trap for the day. The heat wave continued and Trap considered telling the boss it was too hot to haul fish, but he thought better of it at the last minute. They headed out.

The pavement was so hot on the freeway it was as if the rubber tires on the tanker would melt into the roadway. On this day the breeze coming from the north smelled of smoke. For a hot sunny day the visibility was poor, terrible in fact. Trap asked Tom to drive, saying he was not up to par today, but he didn't say why. He was just as foggy as the day was thick with smoke. Trap looked down at the floorboards.

"Let me guess," said Tom. "I would have to say woman trouble from the pathetic look on your face."

Trap looked over at Tom and turned his head staring out the window.

"Yeah, lucky guess," said Trap.

"Is it that beauty you had in the office on a volunteer trip a while back? You didn't goof it up with her did you? Why she makes most people look plain. How could you screw that up?"

"Oh, she hasn't been truthful with me," said Trap.

"She's been cheating?"

"No, lying. Tom, I don't want to talk about it right now. Maybe we'll talk some other day when I'm feeling better. Right now I feel like hell," said Trap. "Let's just get these fish hauled."

Down at Bloods Creek Hatchery they took on 400 gallons of cool water, 5 pounds of salt, and 25,000 coho salmon who had reached a great weight of 500 fish to the pound. As they loaded up the sun grew hotter. Trap was losing confidence in the success of the trip. He took the wheel and inched the truck into compound low. He slowly climbed the access road from Bloods Creek and was on the way up river to the 'Fins For All' ponds.

At last they made it up to the main highway in the old flatbed. Trap could hear water sloshing only a few feet from his head. It made him worry about his load as the truck's leaf springs squealed under the heavy load. Once underway the truck settled down and began gaining speed, cruising just under the speed limit. Wary of the hot sun, Trap pulled over to check the tank after only a few miles. He climbed up and opened the hatch to examine the fish. A light color on the backs of the little fry meant stressed out fish. So far they were looking okay.

Trap took the water temperature and it had climbed by 3° Fahrenheit. Warm water means low dissolved oxygen, so Trap knew he was in a race against time. He climbed into the cab and pushed the truck harder. A mile up the road Trap pulled off at a little quick stop where he bought four bags of party ice and added them to the tank. Trap jerked the truck into oncoming traffic but he had to wait for a diesel truck and lowboy filled with hay. The driver must have stacked 300 bails of hay on his machine about eight rows high. Trap pulled the tanker up behind the hay truck. It was slow and wide. Trap was having trouble spotting a place to pass, and he wasn't sure he had the power to pass with the tanker fully loaded, so he just followed behind. The hay truck was weaving in its lane, as if the driver was having trouble controlling his load.

It may have been a sudden gust of wind, a rut in the road, an unlikely acceleration, or a poorly secured load, but suddenly, a quarter of the stack of hay came off the truck ahead, spilling on the roadway like a big yellow avalanche. The bales flew into the air, skidding and tumbling across the pavement.

Tom bellowed, "for Christ's sake look out! Hit them, go ahead and hit them!"

Some bales were still airborne when the truck slammed into them. A few went over the cab, some went under the truck, and some collided with the front grill. Trap tried to keep braking and hit the bails head on, hopefully to knock them out of the way. The tank truck rammed into the tumbling pile of bales as Trap and Tom both covered their eyes with their forearms. The cab of the truck lifted upwards on impact, the front tires three feet off the road. Then the rear wheels bucked up high in the air and the hatch flew open. Most of the water and fish came over the top of the cab. Salty water, salmon, and hay slid down the front windshield, spilling over the hood and splashing on the pavement. The hay truck slowed to a stop and two men stepped out looking like ranch hands. They spoke briefly to each other and got back in the truck, leaving the accident.

Tom put his hands to his mouth to make his shouting heard. "You lowlife wetbacks, stop that thing before your whole load comes off!"

Trap cursed his filthy luck. To top it off, he got another little taste of bigotry. It was as if everything—every branch of his life—was caving in on him. Most of the fish were dying on the scorching road mixed with sheeting water and many broken bails of hay. In desperation, Trap and Tom tried to gather up the struggling fish. Both men looked at each other and knew it was hopeless. About 20,000 baby coho salmon were sprawled on the scorching road and would certainly die in the next few minutes. There wasn't a thing they could do about it. In the interest of public relations they headed back to Bloods Creek with the few remaining fish they still had on board. The day was shot.

When Trap arrived back at his apartment, disgusted with the day, he flopped on his bed, face down, and just as quickly rolled over on his back, staring at the ceiling. Finally, exhaustion took over and Trap drifted off into a troubled sleep.

He got in a couple hours' rest when the phone jerked him awake. It was Bruce Hills.

\* \* \*

Riley sat down at the dining room table. René sat beside him. Her face was pasty white despite the relentlessly hot and sunny days. Her hands were shaking. She spoke in a weak whisper, her breath short and abrupt. She tried to mouth a sentence. Riley looked hard at his mom and leaned over to her, hugging her around her neck.

"Come on, mom, it's going to be okay. Trap is head over heels about you. I never told you this but I gave him a list of things he could do to impress you. You know he did every one of them, from the snorkel survey to the handmade necklaces. I know I'm only a 14 year old kid, but sometimes I see things. Trap isn't going to leave, count on it. Remember what coach Reuben used to say: when you get knocked down you, get back up and keep fighting."

René stared blankly out the window. She was gazing at all the birds.

"What? Did… did you say something, Riley?" She turned her head slowly in his direction. "Sorry, I just went blank for a second. I can't stop thinking about it. I mean, my father and my husband did this to me."

"You're getting better. I can see it, in spite of your miserable scowl."

René tried to smile. Riley put his finger on the blank sheet of paper sitting on the table.

"Listen sourpuss, I'm going to write a letter to the Blue Angels. I'm going to get this team alive again." René was blinking rapidly. She seemed completely preoccupied.

Like Riley always did, he sniffed and looked up at the ceiling. He shook his head, looked down at his paper and pencil, and started writing.

228

*To all the Blue Angels:*

*I am writing this letter to all of you. You alone: not the parents, not the fans, not even the coaches. A dark cloud is hanging over us. We have lost our coach and we seem to have lost ourselves. Our team is in terrible shape! The amazingly tough and tricky Blue Angels are on the ground. We are belly up and ready for defeat. I can hear our coach saying the same words over and over. When you get knocked down you get back up and you get up right now. There's no time to feel bad, not a spare second. I propose we stop this useless sulking, organize this team, and keep fighting. Reuben would not have it any other way. He would have us running laps until we go to our knees. He would not have us die with him.*

*I propose a players meeting. South Bay Firehouse, next Monday 6/15 at 6. Just us.*

René read Riley's note, nodded, and started organizing addresses and envelopes. They had the letters finished and mailed within an hour.

*       *       *

Exhausted though he was, Trap spoke to Bruce.

"Hello Trap, this is Bruce Hills, the guy you met down at the port a few days back. Remember you asked me to give you a call? Something important?"

"Oh yeah, hello Bruce. Yeah, let's see. Could you hold on a minute?"

Trap stepped into the bathroom and ran a wet towel over his face, trying to wake up.

"Yeah, hello Bruce. You're the guy who tangled with Wade Bode on a tuna boat out of San Diego.

"I'm trying to forget it. Why bring that up now?" asked Bruce.

"Well this might amaze you, but his ex-wife is my girlfriend, or at least she was." Trap ran his hand over the back of his neck. He felt chills over his back. "Not only that, but we believe Wade Bode is here in Olympia."

"Wade Bode is here? What the hell is he doing here?"

"He is an old friend of the late Reuben Sanchez, coach of our soccer team, the Blue Angels. I'm the assistant coach and the team has all but fallen apart since Reuben died. You used to play soccer, didn't you Bruce? Boy could I use you to help coach the Blue Angels."

"Well Trap, I got laid off at work—temporary appointment. I really was calling you for job leads."

"I'll see what I can find out... what do you say, Bruce? Have you got time to do a little coaching? It's all after 6:00 except the northwest regional tournament, and that's all a weekend affair."

"Yeah, okay Trap, I'll give it a go. What the hell, I've got some time on my hands. Where do I meet you?"

"Well that's a hard one for now. Like I say the team has all but fallen apart. I'll have to let you know."

Trap smiled as he hung up. Finally something was going right. The Blue Angels had a chance.

Almost immediately the phone rang again. Trap stiffened. Maybe it was René? No, it was Riley.

"Hello, Trap." There was an awkward silence as Riley tried to compose himself. "Trap, I just wanted to tell you the Blue Angels aren't quite dead yet. I arranged a players meeting. Just the players. I'll call you when we get sorted out."

"Well I'm glad you called," Trap exhaled a breath of relief. "I just found a soccer player who is willing to help me coach the team. Tell that to the players in your meeting. It might light a fire under them. Call me back when you decide what to do."

There was another long awkward silence. Trap's face grew tight. He was trying to find the right words. Something told him to keep his mouth shut, but he brushed the thought aside.

"Riley, how's your mom doing?"

Riley inhaled a weary breath, blowing air out his nose. Another silence came.

"Well, I… I guess she isn't doing well at all. She seems to be slipping back to her old PTSD patterns. She can't seem to concentrate on anything. She's stuttering, and when I try to bring up a conversation she just stares out the window. It would be great if you could stop by and talk to her."

"Well, we'll see. Is she working much?"

"No. All she does is shake and twitch around the house. She's at the gym a lot these days."

"Hey Riley, I need some rest. I'll talk to you after the meeting," said Trap.

"Hey Trap, don't you want to talk to my mom?"

"Probably better if I don't for now… see you, Riley."

Trap nearly went to bed, although it was only about 9:00. Instead he decided to go for a walk. He peered out his apartment window and saw it was still light outside so he stepped out into the evening. The sun was set and the air was beginning to cool down. He went over to the high school track adjacent to his apartment building, and started to walk the rubberized asphalt, but was soon running. The heat was still pretty formidable and after 12 laps he was laboring for air. He sat down on the bleachers, putting his elbows on his knees and his hands on his forehead. All he could think about was René. Just watching her made his stomach dance with butterflies. Although still feeling somewhat down, he felt better after the run. He walked home and finally slept hard the whole night.

A few days passed. The 15th of June rolled around, the day for the players meeting. At 6:00 pm, virtually all of the Blue Angels walked into the meeting room at South Bay Firehouse. They looked a bit different to the parents without their soccer uniforms. The parents flooded the parking lot, gathering in small groups among their parked cars and talking amongst themselves. Meanwhile the team collectively seemed to carry a feeling of shame and silence. For the first time since the team fell to pieces, the Blue Angels looked at each other. Many went to staring at the floor looking like the team was history. Riley finally walked up to the front of the room and cleared his throat. He had a bad feeling, and spoke slowly.

"Okay," he rubbed his face with his hands. "We have to decide today, right now, in this room. One more forfeit and we're disqualified from the league. That's the rule. One more. Most of you have quit coming to practice. Here's the team. Over there is the field. I swear I don't know what you want to do. You're going to have to help me. Speak up."

"The team is dead," said Gabriel. "Nobody wants to play any more. Why beat a dead horse?"

"The team is dead because the coach is dead," said Willis. "He was the leader of the team. Trap knows the game better, but Reuben was the heart of the team. He made me want to try. Now I don't care!"

Babar spoke up. "I don't feel like playing either. But I know I won't always feel this way, and I know what Reuben would want us to do."

"Reuben doesn't want anything. He died!" said JR.

"Yeah, but he's watching us," said Deshaun. "I can feel him watching. His eyes are on me and I can feel him telling me to run laps until my head is right. You're his godson, Gabriel! I don't know where Reuben is but I think I know what he would say right now."

Kyle spoke up. "Look, we're just a bunch of 14 year old kids. What about when we grow up? Are we going to look back happy, or are we going to remember when we were wimps? You know we stand for something. We are Blue Angels. We were dominating the league. Why do you think the crowds were so big? People were being taught a lesson! You don't have to be the same race to be a kick ass team. In fact it's better if you're not!"

Riley spoke up again. "By the way I should point this out. Trap has found a new coach, and he's a for real soccer player. He's willing to help us get back on our feet."

Some of the parents were close enough to the door of the meeting room to hear. The kids remarks sounded rather cliché to them, but that wasn't so for the kids. It was just what they needed to hear to clear the brain fog that comes when young kids have a grown up problem.

Babar spoke again. "What if Reuben was right here, right now? He's right over there standing in the corner! Can't you see him? What would he say?" Babar kicked the chair in front of him. Deshaun jumped at the sound of a chair falling across the room. He grabbed Babar by the arm. Babar put his hand on Deshaun's chest and shoved. Babar made a fist, but then relaxed a bit, remembering his poise.

"Remember, this is just the beginning for us. If we quit now where are we going to end up? Some of us have the potential to be pro soccer players. Where are we going to finish? Here, crying like babies? This is just a start and we are a good team! Do you understand me? This is just the start!"

An early summer west wind suddenly picked up, bringing with it dust and cooler ocean air. It slightly bent the alder and fir next to the firehouse. A few alder leaves tumbled across the street towards the meeting room. It blew the door shut with a loud slam. Jaylen, Deshaun's father, opened the door and stuck his head in the room.

"We want you back!" he shouted in his usual husky voice.

The kids looked at each other.

"Let's take a team picture," said Riley.

Outside Caro was panting in the summer heat. She turned her face into the wind.

\*   \*   \*

By Tuesday night the heat wave was nearly over. The temperature dipped into the mid seventies for the coming game. The gentle breeze kept coming in from the west, particularly in the evenings.

After the meeting Riley called Trap and told him the good news. The Blue Angels were back on their feet. Trap subsequently called Bruce and told him the time and place for the next practice. Trap had enjoyed his run over at the high school track. After he hung up he got into his shorts and went over to do it again. It was a good distraction from constantly thinking about René. He kept seeing her face and the dimness in her smile. Trap knew she was on the road to recovery when he walked out on her. *What are you some kind of self righteous jerk?* he thought to himself. *Has the great Stream Walker ever told a lie? Come on Trap. What is this high and mighty self image all about? Come down, man. You lie to landowners all the time to get access to the creek you need to look at. She was just exaggerating her job because she didn't want to tell you she earned money from her good looks.*

Trap went home and picked up the phone.

"Hi René, this is Trap." There was a long pause.

Back at the trailer a flock of crows were sounding off in the woods to the north. Caro listened to the sound of the birds, her head and ears erect. She lowered her head and began to growl.

"Trap, there's somebody in the front yard! Get over here!"

René put Caro on the leash. She wrapped Caro's leash twice around her hand and gave a quick glance at the baseball bat leaning on the wall next to the door. Her hands were trembling. She could see the black shadow of a man in the front yard.

Riley called to his mom from the other room. René slowly opened the door. The night was still, just a few crows not yet bedded down and a gentle lapping of the waves.

"Who are you?" René yelled at the man. "What are you doing on my property? Is it Wade?"

"You've lost weight," said the man quietly. "You turned out really well, didn't you?"

"Wade, I'm gonna let this dog tear you apart if you don't leave right now!"

"Ever seen a dog fight a man with a club, Libby?"

"My name is René!"

"And I'm bugs bunny!" The man held a wooden club in his right hand: the kind tuna fishermen use. He pulled a flashlight out of his coat and shined it right in René's face.

"Just checking," He said. Then he shined the light into Caro's face. Wade took a step forward looking at the yellow in the dog's eyes. Caro was showing her teeth, her lips pulled back.

René yelled to Caro. "*Voran*, Caro, *Voran*!"

Caro jerked at her leash, and let out a vicious series of growls and snarls. Her leash was tight and she was ready.

Two headlights appeared on the crest of the hill as Riley stepped out on the front porch.

"Well hello, Morten. Long time no see," said a voice from the black silhouette of a big man.

"You're Wade aren't you? W—Wade Bode! My bastard father! You're the one that screwed her head up! You know there's a restraining order against you! You can't come within shouting distance of my mother!"

"But here I am. I turned the order into hamster bedding a long time ago. Some of it I used for cat litter. Have you got another copy? I'd love to shut that dog up!"

Caro seemed to understand the threat in the man's voice. She hackled, the hairs on her back growing stiff. She crouched and let out another snarl.

"Riley! You back off! Go inside and call 911."

Riley stepped in the front door and turned on the outdoor floodlight. He looked for the phone, but it was missing.

The floodlight lit up the front lawn, drowning out the headlights of the car coming down the hill.

René and Wade looked at each other. Wade was silently waiting.

"Well now look at you, and look at that body, and those hooters; you're a real man-killer aren't you? I can't wait to get my hands on you! You'll be coming with me now. Looks like I'll have to put you back home where I left you. You're my wife! Do you need a leash of your own!" Wade pulled some snap ties out of his back pocket.

"Stay back you wife beater, you damned monster! I see your knuckles healed up just fine! I remember my teeth on your fists, Wade. Well I still have every one of them! All you've got for your trouble is scar tissue on your fingers!"

A voice came from inside the trailer.

"Mom, the phone is gone!"

Wade tightened his hands, breaking the phone, looking sinister. He took two steps towards René.

"*Voran!*" shouted René again and Wade stopped in his tracks. Caro flattened her ears, continuing to snarl. Caro looked menacing.

"Take one more step, Wade, just one more."

Wade did not hesitate, as if he wanted to fight the dog.

"Caro, *fass!*"

She was on him in two great bounds. The dog locked her fangs on Wade's mid calf and let her grip slide down to his ankle. Wade kicked his other leg high in the air trying to keep his balance. He fell on his back and put both hands on the ground, trying to get up. Caro saw the club in Wade's right hand. She released her grip on Wade's ankle, went for his right wrist, and locked on, shaking and tearing. Unable to swing the club, Wade clenched his teeth. Caro could feel the man's strength, and she pulled back hard on his arm, nearly dragging the struggling man. Dirt, grass trimmings, and rotten leaves flew into the air over the fight, making it hard for René to see. Still snarling, Caro viciously shook her head and Wade screamed in pain. Caro was enraged and she gave Wade loud menacing snarls beyond anything he had yet heard. Caro was all over him. The headlights were down the hill, approaching the driveway. Hoping to get the tuna club in his left hand, Wade rolled over on his side and reached it. Caro's head was right in the way so he pounded his left fist at her neck and head. After struggling to get to his feet he looked down at her. Caro held on to his wrist. Her grip slipped to his open palm and she sunk her teeth deeply into Wade's hand. Caro was furious. He dropped the club and Caro bit down harder. The man again screamed in pain as he raised his right arm, nearly lifting the dog off the ground. René saw the club fall to the ground. It looked like she might be able to get to it. After a moment's hesitation she sprinted across the lawn grabbing desperately for the club. Wade lifted the dog and slammed Caro into René's arms as she reached out. Wade beat her to the weapon with his left hand. René grabbed his face, shoving her thumbs deeply into his eye sockets. He reached up with the club, attempting to knock René's hands out of his eyes. Seeing her chance, René kicked Wade in the groin as hard as she could. Wade groaned in pain and went down on all fours, his forehead on the grass as he gaged several times. Caro would not let him go. She pulled back and jerked Wade's arm out from under him. He got to his knees again using only his left hand. From a kneeling position he took a viscous swing at Caro. He missed his mark but caught the dog with a sharp blow to her hindquarters. Caro let out a sharp yelp between her teeth, but would not let him go.

"Let go of me, you rabid beast!" he shrieked. Caro snarled back at him, closing her fangs.

Wade began wheezing now, overweight and out of shape. A loud voice came from the head of the walkway.

"All right, hold on here!"

Wade paused as Trap ran down the walkway and onto the lawn.

"Riley, call 911!"

"He got the phone!" yelled Riley.

"Go to Lester's! Riley Go!" yelled René

"René, call off Caro!" yelled Trap.

But Wade was standing now and he rifled his club at Caro's head. The blow landed behind her ears, right on the back of her neck. Caro fell back on her side, her body jerking in convulsions.

Trap got between René and Wade. He turned to Wade and looked him in the eyes.

"So, you're the one that beat her when she was with a child! You're the slob that wrecked her life! The police never saw that beating did they?" Trap pulled off his own T-shirt, throwing it aside.

"Okay mister boyfriend," said Wade, "Buddy you want some bare chested, bare knuckles, huh?"

Wade reached down to pull off his sweatshirt. At that moment Trap smashed his right fist into Wade's face. Wade staggered back and rolled his lips. He dropped his club.

"Hey man, I waited for you!"

"That's big of you, Wade!" Trap let his right fly again, landing it on Wade's left eye. Wade knew if he pulled his shirt over his head he would take a flurry of punches. Trap drew back he knew he had Wade hurt and Wade went down on one knee. Trap did not want to wrestle him. That would give Wade a size advantage and a chance at some kind of hold. Trap stepped back and bounced on his arches.

"Get up, you slob!" yelled Trap.

Wade charged and the two men started swinging. With blood on his right hand and on his face, Wade was like a cornered animal. His eyes bulged with rage. Trap delivered several hooks with his left and right hands, catching Wade on the temples and forehead. Wade kept coming, and landed an overhead right between Trap's eyes. Trap's mind went numb and he started to go down, but Wade's shoulder plowed into Trap's waist, holding him up. Trap gritted his teeth as Wade delivered two well-placed shots to his face. Dazed, Trap was having trouble staying on his feet. Trap grunted as the big man slammed onto him, driving him against the side of the trailer. Then Wade closed his hands around Trap's lower back and squeezed. With Wade crushing his ribs, Trap was helpless. He couldn't breathe. Holding him off the ground, Wade dug his chin into Trap's chest and squeezed. Trap felt the crushing strength of the man's bear hug. Trap knew he had little time before Wade had him unconscious.

With both hands free, Trap locked his middle and index finger together. With his left hand he grabbed the back of Wade's head and forced it forward. Trap forced his two fingers into Wade's left eye socket and pushed. Wade shrieked with pain and released his bear hug, trying to save his eye.

René was standing about two yards from the two struggling men, screaming. She stepped up to Wade and with all her might smashed her body against his. Fourteen years of rage was coming to the surface in René. She let out a low-pitched scream and kicked at his groin again, but did not make solid contact. René then remembered a defensive move she had just been taught and rushed Wade, going for his knee. She stepped forward and jumped, her body sideways. She slammed her foot into Wade's left knee with all her body weight. She listened for the cracking sound of a dislocated knee, but she missed and no sound came. She had hit him in the lower thigh. Though she missed her target, the kick knocked him down. Trap gained his footing, and shaking his head moved quickly from the trailer out to the center of the lawn. Again he danced on his arches. Wade lumbered in Trap's direction. Trap had a look in his eyes that René had never seen before. He looked like an animal.

"Come on, you slob! Come on!"

As Wade approached Trap he took a roundhouse swing at Trap's head. Trap ducked under it and went for Wade's abdomen, landing several uppercuts in his stomach. Then he came to Wade's face with a wicked cross, landing it square on his chin. Wade went over on his back again, hitting the ground hard. Trap's eyes grew more savage as he tightened his fists. He grabbed Wade's sweatshirt with his left hand and lifted him partly off the ground. Trap would not let him up, but rather started peppering him with his right. Wade was neither down nor up. He was stuck in the middle where Trap held him. But Wade used his strength to get both hands around Trap's neck. Then Wade heaved Trap off him. Pouncing on top of Trap, he locked his hands around Trap's chest, his face at the small of Trap's back. Facing in the opposite direction, Wade now had Trap face-down on the grass, Wade's belly on top of the back of his head. His legs spread wide, Wade squeezed, letting his weight force Trap's face into the grass. Trap tried to yell, but almost no sound came as his face sank deeper into the turf. Trap could not move. He tried to move his legs, but Wade just squeezed harder. Trap was choking, gaging, not getting enough air.

"Eat dirt, boyfriend, eat dirt!" Wade growled as he squeezed harder. Face down, Trap was unable to move and his mind went blank.

René looked at the two struggling men and crouched, her chest and biceps like knots. She had seen enough. She moved from side to side, unsure how to attack. Then a racing thought swept through her mind. She heard Trap yelling on the soccer field over and over again, trying to drive the idea home. *Kick it with your laces!* She took a few running steps backwards and pointed her toe at the ground. She kicked so hard the air whistled past her leg, and she didn't miss.

She connected with the side of Wade's head. He rolled off of Trap and came to all fours, but she had landed her foot so hard he just stayed put, looking lost and semi-conscious.

Trap did not move. For the moment, neither of the men moved. René ran at Wade with her fists clenched. Wade finally made it to his feet but was exhausted. René exploded. Not only was she extremely strong, she had learned to fight. She move close enough for a jab. Wade grabbed her shirt. In a split second he ripped off her entire shirt and threw it at her. René staggered back. Her abdomen was hard and rippled. Without hesitation, she regained her balance. She put her left wrist in front of Wade's face without striking him. Just like she wanted, he grabbed her wrist with his right hand. René rifled her flattened hand into Wade's nose, then quickly grabbed his index finger and twisted her forearm hard. René screamed and Wade's finger snapped. Wade bellowed with pain and looked at his broken finger. She saw his eyes shift to his hand and she brought up her knee.

Two more headlights topped the hill and stopped at Riley's waving hands.

René walked over next to Trap who was still down. To René, Wade looked just like the heavy bag from the self-defense studio. Using her strong arms she started in on him, landing blows to his stomach and ribs. Wade was on his feet, staggering.

"Soooo. I've got to fight both of y—"

René cut his sentence short with a strong uppercut to his chin. He staggered back, slipping and falling again. Though Wade was exhausted and gasping for breath, he managed to get to his feet. She didn't want to get her bat, or pepper spray, or use some fancy ear pop. She wanted to use her fists. She danced forward while her right leg slid back. She jabbed twice, snapping Wade's head back. Wade answered with a clumsy sluggish swing she easily ducked under. René jabbed again and followed with a quick combination. Wade didn't respond so she rifled another combination followed by her hardest left hook.

Wade was hurt. Seeing this, René moved in and screamed with anger.
Her back gleaming with sweat and muscle and she used uppercuts
jarring his head back. "Swallow your teeth, slob!" She hit him with
every punch she had, yelling with every swing of her fists.  Wade was
exhausted and went down. René jumped on his head, locking her
thighs around is neck and squeezing hard.With Wade on the ground
nearly unconscious, René cried out again and continued to pound on
Wade with all she had left.  Fourteen angry years was still there.
Shaking his head Trap coughed and gaged but came to his senses. He
staggered to his feet and lumbered across the lawn away from both of
them. He reached in the drawer by the trailer door where René kept the
pepper spray. Returning, he also grabbed Riley's bat. Trap ran the
pepper spray across Wade's eyes and gripped the bat. Wade screamed
again, covering his eyes with his hands. Rene took some pepper spray
in her face but kept swinging her fists somewhere between rage and a
burning in her eyes. "Don't move, Wade, just don't move a damn
muscle or I'll crack your skull!" slurred Trap, holding the baseball bat
over his head.

The county Sheriff's patrol car pulled up next to Trap's van.

René hurried over where Caro was laying on her side. She put her
hand on the dog's shoulder. Caro was laying still, her convulsions gone
except for a twitching in her lower legs. Growing still, Caro was
dying.

Two sheriff's deputies emerged from the car and ran down to the
front lawn. After forcing the three of them apart, the deputies got
control of each of them. Wade was still gasping for air, his hands over
his eyes.

The two deputies quickly got things under control. Before long
they had Wade in cuffs, forcing him into the squad car. The deputies
made it clear to Trap that he would be asked to come to the station and
issue a written statement. That would take place in a day or two.

CHAPTER 26

June 16th, 1998

Olympia, Cascadia

Wade's club must have caught Caro right in the back of her neck, snapping her spine just below her head. René buried her face near Caro's collar and ran her hand through the top of the dog's head between the ears. She was still warm, her limbs still loose and flexible. René had never had a living thing give its life to protect her, and she sat on the lawn with her hand on the dog, sobbing. Trap could barely walk, and shaking his head went into the trailer. He brought out a sheet. He limped over and knelt at René's side, placing his hand on the dog's ribcage, hoping in vain that he might detect a heartbeat. Caro remained still, her eyes empty and lost. He wrapped Caro in the sheet, leaving her head exposed.

"Let's let her rest here with this sheet around her," said Trap. "Let's leave her face out in the sun for a day or two, while we somehow learn to accept her death. Let's not put her in the ground for a while." Both of them were choking back tears.

René and Trap slid the dog over to a spot on the porch.

Trap looked down at Caro. "Goddamn it anyway!"

Riley made it back from Lester's place. He appeared in the walkway and just as quickly disappeared into the trailer. Instead of coming outside he knelt on the couch, staring out over the water. Riley was having a whole lot of trouble going over and looking at Caro. Her body was so still. He knew he had to go look at the dog. Very slowly, Riley went across the porch and eased over by Caro's body. His throat strained into a lump and his face grew tight. In his youthful wisdom, he forced out a few words.

"Something happens between a human and a dog. Caro was special. She got into my heart more than I would've thought, all in a very short time. Caro was a smart dog and I'll bet she knew when she attacked that big man that she may lose her life. Still, she went after him... to save us."

Riley turned his head away, unable to say another word. A long silence lingered over the yard as clouds passed in front of the sun. No one spoke for many minutes.

René felt devastated. But something inside her had changed; part of her troubled soul came out into the light. René had never cried so hard and so long, but after her tears, and mixed with her grief for Caro, a strange calm crept across her shoulders and rested in the back of her neck. Her whole body was shaking, but she looked up at Trap for a long while before she hung her head. Trap's stomach was a yawning hole as he looked down at Caro, his eyes wet.

"We fought him, didn't we Caro?" said René. "One of the two men who worked me over just took a terrific beating." Her voice was steady. It was as if a door had opened inside René as she looked down at the dog.

Trap looked down at his hands. Both of his fists were sore and beginning to swell. Trap turned his trembling hands over, looking at his palms. "He had it coming. Wait until the authorities get this straightened out. I can see his rap sheet looking really bad. You know something René, I don't think we'll ever see him again."

René's forehead wrinkled as she looked down at Caro. She spoke so quietly she could not be heard.

"I'll never forget you, Caro."

René stood erect, facing Trap. She put her hands on Trap's chest, her eyes pleading.

"Trap, please forgive me for not being honest with you."

Trap looked at René with great empathy, but he was unsure of himself and didn't say a word.

Wade was taken to the County Sheriff's office and placed behind bars. He was in a lot of trouble. The following morning Trap stopped by the Sheriff's office and gave the deputies a statement. Wade was booked on four charges: violation of parole, violation of restraining order, felony animal cruelty in the first degree, and felony assault with a deadly weapon.

On that day, René started to change.

*   *   *

Trap's face was badly bruised. He was full of grief for Caro, and full of confusion about René. He tried hard to pull himself together for soccer. Bruce arrived, and he looked hard at Trap. With a serious look on his face, he said nothing in front of the team. Trap explained to his team the bruises on his face and hands. He let them know that he'd struggled with an attacker, and that René's dog was killed while protecting her from a violent intruder at her home. Trap stood in front of his team, refusing to give up. The soccer players were also silent, staring at Trap earnestly.

It was Wednesday evening, the first day of practice since the team had agreed to reunite. Almost immediately Trap noticed that Bruce had a set of skills which he lacked. Trap was outstanding at talking to the players, and he could motivate them by making them proud of themselves. But Bruce had amazing footwork. Effective as Trap was at coaching, he was still no soccer player. In that respect, Bruce and Trap made a good match. It was the difference between them that made them a powerful pair.

Before long Bruce had them doing a series of rolls, drags, step-overs, and fakes. The players loved the fancy footwork and took to it without delay. The team was still understandably low in morale. But this was something new, something that had a refreshing quality. It got the team moving forward again, knowing they were still the team to beat—still undefeated despite the forfeit they took in their last game. The next game was tomorrow, June 18th. They practiced hard, getting ready to compete.

Trap looked over along the sidelines and watched the wind singing through the row of cottonwood trees that separated the two soccer fields. June in Cascadia is an odd month. It could be bitter cold or

244

sweltering hot. It could be peppered with heavy rain or hale, and the wind could blow like a storm in November. Just as often, it could be the most perfect day of the year. The cottonwoods were extremely tall and bent gracefully in the wind. Trap could hear flickers and mocking birds sounding off in the tree branches. He looked down and saw René standing in the breeze. Wearing tight levis and thongs, she tried to hold down her hair and shifted her hips against the wind. Gabriel ran up to René and told her he and the kids on the team were sorry she lost her dog. She thanked Gabriel, looked at Riley, and nodded her head in gratitude.

"Well Gabriel," she said, "Caro was like a Blue Angel; she wouldn't go down easy."

Trap just shook his head. She was still grieving for Caro and her face had a weary look, but Trap instinctively knew she would get through this. She seemed so sad, Trap had to look the other way. He pressed his thumb and forefinger on the bridge of his nose and held his breath for a moment while he shared her grief. Her face was as dim as Trap had ever seen. Despite her lean muscular body, she looked completely vulnerable. Trap locked eyes with René and she gave him a little fist pump in return. They held each other's gaze for a few seconds.

Bruce had more tricky soccer up his sleeve for the team. He was showing the Angels many more moves including foot curls, outside the foot pass, side scissor kick, and the dangerous diving header. Momentum was building rapidly for the Blue Angels as Bruce helped fine-tune their skills. Trap could see that the relentless attack soccer they were so well known for was still alive.

The late afternoon wind was picking up. Cottonwood seedlings were lifted off the bending trees, tumbling through the air and across the soccer field. They looked like flakes of snow in the summer heat. The team practiced an hour later than usual. Tomorrow was the big game. They would face Benders West as the last games of the regular season were in front of them. Trap knew Benders West was a really tough team.

After practice René walked over to Trap. She was watching every move he made.

"Thanks for helping me out last night. You really saved me. If he had gotten hold of me I don't know what he would have done. Thanks Trap, from the bottom of my heart. Say, could you loan me a quarter?" she smiled on one side of her face.

"Sorry, I got no quarters," said Trap. Then he reached into his pocket and pulled out a shiny half dollar, putting it in René's hand and closing her fingers over it.

"You've got some bruises on your face," he said.

"Yeah well, I got in a fight. How are your hands doing?"

"Well, I got in a fight too. Next time I'll wear some gloves. They're a bit swollen."

René turned her head into the wind, her long brown hair blowing straight back. She changed the subject. "You know something Trap, I was planning on taking the GED. I'll need somebody to help me study. You would be my first choice." She regarded Trap seriously. He paused for a few seconds, looking at the ground.

"Well, it's gonna cost you some corned beef and cabbage."

The next morning Trap decided to stay in the office, editing his stream surveys and going through a pile of interoffice memorandums sitting in his in-basket. One in particular caught his attention. It called for a unit all hands meeting on Friday to discuss three letters sent to Hughes Associates requesting better employment opportunities for minorities. Trap shifted in his chair and read the memo again. He had an idea.

Benders West players were already warming up when Trap arrived at the soccer field. Some of the players were lean, big kids, looking more like fifteen year olds. Word had it some of the players on Benders West were select team players organized to wreak havoc down in the recreation league. Putting a select team in the rec league was usually like matching up a welterweight with a heavyweight. One thing the Blue Angels didn't have was the vast experience of a select team. Then again, Benders West had never seen the likes of the Blue

Angels. Chances are they were in for a surprise. Benders were big. A couple of kids on the Blue Angels team were big, but a little overweight. The main weaponry of the Blue Angels was small and quick. Soccer is sometimes called the little man's sport. Trap said to Bruce that he thought the game was going to be real interesting. Ordinarily Trap would play a team like the Benders with the strongest possible defense. Instead, Trap organized a lot of power and speed within the midfielders, telling them to be spot on defensively. Trap felt he could do this because some of the midfielders had very strong kicks. Riley, the lead midfielder, did not have blinding speed, but he could kick like a mule. Trap also named one kid to a sweeper position. He would by assignment never leave the defensive side of the field, and would defend wherever needed.

Trap gathered his team into a tight circle and spoke evenly. "Okay Blue Angels, this is the toughest team you are going to face. I suspect at least five of them came down from the select league to pump up their sagging egos by beating up on the rec league. I vote we send them back to the select league where they belong with a loss! Now you've got to stop them from shooting! They shoot a lot and they shoot hard. Midfielders, you've got to run them down. Run hard and I'll sub you often!"

As the team broke to take the field, he could see the Angels were more serious than usual, their eyes hard in the evening light. The whole team knew they were in for a battle.

Trap felt nervous, because for the first time he was head coach. And he knew from the league how tough a team he was facing. As the starting whistle blew it soon became apparent that the Benders West team had very physical, almost dirty players. They were using a lot of body contact, slamming into Blue Angels strikers and entangling players' feet. Slide tackles were illegal in the youth league, but the Benders were coming close to doing just that. The referee was too lenient, way too lenient. He was looking the other way at hair pulling, straight-arms to the chest and face, and kicks to the lower body. Babar was a polite and restrained boy when it came to trouble on the field. Gabriel was different. Gabriel had a bit of a chip on his shoulder and always felt anger right from the beginning. Trap could see Gabriel baring his teeth and he started to expect trouble.

Gabriel was getting more and more angry at the Benders' overly aggressive style. What started as a little rough stuff was really getting ugly. During one corner kick Gabriel picked up the ball and rested it on his hip.

"You guys want to play soccer or UFC?" he said in a low voice. "Just let me know cause I'm game for either one!"

Any major league soccer ref would have out his yellow card, demanding both teams lighten up. Gabriel had been hooked, shoved, and spiked plenty of times and the ref didn't utter a word. *Just one more time*, Gabriel thought to himself, *just one more time*. Before long it happened. One of the Benders hooked Gabriel in both shins, knocking him off his feet. Gabriel came up swinging. He let the Benders player know he had crossed the line. Gabriel whistled an uppercut to the solar plexus. Though Gabriel was four inches shorter than the kid who kicked him, he used his speed and fists to work the player over. The two went down on the grass as Trap and the whole Blue Angels team sprinted onto the field in a cloud of dust, white chalk, and grass. Both teams were pushing and shoving each other. Trap shot a look at the Benders coach and yelled at him.

"Let's knock off the martial arts, Coach!" said Trap.

"Tell your team that!" said the Benders coach in return.

Trap tightened his hands and took a couple of steps forward. He held a steady gaze on the Benders coach when Bruce got in front of him.

"Oh for Christ sake chill out, Trap. That's not your style, I don't think!" said Bruce.

After last Tuesday night Trap was beginning to wonder what his style was, but he moved in to help break up the scuffle. The referee didn't know what to do. He stood at the edge of the brawl blowing his whistle until he was beet red. Eventually both teams started listening to the shrill whistle and sourly returned to the sidelines. The coaches tried to disperse the anger to minimize the tendency to play dirty.

"If there's one thing I can't stand it's a cheating bunch of kids acting like the match is a hockey game!" said Kyle.

"Hey, that ref is a bit too meek," said Bruce. "You Blue Angels need to tell the ref to stop slacking it! Complain! Mouth off a bit! Tell him he is missing most of the fouls! Tell him if he wants to avoid fighting, take charge of the game!"

Trap smiled at Bruce. "Well done, amigo," he patted Bruce on the back.

The two teams played on. The Benders continued to commit fouls and the ref continued to ignore it. The Blue Angels kept fighting for the ball. Trap could see there was a real battle going on. Angry shouts echoed across the field. The ball was flying about with more speed than usual. Kids were falling in the struggle, quickly jumping to their feet. The crowd was smaller at this match, because the Blue Angels forfeited the last match. Many fans thought they had quit the league. But those who did show up were much more vocal than usual. After substitutions were made kids were coming to the sidelines totally gassed. Wheezing and gasping for air, they were collapsing to all fours or guzzling sports drinks. One of the kids was so gassed he ducked into the brush and vomited.

As the game continued in a fury of dust and cleats, the Benders started to weaken. They only had two subs. The Blue Angels were rarely at a loss for kids, so they were able to get each of them some rest. Particularly in need of a break were the hard running midfielders.

Getting control of the ball at midfield, Diego dribbled all the way to the penalty arc of the Benders goal and sprinted outside the near post. He kicked it high and to the far post. Babar was there with a perfect header into the net. Blue Angels 1, Benders 0.

The score stayed that way until half time.

After cold sports drinks Trap sat down with the team. Again he emphasized that the Blue Angels should hold their ground and learn to deal with rough stuff going on out there. He then asked Bruce to let the ref know that the Benders were fouling them to gain advantage. Bruce walked over to the ref and reminded him to look for fouls and verbal abuse. Bruce was tactful and spoke to the ref with the utmost restraint.

Trap told the Blue Angels that they had more stamina than the Benders, who were beginning to slow down.

"They're tired!" said Trap, "and you are a second half team. You're tired too, but they are really tired, probably because they don't practice aerobically. Look at them. Half of them will play the second half dehydrated!"

The second half whistle blew. The Benders came hard and the body contact continued, along with lots of yelling. Trap could hear the pounding of soccer cleats impacting the ground as the kids struggled to hold off the Bender's powerful strikers. One of the Benders took a hard shot at the goal. Deshaun jumped high in the air and blocked the shot, but the ball bounced off his hands and out into the penalty box. A huge pile-up of kids fell in the middle of the penalty arc. About eight kids from both teams were on the ground struggling for possession of the ball. Deshaun moved far forward trying to sort out the mess and get his hands on the ball. One of the Benders, sprawled on his side, punched the ball past Deshaun. Ever so slowly it rolled into the net to even the score at Blue Angels 1, Benders 1. Of all the kids, Deshaun was one of the best players. But his enormous sensitivity sometimes got in the way. He cursed himself for moving on the ball too quickly. His jaw grew tense and his lips trembled. He was fighting back the tears. As usual, Deshaun blamed himself. He always gave himself a beating at times like this.

"Come on Deshaun, shake it off!" yelled Trap from the sidelines. Deshaun slapped the ball with his open hand and tossed it to the ref, shaking his head.

As the Benders walked back to kick off, Babar whispered to JR and the team. "Hey guys, Blue Angels B!"

After intercepting the kickoff, Babar ran hard with the ball, but instead of kicking the ball a good distance down field, he just nudged it ahead three feet. Then Babar, Gabriel, and Diego took off running toward the Benders goal as fast as they could go. JR, the strongest kid on the team, kicked the ball hard and high. The three strikers raced downfield, the midfielders close behind. The Benders were caught off guard at seven Blue Angels rushing the goal. The goalie had one shot at the ball as it arced high in the air, and he rifled it back upfield. Riley was there and volleyed the ball from three feet off the ground back to Diego. Diego sailed a high kick toward the far post. Gabriel was there and pounded a full volley scissor kick into the goal. Blue Angels 2, Benders 1.

The score held for the rest of the game. The Benders were a good team but could not score another goal against the high-energy team they were facing. At the end, knowing they had taken such a tough team, the Blue Angels mobbed in celebration. Bruce and Trap looked at each other, then both of their eyes went to the skyline. Both wore euphoric expressions. Up to this point it was the Blue Angels' biggest victory. The Benders were as tough as nails and were loaded with select team players. But the Blue Angels made their mark on them. Until today, the Benders had been undefeated also.

Visibly disappointed, the Benders team slapped hands with the Blue Angels, telling them "good game, good game, good game" as each player passed the other. René walked over to Trap and looked him in the eyes, but she didn't touch him.

"Good game, Coach," and without anything further, she walked away.

Trap walked over to Bruce and shook his hand, telling him he was the one who made the difference.

"Three games to go Coach." Trap downed the last of a sports drink. He was thrilled with the victory, but he thought to himself about how life comes at you. He watched René walking away, her hair to her waist. She swayed like the cottonwoods. Even the way she walked was beautiful. The smallness of her waist made Trap's heart beat a little faster. But she had not asked him over tonight. He felt the trouble between them was coming to an end, but now he wasn't sure. He watched the athletic V to her back, taking a few deep breaths. René had a nagging feeling she was being watched and pivoted around quickly. She caught Trap and several other men looking at her and she smiled. Trap smiled back.

As René climbed into her Astro, Trap's thoughts drifted to the all hands meeting tomorrow at Hughes. What was going to happen next? Trap headed back to his apartment and went for another run on the high school track, then returned home to take some notes for the meeting to be held tomorrow on the subject of equal opportunity. Trap smiled a deep inner smile, knowing he had learned much from being a coach of the Blue Angels. He felt more than ready for such a meeting.

Trap was exhausted, but in a good way. He kicked back in his easy chair and felt the glow of victory resting in his mind. Now it all seemed worth it, and he knew he would never forget this day as long as he lived. They had taken a select team. He let his head fall back against his chair and closed his eyes. He thought of René and how the men watched her. He would call her tomorrow and ask her for a date, maybe a Friday night at the Gold Temple Thai Restaurant. Afterward they might go to a good movie where they could just enjoy being together again.

CHAPTER 27

June 17th, 1998

Olympia, Cascadia

Trap got ready for work feeling the same glow he had gone to bed with. He was kind of looking forward to the day's work. A meeting to discuss the racial undertones that ran through his place of work left him eager and curious. He was hoping this toxic subject would come up and it was the perfect setting to bring up the idea he had. As he stepped out of his front door a very light misty rain fell on the driveway where he parked his van. It was a warm rain and Trap thought it would burn off shortly in the June sun.

The staff meeting started promptly at 8 o'clock straight up. The boss seemed a bit tense, surely because the subject of race was such a delicate one to handle. The construction crew attended, as did the biologists, engineers, technicians, and support staff. Graham Hughes, founder and president of the firm, stood at the head of the conference room table running his fingers through a few papers in front of him. He cleared his throat and shoved a box of doughnuts down the table.

"Here, dig in," he said, "and thanks for all the hard work. Okay, let's get started. I have several letters here asking our little consulting firm to give better employment opportunities to minorities." Hughes nodded slightly as he looked around, painfully aware that every face in the room was white.

"One of these letters is actually a complaint from a Latino intern graduate who did some site visits with us. He complained of racial language at a job site he visited. Does the Slade Creek fishway ring a bell? Look, I'm not going to accuse anybody here of anything. Ed, you do the hiring for the temporary construction help. Be aware we are an equal opportunity employer. How many women do we have on the crew? How many African-Americans? How many Latinos? None,

none, and finally none. I want to see some changes for this year's summer construction season before we get into a boycott situation."

Trap looked at the floor, closed his eyes and very slightly shook his head. Listening to Hughes, he did not sound like he was interested in a strong inclusive community. He sounded like he was afraid of a boycott at the front gate. Hughes was afraid of something that would cost the firm money and lost business opportunity. Trap didn't say a word, but shifted his eyes evenly to Hughes, listening to every single remark. He was frowning, fully aware that he had closely held beliefs about racism.

There was silence in the room. Finally Ed, the construction foreman, spoke up. He spoke loudly because his hearing was impaired from the constant noise of the heavy equipment he worked with. He laid his right palm flat on the conference room table. He sniffed and rubbed his nose. Clearly uncomfortable, he patted the table a couple of times with his hand.

"Well boss, the last time we made some equal opportunity adjustments we got all the credit cards stolen from the dump truck, not to mention some of the tools. I don't have time for that sort of nonsense and we can't afford it."

Graham Hughes was quick to respond. "That is a separate matter. What would cause an employee to do something like that when he would clearly lose his job? I can't help but wonder what caused that situation. What caused a temp to react that way? One might wonder about cause and effect when something like that happens."

Hughes got to his feet and began pacing back and forth behind his chair, clicking his pen.

Ed snapped at his suspenders and said in an even voice, "Well let's face it Graham, minorities just aren't interested in this kind of work."

"I don't buy that at all!" said Hughes. "I want everyone in this room, myself included, to make a fair-minded move to diversify our workforce. We are a sitting duck for protests from many organizations."

Trap was biting back his feelings. Quickly he got control of himself. As sore of a subject as this was, he forced himself to speak up. Trap frowned again, his forehead full of creases.

"When I'm not working here, I'm working with young people. I coach a soccer team that is the most diverse group of teens you will find anywhere. I'd like to take an opportunity to invite everyone in this room to go to the Northwest Regional Soccer Tournament coming up the end of July. Come and watch the Blue Angels: a very integrated team playing in competition. It probably would be a good learning experience for all of us. I know it has been a real eye opener for me."

The employees looked at each other, some thinking it was a very unusual idea. Some rolled their eyes, while others acted interested.

"I would love it if I saw you all at the tournament. To tell you the truth I think lots of you might really enjoy it," Trap offered.

There was a silence in the room. For some reason Trap's colleagues looked at him then spent a few moments looking out the conference room window.

"Well, you would of course be on your own time," said Hughes. "That sort of thing is totally up to you. It does sound like a good idea, though. Thanks for the suggestion, Trap. Any of you think you might like to go to a soccer tournament? Sure couldn't hurt."

The meeting broke up quickly. Some of the employees were angered at the subject of the meeting.

On the way back to the shop, one of the construction crew foremen mumbled to the building superintendent.

"Did I just get called a bigot?"

"I wouldn't say so," said the superintendent. "Are you going to go to the tournament? The Blue Angels are a local hit around here you know."

"I don't know, maybe. It sounds like fun. Better than one of those all hands trainings they put on sometimes. It's something different. But I'll tell you one thing: I ain't going to hire no niggers! I tried that once already several years ago."

The superintendent's mouth grew rigid and his eyes wrinkled into crow's feet as he stared at the foreman.

255

"You know something fella, that word is the most offensive word in the English language. You better rethink that, or consider yourself part of the problem, not part of the answer."

When lunchtime came around Trap picked up the phone and called René. Like a perfect gentlemen, he asked her out for dinner and a movie.

"I know it's been rough lately, René. I got this feeling today. It was like I got up on my soap-box when I should just sit down and shut up. You know everybody messes up. It's like I tell the Blue Angels. When you get knocked down, you get back up and you keep fighting. Getting knocked down is the hard part. Getting back up is all you can do. There isn't anything else to do."

René hesitated, unsure of what to say.

"Well that was well spoken, Trap. You still mad at me?" she asked.

"Does a duck have a butt?" said Trap in a kidding voice.

"Well that's clever. Do you want a really big yes?" she kidded back. "Seriously, Trap, are we ready to put this blip behind us? I'll tell you one thing, I will continue to wear my bikini any time I want."

"Well that's being honest, René, and that's what we've been after all along."

"Aren't we just cute. You ever told a little white lie there, goody two shoes?"

Trap turned his chair back and forth. "Seriously, I guess I'm over being angry with you. Haven't we been through enough? We're over the hump and we should celebrate. You feeling okay?"

"I'm feeling good, Trap. I've got a good feeling inside me. Something has come back for me... like a light coming on."

"Let's talk about it over dinner, okay? See you around six."

After work Trap pulled his van up next to René's car and quickly got out. There was a mackerel sky casting orange lights over the trees and reflecting beautifully off the sound. Trap paused and looked at the small box-shaped clouds spreading from horizon to horizon. They were signs of more rain.

"Hasn't it rained enough already?" he mumbled to himself.

256

René opened the door before Trap could knock. She looked
different. Instead of the tense unhappy face he was used to seeing, she
wore a calm contented expression. She was grounded and in the
moment, and she spoke more slowly. She was dressed simply, with a
baggy flannel shirt gathered at her waist with her faded levis. She wore
elongated brown earrings and a matching beaded necklace. Trap
noticed that she was not trying to drop his jaw with some tight sexy
outfit.

She gave Trap a serene half smile, her voice low and even.

"Hope you don't mind, Trap. I'm not into getting dressed up these
days."

"No not at all. You look like a farmer's daughter," said Trap. "I
hardly ever get dressed up either."

"We're leaving, Riley. We'll be a while. Don't wait up."

"Corin is coming over later, mom," said Riley.

"Do you need supervision?" René joked.

"No, but you do," Riley countered.

René held Trap's arm with both hands as they walked up to his van.
She seemed a bit quiet, her face growing serious and preoccupied. She
looked younger.

They both ordered curry dishes at the Thai restaurant. René fixed
her eyes on Trap.

René rested her palm under her chin. "I feel different now, Trap. It's
like a great weight has come off me. I still have occasional panicky
feelings, but they're diminished. It's the strangest thing. I can talk
about my past now without getting so upset."

"I'm glad, René. You were always the beautiful girl with the dim
smile. Now you've changed. The dimness is gone and the beauty has
taken over." Despite her plain clothes, René looked absolutely radiant,
her eyes big and rich brown, and her high cheekbones looking golden
in the light.

"There are some things you already know about me, Trap. I told
you, I was badly beaten by my father and my husband both. The
doctor said many times a battered woman will leave a cruel monster
only to move in with same type of man she left. Have you ever found

yourself doing the same stupid thing over and over again? To make matters worse I was pregnant when some of the worst beatings took place. The doctor told me women are very vulnerable to PTSD when they're going to have a baby. God, I hated men so much for years. I wouldn't even go out on a date even though guys were always pestering me, especially after I lost the weight and hired a personal trainer."

"Do you feel that way even now sometimes?" asked Trap.

"Sometimes. You saw what happened to me on *Mornin' Mist*. Remember that day when we were having such a good sail and suddenly I had a kind of panic attack? I'm not sure, but I think all that is behind me now. I'm still not sure I will ever marry again."

"Well, you sure did well as a mother. Riley is a great kid, and he's the smartest kid I've ever met! It's almost like he was born grown up."

"Yeah, he's really bright. But did I tell you his day care provider Privina was a shaman? She helped me see a world I would have never dreamed of. She claimed many animals we encountered as we hiked around in the hills were actually spirit messengers. They were telling us where to go and which way to turn in our lives. They were bringing us advice just like the stars do if you believe in horoscopes. She also knew how to send messages. That's why I pay so much attention to the animals around me. She was a terrific help to me when I needed it most. I owe her lots, but it's too late to repay her now. God, I can't believe she left me money in her will. I think she gave Riley some of her gift. In fact, I know so. She told me. You can tell by the way Riley acts, by the wisdom he has. It goes well beyond his age."

Trap nodded silently as René continued. "Did you know why I dropped out of high school? I had to work. Wade left us to go tuna fishing. I had no money and no way to earn a living. Privina found me a job as a student painter with a crew working out of Northridge. We made a go of it, Privina, Riley and I. I never set foot in my father's house again. Never."

Trap listened quietly to every word she said. Being a scientist, he was slightly reserved. But as a Native American he had come to appreciate the value of belief. He could see a kind of rebirth in her eyes. She seemed to be feeling better, but Trap remembered his rule: if you want to know how someone feels, you have to ask.

"So how do you feel about all this history now? I mean right now, this minute?"

"It's all coming clear to me Trap. It seems like all of a sudden I can think straight."

"You look better too. That troubled look on your face is gone."

René exhaled a long, cleansing breath. "I'm sorry I pulled such a stupid trick, lying to you about my line of work. I guess I was always embarrassed about being a bikini model. I didn't mean any harm, honest. Trap, I'm serious about taking the GED equivalency test. You think you might find time to help me get ready?"

Trap leaned over the table and gave her a kiss on the mouth. "Soccer is over in a little less than a month."

"Okay, I'll start cramming on my own until you get enough time to help. Deal?"

"Deal," said Trap. "You're still going to come to the games aren't you?"

"Yeah, you bet, in my skin tight dress."

Trap didn't know what to say.

"Kidding, just kidding."

"And what comes after the GED? College?"

"Well, first things first. But yeah, maybe I will. If I can pull it off." René smiled ever so slightly. She wore a look of determination as she finished her curry. She was quiet and sedate as they finished eating and headed for the movies. They watched the film in complete silence, René wondering if she should ask him to spend the night. Trap couldn't get over how good she looked. It was her face. It had changed. There was a great calmness and confidence in her eyes as she glanced about in Trap's van, mostly studying his face. All the anger, resentment, and despair had melted away. Later that night there was no playing or teasing, just humming erotica all night to the sound of small waves on the gravel. Trap and René made love in a way they had never done before. Never before... not even close. René was so deeply in love with Trap that she plunged into his being. She was frightened at such a strong feeling. She had him back, and held him tightly all night. When the sun came up the next morning, they were not finished.

CHAPTER 28

July 8th, 1998

Lacey, Cascadia

A few weeks passed and the Blue Angels simply overwhelmed the last three teams they played. With Bruce's help the team started blowing out the opponents they faced. The kids seemed to burn with energy and aggression. One team they beat 10 – 0, scoring a goal within the first 20 seconds of the game. They reached a point where their attacking form of soccer was hard for any team to deal with. They shot on goal much more often than their opponents. High shots sometimes crashed violently into the cross bar, making it vibrate from the strong impact. Some wide shots crashing into the uprights of the goal were quite loud, intimidating to the other team. The Blue Angels pounded the field. They played without speaking for the most part unless they were being fouled too often. They reached a point where they didn't need to speak to one another, knowing full well what their fellow players were going to do.

As the days and weeks passed and the crowds grew larger, the Blue Angels continued to be a force in the youth soccer league. But all the while they rarely gave a thought to the thing that made them perform well: the fact that they were having fun with Trap and his unusual approach to the game. It made them feel like major leaguers.

As a team, and in general, they weren't distracted by anything. They were still children, though their voices were changing to the deeper tone of young men and women. They had distractions of all kinds, but were not preoccupied with anything other than winning.

Trap had a kind of magic with the players. He simply made them feel strong. Towards the last games of the season Trap referred to his team as "the deadly Blue Jets." There were times when Trap wondered about the future of his team. He had to admit he was tempted to register them with the Thurston County Select Soccer League. This would be a giant step forward in youth soccer, but perhaps the Blue Angels were ready for it. Perhaps.

René came to all the remaining games, but she was introverted along the sidelines. Rather than showing off her good looks, she dressed plainly so as not to attract much attention. Sitting near the sideline she seemed preoccupied, cocking her eyes to the side and down. She seemed to be looking inside herself rather than watching the game. On one occasion Trap sat down alongside her and asked how she was doing.

"I'm okay," she said. "I'm really fine, honest." But at times Trap saw her folding her arms over her knees with her forehead resting on her wrists. She looked awkward at times, but when Trap spoke to her, she looked up with a contented dreamy expression.

The July summer heat settled over the lowland, leaving behind the summer solstice. The stiff winds of spring were turning to a gentle rustling of the bright sunlit poplar trees.

The regular season was over, but the Northwest Regional Soccer Tournament was just around the corner. It marked the climax of youth soccer in several states in the Northwest. The vernacular for this big event was "Header and Footer," and it attracted soccer teams from Idaho, Montana, and Cascadia, making it the biggest youth soccer tournament of the region. As the tournament drew near Trap put up a flyer at work inviting all employees to attend. He placed the flyer next to the minutes of the last meeting posted in the hallway so it would not be missed.

At the end of the workday Trap phoned René, asking her to meet him at the sailboat. She beat him there. She brought a cleansing drink made with citrus, cinnamon, and grated ginger. She also picked up a couple of submarine sandwiches so they could have dinner on the water. When Trap arrived he was struck by René's expression. She looked different on this day. The July sun had streaked her light brown hair with blonde. René tanned easily, her face and legs a golden brown from soaking up rays in her front yard. Her skin had turned darker than her hair.

They sailed up the inlet. The wind was westerly and light, barely leaving a lens of tiny waves on the surface of the sound. *Mornin' Mist* leaned gently and steadily into the wind. A harbor seal poked its head out of the water and René watched it carefully. The seal seemed to be passing to her a spirit message: that a cycle of hard times and urgency was ending, and her subconscious would be reaching her in wandering thoughts, feelings, and distant, hard to fathom dreams. They seemed to be telling her also that her imagination was spilling over now, but to stay present in the earth and in the sea. René looked up at the gulls circling above the masthead; their sharp cries reminded her to clear up confusion with those close to her. She looked over at Trap, studying the graceful line of his jaw as his long black hair fell over his neck.

René was quiet. She sat down on the leeward side so she could feel the vapor of the water surface touch her face. The water rose almost imperceptibly under her as she stared at the wake of Mornin' Mist and listened to the peaceful sound of moving water beneath her.

Trap nudged her shoulder. "The little lady moves pretty well in this light air, huh?"

René hadn't felt this way in years. She reached over to Trap and wrapped her arm around his waist.

"Hey, you're sweeping me off my feet," said Trap. "But of course you always do, don't you? Whenever I'm with you I feel your presence inside and out. Even when I'm mad you seem to melt me down. It's hard for me to understand you sometimes with your troubled spirit. But something seems to be shifting in you. You're becoming someone else; something like your big weight loss when you were a teenager. So let's be sure we understand how both of us feel. We've been through quite a time, you and I. A lot has happened."

"Okay Trap, sounds like a plan. But could you come over more often?"

The early evening summer wind suddenly came rushing across the sound. *Mornin' Mist* responded immediately by healing over twenty degrees. She galloped up to her hull speed. The shrouds were singing slightly and the clue of the genoa rattled along the leech until Trap secured it.

Trap tacked and let the boat fall off into a starboard reach while René took the tiller. *Mornin' Mist* went charging home. Because it was growing dark, tiny pieces of glowing phosphorescence turned over in the boat's wake and lit the water along her bow. Thanks to the narrow passage of the inlet, the sound surface remained fairly flat. The stars were coming and Venus appeared to the east. At least for the time being, René was healed. She looked directly into the flakes of phosphorescence as she held the tiller a few inches to weather. She thought she saw the black silhouette of a mature sea lion swimming alongside the boat. It seemed to be communicating with her too, telling her to pay attention to everything around her. Was the sea lion speaking to her? She couldn't be sure. In a flicker of a second it was gone. The lights of the State Capital loomed ahead of them and the marina was well lit. After tying up they realized they had forgotten to eat. Talking quietly, they sat in the cockpit eating their submarine sandwiches and sipping the ginger drink René had made. The night was quiet except for the slapping of halyards against the many masts in the marina.

After finishing up, Trap headed home. Saying goodnight to René, he let her know he had to do some planning for the last practice before the Header and Footer tournament. As he pulled up to his apartment he checked the mail and found a letter waiting for him from the Soccer league steering committee. The letter read:

*Special thanks to you and your team Blue Angels for enrolling in the upcoming Northwest Regional Soccer Tournament. All teams competing in the tournament are now pre-registered. Unfortunately we have a shortage of U-15 teams wishing to participate this year. Because your team has the best record in the U-14 bracket and have completed the regular season undefeated, we are requesting you compete at the U-15 level for this year's tournament. Please give this careful consideration. In spite of the fact you will compete against teams with older players we have permission to make this*

*change from the committee. Because of your impressive season*
*we are confident that you will be competitive at the U-15 level.*

Trap was surprised at this news. At first, the idea of moving up in age group did not appeal to him. U-15 kids were certainly bigger, stronger, and faster, but the more he thought about it the more it seemed like an enticing challenge. Standing out in front of his mailbox, he rubbed his finger and thumb over his temples. In fact, it seemed like a real compliment to his team. What if they could compete at the U-15 level? What an end to a truly great season.

Trap went inside, studied his notes, and got out several of his tapes on soccer. Playing against older and bigger opponents would mean stepping up an attack. The Blue Angels at this point in the season were used to pressing hard and could run ragged a team with a more controlled approach to the game. That was their trademark, and that's what they would need to leverage if they were going to pull this off.

Due to his excitement about the upcoming tournament, Trap had some trouble getting to sleep that night. He lay in bed with his eyes closed, rolling over on his side. He couldn't stop thinking about René, either. Could he trust her now? Were all the cards out on the table? Was she being genuine and honest with him, or just pulling the wool over his eyes again like she had done to two dozen other guys in the past? She seemed different now than when he first dated her. She acted like an experienced lover knowing all the wisdom a complete mature woman has. But this time her voice was calm and genuine, as if she meant every word in all sincerity. Thinking about René, he finally drifted off in the early morning hours.

The next day Trap was on time for practice. René thought it was important to lead the team in some relaxation poses, knowing the players were amped up for the battle to come. She guided them through proud warrior, exalted warrior, half moon pose, and others. Trap explained to the team that their level of competition had suddenly taken a big step forward to the U-15 ranks. The team reacted much the way Trap did, taken by surprise at first, followed by a growing determination.

Gabriel was sitting with his legs crossed and his elbows on his knees.

"Why are they singling out the Blue Angels to play bigger kids?" he asked.

"Because the league has been watching us, and because we are undefeated in U-14," answered Trap.

Babar was always a calm team leader. "I feel kind of like we've gotten a huge boost from the league. Really 15 year olds aren't that much bigger than us. Look at our defense. We're big and strong back there."

"Yeah, strong enough to get our little butts kicked," said Kyle.

"Come on, show some guts. You guys are going to have to reach down deep to pull this off. But I think you can do it," said Bruce.

Trap did not ask the team to work out or scrimmage. There were no drills, no kicking practice, no nothing. The team sat in a half circle and listened instead. Trap, Bruce, and René stood in front of them.

"Okay kids, listen. We are facing the toughest challenge we've ever faced. Sometimes in the past I've made a mistake. I tried to change the team around to play against a tough opponent. I don't want you to do that this time. We are well-practiced at a form of relentless attack soccer. I want you to play your game. No wrinkles in the plan, no sudden changes to step up to U-15. Play 'em with your game all the way. That is what you do best, and that is how you'll manage them. We are at a peak. We've never been stronger. I will repeat the same things I've said all season. Play 'em hard. Use some legal body contact. Play 'em rough. I'll guarantee you they won't be prepared or braced for the kind of team you are. They're going to be surprised. They're going to be off guard thinking they will easily handle a U-14 team. They're going to be overconfident. They're going to be shocked at how quickly things are happening. Try to single out the best strikers and mark them. Mark them good, and be ready to defend. Strikers and midfielders, shoot a lot. Pound the goal into submission. Use your false nine deceptions. Use your headers. Never stop grinding the far post."

Bruce spoke up. "I want to do one little warm up exercise. It's designed to intimidate the other team. While you're warming up, get in four lines: goalie in front, then a line of strikers, one line of midfielders, one line of defenders. Form yourselves into a tight group, and as a single unit do a slow jog around the edge of the in-bounds. Keep your knees high and do one lap around the field. Stay in step with each other and you'll make the other team feel they are headed for trouble."

René decided to say a few words also. "You know, I've been watching you all season, nearly every game. I've watched you play with determination and toughness. I would like to have you give a round of applause for the coaches. They are second to none."

The Blue Angels erupted with claps and whistles.

"And while you're at it, let's have the Blue Angels give themselves a hand also! I think you can do it Blue Jets! So does Bruce, and so does Trap! Why don't we all get in the pre-game formation that Bruce described? Get in a tight group and do a slow jog around the field. Then we can go home and get prepared."

The Blue Angels did just that. Then they vanished.

CHAPTER 29

July 25th, 1998

Olympia, Cascadia

It was a clear Saturday morning, July 25, 1998, day one of the two day "Header and Footer" Northwest Regional Soccer Tournament. There was a huge crowd at the Templeton soccer triplex on the south side of town. To Trap's surprise, most of the workers at Hughes Associates came to the showdown. Even the company CEO showed up. Gratefully, Trap shook the hands of each of his coworkers and gave them the news: that they had been selected by the league to play at the U-15 level. Some of the Hughes staff appeared a bit cynical, but at least they were there. Trap overheard some comments to the effect that the Blue Angels looked too small to play against 15 year olds.

There were three soccer fields each surrounded by a noisy crowd: people sitting in the bleachers or standing along the sidelines awaiting the coming battles. The tournament was for U-13 teams on up to U-18. As a rule, the toughest teams in the region would show up at this match thinking they stood a chance at winning. Many but not all of the teams were championship caliber from their own soccer districts, thinking they were the most competitive kids on the block.

When the Blue Angels arrived they were a bit overwhelmed at the number of teams and the number of fans that were on site. But their surprised expressions quickly changed to hard faces, filled with resolve. The team grew quiet and serious. Some felt at first that they were overmatched when they looked over the imposing U-15 teams.

"This is going to be tough," said Babar to Gabriel. "Are you ready for a war?"

Gabriel nodded, "I'm ready! At least I think I'm ready. Boy, what a big bunch of kids. I mean a bunch of big kids! But we can take them for sure!" he said.

This kind of inspired the rest of the team, including Babar, who was expecting to hear fear in Gabriel's voice. What he heard instead were the words of a fighter in the center of the ring. There was no fear in Gabriel's eyes either. They were hardened into a fixed stare as he looked over the opposing teams one player at a time.

"All right, let's get our team together," said Trap loudly, though his voice was tighter than usual. "We're starting first up at soccer field three; game one is in 30 minutes."

Trap decided that this was the time for some encouragement. "Size takes a back seat to cunning in this game. How does the mongoose deal with the cobra? Speed. Well oiled speed! Like I said at our last practice, I want you to play your game. Your style of play is a deadly weapon. It's also gonna be a big surprise. Most soccer teams I've watched go for poise and demeanor. Don't try to play up to them, because they are older. Stick to what you know: our relentless attack. Don't let them up to breathe. Remember to press harder if and when their team is gassed. These are the last few games of the season. Let's show them how to play soccer!"

Trap had the team form a circle. All the Blue Angels reached for the center. He spoke in a strong voice. "God protect these young Blue Angels," Trap broke into a wry smile. "And God help their opponents!" Laughter swept through the team and they relaxed a bit. Trap had a feeling of pride inside him that he could not describe.

Bruce added a comment. "Alright, get in the formation we talked about last practice and do an easy jog around the edge of the field. Okay, make it so." Bruce couldn't help but notice that when the team got elbow to elbow their ethnic diversity was even more obvious. The close proximity of the group highlighted the quick way the team could signal each other, even though their communication was usually silent.

They drew a U-15 team from Boise called the Renegades. The two teams took the field. From the sidelines the Renegades looked only slightly bigger. It was a hot day and Trap noticed right off that the Renegade coaches had no cooler for sports drinks. They were making a big mistake. The dog day heat was oppressive in Olympia due to lack of wind and high humidity.

Game times were shortened to half of the normal time. Trap was concerned about the shortness of the games. The Blue Angels had a way of running the opposition ragged during the second half of the usual 90 minute matches during the regular season. They would often run over the top of teams sweltering in the heat and poorly prepared for the tempo the Blue Angels played.

The Blue Angels won the kickoff and had JR pound an imposing high kick back to the Renegades defense. The Renegades were a talkative team that dribbled and passed back and forth a lot. *Too much*, thought Trap. They were also swarming around the ball way too much and not holding their ground well. Although they were big fast kids, they were making novice errors, and it became very apparent. The team was simply not ready. The Renegades were toe-poking the ball. They were slow to retreat when the Blue Angels went for a shot. This was difficult for the Blue Angels strikers because their attack was fast and relentless. Speed was always the key. This was causing problems, and both Gabriel and Diego were called for off sides during the first ten minutes of play. Eventually Gabriel and Diego got on top of the problem using the deadly wall pass, taught to them by Trap. Both teams pounded the turf and both Bruce and Trap could feel the excitement mount in the game.

Trap temporarily pulled Riley out of the game. His smarts made him very good at dissecting soccer patterns.

"All right Riley, what do you see out there?" asked Trap.

"They don't retreat very fast when we charge them. The midfielders and strikers need to deal with those guys. I say we throw a bunch of deceptions at them. You know, the deadly give and go of soccer. We can use them to get in front. They're relying too much on the goalie. He's a big kid but he's kind of slow. We should work our way down the sidelines and start using headers and volleys to the far post!"

"Good Riley, pass it on when you go back in. Tell Gabriel to go into his offensive sweeper mode."

René brought her camera and was more sociable today than her usual introverted self. She kept herself busy snapping photos of the crowd and athletes and by talking with the parents who were at the tournament without exception. She seemed to be the only calm spirit of the group chatting with some of the mothers and being sure all the folks knew the Blue Angels were playing U-15 teams for day one of the tournament.

Some of the parents were still working on their English, which René kind of expected. She did the best she could. René also took a short walk over by the employees of Hughes. Some of them she recognized from her few visits to Trap's workplace. She made a point of shaking hands with the CEO of Hughes, telling him how glad she was that he took time to come to the match. She pointed out the lanky midfielder standing on the sidelines as her son Riley.

The Blue Angels were holding their own against the Renegades. In fact, they had them 2 - 1 at half time. The Renegades were upset with themselves for being handled by a younger team, while the coach revealed his lack of coaching skills in spite of his soccer talents. He was mostly yelling at his players. Trap learned during the last few months that there was a big difference between playing and coaching the game.

It grew hot, without a breath of wind. The Blue Angels would have been spent without a way to stay hydrated. René was quick to fill paper cups for them. She was catching glances at Trap, wondering if he had put their disagreement behind them.

The local crowd reached a higher volume as they shouted in favor of their home teams. The Blue Angels players were pushing themselves very hard. During the break Trap didn't say much, but he did remind the players that they owned the second half. Over the season they had proven it many times: other teams could not match steps with them when endurance was a factor. They came at the Renegades with a vengeance. The game was growing more physical. From the sidelines the crowd could hear the sound of shin guards cracking together. Blows against rib cages were common, as well as contact tackles coming from both sides.

As in the regular season, the officials were not doing a good job keeping the game under control. Rare for Trap, he and Bruce came on the field yelling about excessive fouls. The physical nature of the game seemed to turn the tide in favor of the larger kids, most of them Renegades. The Blue Angels continued to fight despite the near brawling that was taking place. One of the Renegades went too far, kicking and spitting at Kyle near the Blue Angels penalty arc. Finally an official drew a yellow card, giving the Blue Angels a direct penalty kick. Play was delayed long enough for Trap to get Riley near the sidelines.

"Riley, take yourself out of the play and listen. You can't match blows with these guys, they'll run you down like a front-end loader. You've got to use your speed and you've got to use your own experience. Don't let them bully you! Play them with your game."

Gabriel was outstanding at bending the ball. But this time, instead of scoring a goal, the ball slammed the crossbar and bounced all the way back to midfield where Willis and one of the Renegade strikers were standing. No one was even close to the play other than Willis and the one Renegade striker. The two of them sprinted downfield, the Renegade controlling the ball. The striker was fast, but he was no match for Willis. Willis kicked in his calm composed stride down the field, trying to overtake the striker. The rest of the Blue Angels and Renegades gave chase, but they were out of the play. They watched as the black skin on Willis's neck and legs glistened with sweat. Not quite able to catch his opponent, Willis kicked into a whole new gear. Tears started to blur his vision as he strained to overtake the Renegade with the ball. Way downfield the Renegade tried to shove Willis off balance, but Willis slapped his arm away. In the last few steps before a shot on goal, Willis managed to nudge the ball forward to Deshaun. Standing in the penalty area, Deshaun contained the ball easily and made a skyscraping punt back up the field. The game over whistle sounded. The Blue Angels had taken the Renegades two goals to one!

Out in the center of the field, the Blue Angels mobbed Willis. Fists clenched and arms pumping, they spent only a brief time in midfield, knowing they had two more difficult games to play on that very day. They slapped hands with the Renegades, who appeared a bit somber.

The coach of the Renegades told Trap and Bruce he had never seen such a feisty group of 14 year olds.

The Hughes employees stood together along the sideline. Trap got the kids' attention and singled out the employees he worked with. The men and women from Hughes glanced at each other briefly, then at the Blue Angels coming toward them. Trap asked his players to shake hands with his workmates and give them a special welcome. Willis still had streaks in his eyes as he walked up to the CEO of Hughes and offered to shake his hand. Hughes shook hands and smiled at Willis, but deep in his eyes there was a serious look. Willis paused and looked for a few moments at the expression on this older man's face. As Willis held the gaze of Graham Hughes, his eyes peered through the distance between them. Willis was covered with sweat. He blinked several times, his face holding a question he never asked.

"Thanks for coming to the tournament, mister. I could hear you cheering for us!"

"You're the game winner," said Hughes. "I didn't get your name."

"It's Willis Gray," he said, his face looking bright. The rest of the team joined the Hughes workers and gave them a greeting and handshake. Trap stood beside them, pointing out and naming the Hughes Associates. He introduced his entire team to the employees.

Although a little late, Deshaun's father Jaylen came walking up the sidelines. It being a Saturday he did not need to make his usual swing shift that so much interfered with his coaching on the team. Jaylen saw that the Blue Angels took a U-15 victory. Beaming, he walked over and put his hand on Trap's back.

He said in all sincerity, "Jesus coach, you really pulled one off this time. How did we do that anyway?"

Trap winked at Jaylen. "Everybody helped," he said while raising his eyebrows.

The Blue Angels picked a shady spot down by the corner of field 3. They were given one hour thirty minutes to rest before game two. All in all there were four teams including the Blue Angels competing in the U-15 heat. Each team would play the other once, for a total of three games. The U-15 team with the most wins would advance to play the

2nd place team of the U-16 heat. In the case of a tie the team with the most goals would compete in the next heat.

The next U-15 team scheduled to play the Blue Angels was from Spokane. They called themselves the Pronghorns. Trap was a bit relieved to see they were not quite as big as the Renegades. They looked tough though, with a solid, organized warm up, and colorful bright jerseys that made them look like a professional soccer team. Trap and Bruce watched the coach of the Pronghorns as he led his team in a few warm up exercises. He was a coach more like Trap, not one to do a lot of yelling.

The Blue Angels got a huge boost in confidence once they took out the Renegades. Jaylen walked over to Trap and shook his head.

"They're a U-15 team too, huh Coach?" He shaded his eyes and took a long stare at the Pronghorns. "They look pretty tough from here, Coach. Think we can pull this off?"

"Yeah, I think we can take them, if we stick to our game. I'm not afraid of these older teams. Not anymore."

The Pronghorns kicked off. As they moved downfield they seemed to have a linear approach to the game; they moved upward and backward with little side-to-side positioning. When the Blue Angels got control of the ball they were wild by comparison, sprinting all over the field, making themselves difficult to mark. But it soon became apparent that the Pronghorns were a deep defensive team making a solid effort to block all shots on goal. Trap had seen this kind of thing before. The team would surround the goal and suddenly, when their opponents least expected it, they would explode downfield with very fast strikers.

After ten minutes of play Trap pulled Babar out of the game.

Trap explained to Babar that they were up against a deep defensive team and to watch for a couple of really fast kids. He had Babar tell Willis to take a defensive sweeper position.

The two teams battled into the afternoon. The Blue Angels kept up with their out of control attack. Twice, a fast striker broke loose with the ball and sprinted downfield. But Willis was there every time. Willis had come to believe he was simply the fastest kid on the field. Running down even the fastest strikers, he invariably rifled the ball out of bounds, giving his team time to go into defensive positions before the next throw-in.

To launch an attack against a deep defensive team, the Blue Angels strikers pushed down right in the middle of them. They were so bunched around the goal the strikers chose to ignore the risk of an off sides ruling. The midfielders pressed in close, trying to shoot on goal with very high lobs. Few 14 year olds were likely to head the ball. Headers were scary as hell and everyone on the team knew it. Still, Gabriel and Babar pushed and elbowed their way into scoring position. Babar was not afraid. Wisely, the midfielders started switching sides on the Pronghorns, finding more space on the side of the field opposite the attack. Riley was extremely good at this because he had such a long kick. He was known for shooting a lot from the edge of the playing field.

One thing became clear to the Blue Jets: they were not going to wear out the Pronghorns. With a deep defense they would not be inclined to move around much. They were taking away the Blue Jets' most powerful weapons: the relentless attack, and the ability to totally exhaust the opposing team. There was so much pushing and shoving going on in the penalty area that the ref was having trouble again. The Blue Angels elbowed and bumped between and among the deep defenders. Out of frustration one of the Pronghorns lost his temper and punched Gabriel in the face. Gabriel went down and stayed down, acting like he was hurt. The ref blew the whistle, flashed a red card at the offending player, and declared a direct penalty kick. Gabriel stayed down. Pushed into a corner, Gabriel would fight. He was fully awake, but he stayed down, looking straight into the sky. Gabriel had trouble controlling his temper and it had been a problem the whole season. He knew he had to cool down. If he got up he was sure to work over the offending Pronghorn with his fists. Gabriel waited until Riley came through the crowd. Riley reached down to help him to his feet, offering his hand. He grabbed Gabriel's wrist with his other hand.

"Stay down and be cool, Gabriel," said Riley. "We got them right where we want them."

The two of them looked each other dead in the eye, and Gabriel let go of his anger. He felt a lump on his lip where he had been punched. Moving towards the corner kick area, he walked off his rage.

Babar took the penalty kick, just him and the goalie. It came down to that, and the goalie had no chance.

The sun rose up into the afternoon when halftime came. The whole team was dripping with sweat, but they drank their fill and recovered quickly.

Standing next to Bruce, Trap spoke up. There was some frustration in his voice, mainly because he hated deep defensive play. In the back of his mind he thought it was a chicken shit way to play the game. But there was nothing in the rules that prohibited that kind of strategy.

"Do you all understand what they're doing to you? It's called deep defense. The whole team surrounds the goal and tries to block all shots. The way to deal with them is not to surround them. You have to get in the middle of them. Shoot from the far post and shoot high, real high!"

Bruce gestured toward the center of the field with his hand. "You're going to have to create space within them, not outside of them. Use light body contact to get that space. Try for headers, half volleys, and full volleys. There are a couple of speed players lurking in the bunch of them. Find out who they are and mark them real close. All of a sudden they will break loose and sprint for our goal with the ball. In that case they have to deal with Willis. Draw their midfielders and defenders away from the goal with false nine type plays. Okay, you got them one to nothing. Keep breaking up that deep defense."

In the second half the Pronghorns tried what the Blue Angels least expected. They broke into an open field approach as far away from the deep defense as they could get. They were all over the field, reasoning that the Blue Angels would expect them to do the same thing. Both Gabriel and Babar caught on without delay. Gabriel yelled to Trap that the pronghorns were doing the opposite of what they expected.

Trap bellowed from the sidelines, "Go back to attack soccer, direct forward play!"

The two teams went at it again. Although the Pronghorns were older, they were surprised at how the Blue Angels would not quit. As the second half of the game went on the Pronghorns did tire, much to Trap's surprise. They appeared to be showing a lack of conditioning, perhaps too much finesse and not enough scrimmage…to much deep defense. The Blue Angels pounded away at them, taking every opportunity to rest that they could. The Pronghorns began hanging their heads, some holding their sides as exhaustion set in. Although both teams tired, the Blue Angels had that all-important quick recovery time. The Pronghorns were exposed, and the goals started piling up. Trap watched the game in near disbelief. The Blue Angels were working over the Pronghorns. The final score was 6 to 1. The Blue Angels had done it again. What kind of team was this? Where did their edge come from?

To say the Hughes workers were impressed was an understatement. They looked out on the field with expressions of amazement. Instead of cheering for the Blue Angels some of them were quiet, glancing at each other. The Blue Angels really were looking special. They walked off the field looking for some shade in the growing shadows. As they sprawled in the grass they held a kind of dignity. A crowd gathered around them, asking questions and taking pictures. There was excitement in the fans, and there was a growing confidence in the eyes of the Blue Angels. They had done it again, only this time it was very apparent that a defeat of the U-15 Renegades and Pronghorns both was not a fortunate accident. The Blue Angels were for real, and they were a force to be reckoned with. The Hughes employees were bunched in a group near the Blue Angels. They watched as people in the crowd shook hands with the team. One member of the crowd held his fist high and declared that the Blue Angels were playing a year above their age group. The rest of the crowd stood up in amazement. There was a wave of chatter among them; many hadn't been aware that the Blue Angels were a year younger than the competition.

After an hour and a half of rest, the Blue Angels squared off for the final game of the day. They faced another U-15 team from Winthrop, known as Methow United. As in the other matches, they faced a team of players bigger than them. The Methow team was made fully aware by their coach that they were playing a U-14 team. They were a grizzled looking bunch and Trap got the message that the opposing team had not lost a game in the tournament. The Blue Angels studied Methow. They talked quietly amongst themselves, looking for some bit of information that could help them win. A little later maybe they would get a clue on any Methow weakness, but it didn't much matter. They would bring their attacking game to the field of play and stick to it. It had served them well. If the Blue Angels could make Methow play their upbeat, out of breath pace, they'd have them gassed and off guard.

As the sun began its plunge into a deep brilliant orange, Methow United kicked off. The heat and the brilliant light reflected the Methow faces on the east end of the field. The sun revealed how spent the players were. They looked like they had been battling all day. They were not winded or gassed. They were just tired.

Gabriel, Babar, and Diego had the sun at their backs and the field was easy to see. The Blue Angels would never give in now. They had not lost a game all season in spite of one forfeit. The Blue Angels had enough left in the tank to launch a solid attack on Methow.

They played like a team. Now they were in position to win the tournament at the U-15 level and everybody watching was thrilled at the idea. Encouraged, the Blue Jets pressed harder. Perhaps because of the long day the Blue Angels defenders played a little more kickball than usual. At halftime the teams switched sides, the Blue Angels facing the sun. But as the beginning of twilight came the sun's light softened slightly and the Blue Angels could still see the ball through their backlit opponents. The crowd grew larger as fans of other teams arrived, ready to watch the final game of the day. The Blue Angels were still a second half team and instinctively knew without being reminded by Trap, Bruce, or Jaylen. Just one more game to go. Using their ability to execute wall passes and taking advantage of their second half performance, they pounded the Methow United goal.

The Hughes employees could not help yelling support for the Blue Angels. They were amazed that such a team could be a dominant force on the field. The final score was 4 to 1 Blue Angels. At the final whistle there was an outburst from the crowd as the Blue Angels overcame the odds to beat three teams from an older age group. Both Trap and Bruce were quiet, their eyes watching the opulent horizon. Trap snapped out of it and ran out on the field to congratulate his team. As always, they slapped hands with Methow United. The stunned crowd slowly began moving onto the field. Then Trap asked the Blue Jets one more time to shake hands with the employees of Hughes Associates. People were swarming the field, but the Blue Angels managed to spot the Hughes workers standing in the corner kick area. They ran over to thank Trap's coworkers for their support. The early evening sun was sinking into a far-off lens of clouds. It shined on the Hughes workers' hands. The kids formed into a line adjacent to the employees who were now bending over slightly to meet the players up close. Every Blue Angel was covered with sweat and grinning. Virtually every one of the Hughes Associates smiled back, and from that moment a few of them would begin to think differently about their place of work. A sunset orange light flashed through everyone's hands as the cheering crowd moved in to surround them.

René could not recall ever feeling the way she felt after Saturday's tournament. It seemed to her like the whole day was full of action, and it caused her to remember the beatings she took fourteen years ago. She had a moment of dizziness when she thought back to the time she was holding Riley while being beaten by her father, her palms helpless and flat against the wall. René walked slowly down the sidelines with her fingers on her temples. Amongst all the cheering she felt strange and conflicted. Was she having a panic attack? No. She could face the violence in her toxic past and it didn't hurt anymore. Now Trap was in jubilation. She turned around and held a long gaze at him. He smiled at her and nodded briefly before Nicolás grabbed him around the neck in sheer joy. René walked over to the icebox and filled one of the remaining glasses. Without so much as a smile she walked over to Trap and dumped the drink over his head. "Way to go Coach," she said in a whisper.

On Sunday morning, the crowd was a little smaller. People had a full plate of soccer the day before and were going to church or getting ready for the coming week. But most of the Hughes people came to the second day's competition. Of course, the Blue Angels' brothers, sister, parents and friends came to the game, amazed the Blue Angels had won the right to play the second place team in the U-16 heat.

Many of the visiting teams had already left the night before, having been eliminated from the competition. Some stayed to watch.

The Blue Angels squared off against a team of 16 year olds from Portland called the Chinooks. They were a much bigger group of young men, some of them standing a full head taller than the average Blue Angel. For the onlookers it looked like a mismatch to say the least. The two teams lined up. Gabriel and Babar took a long look at each other. Gabriel rubbed his hands together and nodded slightly. His legs were trembling. There was a look in his Latin American eyes… that he would not be dominated. The Chinooks could not overlook the ethnic diversity of the Blue Angels and it made them uncomfortable. It was something they had not seen often.

At the kickoff, Babar nudged the ball forward. JR moved up and kicked it hard, but instead of rifling downfield as usual, it bounced off Babar's back. The ball flew high in the air. Unhurt, Babar looked up at the ball and cocked his face like he was positioning to head the ball. Instead of heading, he let the ball fly to his inside foot, volleying it to Gabriel. This faked the Chinook striker who was expecting a header. Gabriel let it fly and scissor kicked the ball at the net. It slammed loudly into the crossbar. Gabriel was called for offsides, but the Blue Angels had shot on goal after only eleven seconds. A big midfielder from the Chinooks rolled his eyes at Gabriel. *Soccer players are quick and small*, Gabriel thought. His black eyes shot a gaze back at the midfielder. The player looked at his teammates, signaling by his expression it was time the Chinooks got serious. Though these kids were only 14, there was something unusual about them. At the next free kick the Chinooks toughened up and pounded down the field. The size and speed of the Chinooks was right up front and they scored a goal on their first drive downfield. But they were fresh. Maybe the Blue Angels could wear them down. Riley told his midfielders that they were going to have to run like never before, helping both the defenders and the strikers. He signaled DeShawn to hold the ball as long as possible. On the next throw in, Riley yelled to the coach to sub the midfielders a lot. Trap nodded. Gabriel went into his sweeper mode, playing striker and defender at the same time. This seemed confusing to the Chinooks as it did every other team the Blue Angels played. Gabriel seemed tireless, as if soccer was in his DNA.

The two teams battle on. Nicolás, despite his youth, was the biggest kid on the field. Though not fast, he was using his size to make a lot of legal contact, bumping and body checking the Chinook strikers when they closed in for a shot. The ref was not stopping him. Still the Chinooks seemed too powerful to stop. As the game wore down near halftime the Chinooks showed little sign of fatigue. If anything, they were getting stronger, scoring two more goals before another ten minutes passed. Gabriel bellowed above the crowd yelling at the top of his lungs. "Come on Angels... fight!" Diego slammed a laser shot on goal, but it was a foot wide. The Chinooks goalie brushed the ball with his left hand, forcing the miss, setting up a corner kick situation. Willis pulled the same trick and bent down to tie his shoe, gently nudging the ball onto the field of play. JR was waiting. JR did his high kick. Kyle saw it and raced forward. He headed the ball, but the impact landed on top of his head instead of his forehead where he was aiming. As a result the ball flew high into the air again, coming down right in front of the goal. Babar did a complete flip, catching the ball with his laces.

Babar fell on his back. The Chinooks goalie was a big kid, but the ball flew hard into his face, knocking him down. Both players were on the ground. The goalie got right to his feet but the ball rolled into the net. Babar didn't get up. He was gasping for air, and had apparently hurt his wrist as he hit the ground. Trap ran onto the field and with the help of the Chinooks goalie they got him to the sidelines. Without

Babar, the Blue Angels were in deep trouble. Willis moved up to striker. He was frightened and there were tears in his eyes, but he looked down at the ground and shook his head hard. The halftime whistle sounded. The score was 3 - 1 Chinooks.

Ashar ran over to his son, grabbing a roll of tape from the equipment and putting his hand on his son's back.

"You all right son? What's the matter with your hand?"

Babar was on his hands and knees, coughing at the ground. "I just jammed my wrist. Here, could you tape my hand?" Babar looked up at his father. "Dad, they're just too big!"

Babar got to his feet, his face soaked with sweat.

At the beginning of the second half the Chinooks replaced two of their strikers with boys who had not played in the first half. It looked as if the coach was holding back two of his strongest players. The Chinooks kicked off and it rolled past both the strikers and midfielders. Kyle fell back near his own penalty area and took control of the ball. But instead of passing, he sprinted down the sidelines dribbling the ball by himself. The Chinooks were not expecting this, and Kyle raced towards their goal. The goalie did not stay back, seeing an opportunity to steal. Kyle got his toe under the ball and flipped it high, lobbing it over the goalie's head. The ball landed over near the far post and gently rolled into the goal. The score was 3 - 2 Chinooks.

The two new strikers were fresh and athletic, their eyes narrow and their faces hard. They stood side by side in the center of the midfield circle. They worked as a team, lean and fast and both standing nearly six feet tall. From then to the end of the game the Chinooks pounded the Blue Angels goal. Instead of wearing down the Chinooks, the opposite was happening. Though the Blue Angels fought hard and played the Chinooks with their best game, they had no chance. They were quite easily beaten for the first time in 1998. Though the Blue Jets gomanaged to get two goals on their older opponents, there were ten goals scored against them.

The Chinooks were amazed they were playing a team of 14 year olds, and congratulated the coaches and players for having such a remarkable group of fighters. The Chinooks also had some class, and they did not slap hands, which was the routine. For both teams this seemed like a moment in their lives they would not forget, so the Chinooks personally shook the hand of every Blue Angel. As they reached out to join hands, their skin glistened with sweat, some of their arms white, some yellow, some hands were black, and some hands were brown.

The employees of Hughes Associates who came to the Sunday competition felt compelled to do so. They had to see how it turned out. They had seen a group of youth function with complete unity though they were from ethnic origins all over the world. Many of the Hughes people left the last game of the season with a deep curiosity. They could not help asking themselves about their own work group. One possible answer still burned in the form of a question: were the Hughes people going to learn in the future? How did these young people feel about the color of their skin when they were born? What did they feel like now that they were 14? What will they feel when they look back on this day when they are 50? Would they rearrange their minds as they grew older? Trap thought not. They were the beginning of a new Cascadia, and they would see things differently.

Trap looked at every corner of the soccer field: at the grass, the bleachers, and his team shaking hands with the Chinooks. He savored the moment, because he had done something he never dreamed he could do. Then he looked at René for a long while and he knew she would be all right.

Trap's eyes shifted back and forth as if looking inward, as if the world was looking in at him, rather than the reverse. For a moment, only in his thoughts, racism was a useless relic of the past.

Rene would not take her eyes off of Trap. Her face was even, as if the sadness and joy of the moment had cancelled each other out. But her eyes were loving and earnest. She looked to Trap more calm than he had ever seen her.

"You know Trap, I never would have believed it. How did you pull that off? How did you do it, Coach?" René pressed against him and brought her mouth close to his. "Can I borrow a quarter?" She smiled. "Now what are you going to do?"

Trap's stomach did a hairpin turn looking at René's pretty face. There wasn't any dimness. He stroked her arm and squinted at her. "Walk streams, I guess. And just maybe next year you could help us coach U-15 soccer!"

## ACKNOWLEDGMENTS

I would like to thank Dr. Steven Farmer for providing to me permission to use his works and insights into Spirit Animals and shamanism. Visit his site at www.EarthMagic.net. I am also grateful to John Hurtado, Anthony Hurtado, Bob Gowan, Molly Lee Gibbs, Michael Graham Johnson, Oscar Ward, Alex Ward, Angelo Gray, Azziz Haq and his brothers. Thanks to Chinqually Booters, John Carlton, and all the young men and women of the Blue Angels U-14 Soccer Club.

---

You are invited to comment on this story. Please write a review of *Streamwalker* on amazon.com for other customers who may want their own copy.

Greg Johnson is a marine biologist currently living with his wife
Molly in Olympia, Washington. He graduated from Humboldt State
University in Arcata, California, where he studied fish biology and
creative writing. He has worked in salmon enhancement for decades.
Greg has always celebrated sports and spent years as a youth soccer
coach, which he claims was one of the most rewarding things he has
ever done. Greg loves living near the ocean and has worked as a
merchant marine, and commercial scuba diver. Greg is also a folk
musician, abstract artist, and is addicted to fishing with his son
Michael. He was born and raised in Crockett, a small suburb of San
Francisco, California.

Made in the USA
Middletown, DE
29 August 2020